CROWNE RULES

CROWNE RULES

CD REISS

Crowne Rules by CD Reiss

Copyright © 2020 Flip City Media Inc.

All rights reserved.

Cover art designed by the author from a photograph of Christian Balic as taken by Raf Garcia.

No part of this book may be reproduced in any form or by any electronic or mechanical means, including information storage and retrieval systems, without written permission from the author, except for the use of brief quotations in a book review.

This came out of the author's head. Any similarities to persons living or dead makes you a lucky dog—no more, and no less.

Dear Jana Aston—You make me a better writer.

THE NY TIMES BESTSELLING GAMES DUET

He gave up his dominance when he married her. He wants it back.

Marriage Games | Separation Games

THE EDGE SERIES

Rough. Edgy. Sexy enough to melt your device.

Rough Edge | On The Edge | Broken Edge | Over the Edge

THE SUBMISSION SERIES

Jonathan brings out Monica's natural submissive.

Submission | Domination | Connection

CORRUPTION SERIES

Their passion will set the Los Angeles mafia on fire.

Rogue | Ruin | Rule

CONTEMPORARY ROMANCES

Hollywood and sports romances with heart and a lot of heat.

Star Crossed | Hardball | Bombshell | Bodyguard

CHAPTER 1

MANDY

"You're letting them tell you who you are, Mandy." My best friend, Ella, shook her fists in frustration.

"I'm a homewrecker." I yanked my suitcase from the closet, repeating the paparazzi's accusations through a mouth dehydrated from hours of crying, and threw it on the bed. "I came between Renaldo the perfect and his perfect wife, then he dumped me, which makes me look even worse. Somehow."

A photo of the love of my life, Renaldo DeWitt, almost kissing Gertrude Evans lit up my phone's screen. A crack in the glass split his face in two, and as much as I wished he was the one who was broken, I was the one who was broken.

"It makes no sense," my mother said as she unzipped the case. "They file for divorce, then you two go public." She flopped open the top. "Then he's seen with Gertrude, and they're calling *you* names?"

When Ella and I arrived at my house, Mom's Mercedes had already been parked in my driveway. The minute she heard my life was being spread all over the internet, she'd driven over and waited, rushing out in her Uniqlo sweatshirt and NYDJ jeans to chase away the paparazzi, admonishing them to get a real job while I ducked my head and Ella led me inside.

"It makes perfect sense," I said, slapping a drawer open and throwing clothes on the bed. "I was just there to wreck his marriage, and now it's no fun because I'm just a homewrecking slut."

But that wasn't what everyone hated me for. They hated me because they didn't know the truth about Renaldo's marriage.

Renaldo's wife, an A-list actress with a string of blockbuster romantic comedies and an image so sparklingly all-American I wanted to put on sunglasses just to look at her, was a lesbian, and Renaldo was her handsome, devoted beard.

"There's a silver lining here," my mother said as she folded a shirt. "When the clouds break, you'll see it."

"There's no silver lining, Ma. This is *my life*." I mimicked a woman who'd taunted me on the street. "Bitch can steal a man, but bitch can't keep him."

I had to get out of Los Angeles. I was already being threatened by a hive of fans who'd ruin me before they knew the truth.

"It'll die down in a week." Ella put her hands on my arms and tilted her gaze up to meet mine. "Don't let what people think of you change what you think of yourself, okay?"

And what did I think of myself? The fashion designer whose signature color was a sunny-bright shade of yellow wasn't that sunny or bright.

"I let men use me," I said, saying things that were going to make me cry again. "I let them manipulate me. It's not even about Renaldo. It's about me. Why am I this way?"

"It's your father's fault," my mother said because everything was my father's fault, apparently. "Let me get you some water."

She left for the kitchen.

Ella waited until Mom was gone to whisper sternly, "Go to *Town & Country* and tell the truth." She was the only person I'd told the secret about Renaldo's wife.

"What would that make me?" I said, wrapping the cord for my toothbrush charger around the handle, each twist ending in the same humiliating fact. "I'd been enough to fuck, but not enough to leave his sham marriage for?"

"It'd make you not a homewrecker?" Ella answered, peering into the backyard again as if she'd heard something.

"You don't just drag a person out of the closet."

She knew that. I stuffed the toothbrush apparatus into the side pocket, where my now-useless birth control pills were packed, and the cord unraveled as soon as I let go. I was furious with him, but some part of me still thought that maybe there *was* an explanation, or at least an apology, coming my way.

"They wouldn't believe it anyway," I continued. "Everybody loves Tatiana and Renaldo together, and it's *my fault* because I'm some kind of"—I slapped a handful of underwear into the suitcase as if I could break cotton and silk—"some kind of sex goblin."

"No one thinks that."

"I've been dumped again," I whined. "I can't take it here, and I miss him already. I miss his laugh. The way he called me sweetheart. The little crooked incisor I could see when he smiled. I even miss the constant gum-chewing."

"You do?"

"No. It's gross, and I hate it." I stuffed a yellow bouquet of clothes in the bag. "But it's like I forgot what I ever wanted and just did what he wanted."

"A week at a Crowne estate and you'll forget all about forgetting."

"Have you been?" I asked, hoping Ella's husband, Logan Crowne, had shown her a good time there. "Is it nice?"

"No clue. But it's a Crowne place so... probably?"

"Logan said it's off the grid."

"He also said it's so updated and modern you won't even notice."

I sighed, looking at my pile of clothes and wondering if I was missing anything.

"You know," Mom said, blowing in with a glass of water I didn't want, "we have that place in Lake Tahoe. We haven't sold it yet. You just have to have the electricity turned back on."

"Cambria's closer." I sipped the water and ended up drinking the whole thing. "Thank you."

The little beach community of Cambria was closer than Lake Tahoe, halfway between LA and San Francisco—the exact distance between an efficient commercial flight and an easy drive—and though the Bettencourt name implied private jets and luxury vacations, we hadn't been private-jet rich in a decade.

"Plenty of fish in the sea," Mom chirped, zipping up a side pocket. "You have your pick of Hawkins's boys now, though there's always the one that got away."

Mom was tight with Will Hawkins's new wife, and she tried to sell me Caleb Hawkins like a fabric salesman with too many loose bolts, even knowing he'd broken my heart in eleventh grade. And twelfth. And repeatedly in college until ghosting me completely.

"I'd rather be alone," I said. The suitcase yawned like a big, open mouth full of dandelions. The cheerful yellows annoyed the hell out of me, so I didn't fold a thing. Every garment was going to look as wrinkled and wretched as I felt.

"You will be," Ella said, peeking out at the calm of the backyard again. "Logan says it's pretty secluded. Just you and the house."

I flopped the suitcase closed, revealing my phone. The tabloid photo had darkened and was replaced with the home screen. My sister, Samantha, and I hugged, smiling at present-day me from eight years ago. The crack in the glass cut across the last picture of us together before she took her life into her own hands and committed suicide, leaving me really and truly alone. After that, I never chose to be alone if I could avoid it.

"I keep thinking about when I went to Greece with Renaldo last summer."

I was supposed to go to Monaco with my girlfriends Aileen and Millie. We'd planned it for months. Then Renaldo yanked the rug out from under the entire thing with a surprise birthday trip to Greece. His birthday. Just the two of us cruising from remote island to remote island, staying in resorts where the staff knew it wasn't worth their jobs to photograph an adulterous couple skinny-dipping in the infinity pool. The whole week had shimmered—aquamarine water, yellow sun, cold glasses of white wine. Renaldo's body gleamed as he swam out of the ocean and came to kiss me where I lay in the sand. Every bite of fruit and sun-touched glance was jewel bright.

"He said he wanted me to belong to him." I sighed.

"Only true thing he ever said." Ella snorted, stepping away from the window. "You want to get control over your life? You're not going to find it in Cambria, but you're preparing for it. You're getting ready to become the best Mandy. Couture Mandy."

I scoffed. Only Ella could come up with "Couture Mandy" as the top of the line. "And what am I now? Irregulars Mandy? Chargebacks Mandy?"

"Well," Mom said, "obviously it's Discount Mandy."

"Obviously," I grumbled.

"You have to fortify yourself to own your power," Ella added. "Don't give it to them just because you're sleeping with them."

Ella was my best friend, and this wasn't an empty *you go, girl* speech.

"You're saying I should use them the way they always use me?"

"She's saying," Mom cut in, "it's not always about love. Sometimes it's just about sex, which—if you ask me—you're not going to solve in a house alone."

"She can stand to be single for half a minute," Ella said, snapping her head around to look out the glass door.

The movement in the backyard distracted me as well, and I froze in a dead panic as two figures—female, from the looks of them—crested the top of the wall. Before I could think, my back patio door shattered.

Ella and I screamed. Mom rushed out, shaking her fist, but the vandals were gone.

On the carpet, a red brick was lying in a spray of broken glass with a note wrapped around it. I didn't have to pull it out of the rubber band to read the one-word message written in all-capped Sharpie.

WHORE.

"We'll get security," Ella whispered, staring at the brick with wide eyes. "Logan has people."

I couldn't find a word to say.

"You should go," Mom said, pulling my suitcase off the bed. "It's better than Lake Tahoe. No one will know you're there."

Suddenly grateful to have someplace to go, I took it from her, and we headed out.

CHAPTER 2

DANTE

THE CLOUDS THAT COVERED THE MOON AND STARS HAD REFLECTED Los Angeles's lights in an orange-gray, but now—coming out of Malibu—they draped an opaque hood over the sky, leaving me to navigate by the headlights' reflections on drops of rain.

The route to Cambria was etched in my mind after so many trips. The beachfront would turn to truck stops, outlet malls, and billboards before it straddled the sea, then opened into desert and found the ocean again.

The Lordstown didn't handle as well as the Bugatti, which took turns without a hint of drift. but lately, the Cambria house always needed work, so I'd brought the truck and took the turns nice and easy to keep an accident from spraying the contents of the truck all over the freeway.

When my phone rang, I jumped a little. My cell signal had often dropped along the route until I invested in a better service provider.

The upside was no dead spots when I needed to make a call.

The downside was incoming calls.

Logan's name flashed on the screen. Unlike my brothers, I'd

never worked in the family business, but like them, I used its resources and answered to its needs.

"What?" I asked.

"You didn't tell me you were going to Cambria."

I never told anyone where I was going. He knew that.

"Because I don't answer to you."

"Actually, you do."

I snorted my contempt loudly enough for him to hear. "You loaned me your fixer, and I paid him. We're even."

"What's in the box?" he asked.

"I didn't hang around long enough to read it all. But there are some untranscribed dictation cassettes that look promising."

"There might be a player in the garage."

"I know."

"I want to help you," he said. "You know that, right? You didn't have to take off like that."

He did only want to help, and I did know that, but I didn't have to like the fact that I'd needed it, and I didn't have to stick around with that box in my hands, unpacking my adolescence one piece at a time. I needed to be alone to do that, and not just alone, but isolated like a contagion.

"Thank you." I was grateful, but that didn't change anything.

"I gave Mandy Bettencourt the keys," Logan said. "She's already on her way."

A flash of lightning lit up the road just before the pound of rain doubled.

"Who?"

"Mandy. My friend. You know her."

"Amanda Bettencourt?" I sought clarity as if the Bettencourts had an extra daughter lying around and the one headed to Cambria wasn't the one I remembered from a dark closet ages ago. "She's on her way to the Cambria house?"

"Yes."

I knew Amanda Bettencourt as well as anyone knew their

brother's best friend. She swam like a swan, honked like a swan, and looked as beautiful as one, but she was a porcelain likeness—lighter than the real thing, hollow and breakable.

"With who?" I asked. That house wasn't big enough for three people, and Amanda wasn't the type to do anything without a girlfriend at each elbow.

"Just her." His exasperation was as audible as my contempt had been.

"It's a small house."

No one knew that house better than I did. Even our parents, who'd bought it, updated it, and lived in it long enough to decide going off-grid was too much trouble, didn't know that house the way I did.

"Tell her not to come," I added.

"She left. Her phone's not getting a signal. You'll have to tell her when you see her."

I let my silence communicate how I felt about that, and his silence let me know he wasn't making any more effort in the matter.

"For what possible reason would you send a woman like her to a house with no connection to the outside world?"

"What's 'like her' supposed to mean?"

"There isn't a nail salon in a forty-mile radius."

"Can you just not be an asshole? She's having a bad breakup."

"I'm thrilled to be managing your friends for you."

"If anyone knows how to get rid of a woman, it's you," Logan sniped. "Just deal with it."

"Oh, I'm going to deal with it, but you're not going to like it."

"Do. Not. Touch. Her," he growled as if I cared how angry he'd get. "Don't even shake her hand. She's not a fuck-and-dump."

"You think too little of me."

"I mean it. If she comes home crying—"

I laughed and hung up without saying goodbye. Logan knew

how I felt about being ordered around—not to mention having a woman in my space.

Especially Amanda Bettencourt—everything I hated about LA women in one vain, lazy, incompetent, gossipy little package.

Her sister had been engaged to my brother until she committed suicide, so I'd seen Amanda at functions both happy and sad, but I'd only been alone with her once, and that was what stuck with me. I'd never forget the curves of her body under my hands or the softness of her lips against my fingers. We'd been teenagers then—kids playing a kids' game, groping around in a dark closet. She'd shown me one of my first glimpses of the kind of man I wanted to be, and though I didn't like the woman she'd grown into, it was hard to deny the power of what had passed between us.

She's not a fuck-and-dump.

No woman I fucked was what Logan had said, but I knew what he meant, and I knew he was right.

CHAPTER 3

MANDY

Ella, my mother, and I had switched cars in an underground lot so I wouldn't be followed, but I didn't relax until I was past Santa Barbara and completely alone on the freeway.

The rain didn't start until the last hour of the three-hour drive —long enough to get me out of my head and into an almost-decent mood. I sang along with the radio; at one point I even caught myself wailing off-key so loudly I hurt my own ears.

Piloting my little buttercup Jaguar—my father's last birthday present before he left us—along the wet, narrow road felt just dangerous enough to be exciting and just safe enough to enjoy.

At least my car will always be sexy.

I had to stock up on supplies before I arrived at the house, so I pulled off the freeway and into a tiny town called Harmony, because who could resist a name like that?

My cellular service had just about died fifty miles earlier and was completely gone when I needed to find a grocery store, but Harmony was a lucky break. I found a strip mall with a restaurant specializing in biscuits and gravy, a mom-and-pop convenience store, a hardware store, and Harmony Lights, which looked as though it sold greeting cards and candles. I'd check it all out in a few days, when I was settled and it wasn't raining domesticated animals.

At the market, I picked up reasonable things: yogurt, whole wheat bread, unsalted almond butter—and some less-reasonable things: a carton of salted caramel ice cream and a bag of potato chips thick enough to stay in one piece when they got soggy. I was in charge, I figured, for better or worse. I could do what I wanted, up to and including drowning my sorrows in fat and sugar. The rest of the meals would be tomorrow's problem.

I was waiting in the market's checkout line, craning my neck to see if they had plastic spoons I could use to eat the carton of ice cream in the car, when I saw the *DMZ Weekly* in the rack and my appetite took a hike.

The front was splashed with Renaldo and me photoshopped together in a way that made us both look anxious and upset. The yellow of my leggings was an unmissable neon flag, drawing everyone's eyes to the headline.

RENALDO & THE HOMEWRECKER: HOW MANDY BETTENCOURT'S BIG PLANS BACKFIRED

Those were the pre-humiliation rumors of a week ago—back when I could stand it because he was mine and I was his.

I dumped my groceries on the conveyor belt, then I swept every single issue of the magazine along with them. I couldn't destroy every copy in LA, but at least I could keep my new temporary neighbors from seeing my shame. Maybe there would be a fireplace at the house and I could do a ritual burn.

The goateed guy behind the counter rang it all up, light-brown eyes flicking up at me, then back at the food. I tried to look at my phone while I waited, but the signal had dropped ten miles back and never picked back up again. I really had to switch my carrier

—except maybe it was for the best. If I was getting away, I was getting away.

Goatee Man got to the stack of tabloids. "You wanna pick up just one of these or...?"

He left me to fill in the blank.

"All of them." I put on my sunglasses so he wouldn't recognize me, but that probably made it worse. We were inside, it was raining, and it was night. But I kept them on as I handed him my card, even though my name was on it.

Hooking the handle of the plastic bag on my wrist, I gathered the papers in my arms. On the way out, I found the counter with plastic utensils and plucked a white spoon out of the basket.

I ran across the rainy parking lot and tossed everything in my trunk. When I closed it, I realized I was really and truly alone, behind a windshield obscured with rain and miles and miles from a cellular signal. Cut off from everyone who loved me and everyone who hated me. For once, I was in control of all my relationships.

Rooting around the bag, I found the ice cream. Sticking the spoon in my mouth, I peeled the container open and put it down long enough to pull open the bag of chips. I smashed one on top of the ice cream and scooped it up, letting the cold, crunchy mixture freeze out the loneliness.

When I turned the key, the radio and comforting heat blasted on. The wipers sprang to life, clearing the rain from the windshield. Now I could see inside the market, where Goatee Man stood in front of the rack I'd emptied and slid in a fresh stack of *DMZ Weekly*. A snarling, man-eating version of my face stared back at me from the cover.

* * *

WHEN I FINALLY REACHED THE CROWNES' Cambria house, the rain

had turned to a drizzle, but the sky was still dark with thick, bloated clouds.

Even with the view obscured by darkness, it was obvious the place was a dump. The ten-foot hedges that circled the property were in need of a trim. The solar panel over the security platform had been knocked sideways, making me worry—when I had to put the code in twice—that there was no power to the keypad. The gate creaked, but when it slapped closed behind me, I felt protected and alone.

The long, uphill driveway was so cracked and uneven my Jag bounced and popped over the wet concrete, snapping sticks and smacking into potholes as the cottage came into view.

"Don't you worry baby." I patted the dashboard at the halfway point between gate and house. "We're going to be safe here."

But the car made a liar out of me. The tires slid, and I heard a scrape from the right bumper.

When I got out, the breeze was cool and damp, crisp with ozone. The crash of ocean waves hissed under the rustle of wind in the leaves. I'd scraped the bumper against a low stone wall that bordered each side of the driveway. It wasn't a big deal, but the tires weren't going to stop sliding, and the walk wasn't too bad.

After so long in a heated garage, the Jag would have to spend the night under rainy skies.

After yanking my bag out of the trunk, I grabbed my bag of food, locked the car with the stack of tabloids in the back, and headed up the hill.

The house looked as if it had been built in the seventies, with glass walls on four sides, wood siding, and slate tiles. Unlocking the door, I dragged my bags in and shut myself behind it, laying my hands on the wood as if I couldn't believe it was solid. A *click-click* made me spin, pressing my back to the door.

Click-click.

Movement in the shadows.

Click-click.

A branch hitting a window.

"Girl," I said to myself, "take it easy."

The flashlight on my phone revealed teak furniture, high ceilings, windows on every side. It smelled of cleaning fluid and unlived-in-ness. Undoubtedly, they had caretakers keeping it ready, even though the exterior had gone to shit.

I was in a dump, but it was the safest dump imaginable. With a locked door, an iron gate, and a few hundred miles between the paparazzi and me, I slid down to the floor with my back to the wall. No one could see me. In that dark, musty room, I could finally breathe.

There were bowls of fresh fruit on the counter and food in the refrigerator. The garbage can I threw the plastic ice cream spoon into had a new liner in it. The freezer where I put the remainder of the ice cream was full of meat. The sink was as empty and dry as my tear ducts, and though I laid the half-empty bag of Kettle chips on cans of food that weren't dusty, most of the pantry's condiments looked as if they hadn't been touched in a while.

Weird. If no one lived here, why the fresh food? And why would the cans be new?

I shrugged and went to the master bedroom, opening my suitcase on the bed I'd be occupying alone while I sorted out my life. I put my toiletries on the vanity, including the birth control pills I could stop taking any time now since I was single. In the mirror, past the liberated, in-control woman who fucked and forgot without getting attached, was a bathtub.

A bath would be a beautiful thing.

I left the water to run until it was hot, stripping down and pacing the house naked, eating potato-chip-crumbled caramel ice cream. The windows had blinds, but I left them open. There was no one to see me. When lightning flashed and lit up the outside, I saw a small pool and a garden of sticks. Out of habit, I counted the tense seconds the way my sister and I had before she died, with the melding of our names.

One Samanda.
Two Samanda.
Three Samanda.
Four Samanda.
Thunder.

The Jack-and-Jill bathroom led to the second bedroom. Inside, a manual typewriter sat on a wood desk, a ten-pound prop from a black-and-white movie. A sheet of clean, white paper looped around the tube with the excess sticking out the back like a tongue. I hit the letter W. An arm popped up and lightly tapped the paper. I hit it harder, leaving the fuzzy impression of a W behind.

It worked. Huh. I thought I knew the Crownes, but apparently they had an unexpected commitment to analog technology.

As I scraped the last of the ice cream out of the corners, lightning flashed.

Looking up, I noticed steam curling out of the bathroom door.

One Samanda.
Two Samanda.
Three—

Thunder cracked, and the water heater had probably done its job by now.

When the water was so hot I could barely touch it, I plugged the tub and rooted around under the sink, finding a box of squat, white candles and a lighter and a red satin bag of bath bombs. I lit the candles and tossed a couple of bombs into the water, then threw in another for good measure.

When the waterline was near the top, I shut off the faucet.

My phone had been completely useless for miles already, and if there was Wi-Fi in the house, it was off, but I could still play music. I threw together a playlist of songs with a "fuck him" theme, put headphones on, and settled in, letting the line of scalding heat envelop me to the neck.

Arms floating, I let the music take me away, singing along

with a song about heartbreak and renewal, unable to hear my voice as much as feel it against the sobbing soreness of my throat.

He broke my heart
  When I was so nice
  Forget that asshole
  I mean it, girl
  Forget him twice

I belted it out not to the bathroom tiles, but to the Renaldo in my mind. He was begging to have me back, and I was toying with him, asking, "Why?" Why did he promise to leave his wife only to humiliate me? Turn me into an object of public disdain only to get on his hands and knees and literally kiss my feet?

Not just him, but Caleb, who'd treated me like trash for years, and every guy after him who dumped me and then strung me along so they could dump me again.

In my fantasy, I was telling them about all the other guys I was fucking and how little I cared about any of them. I was walking away from some faceless stud, sated and satisfied and totally unattached. I was never, ever going to get hurt again, and every time I started to cry again, I sang louder.

"No, no, no-no!" I chanted with the music, waving my finger at my imaginary lover. *"You ain't that..."*

The lights went out, and I practically leapt out of the tub in shock, sliding my headphones away from one ear. A moment later, I realized what *must* have happened, and surprise turned to exasperation. Because, of course, this goddamn house couldn't stand a thunderst—

"Hello?" A man's voice came from the darkened doorway.

In a crouch, dripping wet, with female empowerment in one

ear and his question in the other, I grabbed something, anything, in the dark and came up with a shampoo bottle.

"I know tae kwon do," I said in the general direction of the voice, standing up to wield the plastic bottle.

"I'm sure." The lights went back on with a click, and I could see the source of the voice.

Fuck.

Dante Crowne. Gray raincoat glinting with droplets of water, finger on the light switch, looking down at me from the top of Mount Six Foot Four. All the Crowne men had light eyes, but Dante's were deeper set and the iciest blue I'd ever seen.

"Hello, Amanda."

"It's Mandy," I said, pulling the headphones around my neck and lowering the shampoo.

His gaze followed the poorly chosen weapon and took a circuitous route back upward by way of the naked triangle between my legs, my belly, my breasts. When his eyes landed on mine, there was desire there, but I could tell by the way he tightened his mouth that it was an easily dismissed interloper and not something he wanted to act on.

"Logan said you'd be here," he said.

He wasn't going to apologize for scaring me half to death and then checking me out without even admiring the view?

"Well, he didn't warn me about you," I said.

Lightning flickered, and I held my reply for the whipcrack of thunder one *Samanda* later.

"Clearly," Dante scoffed, looking my nudity over again.

I turned for the towel, catching sight of myself in the mirror. I was splotched in patches of bubble. South America drifted down my hip.

Dante grabbed the towel and handed it to me, eyes respectfully averted. I took it slowly, daring him to look again, and he took me up on the challenge, letting his gaze fall all over my body like a steamer pushed under a dress to relax the creases in every corner.

"Logan sends his apologies, but this house is mine," Dante said as I wrapped the white towel around myself. "And I need to use it this weekend."

"Your brother said it was a family house."

"Hm."

After the one syllable, he turned and left me alone in what was apparently his bathroom.

CHAPTER 4

DANTE

AMANDA BETTENCOURT.

Logan's phone call had prepared me—otherwise I would have been furious and not a little unnerved to find her there. I'd come up here to do a sensitive task. I didn't want company.

Not even the kind who drove sexy Jaguars left diagonal in my drive. I could have gotten around, but I took the back way, parked in the garage, and checked the solar cells out of habit.

The sun wasn't going to hit the panels for another week, and the electrical had been turned on full blast without increasing the battery load. Worse, she was running a goddamn bath. Either Logan hadn't warned her about the water tank, or she hadn't listened. If she didn't get out soon, the house would run out of both water and power in a few days.

The master bedroom looked already occupied by the aftermath of a tornado. Apparently, Amanda had grown up to be a slob. Her clothes were everywhere, a scattering of lace and Lycra and cashmere in varying shades of yellow. The bath stopped running, and I heard her get in.

Her suitcase was splayed open on the bed. I untwisted a pair of underwear from their curl, laying them flat on the comforter.

Clearly, this was a woman who had no boundaries. No precision. No control over herself or her life.

From the sound of her singing, she hadn't noticed I was in the house yet. No one with a voice like that would sing in front of another human. It was aural equivalent of brutalist architecture, and letting her finish would have been an aesthetic injustice.

I opened the bathroom door. Though I was glad to smell the demise of the bath bombs my sister had left under the sink for ten years, the room was lit with the emergency candles I kept next to them. Amanda's eyes were closed, and her ears were covered with noise-cancelling headphones as she sang some garbage pop song.

Her voice was truly terrible. Metal scraping metal was more pleasant, but the earnestness of her expression changed the entire tone—turning discord into harmony. Somehow, if she'd been on key, it would have been wrong. But she was real in a way I wouldn't have expected, and I stared at her a few seconds longer than I should have.

"Amanda," I said, but she didn't hear me. She kept on singing, and I kept on staring.

"*No, no, nooooooo...!*"

"Amanda," I said a little more loudly before I realized I wasn't getting her attention because I wanted to keep watching her and listening to her voice when I had no right to do either.

"*You ain't thaaaat...*"

I shut off the light, and she went silent with a gasp, splashing in surprise.

"Hello," I said, trying not to smile as she weaponized a shampoo bottle, crouching in a battle stance, then stood.

"I know tae kwon do," she said over the tinny music coming from her headphones.

"I'm sure." In fairness, I turned the lights on. I'd see her naked, but she'd see I wasn't a threat.

She looked so fierce, with swollen, red-rimmed eyes cupped

by dark circles, reminding me of Logan's warning that she was having a hard time.

"Hello, Amanda."

Knowing she'd be in the bath hadn't prepared me for the sight of her body slippery with bubbles and soft in the steamy air. She heaved with a dose of adrenaline more desirable than her nudity.

My attraction to her didn't portend anything deeper. She was gorgeous, but she wasn't the only beautiful woman in Los Angeles any more than she was the only empty one. She was a host of clichés. A tall drink of water. A long-stemmed rose with not a petal out of place.

"It's *Mandy*," she said, using her leftover adrenaline to fight over her name.

I watched her body as it let go of danger, relaxing one muscle at a time.

She was shallow, vain, and immature. Prideful, but not confident. Useless as a mate and probably dull as a doorknob in bed.

And yet—all that still being true—she'd always piqued in me a pointless curiosity that if ever sated would surely disappoint. There was no there, there. I knew that like I knew the exact location of my own dick.

And yet again—the game of hoodat so long ago. I'd always told myself those minutes in a closet said more about me than her. That had to be as true now as it had always been.

"Logan told me you'd be here," I said.

"Well, he didn't warn me about you." She put the shampoo bottle on the shelf and laid her hands on her hips.

"Clearly."

Lightning flashed. Her lips didn't move, but I could tell she was counting the Mississippis until the thunder came a second later. Her shoulders relaxed as if knowing how close the storm was gave her control over it, and I knew right then that I was watching her too closely.

"Logan sends his apologies, but this house is mine," I said, taking my eyes off her long enough to snap the towel off the ring and hand it over. "And I need to use it this weekend."

It occurred to me too late that I didn't have any good answer ready if she asked me what for, and luckily, she didn't.

She wrapped the towel around herself, and I looked at her again.

"Your brother said this was a family house," she said.

She and Logan had been friends for a long time; she had to know how things worked among the Crownes. Someone was always jockeying someone else for position, and while this house technically belonged to my parents, Logan and I both knew it was really mine.

But I didn't have the energy or patience to get into that with Ms. Lonelyhearts. I had plenty of things to keep me busy, and babysitting wasn't on my to-do list.

"Hm," I said and strode out of the room, leaving her alone to put clothes on that beautiful body.

CHAPTER 5

MANDY

Dante had set his two leather bags by the door of the master bedroom as if preparing to take possession. My bag was still open on the bed, and a pair of my underwear was spread into a butter-colored lace crescent.

I certainly hadn't left them like that.

So, he'd known I was in the house. He knew I was in the bathtub and walked in anyway, turning off the lights to scare the shit out of me. Sadistic asshole.

My family was linked to the Crownes by society. Same parties. Same schools, more or less. Logan became my friend because he could dish out verbal jabs and take them like a champ. When my sister, Samantha, got engaged to Byron Crowne, our families were linked by love. And when she committed suicide, they were linked by grief.

So, I knew Dante well enough, but not that well because no one knew him.

All the Crowne boys were handsome and charming—*blah, blah, yawn*—a dime a dozen, generally. Their wealth made them so desired. But Dante had an emo thing that wasn't emo at all. It was a certain mysteriousness that wasn't broody or melodramatic. In his teen years, he didn't complain about being misunderstood and strain credulity with outlandishness. He stayed within fashion and behavioral conventions, and all that did was shine a light on just how different he was and how that differentness was defined by what he wasn't.

He wasn't a gossip. He wasn't loud. He didn't speak unless he had something to say, and when he did, you listened because you had no choice. Not because you agreed or disagreed, but because his voice came from a place of command and confidence few could access.

Some of my friends had thought he was sexy. The straight boys found him threatening but never admitted it or explained why. He scared me a little, but as intriguing as my fear was, I didn't try to follow it down a rabbit hole of crushes and hookups. I had Caleb to hurt me.

Paula Harris had dated Dante for a while in college, I remembered. With my underwear put aside, I stood over the open suitcase, trying to remember what she'd said about him. Anything at all. We weren't great friends, but she must have—yes. I remembered.

About a year after my graduation from Otis—at the Mayor's Gala. Paula hid bruises on her wrist with a big bracelet that had his name engraved on one side and hers on the other, but it wasn't just her name. It was something that alarmed our friend, Aileen.

BONA

Which—if you were Aileen and had six straight years of Latin under your belt—you knew meant *property*.

That night—that same exact night—I was talking to Irene Martino, walking down the hall to the bathroom, and I turned the corner without looking and crashed into him. Boom. His chest had been a tuxedo-wrapped brick wall, and I apologized right away, but all he did was look at me as if his icy eyes could see right through me.

At least, that was what Irene had said. For some reason, my gaze was glued to the carpet.

Until my friend told me that later, I thought he'd started looking through me when he took my chin in his hand and tilted it up to face him. He didn't take my clothes off with his stare. He peeled off my skin.

"Hold your head up," he said. "And you'll see what's in front of you."

Being in my early twenties, I took that as a scold and slapped his hand away. I wanted to say, *"Yes, sir,"* but managed not to. My second response was, *"Use those eyes to look* at *not* through." But saying that would have been admitting he'd disarmed me, so I closed my mouth around it and—in a single moment of thoughtfulness in a lifetime of impulsive behavior—I chose the third option.

"You could have looked yourself, you know."

"You're right," he said with a nod that was gracious far beyond his years. "Pardon me."

"It's fine," Irene chimed in, looping her arm through mine. "See you later."

She dragged me away, but I looked back. I had to. I could feel him following, pulling at me, and I had to know if it was my imagination.

He hadn't followed. He was ten feet away, down the hall where we'd left him.

It was my imagination, and it hadn't been, because he was turned toward us, looking not at but through me again, as if there was so much to see.

The same way he'd looked at me for a split second in the Cambria bathroom... as if I wasn't covered in skin, but an emotional armor that would crumble if he decided to attack.

"Hm," I said to myself, mocking his last word to me as I shoved my feet through the underwear he'd touched. "'Hm,' my ass."

Dressing quickly in gym shorts and an oversized sweatshirt

the color of a traffic light drivers speed up for, I threw my hair up onto the top of my head with a velvet scrunchy, then I stormed out to give Dante Crowne a piece of my mind.

The house was super small. Two bedrooms and one bath. Nothing like the Crowne's Bel Air estate, which would have been its own zip code if more people lived in it.

When I arrived in the kitchen, Dante was filling a teapot. His shirt was open at the neck. The tightness of the sleeves, as well as the fit of his jeans, did more for his shape than a thousand hours at the gym… though the gym was definitely on his schedule.

He didn't even look at me. The huge glass doors were wide open to the pounding rain. The patio was covered, so the house didn't flood, but it was weird enough to put a hold order on my anger. Lightning struck, and before I could count, thunder split the air. I gasped.

"Another one overlapping," he said as he shut off the water. Another crack followed as if summoned by the God with the Teapot. "It's right over us."

"Can we close the doors?"

"No."

"It's cold."

He turned on the burner, glancing at my bare legs for half a second. "Put on pants."

The chill had visibly hardened my nipples even through the ginormous sweatshirt. Pants might have warmed my core and kept the skin on my thighs from goose-bumping, but I doubted they would make my nipples invisible to him.

Lightning again.

One Sama—

Thunder.

"What are you making?" I asked.

"Hot water."

Infuriating. How could he pretend not to know what I meant? Was it just for the sake of using as few words as possible?

"Once the water's boiling, what are you putting in it?" I said with the faux patience of a third-grade teacher at two in the afternoon on a Friday.

He smirked, making me feel like a child when he was the one being unbearable. "Lemon and bitters." He waved at the bowl of plump yellow fruit on the counter. "If the lemons are good. I had our caretaker pull a couple from the tree when she brought supplies."

That explained a lot of things. The cans. The fruit. The full freezer.

"Bitters are in the refrigerator door if you want," he said.

What I wanted was something to do. Condiment bottles clicked in the door when I opened the fridge. The shelves held the usual, and I plucked through until I found a slim bottle of bitters. I put it on the counter next to him.

"Thank you." He held the lemon under his nose and—finding it acceptably aromatic—slid a knife from the block. He said nothing as he got out a small cutting board and shaved away the yellow skin.

"Are you doing a cleanse?" I asked. "Lemon and bitters? Is that a new thing I haven't heard of?"

Without a moment's pause to decide if he wanted to admit to doing a cleanse, he said, "Amanda, I need you to leave first thing in the morning."

"Mandy. It's *Mandy*. It's been Mandy since middle school."

With expert precision, he separated the zest from the rind without a speck of bitter rind in the bowl. "Did you spell it with an I-E and dot the I with a heart?"

He had no way of knowing I'd done that. Lucky guess and fuck him for it.

"Fine," I said. "Whatever. I'll go in the morning, okay? I can't get any signal here anyway, and there's no Wi-Fi, so it's boring."

Why did I sound like such a dipshit?

Did I feel so safe in that house that I thought the bricks would stop coming through my window at home? I wasn't trying to impress him, but I'd said it for his benefit somehow.

Did I just want to do what he told me?

Dante nodded to himself, satisfied that he had what he needed from me. "You came here for the excitement."

It wasn't even a question, barely a prompt. The word was a command, casually dropped with slivers of lemon into two glass mugs.

If I told him in lurid detail why I was running away, maybe he'd let me stay.

Maybe I could drive to Harmony and appeal to Logan.

The fact was Dante wouldn't be moved, and the Crowne name trumped Logan's permission.

I'd leave in the morning and not a moment sooner. It wasn't my fault he and his brother had gotten their wires crossed. Nor was it his, and down deep, I kind of felt bad about...

No.

Stop.

Post-Renaldo Mandy didn't feel bad about anything she did to inconvenience men, and she didn't stay where she wasn't wanted.

But I didn't have to tell Dante Crowne what I was getting away from just because he wanted to know.

"I'm getting away," I said.

"From." Again, not a question. A command.

"Everything," I said, figuring two could play at this game.

The teapot whistled.

"Specifically." Dante shut off the flame.

I assumed he was going to play the one-word-then-silence game, and I was determined I wouldn't lose it again, but he outmaneuvered me by filling two mugs with boiling water as he filled in the blanks in my story.

"The paparazzi," he said. "The gossip sites. Being held to account for fucking a married man for years."

The words were accusatory, but his tone sliced off the judgment, leaving not a speck of bitterness to taint the facts. I wanted to be angry at him, but without his contempt, I couldn't be, and since the only thing I'd done wrong was keep a secret, I couldn't be offended either.

"Yes," I said with my chin high. "I don't know how that matters to you."

He dropped bitters into the lemon water until it turned the color of tea. "It doesn't." He handed me a cup. "You're lucky I showed up."

"I don't feel lucky."

Leaning on the counter, he finally faced me, and the scalding tea went cold in my hands.

"Warm water's recycled through the pipes to keep bacteria from building up. When the keypad out front is used, it turns off the tank heater so the tankless—which runs on electricity—can go on. You're two hot baths away from running low enough on water to set off the emergency pressure attenuator, and you didn't have the solar cells set to carry enough load to run the tankless more than two days. The entire system would have shut down—including the front gate—and that little car you left in the middle of the drive doesn't have the horsepower to ram it down. You would have been walking on the side of the road in the rain, hungry because the stuff you brought won't make a meal. We don't have servants here. You couldn't get Sugarfish delivered even if your phone worked."

That too was said without judgment or negative emotion. I wasn't sure if he was a sociopath or a god. Both could be handsome, and both were capable of fucking a woman and leaving without a second thought.

"Well." I shrugged, putting on the same lack of emotion. "Fuck you, then."

"You shouldn't need to take such pains for a man like Renaldo DeWitt." He shook his head, and it was the first time he judged me. It was awful, but it was also comforting. Dante Crowne might have contentedly sipped scalding water as if he were impervious to pain, but he was human.

"What he had wasn't a marriage." That was as close as I could come to letting Tatiana's secret slip, but I only sounded like a cookie-cutter mistress making judgments about a marriage based on the lies of the husband she was fucking. "And I'm not here to get away from him," I objected with absolutely zero cool. "I can't leave the house without someone taking a picture of me. I'm everywhere, and they put... *words* over my face. *Whore* and *slut* and... worse. I'm a *meme*. They doxed me, and I had a brick launched through my bedroom window."

Dante washed and dried his cup with practiced grace. All his money, and he did household chores. I didn't know whether to be disgusted or impressed.

"Why don't *you* go back?" I insisted. "Why do you need to be here? Taking a break from owning some snooty clubs a few thousand miles away?"

Of the million ways he could have reacted, the last I expected was for him to step closer, towering over me as he lifted my chin with one crooked finger just as he had when he told me I had to take my eyes off the floor to see forward. Had he smelled like ground coffee beans that night too? Had there been a deep musk and a profound tenderness as he looked not at me, but right through me?

"Tomorrow morning," he said. "You're going to wake up and take a shower, not a bath. You're going to get into that sexy little car of yours, back it out past the gate, and drive away like a good girl."

Of course, he was right.

I was going to obey him. He was the one with the house and the name. He was the one of us who needed the least, so he was the one with the power, inspecting me as if I was a lemon he'd peeled before juicing dry.

He was exerting exactly the kind of control over his life and the people in it that I wanted for myself.

Maybe Dante Crowne was exactly the guy to help me become Couture Mandy.

His shapely lips twitched so slightly I would have missed it if he hadn't been standing so close. Everything was in that twitch, and nothing was outside it. It was a bomb—the pure potential of an unlit fuse contained in a metal shell that would make perfect shrapnel.

What did an explosion look like for Dante Crowne? Had Paula Harris found out and paid for the knowledge in bruised wrists?

"I'm not your *bona*."

"No, you're not." He lowered his hand. "I take grown women. They know what they want. They're mature enough to consent and confident enough to trust me. They're not hollow, desperate little socialites waiting for someone to tell them who they are."

My brows knotted and mouth opened, but when he walked away, the denial caught in my throat.

"We understand each other," he said, sliding the back doors closed, cutting the patter of rain and rumble of thunder that had faded many *Samanda*s away. "I'll be in the master." He snapped the lock. "Rinse your cup before you go to bed."

Oh, no. He wasn't going to walk out with the last word. At least, not those last words.

"I run a business!" I cried.

He stopped, turned, crossed his arms. "What kind of business can you leave for however long you thought you were hiding out?"

"Not that it's your concern"—I crossed my arms to mirror his posture—"but I only have a few employees. I do a few special pieces a year. So, there's downtime while I collect inspiration." Every word sounded silly and trite. I had to hit him where it hurt. He'd insulted my career, so I could at least hit his chain of elite

European clubs. "We don't all need to run empires to make up for our little dicks."

Insulting penis size was beneath me, but I was mad, and he'd never have the opportunity to prove me wrong, so fuck it. I said what I said.

"What you describe isn't a business," he replied with a smirk that was equally sexy and infuriating. "It's a vanity project."

My blood went red hot. How could he think that? I worked my ass off. I'd risked everything I'd been given, knowing my family couldn't afford to throw another dime my way if I failed. My company was the one thing in my life I'd done myself, and it was the one thing I was proud of. How dare he—Dante *Crowne*—say all that made me shallow?

I should have insulted the nepotism, but I was too angry to go high. "Well…" I balled my fists at my sides. "I'm sorry I'm not deep enough to be one of your submissive whores."

It was the worst I could think of. It was meant to wound him, but I hadn't aimed carefully or thrown hard enough, because he reacted as if I'd proven his point.

"If you were my whore, you'd be kneeling at my feet, naked with your ass up, offering it up for my pleasure, hoping I'd hurt you. Afraid I wouldn't. You'd sleep at the foot of my bed to please me. You'd open your legs when I told you and take my cock down your throat to thank me. You'd let them call you a whore if I asked you to because with every orgasm I let you have, you'd know you were only mine."

I was wet. I should have been appalled and repulsed, but I was breathless, covered in skin that tingled as if it was heated from the inside.

"So, no, Amanda," he continued. "You're beautiful and sexy, but you're the only thing standing in your way. You've stuffed your needs into a bag and thrown them into the river because they scare you. But I see them because I am the river."

It was a much cruder way of saying exactly what Ella had said to me back in LA, but I hadn't reacted to her like this. What kind of needs could Dante see in me? Was he looking at my pink cheeks? My nipples, which didn't have the cold as an excuse anymore? Could he tell by the way I shifted from foot to foot that I was trying to stand comfortably with a swollen clit?

No. He wasn't superhuman. He was just another presumptuous man I was handing my power to.

"Such. Pretty. Words," I sneered, walking toward him. "I can't wait to get out of here tomorrow morning."

I brushed by him to get out of the kitchen, forgetting I was supposed to rinse my cup until I was in the master bedroom. If he wanted chores done so badly, he could rinse the cup himself. I grabbed my stuff out of the master, threw it in my suitcase, slapped it closed, and went into the smaller bedroom, slamming the door behind me.

But there was a path between us. A joining point.

He'd be on the other side of the bathroom, like the connected closet where I'd first tasted him.

CHAPTER 6

MANDY

Aileen's house in West Adams was an old Craftsman with Victorian touches and a floor plan that defied logic. The adults were downstairs, drinking wine to celebrate the end of the school year, and their children, ranging in age from seven to seventeen, were upstairs in self-selecting groups, playing video games, who-can-scream-loudest, and for those of us in the older crowd... hoodat.

Hoodat was where the crazy layout of the house made things interesting. Aileen's closet and her brother Connor's were connected by a sliding door. The girls stayed in Aileen's room and the boys in Connor's. We used a random-number-generating app to choose who went into the closet for seven minutes with a boy from the other side. Highest prime number in the group was Dat.

"Five percent chance Mandy ends up with Caleb," Millie said. She held up her phone. Twelve. "Six point six now."

"Eight," Ella said.

"Ten percent," Millie calculated.

"Thirteen." Aileen held up her phone with a look of conspiratorial satisfaction. She was the only prime so far, increasing the odds she'd end up in the closet with Caleb, who I'd given my virginity to and who I was supposed to end up in the closet with.

A knock came from inside the closet. The boys had chosen.

"Go, Mandy." Millie nudged me. "Still at ten."

"If I get Logan, I'm out," I said, hitting GENERATE. "We're friends, and that's it."

But if I got Caleb, I'd be alone with him long enough to ask him why, or make out with him in the dark, or tell him how much he'd hurt me until he said he was sorry and begged for me back. At least I'd know what I'd done wrong, how I'd come up short. There was no talking in the closet—we were supposed to identify the other by feel—but I was going to break the rules to get answers.

"And if you get Caleb?" Aileen teased as my app flipped numbers around for the sake of suspense.

Winning meant you got to either go on a date with the person you guessed or make them go on a date with someone else—usually your friend who liked them—who had to act put upon. The rules were intellectually simple and socially complex.

The numbers on the screen stopped, landing on seventeen.

"Oh," I whispered, suddenly faced with the prospect of being with Caleb in the closet.

"Twenty percent!" Millie clapped.

"If it's Caleb, you should bite him," Ella said after knocking on the closet door to tell the boys we were ready. "Then send him out to me, and I'll bite him."

I'd gone nonverbal. Did I really want to know what I'd done wrong? What if he said it was because I had sex with him and I was lousy at it?

But what if it was me? Like, really me?

"Odds are it's not him," I said, surrendering my phone with the timer set for seven minutes. "There's math on that, right?"

"Try to have fun," Ella said with a wink as she opened the door.

Aileen shut off the bedroom light.

Once I was inside the cedar-lined closet, the door closed behind me. My heart seized. Fabric brushed against my shoulder, and I jumped. My eyes darted, looking for purchase on a stitch of light, but hadn't adjusted yet.

My throat was clogged with hardening concrete, and my lungs shrank to the size of kidney beans. Panic seized me, running my thoughts like a sportscar with broken brakes.

I shouldn't have agreed to play this game, but I wanted to talk to Caleb and I also didn't think I'd get picked, but now I was in a dark closet, and what no one knew was that I was deeply terrified of the dark. Palms sweating, I knocked on the sliding door with two sets of three raps, hard enough to signal the kids in the bedrooms to start the timers.

My eyes adjusted the closet into splotches of gray. Clothes. Boxes. Feeling forward, I touched the door between the two closets just as my silent partner slid it open.

It wasn't Logan. I knew that right away from his smell. Logan had an anise scent. My hoodat was richer and earthier. That was good and bad—good because I didn't want to be stuck in a closet with Logan for seven minutes while everyone wondered if we were making out, but bad because I couldn't just tell my partner it was *me... Mandy*, and we could both win.

Also, I wasn't sure if it was Caleb, which should have alerted me to the fact that he and I had never clicked. If we had, I'd have felt him there and known.

But I didn't.

"Caleb?" I whispered so low it was barely a breath, trying to cheat the system.

He put two fingers on my lips, letting me know he was playing by the rules and expected me to do the same. His commanding manner could have frightened me, but it didn't. The lump dissolved, and my breath entered lungs large enough to sustain me.

I hoped my hoodat was Caleb at the exact same time I knew it wasn't.

His fingers still on my lips, I laid my hands on what I thought was his chest but found solid upper abs covered in a button-front shirt. Tall. Could have been Caleb. Like any young person who hadn't been shattered a few dozen times, I was open to pleasant surprise.

His fingers slid between my lips. Reflexively, I opened my mouth to ask him, "What the…?" and he slid his index and middle fingers between my teeth and over my tongue. He tasted like the rosemary olive bread in the basket downstairs.

Who'd taken that one? Which of the five or so boys?

I sucked off the taste, looking in the general direction of his eyes as he pulled out so slowly I could feel each knuckle bumping against my lips as if it was between my legs.

This was not Caleb.

I let my hands drift down the sides of his body, over his hips. Jeans. Belt. Who was wearing a belt tonight? I couldn't visualize anyone, couldn't imagine a boy who could put his other hand under my jaw, gripping my throat just tightly enough to hold me still and send a shot of electricity down my spine the way this boy did. Which one would lean so close into me I could feel him put his slick fingers in his own mouth, sucking my spit off with the rosemary bread?

His breath hot on my cheek, his body drawing me into him, he wiped his wet fingertip along my lower lip, and I opened for him.

It was so natural to say *for him* to myself that I thought nothing of it until later. Like everything else about the encounter—the way his hand pressed against my throat, the way I opened my lips for him without being asked, the way our flavors mixed when his fingers reentered my mouth, or the way I closed up to suck on them—I dismissed it as a fluke.

I didn't realize I was gripping his shirt until his fingers slid all the way out and he pulled them away, turning me until my back was to his front and my wrists were pinned behind me.

This was more intense than I'd signed on for. We were supposed to be two teenagers fumbling and giggling while trying not to talk. This wasn't a boy trying to cop a feel while trying to figure out who I was. This was a man who knew what he wanted and how to get it, and it had taken him two minutes to render me powerless and so turned on I couldn't do the one thing that would send all our friends into the closet.

I couldn't scream or say, "Stop," because I didn't want him to. Even when he loosened his grip to a more or less symbolic hold or ran his hand between my breasts, not touching the nipples that had furled tight for him as he made his way to my waistband and to my belt buckle.

He slid to the end of the belt, handling the metal end, and letting it drop.

"Yes," I whispered without thinking. My ache had grown past the size of my jeans, pressing against the seams, stimulating me with even the slightest move.

"Amanda," he said in my ear.

I didn't recognize the voice, but we were both talking in breaths.

"Who are you?"

Gently, he lifted my hands and put them on the sliding doorjamb. "I don't have to tell."

He was right. He could win, and I could lose.

We weren't even supposed to be talking, much less giving clues, but I didn't know any of the guys to be so confident they could slide their hands down the sides of my rib cage without making me uncomfortable or self-conscious. None of them—not even Caleb, whom I'd been so sure about loving—had put me in such a state of utter surrender.

"Give me a hint."

He felt over my ass, and I pushed it out toward him for more.

"One day," he said in a voice I kind of thought I recognized for a moment, until he slapped my ass and I gasped. "But not today."

The doors to the bedrooms erupted in knocking. The man-boy and I separated. He slid the panel between the closets closed, and I backed away from it like a stunned animal in the dark, tiny lungs gasping around a thick lump in my throat, terrified again of what I couldn't see.

Behind me, my friends opened the door, and light flooded in. I squinted as if I'd been spelunking for days.

"Well?" Aileen demanded. "Who was it?"

The central question demanded an answer.

I'd have to face each of those guys at some point, and one of them had soaked my panties not with a kiss or a promise, but sheer, undeniable wordless command. None of the guys we knew were that confident.

"Not Jonsi," I said. "Not Logan."

"Caleb?" Sally asked.

If I said no, she'd break down the odds of who it could have been, and I didn't want her to deduce who it was. I wanted to know, but more than that—I didn't want my friends to know.

"Maybe?" I shrugged. "But maybe Sawyer or Connor?"

"We're missing one," Sally asked, counting boys on her fingers. "Jonsi, Logan, Caleb, Sawyer, Connor, Jackson…" She held up the thumb and finger L, wiggling the pointer for the unknown variable.

"Describe anything about him," Ella said. "Height? Weight?"

Like me, Ella was a fashion person but far more technical. She probably could have used the sensory information I had to discern his shirt size.

I shrugged again. What had happened in that closet was too intimate to talk about, and it was mine alone. It would not be diluted or broken. It would not be dragged into the light by me.

Aileen rolled her eyes. Millie had already lost interest and started scrolling through her phone. A bunch of kids stormed down the hall like a herd of wild elephants, screaming, "Ice cream, ice cream!"

The bedroom door opened, and Caleb leaned in.

"Hey," he said in a deep, icy voice, making eye contact with me for a split second—long enough to look away quickly because, even after getting down my pants, he just wasn't interested anymore.

"What's up?" Aileen asked, and the distraction gave me a moment to take in details.

Caleb wore a T-shirt. The guy in the closet wore a button-front. So, not him, though I had to leave room for the possibility that he'd put it on before the game started and took it off after just to trick me.

You know it's not him.

"There's a Coolhaus truck in the driveway," Caleb said, glancing at me again as if reconsidering another go, and suddenly I was game for it. "We're heading down."

"Thanks," I said because I had to let him know I existed.

He winked at me and left.

We joined the flow down the stairs. I caught Logan at the first landing.

"What did your side say?" I asked quietly. "Did you figure out the hoodat?"

"Nope."

The name from his side would never be pried from Logan, so I didn't even try. "Us either."

We passed the adults as they sat at a long table, laughing, drunk on wine and a vodka my father had picked up in Estonia. The fruit and cheese trays were picked over, and the bread basket had a pebble of rosemary kalamata crust left.

A hand reached in and took it. I followed it to the source.

Dante Crowne hung on the periphery of the adults, disinterested in what the adolescents were doing, leaning on the sideboard and talking to Caleb's mother.

Could it have been Caleb? I scanned for him. Found him high-fiving Jackson Schmidt.

No.

As I passed, Dante popped that last crust in his mouth, looking at me with an unsettling maturity.

"What are you looking at?" I asked when it was just too uncomfortable.

"Nice belt." He leaned against the sideboard again.

"Thanks."

The last I saw, Veronica Hawkins was talking to him, and he kissed the bread from the pads of his second and third finger—the two that my hoodat partner had glided along my tongue, leaving a trail of rosemary flavor.

I was pushed forward, away from Dante, toward the side door where the workers in a white truck gave out prepaid ice cream.

Nice belt.

It was Dante Crowne. He'd identified me from the metal tip at the end of my belt.

Dante didn't play silly teenage games, but it had been him in the closet. No doubt. And he'd told them he didn't know who I was when he obviously did.

Outside, Aileen was waiting. Caleb had his back to me but would find me useful a few days later. Logan and Millie hovered over a phone, days from dating.

"Hey," I said as I approached Aileen. "I think I know—"

I stopped when a feeling of wrongness hit me like a slap in the face. If I shared a moment of what happened in that closet, I wouldn't be winning a game but betraying a confidence. And even if I never said it, I'd be exposing my arousal, opening the door to a terrifyingly dark room and revealing the red, unblinking eyes of shame.

"What do you know?" Millie asked, still canoodling with Logan over some app or another.

Shaking the vision from my head, I shut the door.

"Vanilla," I said as if interrupting myself. "I know what flavor I want. Vanilla."

* * *

Maybe because I didn't know exactly where he was, I was hyperaware of Dante's presence in the Cambria house. I wanted to go into the bathroom and brush my teeth, but we were still at opposite ends of the Jack-and-Jill, and I definitely didn't want to run into him there. I'd had enough of the man for one night.

It was pretty late when movement caught the corner of my eye. The wall of windows in my room was next to the other bedroom. Both faced onto the side of the house and cast trapezoids of light on the empty concrete patio, framing my shadow in one. Next to it, Dante's shadow moved about in the next room. It disappeared and reappeared again with a starkly masculine shape that curved in places usually flattened by clothing.

Was he naked?

More importantly, was he looking at the shadow the light in my room cast as it stretched next to his?

The swelling between my legs throbbed in time with my pulse inside a shell of need and skin. I was tired of feeling things I was powerless to act on.

I was tired of keeping my mouth shut and taking whatever was given to me.

I wanted to come tonight.

So, I would.

"I do what I want," I muttered to myself. "Look or don't."

Standing at the window, I twisted off my shirt, making a show of tossing it aside. Lowered my shorts and kicked them away. Pulled out the sides of my underpants as I stepped out of them. I held my arms out in a gesture visible in the shadow he probably wasn't even looking at.

There, asshole. Like that?

I thought he'd reject me by snapping the drapes shut, but he didn't. He pointed his right finger and circled it, rotating at the wrist.

Get on with it.

Get on with what? Was I supposed to know? Because I didn't care. Getting undressed was a *fuck you*, not a *tell me what to do*.

His left elbow jutted from the edge and back in a slow, rhythmic motion while the right said *get on with it* again.

He was literally jerking off. A hot thrill went through me at the realization. He could pretend to be indifferent to me all he wanted, but Dante wasn't immune to me any more than I was to him.

It was dirty to the point of being almost disgusting. He was jerking off to my shadow, and that held me there more firmly than shackles, pinning me to a raw opening in my desire.

What should have been revolting became enthralling. The anonymity of it. The impropriety. The sheer filth of it didn't repel me. It beckoned.

I spread my arms for him and swung my hips to show my figure. "Beat off to this, Dante."

Spreading my feet apart, I leaned forward until my breasts were visible in the shadow, hanging beneath me as I put a hand on the window and another between my legs.

Jesus. I was as wet as I'd ever been in my life. I ran my fingers along my seam, pivoting until my shadow on the concrete illustrated what I was doing because I needed to control how I turned him on.

It was all about me now, but it didn't hurt to know that I was teasing Dante by reminding him of what he couldn't have. However good his fingers felt to him, my pussy would have been better, and we both knew it.

His elbow sped up. My hips jerked in response as I watched, defenses gone, imagining he wasn't behind a wall, but behind me, fucking me like an animal at the speed of his shadow's hand, while his other shadow hand swung to the side as if he was slapping my ass.

Fantasy Dante slapped my ass, and as the real world of shadows and the imaginary world of animal-fucking collided, I came so hard I dropped to my knees. I wasn't unconscious, but I wasn't conscious either. I was as blank as a sheet of paper, writing my moans with fingers soaked in arousal, all pumping hips and tightening muscles.

Then it was over, and I was looking at the ceiling with no idea how to feel about what had just happened. Discount Mandy might have been ashamed, but I wasn't.

Sitting straight, I looked out the window. He'd either shut his light off or closed the blinds. A soft knock at the bathroom door followed.

"Amanda?"

Fuck. Was I going to have to face him? Were we going to have to discuss this? I could barely get my own head around what I'd just done.

"Don't call me that," I barked, snapping the curtains shut.

"We're not going to make this a thing," he said through the door.

"A th—" Wait a second. Was he making sure I didn't want a commitment or a repeat? Did he really think that was necessary?

He did. He really did, and that assumption was going to end immediately.

"This is not going to be a *thing*." I pointed at the door as if it was his face. "I just wanted to get off, and I did, and I didn't need you to do it. So, if you got your rocks off in the meantime, that's great, but I wouldn't have a *thing* with you if you got on your knees and begged me."

He paused so long I wondered if he'd left the bathroom. I put my ear to the door. When he finally spoke, I was so shocked I had to pull away.

"I'm getting washed up," he said. "Then it's all yours."

"Fine."

If I were polite, I would have backed away when he peed, but all I could think about was the size of the dick that had just exploded for me. Not because I wanted to know... of course. But because I could, and I was a free person, and a fantasy didn't mean I expected a *thing*.

He rapped on the door so gently I felt it on my skin. "You're good to go."

The door on his side closed.

I got my stuff and went into the empty bathroom. As I ran my electric brush over my teeth, I realized I hadn't thought about Renaldo in hours. I hadn't been anxious or sad about him or wondered if he missed me. I didn't make up a story about what he was doing without me.

Getting over him wasn't as impossible as I'd thought.

Tomorrow, I'd be forced back home to hell, but at least I was leaving Cambria on my own terms.

CHAPTER 7

DANTE

SHE'D SURPRISED ME.

When I first saw her shadow moving on the other side of the window, it had sparked a flare I'd intended to ignore. *Control* was my watchword, and I'd spent years refining my body's ability to ignore its immediate desires in favor of longer-term pleasures.

But then she'd stripped, defiant and confident, and there didn't seem to be any point in discouraging her. I wasn't ashamed of what I wanted, and there was no reason to turn down the offer of a freely given fantasy.

It was almost too easy to tune into the half-remembered feeling of her body against mine in that hoodat closet all those years ago—her mouth wrapping hungrily around my fingers, the muscles in her throat moving under the pressure of my hand. In some ways, she'd been my first, and as disinterested as my mind was, my body had never forgotten what it had felt like when she'd asked me for more and I had had the power to refuse, to send her away wet and wanting.

Which I would tomorrow. This had been a one-off thing, a way for her to blow off post-breakup steam and rebound without consequence. She'd wake in the morning, remember who she was, and get the hell out of town.

Amanda Bettencourt might have been branded a slut in public, but I knew her, and she would never again let her desires run wild the way she had tonight. She fucked men because she needed them to tell her who she was, and I would never do that for her. Inevitably, she'd run to someone who would, and that wasn't my problem.

My problems weren't romantic. They were strictly professional and needed attending.

After Amanda holed herself up in her room, I'd gone to the back of the truck to move the cardboard banker's box to the closet. Once her lights were out, I placed it on the desk and checked the crusted, peeling label for the hundredth time.

Thoze & Jensen
THG
Q2/2005 - D

Thoze & Jensen was a legal firm.

THG was The Hawkins Group, a media conglomerate. News. TV. Cable. Internet.

The D after the quarter and year defined what type of records were inside the box we'd found in the storage unit of a recently passed—and apparently sloppy—lawyer.

I'd opened the box when Cooper Santon delivered it to me that morning. Folders and files with boilerplate contracts, nondisclosure agreements, and meeting notes that weren't relevant to me.

What was relevant was the folder with two tiny cassette tapes.

W/C H
Quadrant Hold.
5/12/07

If this tape contained what I thought it did, I'd be released from a tense status quo without publicity or fuss. The other, labeled the same day, was probably meaningless.

Hawkins Trust
5/12/07

The second one might be amusing, but it wouldn't get William and Caleb Hawkins out of my life. One dictation tape in an obsolete media box stood between freedom and me.

Before calling Logan, I emptied the rest of the box and found nothing but more irrelevant files.

"Do you know what time it is?" he asked without preamble in a voice as awake as any insomniac's.

"I spent the evening dealing with your houseguest."

"How is she?" he asked more quietly.

How was she? Petulant. Entitled. Sexier than expected.

Logan didn't need to know that. I'd kept my promise to not touch his friend, but when I'd ejaculated into my hand watching her finger herself, I hadn't exactly honored the spirit of the agreement.

"She's leaving in the morning," I said.

"I'll tell Ella to meet her at her house."

"You don't have to baby her. She's a grown woman."

"Did you call to give me advice?"

"No." I sat in the chair and put my feet on the desk. "I went through the box your people acquired for me."

"And? What do you have?"

"Contracts, garbage, the tapes. I'll go through it tonight and let you know if it's relevant."

I didn't have to let him know anything. This was my problem to solve, but my father would expect to be kept in the loop.

"And the tapes? Do you need someone to come up and do the transcription?"

"Maybe."

"I'll send someone up now."

"No!" The refusal burst out of me before I knew why it was so important or how to cover for it.

"Why not? It'll take Ernie a couple of hours."

I tried to smooth over my outburst. "The house isn't ready. The cells are low, and there's too much cloud cover to recharge. We're not going to have enough power for three people. It'll clear up this weekend."

"He'll wear a sweater."

But I needed to make sure Amanda was well and truly gone before Ernie showed up and ruined everything.

No. That wasn't it. Not one hundred percent.

I wanted to know what she'd say in the morning. Would she be ashamed? Would she beg me to keep quiet about it to Logan and Ella?

Would she want a second round?

"Tell you what," I said. "If I find mom's Dictaphone, I'll listen in the morning. If the tapes are worthwhile, I'll call you."

"Call me even if they're not."

"Fine."

"I want to help you get away from them as much as Dad," he said.

My life wasn't supposed to be a family affair—ever. I'd kept myself and my business separate, but the wall I'd built between us was iron, and the Crowne family was a magnet.

"Goodbye, Logan."

We hung up.

It was late, and I wasn't tired, so I took out a folder and started reading. I should have been alone with my problems, but for the night, I was stuck with Amanda Bettencourt, a woman I'd agreed not to touch and barely liked.

Deep into the early morning hours, with a head full of legalese, I still felt the gut punch of my earlier orgasm, the satisfied thrum of my desire, and the keen knowledge that Amanda was next door.

The contracts in the folder were irrelevant to me, so I finished and slid out the next one.

I'd watched her shadow shudder and shake.

I'd watched her give herself everything she wanted.

The experience had opened a door in my mind, and I couldn't shut it. Desire poured through it, flooding me with an obsessive need.

Seeing her silhouette come wasn't enough. I needed to smell her orgasm. Taste her cunt. Hear her moans when I allowed them. I'd play her like an instrument.

We could deny it later, or brush it off, or laugh about it in front of Logan if he ever found out.

The information in the box had lain dormant for over a decade. What was another few days?

Just one fuck, slipped under the door like a dirty note.

Just one time, I needed to own her body completely.

The obsession was physical and powerful.

The need to *not* fuck her, one time or ever, came from my brother and her neediness, which would hamstring me longer than I was willing to commit to her… and it was just as strong.

They pulled against each other all night, each tugging the rope holding them together.

Tomorrow, I'd cut it.

Or not.

CHAPTER 8

MANDY

In the morning, the first thing that came to my mind was the shadow sex with Dante Crowne.

I waited to regret it.

I told myself I should.

But I didn't. Not at all.

I felt good about it, and for once, I didn't feel good because I thought he wanted me. I wasn't validated by the experience. I'd just enjoyed the give-and-take in the shadows, and that was that. I could do it again, or not. It didn't matter.

Dante wanted me to take a shower instead of a bath, which was my habit anyway. Baths are for relaxing before bed, not waking up. The only reason for a bath that glorious morning would have been to spite him, and I had no desire to send a message about my free agency or personal power. Sometimes a shower is just a shower.

Except for my thoughts, which wandered to last night and Dante's silhouette and the way it filled in information about the shape of him under his clothes. While I shampooed and conditioned, I imagined he was watching me, the click of the glass door opening as he slipped in to join me, thanking me with his fingers for being such a good girl as I used my own fingers.

I came with the shower sprayer standing in for his tongue flicking my clit. Satisfied, I put it back with a smile and a sigh.

See? I was fine. I didn't need a man to get off, just an imagination. I didn't have to care what the actual Dante thought of me at all.

After I was clean and dry, I packed my suitcase for the second time in as many days. When I zipped the bag, I held the pull for a moment too long. The horniness was gone, replaced by the throb of my heartache and the fear of what would happen once I was back home.

Somehow, I'd let my moment of control slip away.

I stood in the doorway, bag in one hand as I scanned the room for the last time, trying to make sure I hadn't left anything. Dante would love that—another piece of evidence that I was exactly the airhead he thought I was.

I wasn't supposed to care what he thought of me, but Discount Mandy wasn't going to be conquered so easily. She slipped back into my heart as if every barrier I'd put between what I wanted and how I'd lived my adult life was no stronger than a sheet of wet paper.

The huge hulk of the typewriter sat on the little desk, as pretentious and unavoidable as Dante Crowne himself. Stronger than my resistance. More powerful than my promises to myself.

I found a clean ream of paper in the drawer, and after pulling out last night's page with its wobbly W, inserted a fresh sheet, rolling it up so that I could pick out a sentence with one furious finger, barely looking at the page as I typed.

I've seen rivers, and you ain't one baby.

My compulsion to respond to him needled my every weakness, but as immature responses went, typing a childish note was less harmful than acting as if he owed me something.

I'd bolster my resistance with music and positive thinking on the road home.

Dante was in the kitchen. His hair was still slightly damp from the shower, but I didn't remember hearing him in there. He must have gotten up before I was conscious. Even on a day off in a cabin in the middle of nowhere, he wore designer jeans and a fine-gauge merino sweater over a collared shirt. Good. His formality would keep me from being flung back into the intensity of last night—the shape of his shadow and the knowledge that he'd wanted me when he thrust his hips into his hand and thought of me when he came.

The memory was almost as seductive as the smell of coffee.

"Good morning," he said, businesslike as ever. He tapped a coffee press. The handle was up, and the container was full of deep, black liquid gold. "I have another cup going."

"Thanks." I put my bag down hard, as if reassuring him that I was really on my way out.

"There's bread out for toast."

He was being awfully nice, putting a mug on the counter for me. I pushed down on the press, feeling the satisfying resistance of the grind.

"No, thanks." I'd never been much of a breakfast person—but if I was being honest with myself, I didn't love the idea of lingering with him for longer than I had to.

"All I have is heavy cream," he said, indicating the metal pitcher.

I'd been on an almond milk kick back home, but I deserved a little indulgence before what would definitely be a shitshow of a day. The white stream billowed in the brew.

"Clouds in my coffee," I said.

He tipped his cup to me. "To vanity, then."

We drank. The coffee was still hot, and it tasted a little chocolatey. I closed my eyes as I swallowed. When I opened them again, Dante was watching me.

Wait. He was being nice, and now he was staring at me.

No, no. I wouldn't let him confuse this issue when I was doing so well.

"If you want to talk about last night—" *Everything's chill*, I prepped myself to say. *We're cool. It's not a big deal.*

But he wouldn't even let me get the sentence out. "There's nothing to talk about because nothing happened."

It wasn't defensive—it was a statement of fact, as cold and calculated as his assessment of my life last night, as if what we'd done had barely even registered for him and it shouldn't register for me either. It was just fun. Thank you and goodbye.

I nodded my agreement, then took another sip of coffee.

Not caring was supposed to make me feel powerful, as Ella had said—I was using men, not the other way around—but it wasn't working. I needed him to care, or expect me to, so that my indifference would take him by surprise. The idea that we'd both left each other cold made me feel kind of depressed. It was the emotional version of slipping into last night's panties before heading home after a one-night stand.

I was so tired of feeling uncertain and unworthy. Cambria was supposed to be my retreat, but somehow, getting out of LA hadn't made my life any better or put me more in control.

"Amanda," he said in a tone I couldn't, wouldn't, try to parse.

"My name's Mandy," I replied, trying to keep my voice inflection free the way he did.

I took my bag and left the kitchen, but my feelings flowed like an unraveling skein of scratchy black wool to the living room and out the front door.

Even though I was curious, I didn't look back to see what he'd made of our last exchange because it wouldn't matter. Couture Mandy barely existed, but at least I could pretend I was her.

The rain was coming down harder now, fat drops pelting the

ground outside the range of the patio roof. Getting back to LA was going to be miserable—any amount of precipitation meant snarled traffic and an uptick in accidents. I checked my phone with the intention of checking traffic, but before I could stop myself, Discount Mandy impulsively opened my texts, hoping to see Renaldo's apology as if that would make it all okay. I would have taken a sweet text from Ella too. Anything to make coming home seem less like surrender.

NO SERVICE.

"Good," I said to myself, putting the phone away. If I couldn't handle having a phone up here, maybe I should just throw the damn thing out when I got home.

I tucked my chin to my chest, said a prayer for the state of my hair, and took two steps before colliding with something large and warm and—Dante.

He was in the same gray raincoat he'd worn the previous night and was holding a huge black umbrella.

"You scared me," I said.

"I'm walking you down to the car. It's slippery."

I scanned him for signs that a walk to the car was more than a walk to the car, but he looked no more or less than sincere, and I didn't want to get any wetter than I had to.

When I stepped under the umbrella, the scent of him surrounded me. Ground coffee, delicious and luxurious. The rain on the fabric made a gentler sound than it did on the cement, but it still felt loud in my ears—a percussive drum, *pop, pop-POP, pop.*

"Thank you," I said.

He didn't say anything but reached for my suitcase. Our hands touched, sparking a core reaction in the basest parts of my brain, so I let him take it before I did or said something monumentally stupid. If he wanted to wear himself out being a gentleman in our last five minutes together, I wouldn't stop him. Nothing I was wearing could have been called practical rainwear, and the absolute last thing I needed was to catch a cold or bust my ankle in front of him.

He hefted the suitcase, looked at it, then at me. "Hm," he said and started down the hill.

I followed under the umbrella. "What's *hm* about this time?"

"I thought it would be heavier."

"Are you trying to insult me?" The tease flew out before I could remind myself that I didn't care what he was trying to do.

"No, actually."

I had to keep my eyes forward as we walked, or I'd fall, but he sounded almost as though he was smiling.

"What made you think I usually travel with my rock collection?" I said.

"I assumed you'd bring lotions and creams and whatever you use to keep yourself beautiful."

Was he making fun of me? He was too serious a person to hand out compliments.

"You don't know you're beautiful?" he asked into my silence.

"Are you trying to get in my pants?" I shot back. I didn't add, *If you are, the answer is yes.*

"As much as I'd like to get those yellow pants off you," he said, definitely smiling now, "it's not to get my hands on the woman in them."

I gave him a *hm* of my own.

The rain was still falling around us, each drop exploding off the fabric of Dante's umbrella, *pop, pop-POP, pop*, under a roof—as if we were in a room together, somewhere small and close. My body was unbearably aware of the nearness of his as we walked.

Pop, pop, pop-POP, pop.

I was glad I couldn't hear my own heartbeat above its rhythm.

We rounded a corner, and there it was—my little buttercup car, waiting to carry me away.

"Where's your car?" I asked.

"I came the back way along Siena Road," he said. His pace

picked up slightly, as if he couldn't wait to finally get rid of me now that the car was in sight. "What I meant when I asked if you knew you were beautiful—"

"Don't," I interrupted. Dante's brain had finally caught up with his mouth, and he was about to either retract the compliment he'd accidentally given me or pile it with a metric ton of platonic vanilla encouragement.

"I think I need to explain."

"You do not."

"After I said it, you asked if I wanted to fuck you."

I couldn't help laughing. "Only to find out you don't like my pants."

"I don't like yellow."

"And you don't want to fuck me. I get it."

"I didn't say I didn't want to fuck you."

We were at the car now. I could have grasped the door's handle. Once I did, I was homeward bound, where the paparazzi waited and bricks went through my window.

Home, where I was a whore with a big, red W and the man who said he'd love me forever never actually did. I'd tried to figure him out a hundred times, taking apart every word choice he made and the timing of every message he sent.

Crazy. I must have been crazy.

Well, I wasn't going to be crazy anymore.

"I don't have time to figure out what you mean," I said, holding out my key fob to pop the trunk of the car. "So, say it or don't."

Preferably don't. I forgot to say that part.

He led me to the back of the car, still sheltering me with the umbrella.

"I'd love to fuck you," he said as if he was talking about meeting me for brunch.

But I barely heard him as I looked into the trunk, which was empty except for the stack of tabloids turned facedown. I knew what the front said, and Discount Mandy replayed it just so I'd remember.

RENALDO & THE HOMEWRECKER: HOW MANDY BETTENCOURT'S BIG PLANS BACKFIRED

Dante's statement needed a reply, but I was paralyzed before the stack of shame. That was what waited for me in Los Angeles. The eyes and the cameras. The name-calling. The invasive pressure of never knowing who was watching me or what they were thinking.

My stupid broken heart didn't have the defenses to leave the house. There would be no avoiding Renaldo and his new woman in Los Angeles, no turning away from the knowledge that everyone knew. I wasn't good enough, pretty enough, smart enough, anything enough.

But my promises to myself…

But the woman I wanted to be…

Did Couture Mandy have to be squashed underfoot before she had a chance?

"This isn't about who wants to fuck," I said, slamming the trunk closed. He didn't respond, and for a second, wild, desperate hope set a blaze in my heart. Words spilled out of my mouth before I could stop them. "Please, Dante. I know we—I know we don't get along. But the house is big enough for both of us. I can stay out of your way. I just really, really need to be someplace safe right now."

He considered that, considered me. I felt naked under his gaze, stripped and scrutinized, as though he was trying to figure out how to break me down for parts.

"You really want to stay?" His voice was quiet, but it filled the space between us already steamy with our breath.

"Yes. I need to."

He was obviously thinking, eyes flitting over my face, jaw clenched as if he was biting back words he'd want to take back.

"Then beg me for it," he said through his teeth. "Beg and you can stay."

Beg? My mouth made the word, but my breath was caught in a flood of arousal at the tone of the command and the thought of kneeling at his feet like a beggar.

Any sense of self-worth I'd cobbled together was shouted down by that hidden headline. I was an animal fleeing home to find shelter anywhere else. He couldn't scare or intimidate me out of here. Dante Crowne had nothing on the combined forces of Tatiana, DMZ, and a lifetime of heartbreak at the hands of careless men.

He wasn't careless though. He was anything but. My heart seemed to make more blood, filling my veins with a pounding heat at the possibility of being under him that drowned out the pride of refusal.

"I'm begging you, Dante." I didn't even have to pretend. "I'm begging you to let me stay."

"Kneel," he goaded me, raising the original dare with a double-dog to get the fuck out of Cambria. Run. Go home to a nemesis I understood and pain I'd invite in like an old friend.

His hard, unrelenting gaze was a physical push downward—an ultimatum he wanted me to take but needed me to refuse.

But what did I need? My body ached to comply. The organs between my legs swelled to just let go of pretense and promise for a moment and embrace a freedom I'd been too scared to want.

So, I knelt. My knees protested the frozen pavement, but I also felt a flash of heat go through me. It felt good to finally surrender, to just fucking submit.

Silence. I couldn't go back now. I'd given up on control to get control, and now that I was begging without worrying whether he really wanted me to beg or not, I had to wait for him to decide.

Exactly what I was trying not to do.

As I looked up, my eyes caught on the bulge in his jeans. He was hard for me.

I'd been acting on instinct, and now I understood why. This was where I'd wanted to be all along. My body pulsed with need, my clit as swollen as he was—as if we were connected without even touching.

His erection was a lightning rod for inspiration. My whole escape to Cambria could be more about who I was when I returned home. Was I a pushover who planned her life based on the whims of men? Or a powerful woman who paved her own path with the bodies of men who tried to get in her way?

Obviously, my doormat days had to be behind me. The irony of making this decision from a kneeling position wasn't lost on me, yet I didn't think I could have gotten there on my feet if they were running.

So, I held Dante's gaze steadily even though I was shaking inside.

"I want to stay, and"—I turned my eyes straight ahead, to the rod in his pants, then back up at his face—"you want me to."

Kneeling at his feet, in the rain, I begged for an indulgence he was unwilling to give, and yet I felt expanded, more powerful, taller, in control of my life and decisions for the first time.

No matter what he decided in the next moment, Couture Mandy had arrived.

CHAPTER 9

DANTE

WHEN I ASKED HER TO BEG, I'D EXPECTED AN ANGRY SLAP AND A quick exit. That would have been the end of this whole thing.

Now I was visibly hard just seeing her kneel.

Logan had said she was going through a nasty breakup. The promise not to touch her had been easy to make. I had no time for soft hearts or clingy women. No matter what she claimed, if I touched her, odds were she'd end up getting hurt. It would get back to Logan, who'd use it as proof I was as rotten as he'd always thought I was, a heartless asshole who burned through women—fucking and dumping.

He was wrong. The fucking was always fun, but there was no dumping. Breakups were built into the agreements. A Boy Scout like Logan wouldn't understand, and I didn't care what my brother thought.

His wife, Ella, was a different story. I liked and respected her. If I hurt her friend, she'd be livid, and she was the type to be upfront about how pissed she was. In a family as close as ours, that could make for uncomfortable encounters that would upset our mother.

It wasn't worth it.

It really wasn't.

Amanda Bettencourt had to go. That was the only scenario that worked for everyone.

But there she was, looking up at me from her knees, begging, and all I could think about was how good she looked from that angle, how close her pretty mouth was to my dick, how—in the moment her knees started to bend and I knew she was going to do it—I'd had to resist a need to take control of her body and mind. It was a familiar need, but in that split second, it had been stronger than ever before.

"I want to stay, and..." she glanced at my erection before turning her eyes back to mine. "You want me to."

I'd told her she could stay if she begged. If I threw her out now, I'd be a liar.

I still had time. I could be enough of an asshole between now and Saturday to scare her off. There was no way she could manufacture anything between us in just a few days—especially since she'd made it clear she wasn't interested in sex.

Letting her stay kept my promise to her, and as long as I didn't fuck her, I was keeping my promise to Logan.

I considered letting her stay, my eyes fixed on the glossy, windswept tumble of hair framing her face. She had to be good at keeping her mouth shut—how many years with Renaldo and no one had proof of their relationship until recently?

And again, I'd told her that if she begged, she could stay.

If she ran away from trouble she brought on herself, that was her problem.

If my dick was a two-by-four, that was my problem.

If she begged defiantly instead of submissively, whose problem was that?

"Your knees are getting wet." I held out my hand, and she took it by the wrist, the correct hold to help someone up.

"So," she said when she was standing, "that beggy enough?"

"As begging goes, it was terrible."

"You want me to try again?"

Before she could drop, I grabbed her arm and held her up. "No, but this isn't a vacation for me. I'm here to work. If you stay, you work."

Her eyes narrowed, and she considered me sidelong.

"You can type," I said without asking because everyone could type.

She shrugged as if she'd never thought about it.

"You'll stay and assist me. You'll be perfect and do what I tell you without questions. That's the deal. That's the whole deal. Take it or leave it."

"I'll take it," she said without thinking, yet without impulsive eagerness, as if she knew what she wanted and was happy to get it.

She was getting so much more than she'd be happy about.

"Let's get your bag, then."

She popped the trunk of the yellow Jaguar, and I retrieved her bag, which was still lighter than I expected.

* * *

THE GET-TOGETHER at Aileen's house had been the same as any other year-end party between families attending a certain cluster of private schools. The adults unwittingly separated by gender, drank wine, beer, and whatever the staff managed to concoct out of the liquor cabinet.

The kids divided themselves up by interest, and I wound up with the group not absorbed in video games or watching dailies of Nadia Genaldi's movie in the basement theater.

That night, it was Logan's crowd I wound up with. They were playing hoodat, and I was curious, but I didn't think I'd get picked.

When I stepped into the closet in Aileen's house, I hadn't

known anything about myself. I was sixteen and headstrong, full of desire but not yet gifted with control. All I knew how to do was follow my instincts, which were still clumsy and inarticulate.

I hadn't even particularly wanted to play the game, but Logan had bet me a hundred dollars I couldn't win a round, and I was always eager to take his money. I had figured out by then that I had an eye for detail most of my peers lacked, which made me confident in my advantage. I wouldn't confuse Aileen's expensive perm for Ella's natural curls.

I walked into the closet absolutely sure of myself.

The girl I found in there surprised me—when she sucked my finger into the liquid heat of her mouth once and then again. No one I'd touched had ever opened up to me that easily before, and knowing it was Amanda Bettencourt—from her height and whispered voice—didn't soften the shock.

My pulse throttled up like the engine of my new Aston Martin shifting gears, an increasingly urgent hum in my ears and under my skin. I touched her soft, vulnerable neck, then the space between her breasts. I felt the heat of her body seeking mine.

She wanted to touch me so badly. She wanted to be touched, and yet she waited because I signaled it, and that control over her was more than hot. It slaked my soul. Sex and desire had seemed like no more than a quest for relief from discomfort.

I'd recently lost my virginity to a fellow Crowne Industries intern and Harvard-Westlake classmate named Delilah Doctorow. Nice girl. Great laugh. Came like a champ. We did it against the copy machine, in the stairwell, on the conference room table, and it was a relief every time.

But this? With Amanda in the closet? This was new, and it was huge. More than the push to quell a need, dominance over her put desire on an equal footing with contentment.

When my fingers made contact with the tip of her belt buckle, I imagined the shape of the mark it could leave on the curve of her ass, and I knew there was something wrong with me I couldn't change.

With Amanda's submission still tender on my fingers, Veronica Hawkins struck up a conversation. A week later, she found me in the locker room at the tennis club and taught me everything Delilah couldn't. Veronica—who was married and in her forties—had yanked me out of my childhood by the collar and built me into a man.

Everything my encounter with Amanda had brought to the surface, Mrs. Hawkins skimmed off and taught me to relish.

As I walked back to the house with Amanda, her knees likely raw and my dick still hard, the awakening in the closet came flooding back. She'd wanted to be dominated then; she'd complied with my demands without even knowing who I was. She was the first girl to make me see that my own desires wouldn't be sated by the usual teenage run around the bases—that I wanted something complicated and specific, dark and urgent. She had been my first sub, and all it took for her to draw me out was seven minutes in a closet.

I felt quite certain I'd been her first too, but the difference between us was that I'd spent the years since exploring what I wanted with women who already knew.

It was always dangerous to get involved with someone who didn't understand herself, and that went double for subs, who needed to be so self-assured they could give their will to me fully without confusing vulnerability for intimacy, or trust for love.

What had happened with Veronica wouldn't happen again. I'd been successful in avoiding it so far. Amanda wasn't going to undo it all just because she was willing to beg a little.

If we started playing by my rules, sore knees would feel like nothing before the end of the day. If I punished her for every infraction—I could already think of a handful she'd committed—she was going to collapse before she had a chance to feel anything dangerous.

Which was exactly what I wanted.

There was no way she'd make it twenty-four hours.

"What are you smirking about?" she asked as we got to the front door.

My phone vibrated in my pocket.

"You're in the smaller room," I said, ignoring the question to look at my phone. It was Logan.

"You're getting signal," she observed with a sulk.

I handed over her bag. "Unpack and we'll get started."

When she was inside, I closed the door between us and answered the call, ducking around the side of the house farthest from the second bedroom.

"What?" I asked.

"What time did Mandy leave? Ella hasn't heard from her."

"She's still here."

"Why?"

Because when I told her to get on her fucking knees, she got on her fucking knees and begged me. "She wants to, and she's not bothering me."

"Have her call Ella, would you?" he asked.

"She has no signal. You call Ella."

"Do you know when she's planning to leave?"

"Tomorrow, I believe."

"Tomorrow?" He was far away, but his frustration came in loud and clear.

"It's *raining*."

Indeed, it was. And though it was the proper season for such an ordinary weather event, it was enough to send an otherwise normal woman into paroxysms of worry for a friend taking a long drive.

I was never a liar. I avoided answering questions I didn't want to, and I was skilled at changing the subject. I'd fly to the moon and back to avoid outright deception, but I didn't see any other way out of the situation. I couldn't tell Logan about my deal with Amanda.

"We're waiting until it clears up," I said. "Then she'll go. It's not safe."

Lying wasn't a part-time job. Either it was a daily practice, or you sucked at it, and Logan knew rain wasn't the type of thing I worried over.

"Dante," he said. "You said you'd keep your hands to yourself."

"I haven't touched her." Technically true. She had touched herself for me. I certainly had some plans to lay hands on her but not the way Logan was imagining.

"And you're not going to."

I was saved from telling him I'd do what I wanted, when and how I wanted, by the sound of the phone being put on speaker.

Ella's voice broke in. "Hi, Dante."

"Hello, Estella."

"You're letting Mandy stay?"

"Until it stops raining." Lying on top of double-dealing. I was committed now.

"Aww!"

Oh, God, save me from a woman's propensity to turn normal behavior into cutesy-pie sugarplums.

"See," she cooed. "I knew you had a heart. Thanks for taking care of her."

I had to guess that Logan hadn't told Ella anything about the Hawkins tapes. If she'd known what Mandy could get caught up in by staying here, there was no way she would have been so excited.

"Don't thank him yet," Logan cut in.

I'd had more than enough of this, and the longer I stayed on the phone, the more likely I was to have to lie again.

"I have to go," I said. "I'll call when Amanda heads out. Probably tomorrow or the next day."

She would too. Because I was in control of this situation, and I wanted her to leave. That would be that. I wasn't going to fuck her, as Logan feared, and while I did have a heart, Ella was wrong that it was guiding my decision-making. I knew what I was doing, and I could prove it, if only to myself.

Amanda had pledged to do whatever I asked of her, and it was time to test that promise.

CHAPTER 10

MANDY

I'D FINALLY WON.

I'd beaten Dante Crowne at his own game. I'd given him what he wanted, sure, but I was getting what I needed in return.

The more I thought about it, the more ideal the whole thing seemed. I could hide out and have what promised to be excellent sex with someone I could never like enough to love. I would come back to Los Angeles well fucked and totally in control, glowing and confident and care-fucking-free.

In the midst of unpacking, thinking wistfully of my favorite La Perla bra-and-panty set, which I hadn't bothered to bring with me, Dante appeared in the door of my room holding a banker's box with a smaller box on top of it.

He placed the load on the desk, next to the antique typewriter. "I have audio dictation tapes," he said, opening the smaller box. "We're going to get you set up with this player." He extracted a black plastic device the size of a whiteboard eraser. "You're going to transcribe one."

As he opened the banker's box and got out a little cassette, I bit my tongue against a "Says who?" since I was the one who had agreed to this deal. "I didn't bring—"

"I didn't say you could speak." He snapped the tape into the player and paused, waiting to see if I would be obedient.

Wow. He was really bossy. Well, I could stay silent, but I didn't have to make it that easy for him.

"Like I said"—Dante continued uncoiling the wire on the headphones—"you're going to listen to these tapes and transcribe them. Format like so." He took a typed transcription from the box and laid it in front of me. "The name in caps. Colon. Tab. Type what they say. Nonverbal cues in brackets."

"Got it." It was just dialogue between two people. Seemed easy.

"Your accuracy is more important than your speed. Since I didn't see a laptop in your things, you'll have to use that." He indicated the typewriter on the desk.

My mouth fell open in shock. I'd been prepared to wash a dish or two, maybe clean the floors naked—suck his dick until my lips were swollen, let him fuck me until we were both worn out—but it was secretary stuff. I could live with that.

The typewriter turned all of it into straight punishment, plain and simple.

"You have a question," he said.

"Why?"

"You don't need to worry about anything except making sure that what's on those tapes gets onto paper."

"What's on them?"

"Your next question will be about the process or practicality of doing this job. Any other question will be answered in a way you don't like. Do you understand?"

"Not really."

He pulled my note from the typewriter with a flourish. My words looked too small on the center of the page, and the typos I hadn't seen in my pique glared at me.

Ive seen rivers, and you aint one baby.

"You did graduate from that garbage high school, right?"

"It wasn't garbage." I would have sworn I punctuated it with apostrophes, but I was mad when I typed it.

"It was obviously a waste of money. One sentence, and you're missing a comma and two apostrophes. You'll have to do better. If you ask the wrong questions or you're careless in your work, you'll be punished."

"You're going to have to define punishment."

He flicked the paper onto the desk. "I'll define it, then. And if you don't like it, you can leave."

"Or the comma police will lock me up and throw away the key?" I taunted. It was kind of fun winding him up and watching the fury build behind his icy eyes.

I don't know what he thought he was accomplishing. I had this well in hand. Instead of arguing, I smiled at him with a half shrug, daring him to punish me the way he'd dared me to beg.

"This isn't a game, Amanda."

"Define punishment all you want, but my name's not Amanda anymore."

In answer, he pulled the chair out from under the desk and placed it to the side, leaving the whole front unblocked. "Elbows on the desk."

"Elbows…?"

"On the desk."

I stood there, realizing what position I'd be in if my elbows were on the desk as he commanded. I'd be bent over with my ass out, and for what?

For the obvious punishment.

He tapped the desk twice, not with impatience, but as a way of waking me up to the choice I had to make.

Do it or don't.

Stay or leave.

Yes or no.

Do it, I decided. Stay. Yes.

Stepping to the desk, I laid my elbows on the wood. Part of me couldn't believe I was inviting Dante Crowne to do whatever he wanted to me.

Part of me had been waiting to finish what we'd started in a closet so many years ago.

"Lay your hands flat," he said from behind me. Being unable to see his face made the command harder to resist and, at the same time, more dangerous.

I flattened my palms against the surface, and I felt a gentle—yet commanding—downward pressure on my lower back. My spine curved at its authority, as if it wasn't just pushing but interrupting the message from my brain that it needed to resist.

"If you want to stop," he said. "Just say stop."

"Okay."

I could have told him this wasn't going to happen, but I didn't, and we both needed a moment to digest that. At least, I did, and I took his pause to mean the same.

"Now," he said. "*I've* is a contraction of I and have. The missing letters are replaced with an apostrophe. Spell it."

"Spell what?"

"*I've.*"

"I-vee-ee."

Smack.

I almost choked on the pleasure of his hand connecting with my ass. My pride was furious with me, but it was no match for the pure, luxurious sting.

"I've seen rivers," Dante said. "I-apostrophe." *Smack.* "Vee-ee." *Smack.*

Every time one of his slaps landed, I rocked forward onto my toes, my hips thrusting instinctively. It was like he was getting me in rhythm, forcing my body to move at his pace. It was ruthless, and I wanted more.

"Continue."

"I've seen rivers, and you ain't…"

Smack. Harder than before, as if a new infraction demanded a new level of intensity.

"It's colloquial, but it has an accepted spelling."

Through my clothes, I felt his hand rest on my burning ass as he waited. The stinging skin was sensitive to every stroke.

"A-I-N—" I paused, wanting another smack but wanting to please him more. "Apostrophe T."

"Go on." His fingers brushed the seam between my cheeks. I was so turned on I lost my place in the sentence, and he helped me as if he knew. "And you ain't—"

"You ain't one bab—"

He smacked my ass so hard I grunted like an animal.

"Comma before *baby*, Amanda." He paused, then said, "I've seen rivers, and you ain't one, comma, baby," before giving me two more sharp spanks.

I could barely think. Sure, it hurt, but the sting of his punishment was strangely welcome, as if he knew exactly what I needed and it was more than stimulation.

It was knowing I'd done something wrong and being set right.

It was giving up control so I could get a better grip on it.

"Okay," I gasped. "Comma, baby."

That wasn't good enough for him.

"Okay?" *Smack.* "Am I your hairdresser?" *Smack.* "Your lunch buddy?" *Smack.*

He paused to let me collect myself, but all I could think was how I wanted more. Needed it. My ass was tingling, and my clit was swelling. I felt my nipples stiffen against the lace of my bra, the weight of my breasts begging for him to cup them in one of those huge hands. He could have fucked me right over the desk, and I wouldn't have resisted. I was so wet he could have slid right in.

"No."

Dante leaned down so that our heads were close together. He

wasn't touching me anywhere, but I sensed his body behind me, his weight, his heat as he spoke softly. "The answer is, 'Yes, sir.'"

I twisted my head around so that I could meet his gaze. It was as pale and piercing as ever. "Seriously?"

"When you're being disciplined, yes, seriously."

Disciplined? My brain was screaming at me to tell him to fuck off, that he had no right—no right—but the only thing I wanted more than to tell him to stop was to get him to keep going, to hit me again, then let his fingers slip between my legs where the seam of my pants rubbed against my swollen nub.

He was hard. This time, I didn't have to see it to know it.

"Yes, sir."

He smacked me once more, playfully this time, then pulled away entirely.

"Get to work," he said and left the room before I could check to see if he had the erection I'd assumed.

I rested my head against the cool wood of the desk, resisting the urge to slip my hand into my pants and give myself relief. I couldn't stop thinking about what it would have felt like if he'd just let go of his control and slid into me where I stood. I ached with emptiness. I wanted to be full, bursting, breaking through the membrane of control. I didn't need to love him or even like him. I could use him the way he'd use me given the chance.

I didn't know what he wanted with these tapes, and I didn't care.

I wasn't done with him yet.

CHAPTER 11

DANTE

Without offering aftercare that would confuse her, I left Amanda bent over the desk and changed into work clothes. The gutters weren't going to clean themselves, and I hoped the fresh air would clear my head and wilt my hard-on. Getting carried away with her was so easy. Too easy. But maybe that was a good thing since I was trying to scare her off.

The way she'd sighed acceptance when she knew what the punishment entailed, the way her body had rocked into the rhythm I set for her, was subtle but undeniable. Her reactions were uniquely hers, but they weren't just readable—they went right to my muscle memory. Her every twitch was coded specifically for my senses, and for a moment, I'd lost myself in her pain.

Stopping had taken superhuman effort. The path of her correction was laid out so clearly before me. Taking her pants down to renew the sting of my hand, then her underpants. When she was driven to tears, I'd stroke her wet cunt before—

Stop.

There was no point in even mentally finishing the process.

I had plenty to do to keep my mind off my sore palms and hard dick. The house always needed maintenance, and I always took care of it. I got out a ladder and climbed up onto the flat roof, which was covered in reflective white TPO paper that was sealed against the bases of the solar panels.

The rain's patter against the roof was gentle and constant, syncopated with the sharper, less regular *tappa*-pause-*tapping* of Amanda typing below me. Despite the crawlspace over the ceiling, she could probably hear me walking around up here, my boots thudding over her head. I liked the idea of my presence lingering in the room with her—in the soreness of her ass, her defiance over commas, and her insistence on following my instructions anyway.

She was transcribing the tape that didn't matter. Best not to think about how many mistakes she was making. Not because it mattered—she'd been given the meaningless tape—but because every mistake would be a chance for her to receive or walk away from punishment.

I dreaded and desired both outcomes.

A triangular puddle had formed in the center of the roof, where an inverted slope drew runoff to the downspout. The gutters must have been full of more garbage than usual. Leaning over the end of the house opposite her room, I cleared out the muck and tossed it over the side.

The rhythmic nature of the work helped to soothe and settle my mind. For a while, I thought of nothing as I made my way around the perimeter, focusing instead on the movement of my hands and the cold making its way under my clothes.

But as I traveled the roof's edge toward the downspout, I found myself standing over the sound of her typing, and my body reacted like a teenager's who was peeking into the girls' locker room.

Zero control. Pathetic.

I was slipping with her.

"Yes," she'd said in a dark closet after I took my fingers from her mouth.

I'd been so young and eager, inexperienced at taking control the way I wanted to. Amanda had been my first taste of dominance, and, typical virgin, I'd bungled it. Didn't go as far as I wanted… and at the same time, I'd pushed things too far.

Did I think I was going to make it right? Heal some adolescent wound?

I didn't know, and I couldn't afford to find out.

There was no question she'd deserve a spanking every time I checked her work. All I had to do was keep her ass red enough to get her out of the house and keep myself busy enough not to want anything else from her.

I could do both of those things at the same time.

As soon as the gutters were clear enough to function again, I made my way down the ladder.

I had plenty of work like this to do. I could get the house back into shape and get rid of Amanda without going too far.

Walking around the perimeter, I passed her window. She was biting her lower lip as she paused the tape, then she two-finger typed. Hunt. Peck. Hunt. Peck, peck.

She wiggled in her seat as if relieving pain in a sore ass.

That was mine. That wiggle. I owned it.

Tearing myself away, I went back into the house, where her presence was like a force of gravity. The door to her bedroom was open. I could look in and see her squirm. Step in and demand she stay still. Walk in and check her work.

No. None of it.

Maybe I was moved by her proximity or the lack of choices in Cambria. Maybe it was having a woman in a house I only stayed in alone. Maybe it was the surprise of her willingness.

"Maybe it's irrelevant," I muttered, staring into the empty fireplace.

My hands had to stay busy, and my mind had to stay occupied with tiny details, or I would succumb to the unanticipated, and unacceptable, charms of this woman.

CHAPTER 12

MANDY

After snapping off the tape player, I pulled the headphones away and leaned back in my seat.

With my ass still sore and my fingers confused by the new repetitive motion I demanded, I took a break and turned the phone on out of habit, but no dice. I still didn't have a kernel of reception, even when I stepped out onto the patio. The rain had stopped, and the air smelled sweet, but it was too cold for me to stay out for long in the gathering darkness.

Transcribing phone calls was probably the hardest thing I'd ever done. Stop. Type. Start. Stop. Type. Start. There had to be an easier way, but I wasn't about to suggest it. If Dante wanted it done the easy way—whatever that was—he would have asked for it that way.

I recognized the law firm's name on the box. They were huge. Offices everywhere. I'd hoped for something juicy on the tapes, but the conversation was so boring I wondered why the lawyer would want to record it or why someone who wasn't even on the call would want it typed up.

But the work was so hard I had to concentrate fully. My sore bottom stopped bothering me when my mind was occupied, until the smell of dinner got too compelling to ignore.

If I went into the kitchen and found he hadn't made enough dinner for me, I was going to gnaw his arm right off.

The patio doors from the kitchen were closed this time, and instead of making tea, Dante stood before a slab of meat on a cutting board. The table was set, the red wine was aerating in a carafe, and the chef wore a crisp, white shirt with the sleeves rolled up past his tight forearms. Even with splashing juices, it didn't have a single spot on it.

"How's the work coming?" he asked without looking at me, so I got to stare at the way his objective good looks were elevated by competence as he slipped a knife from the block, spun the handle around his finger, and let it land in his palm.

"Slow." I sat on the opposite side of the bar and watched him slice the meat with sexy precision. "Harder than I expected. My fingers keep slipping off the sides of the keys."

"Hm," was all he said.

I couldn't determine if that was good or bad. Probably indifferent. Not that it mattered, I reminded myself. I wanted to fuck him, not love him.

"Do you have, like, a deadline for all this to be done?" I asked.

"Yes." He lifted the slices, then the bigger piece of meat, onto an oval plate and brought it to the table. "But I'm not going to tell you what it is."

"Why not?"

"Doing it fast is the enemy of doing it right."

His hand rested on the back of a chair as if he was going to pull it out, but he stopped himself, and—with his hand flat—he indicated I should sit in it.

"True." I sat. "Shortcuts are a great way to piss off your client."

"Hm."

Again with the *hm*. It wasn't even a word, but he managed to tell me everything with it. The first *hm* of the conversation had been confirmation that he'd heard me. This one was agreement and—oddly, even uncomfortably—admiration.

He lifted the lid of a serving bowl to reveal little potatoes dusted with herbs.

People with one-tenth of Dante Crowne's money stopped doing their own cooking unless they invested in a restaurant. My parents were dead broke compared to what they had been born with, but God forbid Dad would pick up a pot. Sometimes Mom would make one dish for a dinner party to impress the guest but have the rest catered because—really?

I glanced over the countertops. They were clean. He didn't have staff hiding somewhere. The guest room, where I'd typed and obsessed over commas, faced out into the driveway. I would have heard someone pull up. There were no servants' quarters.

He lifted two slices of steak onto my plate. The burgundy glaze spread evenly into a spice-dotted puddle as if he had personally ordered it to go no farther than two centimeters from the meat. He hadn't left it super-rare, the way purist macho grill guys sometimes did, the way Renaldo ordered it. He pretended to like steak but never finished it—until he cooked for me one time, and it was gray throughout.

I could assume Dante had made the entire meal, or I could ask. We needed something to talk about over dinner anyway.

"So, you cook?" Since he didn't offer to scoop my potatoes, I did it myself.

"Obviously."

I waited the length of time it took for me to cut off an end of steak and spear it with a potato, but he didn't elaborate.

Well, then. That wasn't tonight's conversation starter.

I ate, and layers of flavor exploded like fireworks that burned different colors in the sky. Sweet and tangy and a rich smoke I had to savor before swallowing.

"Hm," I said, lifting the wine he'd poured for us. "And that's a direct quote."

He gave a quiet laugh. Better... because a loose Dante was a Dante who'd give me what I wanted. I was learning to appreciate what men went through to get women into bed—analyzing every breath and movement not as a reflection of my own worth, but to gauge how much closer I was to my goal.

"So," I started. "Why do you need these conversations typed?"

He took a long time to answer, but I didn't press him because either he was thinking about answering or not answering while I was thinking about the strength of his hands, the way his fingers angled around the handle of the fork, his jaw tensing and releasing as he chewed.

I ate. He ate. I thought he forgot the question until he answered it.

"Typing it out makes it easier for lawyers to digest."

"So, there's a court case or something?"

My question wasn't judgmental. Guys like the Crownes—rich guys with deep pockets and multilayered business interests—sued and got sued all the time. That was what retainers were for.

"Or something," he said.

After a gulp of wine, I said, "There's one thing I have to know. When we all played hoodat...was that you in the closet?"

He smiled like a man caught with a pleasing secret he'd waited a long time to be uncovered. "You know the answer."

"You never said anything." I shrugged as if it had meant nothing at all, but I wasn't fooling either of us.

"We were two kids in a closet." He paused to drink his own wine. "What did you want me to say?"

"What I asked. Did you know it was me or not?"

"Yes."

"So, you lost the game on purpose?"

"Did I lose?"

"Kind of."

He leaned his back in his chair and crossed his arms. It was hard to not look at his hands. They weren't the narrow, soft hands of a businessman, but the wide, strong hands of a man who worked with them. "Getting a promotion in the social pecking order isn't a win. I got to spend seven minutes in a closet with Amanda Bettencourt. I felt the curves of her body. She tasted me, and I tasted her. Winning's fine, but that's a landslide."

Nerves dampened my palms, and the fork slipped, clattering to the plate. I picked it up and looked away. I'd gone years thinking it was Dante and sure his dominance in the dark was a meaningless game he'd played just for the sake of it.

Yet, I couldn't be sure he was talking about me and not just one of the girls in the other room. Did he feel like a winner because he'd wanted *me* or because I'd let him put his finger in my mouth? If Ella or Millie had been in the closet, exchanging spit without kissing, would it have been equally successful?

I couldn't put the question together in a way that didn't make me sound needy and insecure. He saved me the trouble.

The salad dressing was made with lemons from the tree. Meyers. Sweet and sour in a way that wasn't forced or cloying. Complex as a series of adolescent questions nagging at me in my womanhood.

"How far did you get in the tapes?" Dante asked.

Of course. He would ask a girl to beg, spank her until she almost came, then talk business over dinner.

"I finished the hello-how-do-you-dos," I said. "Just a page. The typewriter, it's slow."

Staring at him over the rim of my wine glass, I tried to transmit an unsubtle hint. *Why don't you ask me to do something I'm better at?*

"I appreciate you helping me, Amanda." He nodded, his smile sliding dangerously close to a smirk, but there was something warm there, a single caviar egg of genuine emotion glistening in his otherwise distant façade.

I was too distracted to protest his continued use of my full name.

"So, we both know why I was run out of LA," I said, trying to sound cavalier, "but what are you doing up here? Other than tormenting nice girls with boring projects."

"Why do you still think of yourself as a girl?"

"It's just an expression."

"So, you're not a girl. Are you nice?"

"No." I shrugged. "Probably not."

"That's why the work's boring?"

"Sure, small talk between Veronica Hawkins and her lawyer's riveting if you're *nice*." I rolled my eyes at the absurdity of the idea, but I still caught a flash of tension as it made its way through his body.

"You're scared," he said sharply, one stiff finger tapping the tabletop.

Whatever softness I had seen in Dante was quickly hidden. What happened here? I had been making progress, and now I was looking at him through a wall of anxiety.

"I'm not scared of anything." Cowering from the paparazzi in a secret location counted as fear, but fuck him. He didn't have the right to pretend he knew me. "You're the one too scared to even tell me why you can't have your secretary or whatever type up a bunch of blah-blahing from 2005 about"—I waved my hand, reaching for some small detail from the tape—"prenups and infidelity clauses or…"

Abruptly, he stood. "I have work to do. I clean as I go, but dishes need to be done. The leftovers need to get put away. Containers are under the sink. You can scrub the broiling pan with the green brush."

"Oh," I said in confusion.

"We don't have staff here," he said, dropping his arms. "I cook, you clean. If you make the meal, I clean."

"Right." I agreed by reflex, not reflection. "No problem."

"Good. I'll see you later."

I watched the way his jeans fit as he walked out, and I could say without reservation, from a strictly professional standpoint, they were perfect.

I just couldn't get a handle on him. Getting a guy into bed should have been easier, but I could barely keep from pissing him off.

He was single, and so was I. He'd told me I was beautiful and had gotten hard when I was on my knees at his feet. I'd practically offered him my pussy on a platter. What was the disconnect? What was I missing that would get us from this kind of verbal sparring and hard spanking to the hard fucking I was really after?

I collected the dishes and took them to the sink. That was when I realized there was no dishwasher. They had to be done by hand, 1950s style.

"Worst. Vacation. Ever," I muttered, running the water as hard and hot as it would go, daring him to come back in the kitchen to tell me I was wasting it.

CHAPTER 13

MANDY

Dante may have washed as he cooked but not enough to make the job easy. By the time I finished the dishes, my hands were pruney, and I was more committed than ever to the idea that having a full-time cleaning person was not a luxury.

Dante was in my room, playing the conversation I'd spent the day transcribing, tapping a red pen on the desk like a guy with more problems than time. When I walked in, he pulled the headphones off and held up the page I'd typed. It had so many red marks it looked like a creative three-year-old had gotten hold of it.

Admittedly, I wanted another spanking and then some, but I wasn't trying to screw up this badly. I snapped the paper from him. I couldn't have made that many mistakes.

He'd circled misspellings of "prenuptial," "renegotiation," and "anniversary," as well as two instances where I didn't capitalize the V in Veronica and one for the H in Hawkins.

He'd crossed out a hyphen I'd added between "infidelity" and "clause" because it seemed like something a person who knew what they were doing would add.

He'd removed a line break between "If William has an affair, you should be protected," and her laughter.

He'd crossed out commas—which I'd littered all over like cupcake sprinkles—dropped question marks where he didn't know what I was thinking, and crossed out "benifishary" to correct the spelling.

"Did your family even own a dictionary?"

I had no idea but probably not. My mother had thrown a party for Umberto Lario when he won a Pulitzer, but otherwise, we weren't bookish. If we had a decorative dictionary, it was probably on its side with a vase over it.

"If you want to leave," he said, leaning against the desk and crossing his arms, "you don't have to fail. You can just leave."

I scoffed, resisting the urge to slap him right across his gorgeous face. Instead, I slapped open the top drawer and got out my nightgown.

"I'm off the clock," I said, whipping off my T-shirt, leaving my torso bare down to a plain, butter-colored cotton bra. "I sat here all day and typed your transcript." I wiggled the nightgown over my head. "I went slow because I knew I'd make mistakes anyway." I unhooked my bra and pulled the straps through the sleeves—a trick every girl learns in the first five minutes of womanhood. "I tried my best with a sore ass, no thanks to you, but thanks."

His eyes wandered to the natural shape of my body under the thin nightgown, but his arms were still crossed.

Let him look. I shouldn't have bothered changing summer-camp style. I should have just pranced around naked and given him something to stare at.

"I washed your dishes." I wiggled out of my pants. "I let you call me the wrong name. I typed a bunch of garbage on that thing. So you"—I threw my dirty clothes into a pile in the corner—"can correct me all you want, and you can spank me for typing wrong because I like it, but you can back off with the insults."

I stormed into the bathroom, closing the door like a grown-up even though I wanted to slam it so hard this shitty house shook, and twisted the tub faucet all the way to hot. The sound of the water was the music of freedom.

I laid my hands on the end of the vanity and breathed. My hair wasn't half-bad for the humidity, and my braless tits were pretty hot in the gauzy yellow fabric. Good. I'd given him an eyeful.

It would be a minute before the water was hot enough to plug the drain. Might as well spend the time not thinking about Dante.

Standing straight, I snapped my toothbrush from the charger.

My toothbrush was, unfortunately, a piece of Renaldo memorabilia. It had been in an Emmy Awards Show swag bag honoring Renaldo's wife's nomination for some boring historical miniseries she'd done. The sleek piece of rose gold housed a high-powered motor to keep your teeth movie-star clean. Renaldo had kept his in my bathroom for the days chewing gum didn't get the taste of my pussy out of his mouth.

Fuck this thing and every single object that man had ever touched.

When I got home, I was throwing it away and getting a plain white one.

The second beep had just alerted me to the end of the first minute of brushing when Dante came in from his side and shut off the faucet.

"Hey!"

"No baths. I told you."

The cold water gurgled down the drain, and I gave him a solo view of my middle finger.

"Amanda."

"Name's not Amanda," I garbled. "Hang on, okay?"

Dante watched impassively, silent and still for the next sixty seconds. When the brush beeped, I turned it off, spat white foam into the sink, and rinsed my mouth.

"It tells you how long to brush?" he asked, picking up the brush to examine it.

I nodded, hoping that my face conveyed, *How does a rich motherfucker like you not know how an electric toothbrush works?*

"That's impressive micromanagement." His face was all angles, harsh and handsome and unpredictable. If he wasn't so impossible, I would have been in real trouble, but I'd be fine. Totally fine.

"Not as impressive as you coming in here without knocking."

"I don't ask permission to perfect and correct what's mine."

Perfecting and correcting were fine, but had he just insinuated that he owned me?

He had.

How was I supposed to feel about that?

Was I supposed to feel the warm calm his words drew?

Or the stiffened hackles that followed?

Both.

Yes. Both were valid, but only one needed to be expressed out loud.

"You didn't earn me," I said.

He pulled the hand towel from the ring and wiped the puddles of water from the marble counter, nodding as if he agreed and intended to rectify the problem.

"Elbows on the counter." He spoke with a calm command that indicated I'd obey him without question.

So, I did.

CHAPTER 11

DANTE

THE TYPOS WEREN'T THE POINT. THEY HAD NEVER BEEN THE POINT. Ernie or any decent secretary could get everything taken care of for both tapes. If I'd really needed the transcription of the generic tape, I would never have gone to this particular failed secretarial school candidate for them. She either couldn't spell or didn't want to, and her issues with commas went deeper than I could have imagined.

And none of that changed the fact that I wanted her so much it was turning me inside out until I was unrecognizable to myself. At dinner, all I could think about was how badly I wanted to order her to crawl under the table and sit at my feet. The vision of her curled up there, my obedient little secret, made me burn with desire. Or maybe I wanted to get down there myself and put my mouth on her and tell her she had to finish her dinner before she'd be allowed to come.

The flowchart of plans for her body had run through my mind and landed at my cock until the moment she told me Veronica Hawkins was on the call, and I knew I was playing a game I couldn't win. The generic, meaningless tape wasn't meaningless at all.

Veronica had been asking her lawyer about divorcing William. That was all I could put together from what Amanda had said, and I didn't want her to tell me more. I wanted to hear it from my first love's mouth.

I hadn't been able to keep my mind on dinner. I left her with the dishes and went to her desk. I put on her headphones, listened to the words Veronica had said, and was whipped back to a reality more terrible than I imagined.

Forget the infidelity clause. Forget the whole prenup.

Veronica had always told me her husband couldn't find out about our affair. She'd been desperate for secrecy. Best-case scenario? He'd leave her destitute. Probable case? William was a bruiser of a man who'd beat her near to death.

So, we hatched a plan to protect me and give us a way out. I'd own properties we bought together with her savings and my One Big Thing—the one nonrefusable request we got to ask our parents for. She'd cosign as an adult silent partner, hiding behind a Russian doll of shell companies. My parents didn't know about Veronica—my silent partner—and since I was the first sibling to request their OTB and I asked them to keep it secret, they'd made the mistake of giving me the money without asking too many questions.

I'd thought I was keeping Veronica safe.

And yet, on a May 12th call with a lawyer from her husband's firm, she wasn't afraid of William Hawkins at all.

I listened a dozen times and didn't detect an ounce of fear in her voice.

I took off the headphones and heard Amanda washing the dishes. It had been a mistake, all of it—letting her get comfortable here and letting myself get comfortable with her. I had to send her to bed thinking about how soon she could leave in the morning, not wondering if I wasn't such bad guy after all.

I had to push harder but not so hard I broke her.

*\ *\ *

"Elbows on the counter," I said in the bathroom, the electric toothbrush in hand.

Her face went from acceptance to protest, and my uplifted heart went to relieved until she bent over and presented me with the impossible temptation of her ass.

Push harder.

I pulled up her nightgown and slid her underwear down. I couldn't punish her again. She was bruised and swollen and perfect from earlier. When I ran my thumb over the reddened skin, she gasped.

We hadn't seen each other all day, but I'd been with her every second.

This kind of thinking wasn't going to help anything.

I warmed her up by smacking one cheek, then the other, a couple of times, and her gasps sounded so close to moans that I couldn't help myself—I stroked her reddening skin gently to remind her just how good a tender touch could feel.

Her head dropped between her hands. I could smell her body opening up. I was taking liberties, and the cresting waves of my own desire only inflamed hers.

"Look up," I said. "Eyes on me in the mirror."

When she picked up her head, one curl fell over her cheek. That would make her crazy, and if she tried, I wouldn't let her brush it away.

"You're not supposed to enjoy this," I reminded her.

"Then stop being so good at it."

"You have no idea how good at this I am." With a nudge of my foot, I pushed her legs open wider. The heat between us could have powered a city.

"Show me, then... *sir*."

I leaned over her to speak quietly, grabbing a handful of sore ass.

"Don't try to be saucy." I watched in the mirror as the defiance in her green eyes melted away. "If I wanted to…" I filled my voice and body with every ounce of dominance I had, squeezing out hesitation and doubt. "If I really wanted to, I could have you writhing on my cock, begging me to put it wherever I wanted as long as it was inside you. Crying for a taste. You'd suck my fingers until you choked on them, and you'd beg for more because no one can give it to you like I can."

The self-control I'd cultivated since I was sixteen abandoned me, and I acted on pure, uncut instinct, pushing her back down as I stood straight. I yanked off the head of toothbrush and turned it on, feeling the tremor of its eager little buzz.

For that moment, I forgot all about the tapes and the surprises on them.

I forgot about all the decisions I'd made based on what I thought I knew.

I forgot that I was supposed to push Amanda into leaving.

The LED screen on the toothbrush flashed: 2:00.

I had two minutes to keep forgetting.

Running the handle along her spine to the top of her crack, I pushed her legs open even farther so I could run the shaft of the toothbrush over her ass and inside her thighs.

"That document," I said, moving the brush from one thigh to the other without touching between, "was a disaster. What do you have to say for yourself?"

Eyes closed, mouth open, she whimpered, making soft, helpless little noises.

"Look at me." When she opened her eyes, I let the vibrating rod hang just below her sex, close enough to feel it but too far to satisfy. "What's your excuse?"

"I don't have… have—" She lowered her body, but she was too slow, and I moved it away. I knew women, and I knew their orgasms. They'd meet a man halfway.

"You don't have an excuse," I said.

"No." Her eyes scrunched with the need to close so she could focus on the pleasure, but she kept them on me.

"Good girl."

I touched the vibrating handle against her clit. She reached back blindly to tug my body closer to hers. I immobilized her hip against the counter by pushing the pillar of my erection into her ass cheek, letting her melt into my steadiness as I circled her nub and accelerating my own pleasure with little jerks, giving her just enough to keep her right on the edge and myself enough to want more.

"Oh, God," she groaned.

"What do you want, Amanda?"

Was she too close to correct her name?

"I want to come. Please."

"What have you done to deserve that?" I felt how close she was, and I knew exactly what it would take to get her there.

"Please."

The LED said I had eleven seconds, and if I let them lapse without letting her come, she'd be so enraged she'd leave.

Good. That was the point.

I wanted her to go home.

Or I could release my cock and bury it inside her. Make her hate me for pulling her hair, taking her ass, calling her a whore. Anything but this torture.

My belt was halfway undone before I even realized I'd made the decision to take her, and I only woke out of my hormonal stupor after the beep—when the toothbrush motor stopped.

She whispered a soft, strained, heartfelt, "Fuck," because she'd accepted the terms I'd laid out even when I couldn't.

I put the brush back on the counter.

"Hand me a page without mistakes," I said, only realizing how breathless I was when I tried to speak. "And I'll finish you until you scream."

I left before I did something I wasn't supposed to, exiting to my room and closing the door.

My cock ached for release. There was no way Amanda could withstand what I could. A girl like Amanda Bettencourt didn't understand anything less than instant gratification.

All I had to do was sleep it off, but everything Amanda's punishment had helped me forget came roaring back.

Tomorrow, Amanda would leave in frustration, and I'd be alone with those tapes and their unexpected revelations. I'd know the secrets Veronica had kept from her husband and the ones she'd kept from me before everything went sideways.

Pacing the room, I tried not to blame Veronica for everything. We had been doomed by our disparity in age, but I couldn't help but think that if I'd been older, I wouldn't have been so trusting and she'd be alive today.

Needing to get outside, I went to the back patio door and froze, again forgetting any problem I thought I'd had before I found Amanda Bettencourt in my bathtub.

Obviously, she thought I was a dog she could train.

She was wrong.

CHAPTER 15

MANDY

If he thought that was the end of it, I was about to prove him very, very wrong. I'd had plenty of orgasms in my life before I met Dante Crowne. I'd had more than my share before a man even touched me.

I flicked the lights on and opened the curtains to let Dante to see every inch of me so he'd know exactly what he'd done and exactly what he was missing. His drapes were still closed, but in the slit of light between them, I saw his shadow moving as he entered the room. He was there but not paying attention.

Well, I'd have to rectify that... or not. It didn't matter. My orgasm would be for me. His awareness of it was irrelevant.

I dragged the chair I'd been sitting in all day to the window with me. I propped up one foot and hitched up my nightgown to slide a hand between my legs, where I ached for pressure and friction. It felt so good that for a moment, I stopped thinking about Dante altogether. I just wanted relief.

But part of me wanted to put on a show and to demonstrate some measure of the control he clearly worshiped. So, I forced myself to be gentle, grazing my fingers over my clit and then downward, giving myself a whisper of pressure against my slit before dragging them back up. I remembered how he'd stroked me with the toothbrush, firm and commanding, and did it again.

"Come on, you asshole," I said to the place his silhouette had been. "Watch me do what you can't."

Dante's shadow moved across the room once, then twice, like he was pacing, or maybe just ignoring me, getting his things together before going to bed.

I leaned forward, bracing my hand on the window so I could slide two fingers fully inside myself with a gasp of relief. If he wouldn't fuck me, I could fuck myself.

His shadow moved again, this time coming to stand at the slit between his curtains, blocking out the light from behind him.

Now that I knew I had his attention, I wanted him to watch me come before he joined in so we could replay the other night.

I was going to come, then close the curtains before he finished.

I sped up the motion of my hand, giving myself exactly what I wanted—the firm pressure of my palm against my clit and my fingers inside, coaxing my orgasm out with a demanding rhythm. It gathered in my belly, tightening my nipples and pushing my hips forward.

"Watch how little I need you." I groaned, keeping my gaze on the darkness below the slit of light.

And then, in one fluid motion, he pulled the drapes all the way shut.

My orgasm took a step back. I took my leg off the chair and cupped my hand between my legs, resting my head against the cool glass.

My ass was sore, my cheeks were hot, I was dripping wet between my legs, and I couldn't understand how someone who wanted me so badly, who seemed to understand my body better than I did, just kept refusing to give me what I needed.

I wasn't going to win this.

He was too good at this mindfuck of a game.

I realized the difference between who I was and who I wanted to be.

Discount Mandy would stay.

Couture Mandy had no time for this.

Deciding whether or not to go home was moot. My only choice was between leaving immediately, before bed, or after a good night's sleep—but I was definitely cutting my losses and going home before I ended up right back where I began: confused, brokenhearted, out of control.

The next thing I knew, Dante burst into my room, turning me around and pushing me against the glass door. His eyes were dark with lust, and his cock was hard against me. My breath caught in my chest, and as I raised my arms to push him away, his lips landed on me, opening my mouth for his as his tongue probed me, owned me, demanded more of me than I knew how to give—and instead of pushing him away, my hands tightened on his shirt and pulled him closer.

I was a teenager in his arms, wild and desperate. He tugged my head back so that he could keep kissing me as he cupped my breast, fingertips toying with the sensitive peaks of my nipples. Our hips pressed together, and I could feel him, that hard, pulsing length I'd seen but not touched, and all I could think was, *That's for me.*

Pinching open the button on his jeans, I reached inside and found his wet-tipped cock ready for my fist. It was huge and rigid, a column of stone wrapped in hot skin. I groaned when he reached around and under my nightgown to get his hand on my soaking lips, his fingers exactly the rough, blunt pressure I'd been aching for.

"You're so wet for me," he rumbled.

I couldn't even find enough breath to agree—I had to keep kissing him, giving myself up to the sweep of his tongue in my mouth, and riding the flick of his fingers on my clit as he thrust his cock into my fist.

"I'm going to come," I gasped, and he stilled his hand in response.

"There are rules," he said with a smirk. "You didn't give me a perfect page."

Was he going to make me type right then and there? How was I supposed to hit the right keys when my body only lived for the pleasure he controlled?

"I know, but I want it."

He got harder in my hand, gazing at me, holding me up with a flick of his fingers. He opened his mouth to agree to give me whatever I wanted but said something else instead. "Beg for it."

He wanted my supplication. Humiliation. He wanted to turn me into a mess of nerves and flesh without a will for anything he couldn't grant with a twitch of his fingers.

"Please. I haven't earned it, but please let me come. I'll be perfect from now on."

"I like how you beg." He pulled me close, pushing two fingers inside me and using a third to circle my clit. "Do it. Come into my hand."

I hadn't done anything this messy and frantic and bone-melting in years. Maybe ever. We'd been playing chicken with each other all day; now we were crashing over the edge of a cliff together, flying with momentum, too desperate to care if we ended up in flames.

He didn't let up, but he didn't try to keep me on a punishing edge.

My orgasm was sudden and debilitating, ripping through me like a gunshot. Consciousness fell away. The warm honey of satisfaction pulsed through my veins.

Dante stroked me through it, whispering, "Come on, just like that, come for me," against the skin of my neck until every drop of my orgasm had been tasted, savored, and digested.

His cock still throbbed in my hand, thick and hard, pulsing with need.

Couture Mandy put her needs first, but she wasn't a selfish fuck.

I dropped to my knees. This time, when I kneeled at his feet, I wasn't begging for a favor. I started to tug down his jeans, but he swatted my hands away and took out his dick, holding it like a weapon. With his free hand, he took a fistful of hair at the back of my head and made me look up at him past the foreground of the length of his cock. I reached for it, but he slapped me away.

"Hands behind your back."

I did it.

"Open your mouth."

When I did, he laid his cock on the flat of my tongue and slid it back.

"Now open your throat like my good little slut," he said.

The word should have grated against my pride. Instead, it rubbed against the sensitive skin of my resistance, breaking it down to its cause. I wanted to be here, controlled, degraded, a servant to desire.

My eyes fluttered closed with concentration as the head of his cock nudged the back of my throat. He was longer and thicker than any man before him.

"Take it all." He let my hair go to caress my cheek as he pushed deep. "When I let you breathe, tell me you're my whore."

When he pulled out, I gulped for breath.

"Tell me."

He wanted me to say it—the thing I'd been denying to anyone who'd listen.

What would happen if I just said it?

"I'm a whore." I didn't sound convinced.

"No," he said definitively, caressing my head. "You're *my* whore. When you're at my feet, you're mine. Say it."

Every word was a statement of fact, and I sighed as if exhaling doubt about the pure rightness of who I was at his feet and nowhere else. Just like the tabloids said I was, but different because being his whore meant freedom and chains and safety all at the same time, and it was okay.

"I'm your whore," I gasped with an admission that freed me to give him every inch of my throat, my body, and my will.

"Beg for my cock."

This game was new to me, but he was good at it, and it was one I wanted to play.

"Please give me your cock." Too easy to repeat, I took it a step further. "Fuck my throat."

"Good girl." The caress of my cheek tightened, and he forced my mouth open. "Good. Little. Slut." He thrust with every word, and I opened my throat for him.

The hand in my hair tightened, and he shoved his cock another inch down my throat, using my mouth at his pace, his way.

My eyes watered, and he pulled out so I could breathe and waited until I opened my mouth for him to abuse again.

"When I give you my come," he said, with his belly pushing against my nose, "you swallow it."

He didn't wait for me to agree but thrust again and again until, in one last brutal push, he came down my throat, holding me tight against him, moaning through his orgasm with what sounded almost like surrender. His hands loosened in my hair but stayed there with something close to tenderness in the gesture.

Did I feel used?

No. I did not.

I felt as if I'd used him.

I looked up at his face and wiped my mouth with my wrist.

He smirked and helped me up before tucking his dick back in his pants, and I was seized with an irrational fear that I was now exposed to him. I was vulnerable again. My budding agency and self-determination had withered before it bloomed.

I liked him.

His swagger and his dirty talk had only made it worse.

The way he'd casually debased me had been a trick.

I liked him, and I wasn't supposed to.

And now here he was, cupping my cheek, triumphant enough to offer tenderness to a willing target.

That wasn't how it was supposed to be this time.

I'd used him, and now that he'd served his purpose, I didn't need him anymore.

"You can go," I said.

Dante just stood there, blinked, then dropped his hand away.

I couldn't have wounded him. He was too strong for that. But Couture Mandy needed new habits. Better ones. The point was to avoid getting hurt, not to hurt someone else. The point was to build armor, not sharpen my sword.

The point was that what I wanted had to be my first priority, and after that experience, what I wanted was to sleep.

"You were right." I smiled. "I did need that. And now I need to sleep."

"Go on," he said. "I'll tuck you in."

No harm in that, right? "Sure."

He turned the covers back, and I crawled onto the bed, sliding between the cool sheets. He put them up to my chin and sat on the bed beside me.

"Can you leave a light on?" I asked. "The one by the typewriter?"

"Are you scared of the dark?"

"No," I said. "A little."

He glanced at the desk lamp and must have decided it wouldn't drain too much of the solar power, because he turned back to me and nodded. "I will."

"Thank you." My eyes were drooping, and my limbs were made of cast iron. "Hey…" I added as if starting a conversation I didn't have the energy to finish.

"Yes, 'hey'?" With a deft touch that almost relaxed me right into unconsciousness, he brushed a lock of hair from my forehead.

I was too tired to object or remind myself that I wasn't supposed to accept or give bonus affection. "The Veronica Hawkins on the tapes. Didn't she die in an accident? In like, 2000-something?"

"Yes."

"I knew her son, Caleb, in high school." *And I let him break my heart repeatedly for years.*

Dante didn't need to know that.

"He went to Harvard-Westlake with Samantha," I injected before he could say anything.

"Your sister?"

Dante had plucked my sister from the statement, leaving Veronica Hawkins's devastated son behind.

"My dead sister." I added the word because if Dante wouldn't hurt me with indifference or carelessness, I needed to do it myself, and nothing cut me deeper than Samantha's suicide.

"I'm sorry," he said.

"It was forever ago."

"Death is the only forever that matters."

"Is it?"

He kissed my forehead. "Good night, *bona*."

When he shut off the light by the bed, the room went completely dark. I couldn't let it go. It was better than Amanda, but I'd told him what I wanted to be called and he had picked something entirely different rather than use it.

"What's that mean?"

I knew how Aileen had translated it, but that didn't tell me what he *meant*.

"It's Latin, and it means you're mine."

For a moment, that made me happy, and in the next moment, I hated how it made me feel worth no more than a second-string name, then I hated that I even cared.

I was doing the thing I always did. I was setting a straight edge between a nickname and a point in the future where I cried over him and scoring it into my life.

Me first. I had to decide what was important to me and score those lines instead of letting a man draw himself on my choices.

By the time Dante clicked the desk light on, I'd decided against fighting a battle over what he said and did.

"Whatever," I muttered.

"See you tomorrow."

He exited through the bathroom, closing the door and leaving me alone with the desk lamp on and the light patter of a rainstorm that seemed to go on forever.

CHAPTER 16

MANDY

When the rain went from white noise to a steady pound outside, I stirred from a dream, then reentered it.

The desk light was off.

Samantha was in the room, post-suicide. Her clothes dripped, and she smelled of chlorine. Even though—in reality—she hadn't been floating in the pool long enough to bloat, her skin was red and black in the creases, thinned and ready to split open. But when she smiled, she was beautiful.

"You look good," she said, and I believed her.

You look terrible.

I couldn't actually talk in the dream.

"You look strong as a triple stitch," she said, recalling the days we'd sewn together.

The sound of her dripping clothes got louder.

"Strong as a house."

The drip from her sleeve went *plup-plup-PLUP*.

"Strong as a man."

How strong is that?

I still couldn't talk, but she smiled as if she'd heard me. She didn't answer, but I heard her.

Strong enough to carry you if he's strong enough to want to.
Plup-plup-PLUP.
I woke.
The desk lamp was on.

My sister was gone, but the dripping continued. I followed the sound to the center of the room, where a puddle had formed.

The ceiling was leaking, forming little water crowns as the drops fell.

Peering between the drapes, I checked the lights in Dante's room. They were out.

Strong enough to carry you if he's strong enough to want to.

She said I looked strong as a man who was strong enough to carry me if he was strong enough to want to.

Meaning I could carry myself if I only wanted to.

It was two in the morning. Nothing could be done, and late-night shows of vulnerability were unnecessary. I could carry myself.

I pulled the garbage pail from under the desk, dumped the crumpled balls, and set it under the leak. The *plups* turned to *plinks*, keeping me in a half sleep for too long.

Samantha did not reappear.

* * *

When I woke, the desk light was off for real. Dante must have come in to shut it off.

The weather had turned noncommittal. Gray light filtered in through the windows, and a beam of sunlight cast a stripe of light on the wood floor. The leak *plinked* weakly, and when I got out of bed, the shaft of sunlight disappeared into shadow as if the clouds had decided that was quite enough of a tease.

When I was done with the morning's bathroom business, I peeked into Dante's room. The bed was neatly made, and the curtains were open, but he wasn't there. If he'd had a restless night, there was no sign of it.

At eight in the morning, the water in the teapot was cold, so I started a fresh boil and rinsed out the press.

As I pulled out a mug, I heard *clop*s and *thwack*s and scrapes I didn't recognize from outside. That must have been him. We'd have to talk about last night eventually, even if to reiterate that we'd had an entertaining hayride but we didn't have to buy the hay.

Outside, the air was misty with a bite of salt, and the ocean crashed somewhere far away. Wet branches hung overhead, and mud squished underfoot. Birds chirped like a chorus coming together after a long hiatus.

There was another sound too, regular and rhythmic—a *hup*, a crack, the rustle of something falling.

Following the sound around the bend of the driveway to where it ended just behind the house, I found the back of the property, where the bare concrete patio jutted out into spotty grass that extended to a stand of tall, dark trees.

It was easy to imagine an awning stretching over the fully furnished patio, between the Crowne family and the summer sun —the scent of smoked meat mingling with expensive perfume, everyone drinking rosé champagne in the sunshine. A small pool was closed over, another reminder that we were alone in a place no one wanted to be in winter.

Hup. Crack. Clop.

Beyond the pool was a woodpile, and next to it was Dante, axe in hand, chopping logs.

His T-shirt was sweat-soaked and clingy, half-untucked from his jeans. His face was flushed and ruddy—nothing like the buttoned-up society boy I knew in LA, always slicked into a suit, sitting behind the wheel of something shiny. Instead, he was putting all those gym-toned muscles to use—as if he knew exactly what he was doing with his body.

Which I knew now he definitely did. I shivered…and not from the chill.

He noticed me watching as he placed the next log on the stump, ready to be split. "It's going to get cold tonight."

I took my hand off my coffee cup long enough to wave. It was cold already, and I was about to go back inside, but when he hefted the axe, I wanted to see him finish the job. His body extended, arced, and brought the force down with a *thwack*. The wood cleaved in two parts that spilled over each side.

"Don't want to waste the propane." He leaned the axe against the stump and picked up the pieces.

Well, good, then. At least we were on the same page about acting normal. We were just two people who'd kind of had sex with each other. No big deal.

"I was just seeing where the noise was coming from," I said.

He tossed the smaller logs onto the pile. "You want to give it a try?"

"Chopping wood?"

"No," he said, reaching for another big log. "Roller skating."

When he picked up the wood, the muscles in his arms bulged and flexed, and I thought, *I'd rather watch you do it.*

"I have work to do," I reminded him. I didn't need to stand around and get myself worked up for no reason. "Thanks for the offer."

"It can wait."

He motioned for me to join him. I shook my head. I didn't want to make a fool of myself—there was no way I was strong enough—but I had to admit it was a little bit appealing, at least compared to going back to my room and spending the afternoon listening to other people's boring conversations.

"I'm not going to be good at it." I put my cup on top of the wall around the patio.

Dante stepped away from the stump as if he wasn't going to

acknowledge my refusal. I heaved a sigh and walked over to where he was standing.

"Gotta be better at this than typing," he said.

"Do I get punished if I do it wrong?"

He handed me the axe by the handle. "Do you want to be?"

I took the axe. It was as heavy as I expected and twice as awkward. The handle's wood was smooth, but if after fifteen minutes it didn't cause as many blisters as cheap shoes, I'd eat the shoes and the box they came in. "This is punishment enough."

"Over your shoulder," he said, tapping mine. "Then it's halfway there."

I had to bend my knees a little, but I got the blade to rest on my shoulder

"Okay." I was resigned to failure, but I might as well do what I said I'd do.

Dante made sure the wood was vertically stable, then stepped away. "Aim for the middle."

Picking the blade off my shoulder as much as I could, I heaved it forward and down, missing entirely, embedding the edge in the stump. I let go of the handle and let the blade stand straight up in the stump.

"I did it!" I cried in victory. "I saved that helpless log!"

Dante laughed. "Well done."

"High fives!" Two hands splayed and raised, I expected him to leave me hanging, but he actually returned the high ten with a smile that was so close to relaxed and normal I froze when our hands were against each other.

Maybe the brightness of the light made him seem more approachable. Or maybe it was the night before. Or not caring what he thought.

Maybe something had happened to make his eyes seem less cold and icy and more clear.

Maybe all of those things, but it didn't matter, and that wasn't a maybe.

I snapped my hands away, and he broke eye contact.

"Now," Dante said, bracing his foot against the stump to jerk the axe free. "It's time to murder this thing."

He extended the handle in my direction. I didn't take it.

"I'm not prairie enough for this."

He pulled back the handle. "Let me show you."

No demonstration would make me strong or coordinated enough for this job, but if he wanted me to watch his body a little while longer, I could accommodate him.

Instead of picking up the axe himself, he swung his hand for me to get back into place.

Fine. Whatever. This was better than sitting in that uncomfortable chair, trying to work the antique typewriter and tape machine at the same time.

He placed the blade over my shoulder, then—keeping his hand on the blade so I didn't chop off his face—he stood behind me on the other side, pressing his body gently against mine. He was ferociously warm all over. After last night's release, I'd hoped being around him today would be a little easier, but instead I couldn't stop remembering how good his fingers had felt inside me, how expertly they'd manipulated me, and how I'd called myself things I never thought I would.

"You don't have to come up with excuses to touch me, you know," I said.

"As you come down, let the weight of the blade do the work."

"You're making it"—I pressed my ass against him, a small thrill going through me when I felt the stir of his interest—"hard."

"Concentrate."

I looked over my shoulder. His mouth was close enough to kiss.

"You started it."

"Concentrate, Amanda," he breathed in my ear. "Commit to splitting it."

"Maybe I have commitment issues."

"The log doesn't know that."

He put his hands over mine, and together we pulled the axe up, and I let it fall. The wood split with a sigh and fell. Easy, as though it was nothing.

I stepped out of Dante's arms. He plucked up another log and placed it on the stump.

As far as I was concerned, he'd proved his point, and good for him. I didn't feel any more sure of myself though. In fact, I felt rattled. I was supposed to be in charge here—but the things I felt, wrapped in his embrace, were not the kinds of things I wanted to feel for him—or anyone ever again.

"On your own this time," Dante said.

I shook my head, not quite trusting my voice.

"You're here because you promised to do what I told you," he reminded me. "That's the rule. So, I'm telling you. Split it."

Okay. Fine. All I had to do was commit, right? Let it fall the way I had with him behind me.

"Here's a rule." I got the axe up. "You can't boss me unless your dick's in my mouth."

As I brought it down, he said, "What about your ass?"

The axe got stuck halfway through the log.

"Not cool!"

He shooed me aside so he could pull it out, leveraging his boot against the log and yanking the handle. "You're hesitating."

"You're cheating." I grabbed the axe.

"How?" He aligned the log vertically with the half-split side down.

"Saying stuff like that while I'm trying to chop wood."

"'Stuff like that'? Are you in middle school? Anal sex makes you giggle?"

"I have the axe, Dante. Don't fuck with me."

"Did Renaldo fuck you in the ass because his wife wouldn't let him?"

And *that* was the last straw. I wanted to take the axe to his *head*, but I'd already disgraced myself enough for one week, so instead I brought it down on the log. It split as easily as it had when Dante was wrapped around me. Each side tumbled onto the grass with a soft *hush*.

I felt my cheeks turning pink and sweat prickling the edge of my hairline. I was breathing hard, but I'd done it.

"Attagirl," he said.

"No."

"No?"

"And yes," I admitted. "Renaldo's wife wouldn't let him fuck her in the ass or anywhere, if you want to know. Not that it's an excuse for letting him fuck me, but I did, and you don't know the whole story."

"I'm not judging you, Amanda."

"That's. Not. My. Name." I leaned against the axe as if I'd been at the woodpile all day. "And it's not *bona* either. That's Paula Harris's name. My name is Mandy, and it's fine you're not judging me, because I'm judging myself all the time."

I had no guilt about coming between Renaldo and Tatiana. Falling in love with a man who couldn't find it in himself to love me back was the cause of all my shame.

"Okay." He reached for the axe, and I took my weight off it. "I understand."

"Do you?"

He put a log on the stump and stepped back, spreading his legs before throwing the blade over his shoulder. "I was in love with a married woman."

He brought the blade down with a *thwap* and a *crack*, and a final sigh, collecting the pieces without looking at me. He understood being in love with a married person, not using that person as a weapon against your confidence.

"Veronica Hawkins."

"Wait," I said. "She died when we were…"

Kids? Adolescents? Stupid?

Too young for Caleb's mom?

He set up another log while I tried to make sense of the math.

"She did." *Thwap*. No crack. No sigh. He'd missed.

"How old—"

"Sixteen."

"—was she?"

By the time I'd finished my sentence, his interruption had answered the same question from a different angle.

"You can hardly be held responsible for that," I said.

"Why not?"

"You were a kid. She was in her, what? Forties?"

He smirked and shook his head before he reared back again, as if he was responding to a long conversation with himself.

"Old enough to get it up," he said before unleashing the blade. He didn't miss this time. "Is old enough to stand down. That's what my father said when he found out."

After throwing the pieces onto the growing pile, he stood pensive and still.

"Is that what these tapes are about?" I asked.

He snapped out of whatever reverie he'd been caught in and glanced at the sky as if he was telling the time. "You'd better get back to it."

I realized I'd forgotten all about the ceiling and the *plink-plink* in the wastebasket. "Oh shit, I meant to tell you. There's a leak in my bedroom."

"Since I was there?"

"Since you had your dick in my mouth? Yes, Dante. Time existed between then and now."

Like two people with the same thought, we walked back to the house together.

"Not for me," he said with a casual smile, as if the sentiment was normal and acceptable and not something that would shatter me if I let myself believe it.

"I put the trash can under it," I said when we were in the

kitchen. "But obviously that's not the same as fixing it. And before you say another word." I stopped outside the bedroom, and he stopped with me. "What happened? With us? It was fun, and I'd do it again, but I'm not interested in a whole thing."

"You said that already." He crossed his arms while a torture-slow *plink-plink* came from the other side of the door. "So, maybe you tell me what you mean by a 'thing'?"

"A *thing*."

"Use more words."

I knew two ways to explain what he should have understood right off the bat. The first way involved me telling him I was coming off a breakup and wasn't interested in getting tied to anyone right now.

I did not choose that way.

"A thing is where I get attached and you... everything about you, what you think and what you want, is in my head. If we get involved, it'll replace what I want."

"What do you want?"

Plink-plink.

"Anything but a thing. Okay?"

"If thing is a noun, I don't want it either."

Plink.

"A noun is a person, place, or thing."

He raised an eyebrow as if making it through third grade was impressive. "So, you did learn something in school."

I crossed my arms. The comment didn't deserve a response.

"If a thing is a verb," he finally said, "if it isn't something we *are*, but something we *do*, I want it."

"I'm not clear on this."

"You want me to paint you a picture?"

"Of a verb?"

"Things I want to do with you, including but not limited to..." He leaned into me, reciting a list of words from an index card in his mind. The flatness of his statements rushed blood and fluid between my legs so fast it hurt. "Undressing. Pinching. Sucking. Fucking. Screaming. Begging." He got close enough to whisper. "Spanking. Binding. Blindfolding. Hurting. Lying."

I gasped at the last one because I knew who and I knew why. "Logan. He'd kill us."

"Just me."

Regardless of who Logan would be angry with or why, the idea appealed to my sense of safety and a desire for danger. The rules would tie my hands to protect me from hurting myself while he hurt me to the point of orgasm.

"I don't want to be a thing either," I said with my nose a mere breath from his. "We can just do things."

"And not tell."

We could have kissed, but we didn't. If we kissed, we'd have to close our eyes, and this was an eyes-wide-open conversation.

"And not tell," I whispered right before a lone *plink*. "I'll think about your offer." I opened the bedroom door. "And get back to you in the morning."

I went in before I could see his reaction and before he could see me smile.

CHAPTER 17

DANTE

Amanda Bettencourt, a woman whose entire wardrobe was shades of yellow and gold, whose entire life was built around maintaining the fiction of her family's wealth, and who let men walk all over her like doormatting was her job—that woman had taken control of me.

Games were fun, or I didn't play them, and if I didn't write the rules, I didn't enjoy the game. That simple equation had kept me sane and single.

I only offered myself to a woman when I was ready to take her and she was ready to be taken. If she delayed, I walked.

Until Amanda.

I was going to give her the time she wanted because—standing under the leaky ceiling—I was still figuring out why I'd demanded she choose in the first place.

The wastebasket was half-full under a damp, gray splotch of ceiling that was already mottled with the rust from the nails behind the plaster. A glassy slick of moisture hovered above, the center pulling into a nipple of water not heavy enough to fall just yet.

"Have you emptied the bucket?" I asked, trying not to look at her.

"No. It's just this much since last night."

Not that bad. And it had slowed to a trickle.

"I'll check the roof." Like a petulant child angry at her refusal, I left without making eye contact.

What was happening to me? Why did I feel like this?

The mud room was lined with books because there was nowhere else for them. My mother had dubbed it The Library. The trapdoor to the crawlspace was above. It was dry, so the access and the books were safe. I snapped my coat off the rack.

Jamming my arms into the sleeves, I tried to convince myself I was in control of my ability to walk away from Amanda, say, "Thank you. No, thank you," to what was obviously part of some kind of tactic to make me want her more. Having Amanda was a diversion, not a necessity.

After laying the ladder against the side of the house, I climbed to the top.

Playing into her game wasn't worth the energy. So, why was I still thinking about it?

Cresting the roof, I was finally alone, surrounded by the sound of birds and the sight of trees. On a clear day, the ocean was visible, but not today.

I walked the perimeter of the flat roof, disappointed in the way I'd lost control last night until I was pulling her hair and coming down her throat, ordering her around as though she was really mine. She'd promised to do whatever I said while she was here, and I'd promised myself that I would only use her obedience to drive her out, but cruelty hadn't worked, and neither had teasing her.

She was proving she could tease just as effectively.

At least being on the roof meant I couldn't see her, couldn't hear her, couldn't reach out and touch her. I'd been meaning to come up here again anyway—the TPO seams had looked a little worn when I'd cleaned the gutters. One must have opened up somewhere, but it wouldn't be visible without careful inspection.

A divot in a rush of runoff caught my attention. When I probed it with my fingers, I found a tear—nothing big enough to come from an animal. Probably just natural wear on the material, which meant this leak likely wouldn't be the last.

I stood there, trying to figure out what to do—whether it was worth trying to get a new roll of TPO up here and if the rain would stop long enough for installation anyway. If it didn't—what? A house filled with buckets? Trying to keep the precious tapes and documents dry while keeping Ernie from finding out about Amanda?

Amanda would be gone by then. No matter what I was feeling, that was what needed to happen. Not only for the business's sake, but for mine. The self-control I'd spent decades building crumbled around her.

I didn't understand it, and I didn't need to. I just needed to resist it.

Convinced my attention hadn't been on the roof the way it needed to be, I walked the perimeter again—back and forth over every inch, like a man inspecting the details of a new woman's body.

Our teenage connection—the way she'd awakened me to the possibilities of my own desire—made resisting harder than I would have guessed. That had to be a matter of history and little else. I could overcome that.

I wanted her recklessly. So much that I was almost willing to not only lie to my family, but to give her control. But I wasn't going to play her game.

My phone buzzed in my pocket. I pulled it out. Tiny drops of mist landed on my brother's name.

"Logan," I said, glad Amanda was too far away to make a noise that would expose us.

"Are you alone?" Logan sounded worried, which was unlike

him. We were competitive about business, and if he was sweating, he didn't like to let me see it.

"Why wouldn't I be?" I asked. Technically, I was alone. Amanda was inside. There was no one else around for miles.

"Is Mandy still there?"

"She's leaving tomorrow," I said before adding an explanation to prevent more questions. "The rain just stopped."

"Dad wants to talk to you."

My father. Ted Crowne could cede certain parts of the business to his children, but as long as he lived, he was in charge.

"You've been demoted to secretary?"

Logan wasn't in a joking mood. He just put me on speaker.

"You stole records?" My father's voice cut through the miles of cable.

"No."

"No?"

I said, "I bought the contents of the storage unit at auction, fair and square."

"Fair and... Are you joking? Did you even talk to a lawyer before you extracted privileged documents that belong to the biggest law firm in the country?"

"Dad—"

"Nothing you find in that box is going to hold up in court."

"It doesn't have to. It has to be embarrassing enough to get them out of our clubs."

I caught myself. The clubs didn't belong to an *our*. Not my father and me... or the original owners I meant—Veronica and me. The clubs had been our safety net. I bought them with her, secretly until I was eighteen. She didn't make it.

"The way it's structured," I said, "her surviving family inherited all the benefits but very little exposure. When it catches up to them, it's going to catch up to me."

"Logan," Dad said away from the mouthpiece, "can you excuse us?"

"Fine." I heard a shuffle and a door closing.

Taking Logan out of the conversation relieved me of lying about why Amanda was still in the house and when she was leaving… or not.

"There's one solution," my father said. "Sell them your half and be done with it."

"No."

"The Hawkins cheat," Ted added. "They use a media empire to lie. They cut corners."

"And there's something in this box to prove it. If I can just—"

"Despite how you think you ever felt about Veronica, you—"

Forget the prenup.

"She wasn't like them."

"Is this your way of keeping her alive?"

"No," I barked.

Yes, actually.

"I'm not a lovelorn boy anymore," I added. "I'm not fighting to maintain a romantic ideal."

The next part of the argument involved what I was fighting for, but I didn't have an endgame or a brass ring at the end of this. At least salmon swimming upstream for miles got laid in the end.

Only my motivation would soothe my father's frustration, but what was I supposed to tell him? That I wanted to honor the memory of a woman he insisted had abused me? That selling those businesses meant she'd lost her only hope of getting away? That keeping my shit together when she died was for nothing?

"It's disloyal," I finally said. "That's it. Selling the business back to them is dishonorable, and I won't."

"All right." His tone backed away from a conflict, and I realized my tone had started one. "Caleb's always going to have it in for you. He's never going to let his mother's death go. He needs somewhere to put his anger, and he chose you. They're not changing. Best to sell him your half and wash your hands of it."

"It's not right."

She'd died in her Porsche, half an hour after I'd finished salving her sore bottom. We'd just finished finalizing our escape plan when she misjudged the speed of a freeway merge.

Such a dumb thing, and it was all over.

"Dante," my father said, "I've said this a hundred times, and I'll say it a hundred more: Veronica Hawkins was not a partner. She raped you."

Nothing about it felt like what my father described.

"Jesus, Dad." I clenched my fist as if my fingers could be curled tight enough to hold my anger. He was taking away my agency and turning me into a victim who had never had a choice.

"You were a *child*," he insisted. "What else would you call it?"

"What do you want me to do? Dwell on what you think it was? Or what I think it was?"

He let out a breath. A pause. A realignment.

"I want you to be able to live for a future," he said. "I want to help you let it go."

In front of my father, it was easy to forget I was a grown man and fall back into a position where I had to do what I was told for my own good.

But I was a man, and I didn't have to let go of grudges or outdated loyalties if I didn't want to.

So, I thanked him for his input, said goodbye, and hung up.

* * *

GETTING off the house's grounds was good, even just for a little while—to be reminded of the world that existed beyond the one I'd been wrapped in for the past few days. I wouldn't say I was pussy-blind exactly, but Amanda had a way of making me lose track of myself, so I spent perhaps longer than necessary in the hardware store, comparing different types of TPO sealant, grateful for a problem I knew how to solve.

Procrastination notwithstanding, I was running out of time,

and I knew it. The smart thing would be to let Ernie do the transcription, copy all the documents, and give them to Thoze & Jensen looking unopened.

Before I could do that though, I wanted to—no, needed to—get Amanda into bed once and for all. After I'd had her—tasted her and fucked her, felt those long legs wrapped around my waist and her muscles quivering around me—after she'd made her throat raw taking my dick and begging me to let her come, *then* I'd be done, and it would be easy to send her away. I'd get the tapes back to LA. At that point, a roofer could deal with the TPO for me. I'd never have to see or speak to or even think about Amanda Bettencourt ever again.

The thought soothed my need for solitude while generating an anxiety I didn't recognize.

For now, though, she was still back at the house, typing obediently. There was a convenience store in the strip mall, and as I passed it, I remembered the ridiculous breakup snack she'd brought with her that first night: ice cream and potato chips.

Whatever she thought of me, especially after my behavior this week, I wasn't a monster. I was sympathetic to heartbreak and the bruises it could leave.

She deserved a treat.

So, I bought her chocolate chip Häagen-Dazs and picked up the Kettle chips she'd had before, but put them down in favor of Ruffles, which would work better. She'd be surprised I cared about pleasing her at all, then she'd ask if I was trying to bribe her into agreeing to a fuck. I wouldn't deny it, but when she did agree, I'd spank her for the implication and soothe her sore ass with ice cream.

I was picturing her face when I casually handed her the bag as if it was nothing—or something just to shut her up. She wouldn't be able to hide her surprise and delight, and I caught myself smiling at the thought of her face because the easy transparency that had caused her pain in life charmed the fuck out of me.

Then my mind's screen turned her face bitter, with too-red lipstick twisted into a scowl. I didn't know why until the picture in my mind matched the cover of a tabloid on the rack next to the checkout counter.

RENALDO & THE HOMEWRECKER:
HOW MANDY BETTENCOURT'S BIG PLANS BACKFIRED

The yellow block letters plastered over her and that fuck-clown were the size and shape of her pain, but what really bugged me was that they were in her favorite color, because that was her soul, and it was exposed for the public.

She didn't belong to the public.

She belonged to me.

Only until she leaves the house.

As long as she was sitting in my house, doing my bidding, she was mine. I was buying her food. I had made her come for me, felt her pulse and writhe on my fingers, and I was going to do it again.

She'd made a promise when she asked to stay, and she'd kept it. So, for the time being, I got to decide how she was treated. Once she left, we'd both be on our own.

I swept all of the tabloids onto the conveyor belt. The look on my face must have conveyed that I didn't want to talk about it, because the clerk didn't ask any questions as she rang me up. I dumped the stack in my trunk and turned the car back toward the house.

CHAPTER 18

MANDY

Dante was obviously a guy who didn't like being put off, but I had to think hard about fucking him before I did it.

Yes, I'd sucked his dick last night, but if I was going to get control of my love life, it had to start with not assuming that just because I blew a guy, a fuck was the next thing that had to get done. I had the responsibility to think about it every step of the way, and if that meant he had to stew in his own juices for a while, then that was tough shit.

I got back to transcribing the call, which had moved on to duller subjects, but got held up because I must have left it playing, and I had to rewind to find my place.

I spent the rest of the day transcribing calls about the two-million-dollar donation that was to accompany Max Hawkins's application to Yale, and I didn't get really hungry until about five o'clock, when the sun got low and clouds gathered before opening.

The sky held nothing back, dumping fat, heavy drops that splatted audibly on the concrete.

Dante was nowhere to be found. Good. I'd make dinner, and he'd have to do the dishes in the sink with the green brush that slipped out of your hand every two minutes. When he came in from mending fences or plowing the fields or whatever, I'd have something hot and ready.

Everything except my decision, but I didn't have to rush that.

Since I didn't need Wi-Fi to get my jam on, I connected my phone to the sound system and put my playlist on shuffle.

BABY, baby, baby
    You got the kit, and I got the cat
    Blue sky up and my back ain't flat
    Come on, baby, I got room for your kit
    Put it in the trunk
    Yeah, hiss and spit

"MEOW!" I sang with the lyrics, shifting my hips with the beat as I checked the pantry for something to make.

I found a box of macaroni and cheese in the back of the cabinet, frozen peas in the freezer, chopped meat in the fridge, and a head of arugula in the crisper.

"See?" I said, plucking salad dressing from the door shelves. "Meow!"

BABY, baby, baby
    I'm your slinky tabby
    Your back soft and my claws ain't shabby
    Give it, baby, take me on a trip
    We're just pretty kitties
    Yeah, scratch and nip

"MEOW!"

The water boiled and the meat sautéed while I congratulated myself for getting control of my life. I should have done it sooner. How had I lived like that? Getting tossed from side to side by whomever, letting them make all the choices just so I wouldn't be alone.

Well, those days were over.

"*O-V-E-R*," I sang as I poured the macaroni into the boiling water. "*Over, baby, over.*"

I stirred, managed the meat, chopped the salad, and threw the peas into the boiling water three minutes before the pasta was done. I didn't overcook the macaroni or burn the meat. When I combined them in the cast iron skillet, only one elbow spilled out.

I'd even remembered to preheat the oven.

The skillet weighed a ton, so after topping the casserole with an extra layer of shredded cheddar I'd found, I used both hands to put it in the oven.

"*Meow, meow, baby.*" I shook my ass like it was on sale.

This was going to be great. Mac and cheese. Salad. When he'd made dinner, what did he have on the table?

"Wine!"

I found the wine fridge by some miracle, since it looked like any other drawer, and chose a random bottle of red, and stopped myself before putting it on the table.

"Decanter," I called. "Where are you?"

I checked all the cabinets under the counters, then over. Scanned the shelf space just under the ceiling. Rechecked the cabinets more carefully.

The decanter wasn't in the kitchen.

"No wonder you didn't answer," I joked and trotted out to the living room.

There were decorative vases and urns. A teak bowl and an abstract glass sculpture.

It was a small house, yet no place to easily access a decanter.

It wasn't behind the wet bar or in the glass-doored cabinet.

Not in the sideboard or by the window ledge with the other glass containers.

Dante Crowne didn't keep the decanter anywhere you'd expect. He kept it in a cupboard in the little room with the books, way in the back of the house.

When the back door opened, I screamed and raised the glass container like a weapon. "Jesus, Dante."

"What are you cooking?"

"You scared the hell out of me."

"You're jumpy. And not great at selecting weapons."

"I'm resourceful." I jabbed the decanter in his direction.

His lip curled into the edge of a smirk. "I guess this is better than a shampoo bottle."

"Are you hungry? I made dinner."

"Very."

He slipped off his muddy shoes, and together we walked back into the kitchen.

"What's that music?" he asked as if no one would choose to listen to it.

"Jitter Jones."

He got potato chips and ice cream out of his bag.

"You got my favorite!" I clapped, then saw the labels. "Chocolate chip. Huh." I decided not to complain about the Ruffles, which were too thin for ice cream unless you wanted soggy goop in your spoon. "Thank you!" I said with a smile.

He ignored my backpedaled delight and crunched his eyebrows together as if solving a math problem. "What the hell is she singing about?"

"You don't think about it." I slapped the freezer closed and bumped my hip against his. "You dance to it."

"No, *you* dance to it."

"Don't mind if I do."

And I did, spinning out to the center of the floor, shaking my hips, and singing. I did it because I wanted to and I loved the song.

I danced as if he wasn't watching, and he watched until the awkwardness of it all made us both laugh.

He took me by the waist with one hand and lifted my arm with the other, waltzing in the tight space to Jitter Jones's three-four rhythm.

"You dance better than you sing," he said.

He dipped me, and when I came up, the inertia pushed our faces close together. I had to move an inch to kiss him, and I had forever to do it. He was right there, not pushing me away. Not pulling me close. Just waiting.

Then the song ended into silence.

"Well," he said, still close.

"I guess that's the end of the playlist."

In the silence of the isolated house, his stomach growled. He laughed and pulled back.

I laughed with him. "You're hungry."

"I can wait." He rummaged around the drawer for the corkscrew.

"Where have you been all day?" I asked.

"I had some things to get in Harmony." Dante twisted the screw deep into the top of the wine bottle.

Right. The ice cream and potato chips hadn't come from a tree. Had he seen that horrible *DMZ Weekly* cover of Renaldo and me photoshopped together? Would he even tell me if he had? Just yesterday, I would have guessed he'd take any opportunity to humiliate me, but today, I wasn't so sure.

Though maybe it was more embarrassing that he had to protect my feelings in the first place.

"You all right?" The cork came free with a pop.

"Fine, fine."

"I needed sealant for the roof." He poured the liquid into the decanter with the splash of a hundred ruby crowns. "Then I switched you to Ruffles."

"Thank you," I squeaked, grabbing the empty bottle and

pushing it in the trash so he couldn't read the effort it took me to not ask if he saw me being Renaldo's little whore, or what he thought of it, because it mattered to me whether I denied it or not, and he knew it.

In an effort to keep him from looking at my face and seeing whatever was written all over it, I leaned down and opened the oven. There was a whoosh and fierce bubbling, but the casserole was dotted with perfect leopard spots of crusty brown.

"Is it burned?" he asked with a clink of wine glasses as he pulled them from the cabinet.

I reached for the skillet handle. "Another five minutes and it—" I cut my sentence in two with a yelp of pain.

"What?"

"Stupid!" I cried, standing straight with my palm out.

It had two big red splotches, but before I could get a good look at them, Dante pulled my arm down to see, then he took my hand as if he owned it and ran tap water over it.

"Keep it there," he said with intensity, cradling my hand.

"Isn't this wasting tank water?"

"This restores blood flow and prevents necrosis."

"Are you making that up?"

"Yes, Amanda, I'm maintaining imaginary circulation to your imaginary burn. Is the pain imaginary?"

"No," I pouted. "Command it to go away."

He leaned down and spoke firmly to my hand. "You will feel as beautiful as you look, and you'll stay out of trouble from now on." He stood straight and adjusted the temperature an imperceptible difference.

"That may be the last burn I ever get," I said.

"You'll be more careful next time."

"It didn't look hot," I joked, but he didn't laugh.

"This is going to blister." With the same intensity, he gently spread my fingers open, careful not to touch the spots where I'd singed myself.

"I'm sure I can still type," I replied, assuming his main concern was the job he'd given me.

"Keep it under the water." The look on his face was layered with solemnity, as if keeping my hand under the faucet was the most important action he could trust me to take.

"Okay."

He got square pot handlers, used them to get dinner from the oven, shut the door with his foot, put the hot tray on the table, dropped the squares—all in that order and with such efficient grace that not a single breath was wasted between.

"Give it." He took my hand back and inspected the damage. He was trying to be gentle, but it still stung, and I sucked a breath through my teeth. "I'm sorry."

"For what?"

A frown creased his brow, and my stomach twisted at the thought that he was worrying about me. I didn't know what to make of his apology or his concern, and for once—when he soaked a towel, folded it, and placed it over my hand—I let myself wonder about his feelings.

"I almost took the skin off my palm once a couple of years ago," he said.

"*You*? Made a *mistake*? Alert the media."

"It was a barbecue grill, and—as you said—it didn't look hot."

He slid his hand from under mine so I could see the faint hints of a scar still etched into the skin. His palms looked tougher than I'd expected, flecked with imperfections and thick with calluses. All I could think about was how they'd felt on my bare skin.

"Can we eat?" I asked, holding the towel myself. "It smells good, and I'm hungry."

"You sure you're not smelling your cooked flesh?"

"Gross." I wrinkled my nose, and we did an even grosser thing. We stared into each other's eyes and smiled together. His terrible, borderline-disgusting joke was a risk he'd taken in this kitchen with me. It didn't seem like a gamble or a test. It was a kind of trust that I wouldn't think less of him.

He stepped back, and I looked away, as if we both understood the intimacy of what had just happened.

He rushed to the table. "I'll put dinner on the table." He pulled out my chair. "If you don't mind."

Who was this guy?

He got the salad, plates, flatware, and wine on the table, then sat across from me.

"I did a good page today," I said, letting the wet towel go to scoop up macaroni and cheese with my right hand. "I'm sure you'll find mistakes, but I was careful."

I held the spoon out for his plate, but he glared at the ball of wet towel. "You have to keep that on your hand."

"It's fine. My left hand's useless. Come on. Don't leave me hanging."

Instead of holding out his plate, he got up and stood at the side of the table. "Do you know what I admire about you?" Gently, he took the spoon from me.

"What?" I crossed my arms against the insult that would come disguised as a compliment.

"Keep it cool," he said, tapping the burned hand. "Please."

I sighed and laid my palm back on the compress.

"I admire your transparency." He laid the lump of macaroni and cheese on my plate with the same care he delivered the high-class trash talk I was about to hear. "I can usually tell what people are thinking because I'm good at it. But with you, my talent doesn't matter. I know what's going on in your head because you don't hide." He filled his own plate. "You're fearless. You don't care what I think."

I snorted and tried to grab the wine bottle, but he beat me to it and poured.

"You don't know what you're talking about," I said.

"Right now," he said while putting salad in little bowls, "you think I'm trying to hurt you by calling you transparent, and you're building a defense against it. So..." He glared at my right hand as I picked up my wine. "The compress, Amanda."

"I told you, my left hand is useless." I switched the glass to my left anyway. "It's habit."

When he put down the salad tongs, he paused, then sat kitty-corner from me and took my fork. "So"—he slid the fork under the casserole and came up with a heap—"I'm going to be transparent too. I'm not insulting you. A compliment is just a compliment. Open."

"Are you going to fly the plane into the hangar?"

"If you can't take care of your only good hand, you leave me no choice."

I didn't feel as if I had much of a choice either. My left hand was holding my wine, and I wasn't letting it go. If he wanted to delay his own dinner to feed me, that was his choice.

Also, Dante Crowne had a way of telling a girl to open her mouth. So, I opened, and he fed me. The food wasn't bad. Wasn't great either, but I was hungry.

"Just so you know," I said when I was done chewing. "You said I don't care what you think. You're wrong. I care too much what people think."

"That's obvious," he said, rearranging the macaroni and cheese on my plate before loading the fork again. "But you don't try to fool yourself and you don't try to fool me. I can see how hard you work at not caring. It's a noble effort, and you're honest about it, even when you think you're being guarded."

I believed him when he said he meant it as a compliment, but I wasn't convinced readability was an admirable quality in an adult.

"Well, fun talk," I said before he stuck food in my mouth. I poised my wine at my lips as he prepped another forkful. "Let's do it again sometime." I gulped the wine, wanting to get down as much as possible before I said something stupid.

"You still irritate me." He speared noodles this time. "I never thought honesty would be a frustrating quality."

"You admire the things about me that annoy you?" I said around the food I'd taken. "That's like emotional masochism right there."

He laughed, and I drank my wine, watching him. He wasn't laughing at the humor, but at some kind of recognized truth.

"I have it." With my left hand, I took the fork from him. "Eat already. You're making me nervous."

He leaned his hands on his knees as if he needed the help of his arms to rise.

"I knew you were competent on both sides," he said when he was in his own chair.

"Hm." I ate without help. My right hand was wet, and my left wanted to know why it was working so hard, but the food arrived at its destination without incident.

"This is terrible," he said, chewing.

"Yeah, well, you still have to do the dishes." I sipped my wine.

He smiled as he chewed, then looked away like a man hiding something.

"You said I annoy you."

He looked at me as if to ask why I was picking a fight, but that wasn't where I was going with this.

"I just wonder—" I tried to shrug away the weight of the question. "I can't imagine the women you *do* like."

This wasn't precisely true—I could imagine plenty, and it was maddening to picture such a self-possessed genius, whose hair and commas were never out of place, who fell apart like silken pudding at his feet. She didn't burn her hand and need to be fed. She didn't end up here in the first place, because she wasn't idiot enough to love a man who would never, ever love her back. I could be Couture Mandy all I wanted; there was no version of Mandy who would be right for Dante, and in that moment, in that kitchen, I was realizing that, against my will, I cared to know why.

"How many compliments do I have to give you?" he asked with a voice low and serious.

"I'm not asking for a compliment. I'm asking who you are."

Dante just looked at me. In the silence that fell between us, I felt every inch of my skin, electric with goose bumps. His stare leveled me like a blunt force to my sternum. A weight pinning me in place and unraveling me, strip by strip, head to toe. I couldn't stand being that naked in front of him, yet I craved it.

We both finished eating, so I got up to clear the table. He was in charge of doing the dishes, but I could help. Mostly, I couldn't sit still with him looking at me like that.

Dante leaned back in his chair, expression shifting from open intensity to something more familiar—relaxed and impervious, like a king idling on his throne. His shirt was open at the collar, and I had to keep my eyes on what I was doing so that I wouldn't fixate on the hollow of his throat or the open vee of his legs.

Still, I felt the weight of his gaze as I crossed to him and reached for his plate like a silent, willing servant. Before I could lift his plate, he took my right arm by the wrist, turned it, and ran his fingers over my knuckles to indicate I should open my fist and show my palm.

I did.

He spread the fingers wide, inspecting the red spots, which had settled into a sweet, painless pink. He looked up at me with his ice-blue eyes burning.

"So, Amanda," he rumbled, closing my fist in his hands. "Have you decided?"

"Decided what?"

"About my offer." He let my hand drop to my side, and there it stayed. "We're not playing a game here. It's yes, or it's no. If you say no, you have to leave tomorrow."

He got up and stood over me, leaving scant inches between us, and I was conscious of the length of every single one. His posture should have been intimidating, but all I felt was anticipation. My body hummed like an orchestra he was conducting.

"If you say yes," he continued, "you still have to leave tomorrow. But you'll leave having gotten what you wanted. And isn't that the point of all of this? Forget about me. Isn't the point to finally get exactly what you want?"

All the blood in my body relocated to between my legs. I was light-headed and spiraling. What did I want?

I wanted a controlled loss of power. A safe risk. A freefall into a net I couldn't see but knew was there.

Dante could take me where I needed to go. Whoever I would be tomorrow would be the real Couture Mandy, and she could deal with the fallout—because there would be none.

"Yes or no, Amanda?"

"Don't call me Amanda." For the first time, this demand seemed petty without an explanation. "My sister was the only one who could call me that after I changed it to Mandy."

He knew all about Samantha. She'd committed suicide while engaged to his brother, Byron. The moment's flicker of recognition in his face confirmed I didn't have to go into what had happened, and the way he regained control told me he wouldn't allow himself to get sidetracked.

"Yes or no, *amea*?"

A new name, just for me and just for now. I returned that penetrating pale-blue gaze, deciding whether I trusted the man behind it to let me walk away before I let him hurt me. I didn't want to be chased.

But I did.

I wouldn't be able to resist my worst instincts if he didn't consent to help.

"Just once," I said. "I mean it."

"Tonight," he said, his thumb drawing a line of electricity across the back of my hand. "Once. Yes or no."

Did I have a reason not to? Outside self-preservation, why wouldn't I?

"My answer," I said, knowing that no matter what I said, it was the last time I'd be the one making a decision, "is yes."

I expected his hands to be on me in a heartbeat, but instead, he stood slowly, his appraisal turning blade sharp.

"Don't move," he breathed.

Don't move. *Don't move*. My pulse was pounding between my legs; my nipples were stiff, and my mouth was hungry. He circled me like a shark, his movement sinuous, predatory. By the time he stopped right behind me, I was breathless with anticipation.

"*Yes* means my rules," he said into my neck and waited.

"Yes," I answered, facing the taunt of the dirty dishes. Was he about to make me do chores again? Would he make me love it?

"Rule one." With efficient languor, he pulled up my shirt to expose my bra. "You're in this house until morning, and as long as you're in this house, you are mine."

He was careful not to touch me too much—the full body press of our axe-handling lesson had been replaced by the torture of his fingertips feeling under my arms, along the band of my bra to discover its front clasp.

"You do exactly what I tell you to do. You do *only* what I tell you to do. If you agree, you may nod."

I nodded

"Good girl." He unhooked the bra, and I fell out of the soft fabric. He pulled the bra behind me and maneuvered my arms with it, using the straps to tie them together.

He paused, giving me a moment to see my reflection in the glass doors. The rain had picked up again, but it did nothing to obscure my red cheeks and open mouth or the yellow T-shirt folded up to my neck and my breasts on display. I was exposed, vulnerable, a body made for sex—ribs heaving with every breath —yet nothing I saw truly revealed how much I needed to hand over control to this man right now.

Our eyes met in the reflection.

He saw every one of my thoughts and approved.

"Turn around," he said, more as preparation than command, because he took me by the shoulders and turned me to face him, pulling my body against his so I could melt against him, basking in his solid heat and strength, before kissing me.

His mouth was a vandal, kicking the door open and wrecking the place, corner to corner. I opened my jaw for him, letting him take and take and take while my bound arms couldn't take anything back. His mouth abandoned mine, and I was left with my jaw slack, wanting more so badly that when he leaned into me, my eyes closed with anticipation, but he reached behind me and swept our dinner plates off the table and onto the floor with a clatter and crash. The decanter shattered on impact, but he was kissing me again, and the blood in my veins was louder, a percussive crescendo of desire. The peaks of my nipples rubbed against the cloth of his shirt, and I felt a rush of heat and shame that I was so exposed while he was still armored in clothing.

Pulling away again, Dante trailed his hands down my body, outlining every curve with that same unbearable sense of precision and control. When he found the hem of my skirt, he yanked it up and put one palm flat against the damp strip of fabric between my legs, offering just enough pressure to keep me from crying but not enough for anything else.

"Hold still," he reminded me before pulling down my underwear. "Step out." When I got out of them, he gripped my hips and said, "Good girl."

Then he hoisted me onto the table. I leaned back on my bound arms.

"Are you comfortable?" He palmed my knees, hooking his fingers under them.

"Not really," I said as he lifted my legs. "But—"

I'm fine with it.

The second half of the sentence was lost when he spread my

knees apart, and a thick bolt of electric heat shot between my legs. When—still holding my legs open—he looked directly at the throbbing sex there, my whole body leaned on my arms and canted toward him.

"Be still," he said.

"I can't."

"You can. If you want it badly enough, you'll learn." His eyes were dark, the pupils blown wide. "And you do."

"I do."

"You want what?" He placed my heels on the edge of the table.

"Everything."

"That's a lot." With my feet leveraged, he opened my legs again.

"Everything you want to give. That's what I want."

He pulled a chair in front of me, and he sat and eyed me over the stretched hem of my skirt, then he slid his hands along the insides of my thighs, chasing the image away.

"That's still a lot, my perfect little slut..." His fingers slid along my seam and entered me. I groaned. "Hush. Keep your legs open. Can you do that?"

"Yes."

"You sure?"

What kind of question was that?

I knew when I felt a wet sting of pain followed by an explosion of pleasure. He'd slapped me there. Right there. My knees had tried to close, but he pulled them apart.

"Should I stop?"

"Please," I begged. "Do it again."

"Keep your legs open for me, and I'll do it three more times."

He waited. It was obvious he should go on, but he sat there, waiting for the heavens to open or a herd of wild animals or what, I didn't even know.

"You want me to beg?"

"I want consent."

"I consent. Don't stop. Yes, a hundred times."

Thank God he didn't need more than that. He smacked again, and I tried to keep my legs open for the pain to trade more pleasure. Twice more, harder each time and each time harder to keep my knees apart, until my back arched and I felt like a woman going blind.

Which I was because my head was thrown back and my eyes were closed. So, when his tongue soothed my clit, my brain lagged a millisecond behind what he was doing, compressing all the pleasure into a single moment. He worked me with his mouth and fingers, but he didn't make me wait too long, ruthlessly stretching me with three fingers while gently sucking my nub, making my back arch with an orgasm before I could warn him.

When it was done, my legs flopped open without trouble.

"Wow," I said.

He came behind me, pushed me to sitting, and released my arms before pulling my shirt over my head. "Shake them out," he said, rubbing my arms. "Get the blood flowing."

"They're fine." When he walked around the table, I looked at him. "Thanks for that."

"Don't thank me yet."

Before I could reply, he picked me up, throwing me over his shoulder like a caveman. Carrying me to the bedroom, he took advantage of my exposed ass by slapping it with a *thwack* and a burning sting that wasn't punishment for misplaced commas, but a reward for being his whore for the night.

I didn't just allow it—I allowed myself to love it for one more night.

"Do you ever take your clothes off when you fuck?" I asked from behind him. "Or is it, like, your cock is so magnificent that that's all anyone's allowed to see? Would seeing you totally naked blind me? Is that why you've still got all your buttons buttoned?"

He slapped my ass so hard I yelped.

"I'll take that as a yes."

He kicked open the door to his room and threw me on the

bed, skirt hiked, tits out, underwear long gone. He pulled the skirt down my legs and tossed it aside. Now I was completely naked, sprawled on the bed with him standing over me with that monster rod pushing against his pants. He laid his hands on my knees.

"When you're here and we're playing"—he pushed my knees apart, exposing me again—"you offer yourself. Always." He looked between my legs. "Do you understand the rule?"

"Yes," I squeaked. He took his hands away, and I left my legs open for him.

"I saw birth control pills in your bag," he said, unbuttoning his cuffs. "Are you taking them?" He opened his shirt efficiently and quickly, shrugging it off as if he didn't realize what exposing the perfection underneath did to me.

"Yes."

"Which means you were letting that man fuck you without a condom while he was fucking his wife."

I bristled a little, and I had a split second to choose between being offended or answering his assertion. Discount Mandy would have spat back at him, but Couture Mandy didn't need to be liked on anyone else's terms. Couture Mandy just wanted to fuck.

"Yes," I said. "But he wasn't fucking his wife."

Dante smirked and undid the button and zipper on his pants, extending the thin line of hair that started at his navel a few inches. "That's what they all say."

He was right, of course, but so was I, and I had no interest in arguing.

"Wrap it up or don't." I laid back, put my hands inside my thighs, and spread myself open for him. "Just fuck me with it."

I didn't usually act like this in bed, but for one night, I could be a little more wanton. A little slutty. A little of what I was accused of being.

He pushed down his pants and underwear at the same time, hiding his face so I couldn't tell if he liked it or not.

Couture Mandy didn't care if she was liked, but if you're going to fuck a guy, everybody should enjoy themselves.

When he picked his face up and stood, he was fully naked and magnificently erect. I'd had his dick in my mouth, but the sheer size of him stunned me again. For a moment, I let my hands go slack in appreciation, and he *tsk*ed.

"Open it for me again."

So, he did like it. Excellent.

"Tell me," he said as he reached into a drawer. "What do you want me to do to you?"

"I want you to fuck me."

"That's it?" He extracted a condom and ripped the package open with his teeth.

That was it for the moment, but he was challenging me to ask for more.

"I want…" I looked at the ceiling because the sight of his hand on his cock as he slid the condom on was too hot for coherence. "I want you to fuck this pussy hard and deep."

He crawled over me, his body between me and the world, his face taking up my entire vision. "Not bad, *amea*."

He kissed me again, teasing my lips with his tongue, using his free hand to urge my hips up and against him, where my shape clicked flush with his. Hard pressed soft. Rigid slid along wet. I reached down to guide him in, but he grabbed my hands and pinned them over my head.

"Did I do it wrong?" I gasped.

"You forgot to beg." He pushed along the length of me, every bump and vein a sparking tease.

"Fuck me, Goddamnit!" I strained my arms against his hands, but he only increased the pressure.

"Not even a 'please' for me?"

"Now. Fuck me right now."

"Or?"

I wasn't going to threaten to get up and walk out because getting off this bed unfucked wasn't an option. I was soaked and spread under his endless, impassive gaze while his dick lay on my belly like a threat of pain and pleasure.

"Or nothing," I said through my teeth. "Fuck me however you want. Fuck me slow. Fuck me fast. Stick your cock wherever you want—just do it. I want it. I want it."

"Good girl," he murmured.

Then he pressed into me, the pressure steady and relentless, stretching me to accept him—and yes, it hurt, but it was so good all I could do was bury my face in his neck and try to hang on. I had never felt anything like it before, this fullness, a sensation so filthy, scraping every nerve ending raw, driving me to the end of myself, where all I could do was try not to scream.

"You ready to take all of it?" he said with his lips against my cheek.

"Yes."

"Do you have a 'please' for me?" I felt him smiling.

He was going to win.

"Please."

"Are you mine to use tonight?"

"I'm your whore." I tried to move to get him deeper, but he wouldn't play. "I'm your toy. Anything you want. Take it. Use me. Please," I begged down to a whisper. "Please."

"Good girl."

With a purposeful thrust, he buried himself inside me, his body pushing on my clit. My arms were jelly above my head even after he let them go, and I felt myself sinking into a helpless tremble. He stopped, and I opened my eyes, wondering if he was going to make me beg for him again, but his expression probed, checking to see if I was all right as he slid partway out.

"Yes," I said with a nod, answering a question he didn't need words to ask.

He thrust into me, as deep as possible in one stroke, fucking me with a rhythm that expressed not just his utter self-control and power over me, but his need to fulfill my desires as if he knew them already.

I released even the idea of my own desire, letting him use me exactly the way he wanted. I felt my orgasm approaching, and it was the only thing I could focus on: the fat head of Dante's dick splitting me open as the length of him rubbed my clit, the way my rocking hips fell into a tidal cadence I created and he controlled.

He must have sensed I was getting close, because he pulled me up and repositioned me on top while he crouched with his knees under him so though I was above, I was off balance and he was the top.

"You need to come." He tugged my hair hard enough to pull my head back, baring my neck to him.

"Yes."

"Then fuck me until you do," he growled, giving my hair one last yank before letting go. He leaned on his arms with me impaled on his dick, waiting for me to get it.

He was giving me control over my orgasm, and by doing that, he totally controlled me.

"Go," he said with a jerk of his hips. "Now."

"Okay." I had to hear myself say it.

I was going to use him and be his little whore at the same time. Moving up, I angled myself for maximum contact and slid down him, groaning at how perfect it felt.

Dante grabbed my breast, pinching the nipple until it got a beautiful, agonizing shock that stirred me to move faster against him, breathing in bursts of effort. I was bowstring tight, unable to release the arrow.

"Come," he said.

But the need to keep my balance and move with him was too distracting. "I can't. I never come on top."

"It's okay. I've got you." He held me up, pushing me into him so deep it hurt, taking just enough control to keep us joined. "Come like my slut."

At his command, the bowstring snapped, and I was thrown a thousand feet into darkness but tied to his cock as it throbbed against my own pulsing. From the other side of my orgasm, I heard him groan and knew that, even then, he was anchoring me.

When I washed ashore a few moments later, he was still rock hard inside me, sliding his dick in and out with slow, steady pressure as he finished.

I whined a little bit when he pulled out. Feeling sore, used, and satisfied, I rolled onto my back and spread my arms as if I'd died. When his face darkened, I followed his gaze to the still-fresh burns on my hand. I couldn't help feeling a little proud of myself—after all his obsessive concern for that thing, my pussy had at least temporarily managed to distract him.

When he spread the fingers open for inspection, I said, "I'm fine, I swear."

"Hm."

Lightning flashed through the patio doors, then over the *pit-pat* of rain came faraway thunder.

"What if I want to do something before I leave?" I closed my fist so he couldn't get sidetracked. We only had a few more hours, and I wasn't dead yet.

"What do you want to do, *amea*?" His gaze roved over my body with none of his usual clinical detachment.

"What I want," I breathed, "is to waste some fucking water."

His eyes flicked back and forth over mine as if he were reading a book, then he laughed. "You want a bath?"

"Please. You can scrub me clean, then fuck me dirty."

He laughed as if it was becoming a habit. "All right," he said, rolling off the bed. "But I'm holding you to that."

He grabbed my ankles and yanked me to the edge of the bed before pulling me to a standing position. My knees were still a little wobbly, so he guided me to the bathroom, where I pushed him away to turn on the water as he leaned against the vanity with his arms crossed.

"I like it super hot," I said, smacking his thigh so I could reach the cabinet. "I hope you can take it. Ah!" I found the bath bombs and stood up with two. "These were really nice before you busted in."

Plop, plop. I tossed them into the steaming water, and he grabbed me, pulling me into him.

He was hard again.

"How high are you filling that?"

"All. The. Way."

"You're going to pay for every inch."

He kissed me, and with that, the bathroom ceiling gave way, drenching us in stale rainwater and soggy plaster.

CHAPTER 19

DANTE

When the ceiling fell, I expected her to react with horror and disgust. Maybe feign an injury or otherwise turn the event into a drama starring Amanda Bettencourt as the Inconvenienced Socialite whose Big Night of Subbing for Orgasms was cruelly cut short by The Evil Weather and This Shitty House.

But that's not what happened.

After I moved her out of the way of the thinning stream, she looked up, naked, plaster chips stuck to her shoulders and tits like slow-moving shrapnel, dirty water dripping down her belly, and she laughed.

"This is funny?" I said, suddenly the aggrieved one.

"No." She took her eyes off the almond-shaped hole in the ceiling. "I mean, yes." She flicked a plaster chip off my shoulder. "I think if we ever got married, this house would just collapse in on itself."

"Good thing I'm never getting married," I replied before she barely got out the last syllable.

"Good thing." She plucked off a paint chip that had stuck to my chest with a familiar tenderness I was a little too comfortable with.

She... me... *us*? Whoever was responsible for whatever was happening here didn't matter. The split second of comfort I'd felt was a drug, and I wasn't interested in this addiction.

"We should clean this up," she said, shutting off the tub. It was suddenly too quiet, and I heard the splash of the leak on the tiles, which had thinned to the width of a pencil.

"That's not going to stop until the rain does."

"And it's going to ruin the floor." She looked up with me and crossed her arms over her chest—not to cover it but to posture seriousness—and again I found myself a little too comfortable with her for my own comfort.

"If we put a bucket or a pot or whatever under it, it's just going to get full in an hour," she said.

"I'll change it. You go to bed."

She didn't move. "I wonder if there's a way to get it down the drain. Reroute it to the tub, or whatever."

"There's too much debris. It'll clog the lines."

The debris had lessened significantly, but my point stood.

"Hm." Her hip shot to one side as if she were settling into the problem. "It's just that I saw this fountain in Selena Houston's place. It was like an umbrella here." She raised her hand, cupped upward. "And the fountain part? The bowl or whatever? All the way over here." She made a bowl of her other hand. "And the water came from, like, there, landed in the umbrella thing, and flowed into the fountain."

"Hm," I said, my posture of nude seriousness now mirroring hers.

"So, you have an umbrella, but I think the junk in this water might clog it."

"We could use one of the window screens over the drain."

"I like that."

"It's not permanent," I said.

"Just for tonight."

"Just for tonight."

***

ONCE WE AGREED to set up the temporary fix, everything happened quickly and took a long fucking time. She snapped up a towel, dried off, and went to get dressed. I did the same. We met in the kitchen, where I'd left a shitstorm of broken glass and porcelain on the floor.

I eyed her feet, which I expected to find in shoes inappropriate for the shards, much less the rain outside.

"Where did you get those?" I pointed at the blue Wellies she'd jammed her yellow jeans into. "They're my mother's."

"They were in the mud room. Will she mind?"

"No. It's fine."

"Let's go, then!"

She seemed eager to work, not put-upon at all, and though we had to get moving before the water soaked out into the bedrooms, I also didn't know if I was asking too much from her.

"I can do this myself if you want to sleep on the couch."

She rolled her eyes like an adolescent and slid open the back door.

***

IN ALL OF the previous night's chaos, I'd forgotten to shut the living room curtains, so I woke on the couch to the golden warmth of the morning sun on my face, and the first thing I thought with my eyes still closed was that it was yellow, and yellow was the most elevating color.

God, I must have been sleeping like a dead man to think that.

Amanda and I had been up late, fashioning the umbrella into a leak diverter. So late, in fact, that we could have just gone to bed in the first place and woken up early to fix the ceiling.

But working with her had been—in its way—fun.

She was helpful and competent. She listened. She offered

suggestions. She remembered every single thing she'd seen around the house and in the garage— not qualities I ever assumed she'd have.

When the leak water was properly diverted to the screen-filtered tub, we'd cleaned up the kitchen, and I fucked her from behind against the counter, denying her an orgasm until the casserole dish was spotless.

Eyes still closed against the morning sun, I remembered her looking over her shoulder when I pushed my thumb into her ass —the tremulous, open expression that told me she could take the thumb but no more and how it felt to know I didn't have time to fuck her ass like I'd promised.

Nothing I could do about that.

Except, her gasp when I pushed my cock into her for the first time, how it had felt to have her at my mercy at last, tied up and obedient. She'd do it all again when I tied her down again and took her ass the way I should have last night after we crawled on the couch and did it one last time under the fur blankets.

She wasn't gone yet. I could still own her everywhere.

I opened my eyes.

Everyone looks innocent and helpless when they sleep, but that didn't change the pain and fury I felt when I remembered what awaited her at home. The last man in her life had made her so unwelcome that she was determined to become steely and cold to survive.

I could be hard-edged, but if I was cruel to women, it was part of an agreement; ultimately, the point was our mutual, physical pleasure. Renaldo had been sadistic for his own satisfaction, and she didn't deserve a single moment of the suffering he'd caused her.

Now her curls were splayed across the pillow, and the soft curve of her lower lip was chased with sunlit gold. Her body was warm and soft next to mine. It felt as right to have her here as it had to fuck her on the kitchen table last night.

The rightness was new. I hadn't felt it with Veronica or anyone since. Not like this.

It was Amanda Bettencourt's. She owned it, and it scared the fuck out of me.

She had to leave and take the rightness with her.

But later. We had a few hours.

She was turned on her side, the hand she'd burned last night on top of the fur blanket. She'd worn gloves when we worked in the bathroom, and the dishwater had been cool. I examined the blistered skin. It looked good, but I was going to tend the burns anyway. It was an awkward spot for a Band-Aid, but a ten percent chance of infection was still too high.

She stirred slightly, so I put her hand down again and slipped off the couch.

Hadn't the plan all along been to bring her to a series of rude awakenings? And yet I couldn't bring myself to disturb her.

Outside, the rainstorms had cleared the air, and the sky was a brilliant, crystalline blue. I got dressed and checked our upside-down-umbrella-and-pool-noodle contraption. It wasn't bad.

I climbed up to the roof and found another possible spot for the leak and sealed it. It was too small to account for a puddle heavy enough to break the ceiling unless there were a hundred just like it.

The house needed a new roof. Obviously. But it had to get past the rainstorms first.

The ceiling in the room Amanda had been sleeping in could fall in as well, so it was a good thing she was leaving.

Unless she stayed in bed with me.

Fucking her was clearly messing with my head. She had to go. There was no more time for messing around and playing secretary. It was time to deal with my adult life like a man.

I climbed down from the roof. I'd surprise her with coffee on the couch, fuck her ass so gently she'd beg for it again. Refuse. Send her on her way.

But when I walked in, the pile of blankets was empty. Amanda was in her room—the typewriter room, because it was never really hers—packing.

"Morning," I said, then didn't say anything else because there was nothing else to say. I'd told her she had to leave, and for once, here she was—doing as she'd been told.

Leaving.

My dick was disappointed, except it wasn't my dick.

"I was going to make coffee," I offered.

"I made it already," she said, rolling up a mustard something and stuffing it into her bag.

A drop plinked into the bucket. The leak had slowed in some kind of deference to the bigger problem in the bathroom.

"I'm sorry I can't stay to fix the whole thing." She heaved a sigh, looking up at the same spot I was. She didn't linger close to me, and I wasn't sure if I was glad or annoyed.

"I can't even fix the whole thing."

"Anyway," she continued, "thanks for last night. Always good to get a rebound in sooner rather than later." The smile she offered me was polite, and despite everything I'd thought and said holding her in my arms, I couldn't read more into it than the flat, unlayered truth.

"You're welcome," I said. "Goodbye, Amanda."

She rolled her eyes at my use of her name, but she didn't say anything, just snapped her suitcase closed and started toward the door. Then she stopped, and it took me a few seconds to realize it was because I was blocking her way.

I stepped aside, watching her awkwardly navigate her suitcase with her left hand.

"Let me help you," I said.

"No," she snapped, then softened. "Thanks. I have it."

How was this possible?

We were a puzzle with a piece missing, and she didn't even want to check under the table or between the cushions. She was going to leave this unfinished, with me here, on the floor next to the chair leg, because I was the missing piece, panicking at the thought of being left behind.

I hadn't panicked about that in a long time.

"We should bandage that burn. Before you go."

"It's fine."

She'd already refused help, but I took her bag off her shoulder anyway. "You're going to break a blister on the steering wheel." I sounded sterner than I felt. "Then it'll be infected."

She gave in.

The first aid kit was in the mud room. I bandaged her hand as if she had third-degree burns, not second-degree blisters without even a red ring around them anymore. They'd be gone by nightfall, but as long as she was in this house, her hand was mine.

She leaned silently against the cabinet while I worked, watching me with those big, soft green eyes.

"You sure you don't want breakfast before you go?" I asked. "The food between here and LA is crap. Trust me, I've spent years trying to find something decent—there's nothing. Anyway, you already have to lie to Logan about enough. At least you can tell him I was hospitable while you were here."

I didn't realize I'd been hoping for her to smirk when I said *hospitable*, give me some little innuendo we could build on, until she didn't.

So, I made her toast and eggs and watched while she ate them.

I was about to offer to make her lunch for the road—the food along the Cabrillo really was dogshit—when she pushed her plate away and stood firmly. "All right. I really have to go if I want to beat traffic."

"I'll help you carry your bag."

"I'll be all right."

Just take the bag.

I almost did. When she snapped open the telescoping handle, I was in arm's reach. I was in charge here, and if I decided to help her with her things, that was my decision to make. Period.

"Drive safely," I said.

"I will."

"It's going to start raining again this afternoon."

"I'll be home by then."

The wheels of the suitcase rattled on the floor, then whooshed on the rug. She stopped at the front door, and I rushed to open it for her as if I'd gotten confused between the idea of making her stay and the idea of helping her out. My hand just lay on the doorknob like a movie my brain had paused.

"Don't make any stops. You know how they drive when it rains."

She laid her hand on my forearm, not to move it off the knob or hurry it up, but to convey a kind of sincerity I wasn't offering her. "Thank you. Again. For everything. For letting me stay. For last night. And especially..." Her eyes scanned the house, then she squeezed my arm. "Thanks for kicking me out."

I'm not kicking you out.

The sentence stopped in my throat, right behind the first one.

Please stay.

But she wasn't looking for permission to give me her body.

She wasn't looking for permission to stay or go.

She knew what she wanted to do, and she wanted to leave.

I opened the door for her. She smiled and kissed my cheek. I was an awkward teenager again in the months before our game of hoodat. Long before Veronica and her instruction, I was a man who wanted more and didn't know how to get it.

She left, and I closed the door.

The door click felt like a slam echoing in the hollows of my chest. The house was silent for the first time in days—no *plink* of rain outside or *plunk* of the leak in Amanda's room, no sound of her typing or clattering around the kitchen. Just me and this half-broken space and the tapes full of memories I couldn't bear to relive but had to.

Alone with myself and a miserable sense of ache and loss, I was overwhelmed with the knowledge that I'd made a mistake, given up too soon.

And after all, hadn't I? When I'd said she had to leave today, I hadn't necessarily meant this morning. We could get another twelve hours in before getting too attached. I still had a few things I wanted to do to her, and I just… I wasn't…

Before I could stop myself, I ran out the door after her, jogged down the hill, following the path of her footsteps, cursing myself, praying I wasn't too late.

Her car was where we'd left it a few days ago, when she had gotten down on her knees and begged me to let her stay. Now the wipers were on and she was sitting in the driver's seat, hands on the steering wheel, her bandaged palm wrapped tightly around the leather. She must have heard me skidding along the stones and looked up.

Behind her windshield, I saw her mouth shape my name. "Dante?"

I stood there, looking at her through the heavy, misted air, and found myself unable to speak.

I couldn't tell her I'd changed my mind. We'd made a deal, and she'd stuck to the terms. What would she think of me if I tried to change them at the last minute? That wasn't fair, and even when I'd decided to be a dick to her, I'd never wanted to trick her into anything.

I couldn't ask her to stay. And yet, I had to.

She opened the window and eyed me warily.

From outside my body, I heard myself say, "I need a favor."

"Oh?"

"I just realized. There's a crawlspace between the ceiling and the roof. I won't fit up there, but you will."

She looked uncertain, and who could blame her? In my eagerness to spit out my excuse, I'd skipped steps.

"I just need you to take pictures of the damage," I said. "And to figure out what direction the leak is coming from. Then I'll call a roofer with a full scope of work."

"Don't they make their own?"

"It's my work. I decide the scope."

"That's really controlling, even for you."

I had to get her back on the subject before she talked me out of my own reasoning. "It won't take too long. You'll be back before the rain starts again."

She smirked, probably deciding between asking why she suddenly had enough time to check the crawlspace when—not five minutes before—she didn't have a moment to make a pit stop between Cambria and Los Angeles.

Or maybe I wasn't regulating my expression enough and she saw right through me.

"What do I get for doing you this favor?"

She was being transactional, but I appreciated having something to haggle over.

"I'll fuck you again," I growled, my voice a rumbling surprise even to me.

She raised one eyebrow, a perfectly arched question mark. *Didn't we do that already?*

"This time," I said, "you get to make the rules."

"What if I want you to beg?"

She didn't, and we both knew it.

"I'm not going to sub for you," I said. "But you get to set the scene. Tell me how you want it. Since I'll owe you one, I'll fuck you however you want."

Her smile was as blinding as the sunshine-lemon daymare of her jacket. "Deal."

CHAPTER 20

MANDY

Dante Crowne was going to give it to me however I wanted. Everything was looking a whole hell of a lot better than it had on my way up to Cambria.

"Well?" I said when I was right in front of him. "Go. What are you waiting for?"

"Don't you need your suitcase?"

I looked back at my car. The clear sideways B on my windshield was getting dotted with drizzle. "For what?"

He gave his head a quick shake, as if loosening something that was stuck. "Nothing."

I followed him up the stone path to the house for the second time.

Good sex was just good sex, but the way our bodies had moved together last night, it had been hard not to feel as if something else was going on there, something primal and undeniable and big enough to scare the shit out of me. Couture Mandy was getting what she wanted, but Discount Mandy was screaming to get out. I couldn't risk letting my feelings get the better of me when my plans were starting to work out for the first time in forever.

Once we were inside, Dante closed the door behind us, and I

had to laugh. Just ten minutes ago, I'd been steeling myself against a final goodbye, trying to look forward to Los Angeles and seeing Ella again. Now I was back. This place wasn't my thing. It was too orderly and too rickety. It was unbecoming and unwelcoming, and yet I was developing an unreasonable crush on it.

That was when I realized what I'd signed up for. A trip to a small dark place that was probably full of multilegged creatures with stingers.

"What happened?" Dante asked, obviously concerned. "You look like someone just drained the blood out of you."

"I'm sure there are spiders. Not that I'm scared of them," I lied. "But are there are any super-poisonous kinds I should avoid?"

He laughed. "Nothing exotic. It's the same as LA. I promise."

Great. Same as LA was not the same as cuddly little mosquito-eating spiders.

What he didn't know was that as a teenager, I'd spent weekends with Ella and Millie combing gross thrift stores for old designer clothes to alter and redesign for fun. We'd gotten tight with the manager at the Goodwill on Broadway, and he let us see the super-old shit in the basement. It wasn't dark, and I wasn't alone, so I didn't have the sense to be scared until I was deep in the bottom of a box and I saw all these little brown spiders getting out of the way of the light and air. One fell out of a pant leg.

Millie looked over my shoulder, identified them as a recluse species called *laeta,* which had a bite that literally made your skin fall off, just as Ella told her to watch out for another one, and that was it. Millie noped out, and Ella and I were right behind. I left two vintage Chanel jackets and a leather Brando behind.

I decided to do it anyway because Couture Mandy did New and Exciting Things even if she was scared.

"Where's the ladder?" I asked. Dante looked at me as though he had no idea what I was talking about. "To the crawlspace?"

"There's a trapdoor in the ceiling of the mudroom." He gave me another glance. "You should sit down."

"I'm fine. Really."

"You should change first."

My first reaction was to demand a retraction. I'd changed quite enough already, thank you, but then I realized I was wearing a satin T-shirt and flimsy knit pants—both in a color unsuited to a crawlspace with spiders. "I guess I should have taken the suitcase."

He smiled. "There's nothing appropriate in there, trust me."

"If I'd known I'd be chopping wood and fixing roofing, I would have packed the Handybitch overalls I did two years ago."

"Handybitch?"

"Both clients thought it was funny, okay?"

"You made two pairs."

"By hand. That's the company. That's how it works."

"Not much of a job," he groused, but he sounded less judgmental than he had that first night.

"Not for you, maybe." I followed him to his bedroom. "You don't need custom clothes. You look good in everything."

I remembered our conversation last night about how much I liked his dick. What had I said? Magnificent? Or had I just thought it?

In any case, it was true enough to send a shiver through my body, and I wondered if I could cash in my favor before I faced a brown recluse.

But the sooner I faced the creepy-crawly space, the sooner it would be done. I could delay gratification this one time. Afterward, he could wash the cobwebs out of my hair in the kitchen sink. Or we could get a hotel room and make up for last night's lost bath.

Dante gave me a pair of his sweatpants. He was much taller than I was, so I had to roll up the waist and stuff a few feet of leg into the Wellies. His old, blue hoodie smelled like him and was so big it swallowed me in an ocean of fabric.

When I came out of my old room, he was waiting in the hall.

"Wow," he said.

"Shut up." I fell in beside him as we walked to the mud room-slash-library.

"I barely recognize you in a flattering color." He took a pair of black kneepads from a cabinet and indicated I should sit on the bench.

"Yellow happens to be the color of happiness and positivity."

He crouched at my feet and lifted my left heel. "Happy and positive." He laid the plastic shell over my knee and strapped it closed over the sweatpants with sharp efficiency. "Those words describe you"—he let my foot drop and took the other—"not at all."

"You think you're insulting me."

"I think I'm showing you respect for being a serious person," he said, whipping on the second kneepad, then standing.

"I'm flattered," I said sourly.

He stood and took down a pair of yellow gloves. "Your favorite color."

I stood and tried to take the gloves, but he pulled them away and took my hand so he could put them on.

"When you want to fuck a woman," I said as he Velcroed the gloves tight around my wrist. The top of the thumb had been cut off. "Do you make sure she's too boring for words? Does she have to be dour and frowny all the time?" I gave him my other hand. "Asking for a friend."

He turned my palm up and ran his finger over the edge of the bandage. "When I want to fuck a woman," he said as he slipped on the second glove, "I accept whatever she is. Boring, dour, or happy and positive." He reached for the string hanging from the rectangle in the ceiling and pulled down. "It's not my business."

"I don't understand you. Like, at all."

He didn't care. He had a cord to pull. The trapdoor above creaked as a split of blackness widened into a gaping, damp maw with a folding staircase for teeth. He snapped the ladder into place while I cringed and tried to look away from the blackness above, but it had its own suction. Only a *click* to my left turned me away. It was Dante checking the flashlight.

Seeing it worked, he turned to me, ready to say something, then stopped himself. "You shouldn't go up."

He read me like a bad billboard on Sunset. Not that I was trying to hide the fact I was scared, but I didn't want his sympathy.

"I'm fine."

"I'll fuck you anyway."

Oh, no way. I wasn't a charity screw. We had a deal.

"Thanks." I snatched the flashlight from him. "But no thanks. Am I using my phone with no connection? Or should I take yours up? Because I can't email them to you from here."

"We can AirDrop."

"Is that the one where your phone touches mine inappropriately?"

"Only with consent." He stepped away from the ladder so I could mount it. "Once you're up, I'll go up to the roof and track your progress from there. We should be able to hear each other— you can tell me where you are and what you're seeing."

"Okay." I laid my hand on the wood. "Do I get your number?"

He looked at me from the tips of my toes to my eyelashes as if seeing me for the first time. "For?"

"For to call you, duh."

His lips tightened, and his eyes narrowed as if he was focusing on something blurry in his head. "Since I'm right here, I assume you mean once we're back in Los Angeles."

"I might… you know…" I shrugged. "Have a clogged drain or a spider in the tub or… whatever. So." I pressed my thumbprint to the home button, unlocking it.

He took my phone out of my hands.

"I'll make sure the plumber's not ripping you off," he said, tapping in his number. "And if I kill a spider for you…" He tapped the contact closed and handed back the phone. "You dispose of the body. I'm not a mortician."

"I had a squirrel in my bathroom once," I said, sliding the hard rectangle into the back pocket of the loose sweats. "I hit it with a curling iron."

"You really do need someone to come over and take care of you." He reached around me and took out the phone. When I grabbed for it, he yanked it away. "It's going to slide out of that pocket."

"The squirrel ran out the shower window with a burned nose."

"Mammals are tough like that." He unzipped my hoodie a little, then stopped.

"He was never the same again."

"Not surprising." He smiled, slipping the phone into a hidden pocket inside the sweatshirt. "Call me before you traumatize another small animal."

He pulled the zipper all the way to the top and smoothed the front down tenderly, then flipped up the hood and tucked my hair in. Though that felt nice and seemed affectionate, it also seemed as if he was doing it out of necessity.

Spiders. He didn't want my hair to catch spiders.

"Put your weight on the beams," he said.

"What are those?"

"They're the thicker wood pieces." He swung his arm toward the kitchen. "There's insulation between them, and it's just lathe and plaster. It's not strong enough to hold you."

"Got it." I looked at the ceiling, distracted.

He stepped away, giving me a look I recognized.

He thought I was going to nope out.

Well, he had a lot to learn about Couture Mandy.

"Get up there before it's too late. I don't want to rush your reward."

I took a deep breath and climbed. I got far enough to peek into the dark emptiness of the crawlspace before my head hit the ceiling. He stood all the way down there, at the base, where it was light, holding the ladder steady, which he didn't need to do. It wasn't that kind of ladder.

He was making sure I was going to do this.

"Are you going to the roof or no?" I tried to keep my voice from shaking. One more step up this ladder and I would have to get on my hands and knees. "I'm fine," I added as if I was.

"Good girl." He gave me a lazy swat on the ass. There was no real force behind it, but there was an edge of warning in his voice that sent heat streaming through me, that promised pain and then pleasure I wanted very badly.

He got out of my line of sight, and I heard the rustle of fabric as he got on his coat. Without him there, I flicked on the flashlight and swept it across the space.

I was sure it was a damn fine flashlight, but it somehow only managed to illuminate what was directly in its cone of light. Outside that, it was pitch dark, which meant I couldn't keep anything I saw in my head long enough to relate it to what I'd just seen.

Wood. Dripping sounds.

Insulation. Nails.

The door closing behind Dante.

A dead hornet's nest.

Wet wood.

A cardboard shoebox.

Spiderwebs.

It's fine. Absolutely fine.

When I heard a knock above me, I jumped so high I hit my head. "Ow!"

"You all right?" Dante's voice came from the other side of the roof.

"I'm fine." I sounded annoyed, but I was relieved to hear him. "So, what am I doing?"

"Crawling."

Coming out of his mouth, even through the roofing, the word had a physical presence that was honey-sticky and thick with promise.

"Where?" I asked,

"See anything wet?"

"I'm ignoring the double entendre."

"Good, because I didn't make one."

His presence made me comfortable enough to forget the darkness and the flesh-rotting spiders. I shined the flashlight around the corners until I found a beam above that got darker at the top.

"This way," I called. "Toward the kitchen."

"Go and I'll follow."

Pulling myself fully into the crawlspace, I took a deep breath full of stale air and old wood, held it, and crawled.

CHAPTER 21

DANTE

"Go," I said, "and I'll follow."

As I walked slowly above her, I tried not to think too hard about what I'd just done. The sight of her in my clothes, her collarbones revealed by the shirt's gaping neck, the sweats slipping off her hips... She looked *right* that way, the same way she looked right in this house and in my bed.

Knowing she was under me, crawling, made me want to rip the boards off and take her like an animal.

Patience.

We had a deal in place. Maybe we would make another one. We lived in the same city and traveled in the same circles. I'd check in on her in LA. See if the paparazzi could leave her alone. Make sure the burns on her hand and heart had healed.

It was a big city. It would be fine. Good, even. As long as she could keep a secret, which I'd know the next time I saw Logan.

The phone's chime was a merciful distraction. Lyric's name was on the screen and, next to it, a photo of her sunbathing in St. Tropez.

She had, of course, set that photo on my phone herself. Lyric was both the only sister I had and the baby among her five brothers—which meant she usually got what she wanted from us, our parents, and everyone else.

A spoiled brat and my favorite.

No one ever expected us to be close—she was as silly as I was serious, lazy where I worked. I didn't understand Lyric's priorities or her life, but she was the only person who could always make me laugh and probably one of the only people in the world who understood my sense of humor.

I crouched and got my voice close to the roof. "I'm going to take this," I told Amanda.

"Okay. Wait. What does that mean?"

"It'll be a minute." I walked to the other side of the house and answered the phone. "Lyric."

"Hey, nerdbro," she said. "How's no-man's-land?"

"It's all right. The rain finally stopped. Roof's having some problems though."

"Wow, yeah, I really don't care. Listen, I'm at Crownstead." She invoked the name of the estate in Santa Barbara. Our parents had lived there for a while, but now it was Lyric's personal hideaway, the same way the Cambria house had become mine. "On what's supposed to be a vacation from you people—"

"Implying you're gainfully employed?"

"Okay, so being a Crowne is a full-time job because even from up here, I know *waaayyy* too much about who's gonna win gold in the Family Olympics and which of you sorry shitsacks are gonna be eating dirt. That's you, by the way."

"What did I do?"

"Logan says Mandy Bettencourt was up there with you?"

"Logan says?" If I'd let Amanda leave half an hour ago, I wouldn't have had to deflect, but instead, I'd let my impulses run the show.

"Do I stutter?"

"Stuttering's a normal condition a normal person might have."

"Whatever. Logan said when he called me. Ella says Mandy

was supposed to be home last night, and Ella posted up at her house to ward off the paps, but apparently Mandy never showed. So, now Ella's freaking out, which of course means Logan is *extra* freaking out, and now, instead of picking up their fucking phones and grilling you themselves, they want me to drive my ass up to Cambria, grab you, and scour every ditch on the side of the highway for her car, but I think she's still there and there's things happening." She took a deep breath. "Which, if they are, please don't tell me, okay? Call them and either tell them she's there or you're sure she's alive somewhere so that they leave me alone and I can enjoy my vacation, which I earned after that nightmare of a press trip to the Maldives. Please do not ask."

"I won't."

There was a pause, giving my mind the fuel supply for an unhelpful thought. *I'm not fucking her right now, but I could be*, and then, *Maybe when this is all over, when the Hawkinses have been defeated, my victory lap will be fucking Amanda Bettencourt like she deserves*, and then—knowing the dangerous part of the conversation had passed—I wondered if Amanda was still where I'd left her.

"Kidding aside," Lyric said. "You get so boring when you're brooding. You aren't having another existential crisis?"

Finally, a question I could answer honestly. "I've always been very sure that I exist, so crisis averted."

Of course, Lyric couldn't accept the agony of rhetorical defeat. "You know what I mean."

"Yes." I crouched at a rustling sound and knocked on the roof three times. "But do you?"

"Maybe. I don't know. Whatever. Is she alive or not?"

Three quick, impatient knocks came back, and I smiled. Her bratty streak was adorable.

"She's fine."

"Call Logan and Ella, okay?"

Maybe we wouldn't fuck, but she could still be my sub. I'd

show her self-regulation, and she'd be a fun-loving brat who'd make me nuts.

"Dante," Mandy called from below, "where have you been?"

I hung up the phone without saying goodbye to my sister and checked the length of the call. "It's been forty seconds."

"You said you wouldn't leave."

"I'm sorry." I put my hand over where she was as if that would transmit sincerity and regret. I shouldn't have taken the call. It wasn't important, and Amanda needed me.

"Wow."

"'Wow' what?"

"You apologized."

"When I'm wrong."

"Huh," she huffed as if surprised and interested.

"Have you found anything?"

"Yeah," she said with a squeak. "It's huge."

This time, I knew she wasn't making a double entendre.

CHAPTER 22

MANDY

THE FLASHLIGHT ILLUMINATED A WEB TUCKED IN THE CORNER OF A damp wooden beam. In the middle of it sat a hulk of a spider with translucent red skin and legs that didn't splay, but held the bulbous body over its web as if using the length to get enough spring to make it to my eyeball.

Dante asked me if I'd found anything just as the creature moved, and I was trembling too hard to answer. It was coming for me, and I was belly-crawling over beams, leaning on elbows and kneepads, unable to run or feint when it came for me.

There was darkness in every direction, and I couldn't move my flashlight off the spider because I had to be able to see it if it took advantage and struck. Spiders almost never attacked humans—people had been telling me that for years—and yet it didn't make me feel any better. Fear wasn't rational. Fear was something soft and crawling moving closer in this inky dark.

"Amanda?" Dante's tone had gone from brisk to worried.

He was standing almost directly above me, but he still sounded impossibly far away. The spider bent its legs, revving up to pounce, then walked up to the top of the crossbeam for a better angle. My attention followed it, noticing the wet streak where it met the planks and not caring one bit.

"Are you okay?" he asked, a little farther away now, as if he was looking for me. "Do you need to come down?"

The spider didn't launch itself but resettled, and I let the sound of Dante's voice wrap around my mind. He'd guided me through all kinds of shit in the last few days, and either he'd soothed the spider, or he'd soothed me.

I could trust him. I would get this done.

"I'm okay," I said. "Where are you?"

The roof creaked as he walked back to me, and the spider seemed not just smaller, but harmless.

"Right here," he said from just above, so close he must have been kneeling. I put my hand on the raw wood to feel the pressure of his weight.

"Just a spider," I said.

"Tell me what it looks like, and I'll tell you if it's a problem."

Size of a Humvee. Translucent membrane over a bag of blood.

Did I really want to know?

I did not.

"I can see where the wood's wet," I said.

"Good."

"Should I go toward the bathroom or the other way?"

"Go to the source." His voice was equal parts authoritative and soothing, and I melted into its embrace. "You sure you don't want to come back down again? I can hire someone to do this. It doesn't have to be you."

"You're not the only one who can keep a promise around here," I reminded him, sounding much more confident than I felt. "I said I would. So, I'm going to."

"I can follow you. Which direction is it?"

Well, I had no idea, and in order to find out, I had to move the light off the spider. It was sleeping or dead or more focused on catching a bug than biting a giant.

"Come on, Mandy," I whispered to myself. I'd never know if there were more spiders if I kept the light on that one.

That logic got me to trace a path of light along the wet wood until it disappeared.

"Toward the front door," I said.

The ceiling creaked. He was standing. He was going to walk faster than I could crawl.

"Stay with me!" I cried.

"Okay."

"Okay."

"You have to keep making noise so I know where you are."

I tapped on the ceiling above me as I shuffled along, and Dante followed the noise, his boot steps heavy and reassuring. Tapping meant I had to stop, so I talked instead.

"Did you ever have such a gross excuse for a fling before?" I asked, noticing a dozen or so tiny spiders in a wet patch. Different species. Too small to bite.

"I've never had to send a woman to war with an army of spiders, no."

"It's just a platoon."

"Hm," he said, and I noticed his voice was close again. The creaking spanned a wide area, as if he were riding a four-legged animal or crawling on his hands and knees. "We had an army installed."

"Maybe the rest are under my clothes."

"That's where I'd like to be."

His comment reminded me of getting naked and checking my body for tiny spiders, then a bath, but reality cut into the fantasy. It was still a mess in the tub.

"Are you taking pictures?" he asked.

Shit. Right.

"Yep." I took out my phone and realized immediately why the thumb of the glove had been cut off. Dante Crowne thought of everything.

I aimed into the darkness, hoping that the flash would scare off any further would-be spider assassins, and the crawlspace was drowned in light.

"One *Samanda*," I said, knowing the thunder wouldn't come. Counting was just comfort, a joke to myself that lightning had struck inside the crawlspace and made me less afraid.

Dante did too. He chased the fear away, but right then, I knew I had the tools to do it on my own. That was so shocking that I tried it again, taking more pictures and counting off the seconds before thunder didn't come.

It wasn't as funny as the first time, but nothing ever is. And though I knew I could chase away my own fear if I needed to, fear was courageous, coming back like a leak you patched but never really fixed.

"Good thing we set an expiration date," I called up to Dante. "On us."

"Oh?"

"Rules are helpful, you know?"

"They are. Are you all right?"

At his question, I realized I'd stopped moving. It wasn't because of the spider that looked exactly like the one that had threatened me earlier. It was all me, realizing I was going back to LA without the rules I now found so helpful. The attackers back home were larger and had two legs. They ambushed, pounced, bit, and stung.

Under pressure, I'd go back to my old self. I knew I would.

Maybe I didn't need Dante, but I needed the boundaries.

"That's why you hooked up with Veronica," I said. My voice gave my limbs the will to move.

"Excuse me?"

"Veronica Hawkins," I said as if he needed to be reminded of her last name. "I saw her… I was maybe twelve, at the mayor's mansion Christmas party. One of the first big events my mother let me go to. I got lost coming out of the bathroom. It was late, and my cousins were gone, so I followed grown-up voices and ended up outside, and there's this fountain. You know the one?"

Though I heard the creaking of him crawling above me, I asked to make sure he was still paying attention.

"Yes."

"She was with Mr. Hawkins. William. And he's like... you know, this really tough guy. Even in a tuxedo, he walks around like he can either kiss you or kill you."

I could barely hear the little derisive laugh that shot out of him, but it was definitely there. And who could blame him? William Hawkins was known to be a toxic mix of smooth entitlement and pent-up anger.

"And he was—well, I hadn't really thought about it until now—but he was being kind of an asshole." I ran the light along the top corner of the crossbeam, which was wet all the way down to the bottom edge. "He was grabbing her wrist really hard. You could tell it hurt. And it wasn't what he said, because the fountain drowned it out, but there was this danger, this threat coming off him in every direction. I was literally too terrified to move."

The water collected at the bottom of the beam in a silvery rivulet that ran in the direction I'd come from and split in two directions. If I had to guess, I'd say one path led to my room and the other to the bathroom.

"But," I said, "she was amazing. Totally together. Once I saw her face, I was like, 'Oh, he's having a temper tantrum,' and I just went back to the party."

"Did you find it?"

It took me a second to realize what he was talking about. I was on a roll now, imagining how Veronica must have appeared to Dante then, as a boy learning how to be a man.

"She stayed in her lane because she was afraid of her husband. She followed the rules. And that's what you want."

"Amanda." Dante's voice was severe again, and I thought I'd overstepped some boundary. Instead, he asked, "Did you find it?"

"I think so." I knocked on the place where the dampness spread into a dark almond on the planks above.

"Okay," he said. "You can come down."

"Don't you want me to see the damage over the bathroom? For the scope of work or whatever?"

"I don't want someone like her." He avoided the practical question I'd asked in favor of an emotional one I hadn't.

"Oh?" I turned my body around like a clock, leaning elbows and knees on the beams.

"You sure you're okay down there?"

"I'm heading toward the bathroom." If he wasn't going to worry about the job, I could do it for him.

"Did you hear what I said?"

"You said you don't want someone like Veronica."

"Good."

Going back over familiar ground went quickly, but following the stream to the bathroom was slower. New spiders. A hornet's nest. A dry stalactite from an ancient leak.

"So," I said because one of us had to talk before I freaked out again, "what do you want?"

"In a woman?"

"No, in a new car. Of course in a woman."

The kneepad slid off the edge of a beam and hit the insulation. The ceiling didn't break, and I got back up on the beam. This crawlspace was treacherous.

"She's fun," he said. "She doesn't take herself too seriously. She holds onto friendships but lets go of grudges. She lives life as it's handed to her, and she forgets herself all the time. Says the wrong thing because the truth isn't always the right thing to say, but she says it to me because she trusts me."

"I like her."

Either the kneepads were really working, or I was getting used to discomfort, because the wood didn't bite as hard. The view was getting grosser.

"I like her too."

"When I get back to LA, I'll keep all that in mind. Maybe I'll hook you up on a date." The words were barely out of my mouth when I identified them as lies.

Sure, I'd used his body, and he'd used mine for emotion- and attachment-free sex.

Sure, we were parting ways by nightfall.

And sure, I was feeling more like the woman I always wanted to be.

But I wasn't a saint. Dante was going to find a woman like he'd described—one who wasn't anything like me—and he would be fine. I would run into the happy couple at some thing or another, and he and I would pretend we were old friends.

I didn't have to like it, and I certainly didn't have to make it happen.

"What are you looking for?" he asked. "Another Renaldo DeWitt?"

"Ugh."

The disgust was for my ex and the black mold growing on the insulation between my elbows. No wonder there were fewer spiders this way.

"There are plenty of men like him out there."

My pupils tightened. The light from the flashlight seemed dimmer as the hole in the bathroom ceiling chased away the dark. "No, thanks."

"Some are even single, if you're into that sort of thing."

Fuck him for judging me, even if he didn't sound judgmental.

I needed this conversation to keep going so that I didn't lose my mind. But also, I needed to tell Dante the truth. If I died of an undiagnosed mold allergy or the venom of a spider bite, I wanted him to think well of me—to understand why I'd done what I'd done, that I'd had a real reason and not just shallow, selfish desires.

"Every man I've been with has been Renaldo, one way or

another," I insisted, opening my mouth to say things I shouldn't have because the dark space was tight and cold and I felt utterly alone and squeezed in—yet secure in my limits here. "He was the only married one, and it was a sham, and I'm not the reason it fell apart. It was window dressing because his wife is gay, but she wanted to be America's sweetheart, and she thinks America's sweetheart isn't a lesbian."

"Wait."

"I was his consolation prize for a loveless performance with her that made him famous and miserable, and he always treated me that way."

"Hold on."

"And I'm done with guys like him."

"You kept this secret?"

"Of course!" I pushed forward like a soldier through the trenches. "What was I supposed to do? Out her? Why? So everyone would hate me ten percent less?"

"Amanda—"

"Stop calling me that!" I glared at the black-spotted ceiling six inches from my face. "I hated when Renaldo chewed gum, so he did it more to spite me, and when you call me Amanda, you're no better." Knowing he wouldn't apologize, I continued forward, grumbling, "Men. All the same."

"He could have stood by you when everyone found out," Dante said, following.

"Yeah. He coulda. And for the record, I'm telling you all of this because I want you to respect me, which I shouldn't care about, but I do because I'm an insecure half person. My emotional thermostat's broken. That won't change your mind about me, and that's fine, but I thought you should know that I care too much, and yes... it's embarrassing."

Adrenaline and bone-deep fear were turning out to be a hell of a drug. I was babbling as though I'd just swallowed a truth serum.

"I know I can come off as disapproving, but—"

"I can't imagine why." I felt bad as soon as the words left my mouth. Dante had been legitimately kind to me during this conversation; he didn't deserve my sarcasm. "The sex aside," I said with the sharpness removed, "letting me stay was decent. You took care of my hand last night and this morning. I see that you care. I want you to know I care too."

"I do care." He laughed. "My last girlfriend called me 'intentionally cold and emotionally unavailable.'"

"I'd call you more… aggressively controlled."

"If you must."

"No. Emotionally precise. Passionately guarded, maybe."

"It's a habit. A bad one."

The wooden beams were soaked through, and the insulation squished when I poked it, releasing a little pool of mold-flaked water in the indent. The damage started here. I took out the phone and took pictures of everything.

"When Veronica died," he started, then stopped himself. I got took three more shots before he continued. "I acted out. At home, I was angry and cruel. But I couldn't grieve in public because I loved her and I had to protect her."

Death was immune to his protection, but I knew what he meant. As a teenager, Dante had shown more chivalry to Veronica's corpse than Renaldo had given my still-living ass.

"When Samantha died," I said, "I imagined she saw me crying and she'd know I loved her. She'd feel good about it, and at the same time… she'd regret how much she hurt me. She'd know she committed suicide for nothing. Was it like that?"

"Something like that. If I showed one ounce of sadness, I'd break apart and everyone would know. I wanted them to know so I could finally claim her. But I also didn't want anyone to accuse her of being a cheat when she couldn't defend herself. I wanted her to be at peace."

"And that meant not showing anyone how sad you were."

"My parents' hatred for her was unbearable. It was easier to stay... what did you call it? Aggressively controlled."

I'd stopped taking pictures. The intensity of his confession pinned me in place.

"Now," he continued, "some days, I don't know whether I've forgotten how to show what I feel... or if I've just stopped feeling altogether."

The last four days flashed in front of me, a stuttering montage of our strange, intense time together: Dante putting me in my place in the kitchen that first night, then bursting into my room, kissing me as if he was starving for it. The way he'd teased me and spanked me and fed me when I'd hurt myself. I had all of those memories, but I didn't need them to tell me which option was true. The tone of his voice said everything I needed to know.

They were all true.

The closeness and the distance. The intimacy and aloofness.

He wasn't any one thing.

"Your emotional thermostat's broken," he said, waking me from my thoughts. "I turned mine off. I didn't even see a woman for a long time after. I put all my energy into clubs, traveling back and forth. Feeling nothing for years."

With difficulty, I turned to take more pictures, and every time the flash went off, I saw more damage in the corners of the light that needed attention.

"I tried to get right back into it," I said, taking pictures. "She died, and I called Caleb. It was Christmas break. He returned the call at two in the morning. Told me to meet him at some party, and I went. We spent two days together. He said he missed me and he thought about me constantly. It was the first time in months I didn't feel like I could burst into tears at any moment. Then... poof. Gone." I got up on my knees between two beams so I could shoot around a corner.

"He's worthless," Dante said. "You know that, right?"

"I know, but what does that say about me?"

"Who the—"

The rest of the sentence never happened because, right then, I lost my balance and managed to get my elbow under me. All my weight landed on it as it jabbed the insulation between the beams, which felt as soft under me as wet bread.

What had felt merely gross was genuinely unstable, and with a crunch and an increase in the amount of light, I lost my sense of the walls around me, realizing as I fell that spiders and the dark weren't half as dangerous as gravity.

CHAPTER 23

DANTE

THE BIG LEAK THAT HAD DROPPED THE BATHROOM CEILING WAS caused by a ragged gash in the roofing, and by the time Amanda and I were over the bathroom, I no longer cared that it was too complex a job for me to finish myself.

I'd told Amanda too much, and she'd countered by telling me everything.

Shamelessly, completely, with a humility I never would have given her credit for, she'd crawled beneath me with only a few planks of wood and a sheet of roofing between us and opened herself up to derision and ridicule.

"He's worthless," I said. "You know that, right?"

"I know, but what does that say about me?"

It said she was trusting and whole and reckless with her needs because she only knew how to commit fully. She was so rare and beautiful in a world of charmingly armored emotions that I wanted to stand between her tender heart and the world's betrayal. Her protector. Her safety.

The only thing that could have distracted me from telling her everything was the sound of a car coming down the drive. I would have assumed Lyric was finally convinced to come check on me, except the car—which I couldn't see over the HVAC unit—rumbled in a way my sister's Prius couldn't have even if it had the horsepower.

"Who the—"

I stood up to see over the HVAC, but the car had come too close to see. "Who the fuck is that?"

In the middle of my sentence, I was drowned out by the sound of wood splintering and crumbling, then a crash, then her voice, distinct and plaintive, saying, "Ow!"

"Amanda!" I shouted into a wall of wet roofing. "Amanda!"

No answer.

I was moving before I knew where I was going, running to the edge of the roof and leaping onto the patio overhang by her room with the assumption it would hold—which it did. My rational brain knew it would have been safer to cross the roof back to the ladder, but I couldn't wait. If she needed me, I needed to be there for her immediately. From the patio overhang, I shimmied down a concrete pillar that painlessly scraped the skin off my palms.

At last, my feet were on solid ground. As I threw open the huge glass doors of her room, I kicked past the debris at the threshold to the bathroom to find Amanda leveraging herself against the tub to try to sit up straight.

In the bathroom door that led to my bedroom, looking as if she was ready to kick the next pair of balls that got in her way, stood Ella Papillion-Crowne.

* * *

FOR AN ARTIST, Ella was a practical woman. She didn't make a fuss or ask questions until the fire was going and Amanda was settled on the couch with ice against her forehead and left knee.

"Do you need more pillows under your leg?" Ella asked. "It's going to bruise."

"I'm fine," Amanda said, leaning back with her eyes closed.

"Let me get more ice."

"She said she's fine," I growled.

I didn't realize how aggravated I was until I heard it in my own voice. It wasn't caused by the promise of sex I couldn't deliver now or even the deal we had to break, though both of those things frustrated the fuck out of me.

Inside this house, Amanda was mine to care for, and I had to sideline myself to let Ella take over.

If I sat next to Amanda on the couch the way Ella was, I had enough control not to touch her. If I tended her forehead, I had enough control to not kiss it. If I put my hand on her knee, I could easily hide that I hadn't kept my distance, but I wasn't the problem. Amanda didn't know how to be as reserved. She'd give it away, and when I growled, our eyes met, and I knew she was letting Ella play nurse for the same reason.

So, I held back every instinct I had and let Amanda's friend take the lead, which should have been easy. Holding my instincts in check was what I did every day.

My impulse to control was under control.

And yet, with Amanda, every second of surrender was mentally painful.

"Dante," Ella said, "where's the Advil?"

"In the cupboard over the kitchen sink." I jabbed the logs even though they were glowing.

"Show me. Please."

"There's only one kitchen sink."

Fact: I didn't want to hear whatever Ella had to say when Amanda was out of earshot.

Also fact: Ella knew it.

She was barely in the kitchen when she called, "Can't find it."

When I stood, the sight line between the living room and kitchen was clear, and Ella was leaning against the counter with her arms crossed. The back of the couch blocked Amanda's view, but when she looked at me with her big, green eyes, they told me she knew Ella was trying to get me alone.

This was ridiculous. I was acting as if I had no power in this little triangle. We were in my house. I could handle my sister-in-law.

I strode to the kitchen.

"This is a sink."

"You came here to work," Ella said.

"And above it"—I snapped open the cabinet—"is a cabinet."

"Did you get anything done?"

"These"—I took out the bottle of pills—"are on the bottom shelf." I smacked it on the counter. "For short people."

Ella did not take the bait. "You said you were sending her home. I was worried."

"She's a grown woman." I closed the cabinet. That would have been the time to leave, but I stayed so my sister-in-law could berate me.

"Listen. When you hide it so hard I panic she's dead, I start to ask myself why. And the answer I get is that you're just gearing up to have some la-di-da fuckfest."

"Did I mention she's a grown woman?"

"You have no idea what she's been through. This isn't just any heartbreak, Dante. This is very serious, and it's playing out in public. You have no business doing whatever it is you think you're doing with her. Maybe later. In a month. But now?"

If she'd just said Amanda had been through a lot, I would have walked away like I should have, but she tacked on the assumption that I knew nothing about it, and I did. I knew damn well what Amanda had been through, and Ella was the one who didn't know the half of it. Amanda had dedicated herself to a man who couldn't give her what she needed in bed and who couldn't love her the way I could.

Which was not the train of thought I meant to get on.

While I rooted around the pockets of my mind for the right one, Ella jumped in in a hard whisper so Amanda couldn't hear.

"Logan said you wouldn't last five minutes in a house with her."

"Tell your husband I'm not an animal who constantly needs my balls emptied." My answer didn't address her assertion, which was intentional and also not a strategy that would withstand direct questioning.

"Nah, nah," she said, wagging one finger. "That's not what I'm talking about. I'm talking about her." She jabbed that finger in the direction of the living room.

"What's that supposed to mean?" I crossed my arms and leaned on the counter to mirror her earlier posture—one of cool, dispassionate inquiry.

"I didn't believe him until the wedding. The way you look at her?"

Which wedding? The one where she wore a yellow-gold sheath gown that melted onto her body like a stream of molten metal? Or Ella and Logan's wedding, where she wore a buttercup jacket dress I imagined her opening when I told her to and not a second sooner?

"You're imagining things," I said.

"Are you serious? You're going to deny it?"

"Deny what?"

Deny, deny, deny.

"You look at her like you want to eat her alive, and Logan says you always did."

I scoffed. This had to be a fantasy my brother had about his friend and projected onto me. Maybe it was something he'd convinced himself was the truth, or maybe he only had to convince his wife.

"And you know what? It's great. I'm happy for her. Happy for you. Just thrilled she's not dead on the side of the road and you guys are hooking up, but swear to me you're being nice. Swear it's serious and not just a conquest?"

"Okay," I said. "Ella. This is cute, but is there an actual problem here? She needed to stay. I let her stay. The roof leaked, and she offered to go into the crawlspace to assess the damage. She fell. She's fine."

No lies detected.

"Then swear to me you're not fucking her, right now."

"I swear I'm having an irritating conversation right now."

"I'm not mad, I just don't like being lied to."

"I'm not fucking her right now."

"You're telling me to mind my own business."

"I'm telling the truth."

Ella was about to drill down to dates and times, and I was going to have to decide whether or not to tell a direct lie to protect Amanda from being infantilized or stand up for both of us and tell the truth that we were two consenting adults and—

"Hey," Amanda said from the living room. I whipped around to find her standing with an ice pack in one hand. "I think the knee's okay."

My attempt to rush to her started right after "hey," but Ella pushed past and got there first. "Can you put weight on it?"

Amanda glanced at me and walked two steps, favoring the bad knee. "Yeah." She took two more in my direction with less of a limp. "See, I'm fine. And my head too. I don't think I'm concussed or anything."

"No dizziness?" I asked. "Nausea? Do you know your name?"

"Amanda Jean Bettencourt." With a quick glance, she acknowledged to me that she'd called herself what she told me not to call her. "It's Friday, March 13th, blah, blah, blah. I'm fine."

"Cool!" Ella slapped her palms against her thighs. "Well, you don't need me to drive you home, which is great."

"And she's fine," I added.

"And you"—Ella pointed at me—"are also all good. Yay. Dante, once Mandy's home, I'll grab these clothes from her and get them washed. Logan can return them to you, and no one has to go out of their way." She turned to Amanda. "Have you packed up?"

I started a denial. "No—"

"My stuff's in the car," Amanda interrupted me with the truth. "So, you don't have to worry."

"Okay!" Ella said with enthusiasm. "Great."

We all stood there as if we'd ordered a shoe that was about to be dropped.

"Okay," Amanda said. "Let me get my shoes on."

In the blink of an eye, a decision had been made, and I wasn't the one to make it.

I had no power, no choice, no control.

CHAPTER 24

MANDY

This was going to go on all day unless I made some kind of decision.

Ella thought I was getting sucked into something I couldn't handle.

Dante thought I was too weak to say no to Ella.

They were both wrong, but if I asserted what I actually wanted, I'd be setting them against each other, and the animosity and drama would bleed into our lives in Los Angeles.

I had enough in my life, but another ten percent wasn't going to bother me much. Dante, on the other hand, had his own trouble with whatever was going on with these tapes. Family drama wasn't going to help him any.

So, though my head throbbed and my knee ached, it was time to call it off. I had hoped I could get Ella alone long enough to explain, then she'd leave, then Dante and I would be alone. But Ella had her keys in her hands, and it was clear that she would only be satisfied if I walked out the front door while she watched.

"Okay," I said. "Let me get my shoes on."

With that, I got control of the situation.

It felt great, but Dante looked as if I'd slapped him.

Being in control was fine, but it didn't fix anything.

* * *

For the third time, I walked down the hill to my car, and for the first time, Dante wasn't with me.

"That was weird," Ella said after we passed her blue El Camino. She'd refused to get into it, insisting on walking me all the way down to where I was parked.

"What was weird?"

"The way Dante just said bye and walked off."

I shrugged, unwilling to share the necessary details to pick apart the man's motivations.

"I mean, you've been there how many days? You'd think he'd do a hug and a 'nice to have you,' but…" It was her turn to shrug. "I guess Logan's right. No feelings."

I felt, more than saw, her check my reaction, so I made sure I had none at all.

"Anyway, we got some security at your house, so no more brick envelopes through the window."

"Thanks."

Up ahead, my yellow Jag was a spot of sunshine in the gray landscape, still parked in the drive exactly as I'd left it, at a funny, frantic angle. Tire tracks arced in the mud around it where Ella had driven the El Camino.

I ran my thumb over the key fob. The button for the doors was right there, but I didn't press it.

The way he'd said goodbye was too curt, even for Dante Crowne. Had I hurt him? I didn't want to do that. I didn't want anyone to do that. I didn't want him to hurt at all.

Or maybe he was just angry with me for leaving?

Wasn't that the same as hurt?

Why did I care what he thought of me?

I didn't. It wasn't that.

My mind shuffled my heart like a deck of cards. If Renaldo had said goodbye like that, I would have run back to him and begged to know what was wrong, what I had done, and what I could do to fix it. And I wanted to run back to Dante with the same questions, but it didn't feel the same. This need ran deeper. It called without the driving force of an anxious, tightly wound chest. I needed to see if he was okay for him.

Couture Mandy was supposed to take every inverse action. Where I would have begged for affection, I'd give or take it. Where I would have hung by the phone, now I'd call when I had nothing else to do. And if I did something that sent a man into a mood with a sullen pout or a derisive scowl, I would turn my back on his manipulative bullshit instead of running to him, begging to know what I'd done wrong.

But Dante wasn't manipulative, and I knew Couture Mandy wasn't going to *do* anything different. I was going to *feel* different.

I popped the trunk and approached the back of the car.

"Mandy... what are you doing?" Ella gestured at the suitcase that was already in there, ready to accompany me back to the city. "Oh, do you need something? Whatever it is, I can—"

"No." I pulled the bag out of the trunk. She'd watched me pack all of this crap on one of the most miserable days of my life. When I'd left LA with this bag, I'd been running away from people's opinions. Now, I was going to run toward something. "I'm a grown woman, and I really appreciate you coming to get me, but I don't need you to..."

I realized her gaze had drifted down, and mine followed it to the stack of magazines I'd bought in Harmony what felt like a hundred years ago. Taking the bag back out again had dislodged the copies so that they were now a disordered spill, slices of my miserable face staring up at both of us, reminding us how much help and support I'd needed lately.

For the first time though, I looked at them without feeling any shame. Those headlines were basically about someone else—someone who cared about what people thought of her.

I didn't care.

Like, at all.

I slammed the trunk closed on those images. They weren't going to be a part of my life anymore. Ella watched me with a wariness I'd only ever seen her direct at teenage boys being reckless on skateboards and businessmen who left the tacking stitches on their suit vents.

"I'm going to stay for the rest of the day," I said simply. "I'll be back in LA tonight, and I'll see you then."

"I'm not sure—"

I held up a hand to stop her. For once, I felt certain about what I needed to say and what I wanted to do. "I can't tell you how much I appreciate you, El. Not just this last week, but all these years—you've really stayed in my corner, even when I was making it harder. I never could have gotten through any of it without you." I didn't have to butter her up; it was the plain truth, and we both knew it. "And I know you came up here to get me because you were worried. But I'm leaving here on my own terms."

I wanted to say, "You understand that, don't you?" but that would have been like asking for permission, so I didn't.

She stood there for a moment, clearly waiting for me to elaborate, but I didn't do that either. She'd have to tell Logan, and that would only make things complicated for Dante. Our relationship —or whatever it was—was outside her purview until both he and I decided it was.

"Okay, then." Ella clearly didn't like it, but whether she respected my determination or not, she had no choice but to honor a decision clearly stated.

One day, we'd talk this all out, but not now.

We walked up the hill again, footsteps crunching together as if she and I had found a sort of rhythm.

"I just don't trust him," she said. "He's going to hurt you, and the *last* thing you need right now is someone else sticking his fingers in your wounds. I'm sure the attention feels good, but you just got your heart broken. *Shattered.* You're barely in your right mind." She stopped walking and turned to face me. "He's not the right guy for you right now. I don't trust him."

I shook my head and kept walking, and after a moment, she followed.

"Is it him you don't trust or me?" I asked. "Because seriously, I'm okay. I'm..." How could I say this without letting on what was actually happening between us? "I know who Dante is and who he isn't. I'm not asking for anything he can't give me, and he's doing the same for me."

"I hate the idea that you might get hurt."

"And I love that about you." We'd reached the El Camino, which was also parked haphazardly. It looked as though it had skidded the last few feet of its stop. I realized that Ella had probably been pulling in when she heard me fall. No wonder she was being so protective—I had probably scared her half to death.

"I know you're a big girl," she said. "If you need anything—"

"I appreciate it so much, El. I'll need to see you in LA tonight. I'm absolutely dying to get too much takeout and drink a big old martini. We can order from Jaxy and eat on your roof. Under the billboard. All right?"

"All right." She admitted defeat with a huge, long hug, lingering to check my bruises once more, before she got into her car and backed down the driveway.

* * *

I EXPECTED to find Dante inside, dealing with the debris on the bathroom floor. The master bedroom was still relatively unscathed, so I figured it wouldn't be a long commute to get him into bed for the sex I had been promised. Not that I needed an orgasm at that point. I felt as good as I had in months—years, maybe. Couture Mandy wasn't just a character I was inhabiting—she was starting to feel like a person I could actually be.

A person I *wanted* to be.

But Dante wasn't in the bathroom or either of the bedrooms, the living room, the kitchen, or the mud room. When I found him, he was out back, loading the banker's box of tapes into the trunk of his truck. Startled, he straightened when he saw me.

Next to the banker's box was a stack I recognized because I had a matching set: every issue of *DMZ Weekly* that they'd had out at that convenience store in Harmony.

"That magazine any good?" I asked. "My phone doesn't work up here, so I've been looking for some reading material."

The smile I expected didn't arrive. Instead, his face was stern and stormy, and I remembered why everyone was intimidated by him.

"I appreciate your help," he said. "It'll be a lot easier to get the contractor to fix the roof if they know what they're dealing with."

I stepped closer to him. "I'll send them when I have signal."

"Good." He was rigid, tin-soldier stiff.

"Are you forgetting what I'm owed?"

I was ready to fuck him on the hood of his car—the cold metal biting at my thighs, my body bare to the sky above as I let myself be taken. I didn't want anything more than his cock inside me, my pleasure our mutual priority, and to drive back to Los Angeles with the ache of him still thick between my legs.

He said, "No."

"*No?*"

"I don't break promises, but I'm doing it now. I took advantage of you. I don't feel good about it. I don't feel good about any of this. I've lied to be with you. I've let myself want you, and not just your body, but your *time*." He restacked the tabloids with one swipe of his arm. When he turned back to me, his eyes were so cold they burned. "I've been bargaining with myself, trying to find ways to make myself believe that when we get back to LA, I can have this." He flicked his hand between us. "I've been playing games with myself, and you."

He stepped forward, halving the distance between us. Something in the air unraveled. I hoped it was his self-control and his commitment to refusing to pay his debt to my body.

"I'm taking this thing with both hands," he said, "and breaking it. No more sex. No more anything. All there is now is the part where we part ways before I hurt you."

I was breathless with everything—his speech and the aching freeze of his gaze on my skin and the overwhelming nearness of him, the way his body was still hot and almost close enough to touch.

"Wait a minute," I said. "This is your stupid way of protecting me?"

"Maybe."

"Maybe? That's the first unsure statement I've heard you make, and let me tell you, Mr. Maybe, Mr. Dealbreaker... if I get hurt, that's my problem. Logan can—"

"I'm not afraid of Logan," he growled with impatience.

"Then what?"

He tried to punctuate the end of the discussion by slamming the tailgate closed, but the car's hydraulics eased it back into place, and he was left frowning at its noncompliance while I wondered what exactly I wanted out of him.

"I'm not going to beg you to fuck me when you already agreed to it. And whatever, I'll find someone else to do your job." The thought of anyone else touching me seemed wrong, but I said it anyway just to soothe myself. I wasn't trying to make him jealous. That wouldn't have even been a plan B. Or a plan X. You can't impose jealousy on a man like Dante.

So, when he took me by the arms, gritting his teeth with eyes big as doorknobs, I was shocked at being grabbed, but more than that, I'd made him jealous. It wasn't like him, and it wasn't like me to play that card. We weren't ourselves.

We'd left the Cambria house and become two people who never would have liked each other in the first place.

"I'm—" I started.

"Don't—" He stopped himself, tightening his lips into a line.

I lost track of which of us was moving, who had taken which step; all I knew was that we were separated by no more than an arm's length and he could have pulled me close and kissed me. All I knew was that I would not resist.

My brain formed the words *let me go,* but my mouth wouldn't say them. I didn't want him to let me go. Ever.

"You care," I said.

He neither confirmed nor denied. Not with words. Not with his expression and not with the suddenness of his next move.

He pulled me into him, planting a hard kiss as if he were trying to get it to seed and grow. I clasped his lapel, softened my jaw against his, and let him rule my mouth with his. He released my arms but not my mouth, moving his cold palms up to my face as he pushed me against the car.

We kissed for a month, through spring into summer's heat and winter's damp chill, unwilling to let go of each other and deal with the inevitable, until he pulled away a few inches to yank us back into the moment again.

"I care." His lips moved so close to mine I felt the words. "I don't know who I am with you. I make decisions without thinking. I break my promises to myself. You make me weak, Amanda."

Breathing in his scent, rich with the smell of ground coffee mixing with the ozone of more rain, I let him brush my cheek with his soft lips and unshaven sandpaper skin.

"My name is Mandy," I whispered.

The ice started in his eyes and spread through his entire body. He stood up straight and backed up a step, letting the mouth that had just kissed me curl into a smirk.

"Thank you for your help this weekend," he said.

Wow, he was really cutting this off. In the interest of

protecting our hearts, he was breaking the deal. I didn't know whether I admired him or despised him, but I knew it didn't really matter what I thought. It only mattered that he chose.

"My pleasure."

"The pleasure's all mine." He spun his keyring on a finger, and when it landed, he hit the fob button that started the truck.

This wasn't supposed to hurt, but it did, and I had to hide it from him and myself.

He needed to get the hell out of here before he got an eyeful of me losing my composure.

"Yeah," I said, stepping away. "Bye."

I walked away and got five steps before I had to turn back, just to check.

He was at the open door, getting into the car, then closing it with a slap. The white lights in the back flashed when he changed gears, then went red, and he drove away without looking back.

And that was that.

The truck was nearly silent. I watched helplessly as he drove away, turned a corner out the back way. I heard the clack of the rear gate sliding closed.

At last, I was alone at the Crownes' Cambria estate the way I'd planned—back when I was a different woman and so much the same.

CHAPTER 25

MANDY

I'd been right about Dante when all I'd wanted was to be wrong.

He'd done the correct, mature thing that I hadn't been able to do myself.

Though I could have gotten myself inside and finished the week away alone, in a leaky house, I didn't want to. My bags were packed, and I was ready to go. All signs pointed to home, where at least I knew the rules.

The drive home was dry, with spots of sun through the clouds. I cranked the music as I headed south.

About ten miles south of Cambria, my phone sprang to life, and my first thought—the one I wanted to pry out of my head with a grapefruit spoon—was that maybe he was calling me.

I pulled over.

No. It wasn't him. It was Ella from days ago, sending a picture of a gown she was working on for the WearHaus event, which took all of her time in the months leading up to it—yet she'd spent a day she couldn't spare coming up to Cambria to find me.

"You're a good friend," I said to the phone, swiping one picture too far, to the spider in the crawlspace, the hornet's nest, the creepy things in the shadows.

The leaks and damage were there, but somehow, I'd gotten my fears into every frame.

I sent them to Dante, captioned, and tossed the phone onto the passenger seat. As I pulled out, the gas gauge caught my attention. It had read low when I left, and the tank wasn't getting any fuller. I needed to go electric. Off the grid. Like Dante.

"Like me," I said, hitting the blinker. "Not like anyone else."

I got off at the Harmony exit and pulled into the gas station. A pubescent girl eating a granola bar while her dad pumped gas stared at me. Had she seen the gossip pages? Did she recognize me?

I caught my reflection in the pump's chrome… wearing Dante's sweats and his mother's blue Wellies. I looked like a kid in her father's clothes, and I laughed. I would have stared at me too.

Once the tank was full, I decided I was hungry and parked in the little strip mall with the grocery and hardware stores. I picked out a bottle of water and a bag of cashews, standing in line and staring into space as I mentally replayed everything Dante and I had ever said to each other.

Stop.

Why did I keep asking myself how he felt about me? That wasn't knowable, and telling myself I could figure it out was a bad habit I had to shake.

How did *I* feel about *him*?

The guy behind the counter rang up my cashews and water with a series of *boop*s and *beep*s.

I liked Dante.

I cared about him.

I wanted him to be happy.

Getting out my card, I huffed a laugh at myself. Liking, caring, wanting his happiness made him a friend, and though I'd confused friendship and romance before, I wasn't now.

Whatever he and I had was more than friendship, but somehow, the loss wasn't anxious and desperate the way breakups were with me. I didn't feel alone or rejected. I wasn't mentally beating myself up over things I'd said or done with him.

Losing him hurt, but it was less frantic. It was a testing tug of a rope around a lassoed heart. A seamstress gently ripping open a seam that was sewn too loosely.

Gathering my stuff, I was caught short at the magazine rack.

BRAD SINCLAIR SEEN SPINNING IN TEACUPS WITH BABY NANNY
SHE REALLY LET LOOSE!

THE EVER-HANDSOME ACTOR was blurred inside the Disneyland teacup ride. To his right, a little girl gripped the center circle, and to his left, a woman bent over at the waist, possibly letting loose by puking out her guts. The surrounding headlines included Michael Greydon with his paparazzi girlfriend, Fiona Drazen with a cup of coffee, and Justin Beckett generally being a douchebag.

No Renaldo.

No me.

I opened a copy and scanned the inside pages.

Nothing. Not even Tatiana made it.

Like that, it was over.

I hadn't realized how much my infamy had been weighing on me. Ripping it away had been like a giant leaf blower in the sky, pushing the clouds from the sunlight. I could see. Finally, even as my eyes fogged, what was right in front of me got very clear, and it wasn't celebrity gossip.

It was Dante. How he'd made me feel safe in the crawlspace.

How I'd trusted him to do things in bed that I'd never trusted another man to do. How he'd felt against me when he taught me to chop a log. How—all those years ago—I never forgot the emotional release of control in those minutes in a dark closet.

"Hey there," A man's voice came from my left. "You all right, miss?"

I rubbed the tears away enough to see the guy who spoke. He was built like a truck and covered in a plaid flannel tarp, had a thick, reddish beard and a matching head of hair that was starting an early retreat.

"Yeah." I closed the paper and put it back in the rack. "I'll be okay."

"Harmless, I swear." He held up his hand to reveal a wedding ring. "My wife likes knowing I'm a gentleman when I'm on the road."

"She seems like a nice person."

"Been eleven years."

"And you're on the road a lot?" I asked, eager for the pleasant distraction of a decent man.

"Trucker. We broke up over it a dozen times, but it don't stick."

"That sounds painful."

"Nah. I mean, yeah, but I always figure we'll straighten it out. Takes the edge off."

Was that what I was feeling? Or *not* feeling with Dante? Hurt without the edge of a permanent separation? Where would I get that idea from though?

"When did you know?" I asked, trying not to cry all over again. Maybe chatting with Plaid Man was a bad idea. "That you'd always straighten it out, I mean?"

It was too familiar a question, but he had a soft approachability found in the most expensive therapists. And when he smiled with the memory, I knew it would be okay.

"First time she told me I was full of shit. Pardon her French."

"First date?" I joked.

"Second. She was a truth bomb. That made her maybe"—he tilted his flat hand this way and that—"seventy-five percent prettier, which I woulda said was near impossible."

I laughed and punched his arm. "Yeah, you—"

The rest of my sentence was lost in the clatter of the magazine rack as the kind, burly man in the plaid shirt found himself pushed against the counter by none other than Dante Crowne.

CHAPTER 26

DANTE

By the time I got to the Harmony exit, the power lines cast afternoon shadows along the two-lane Cabrillo Highway, and the endorphin rush of making a decision about Amanda had worn off enough for me to doubt myself.

I thought I'd made the right choice, even if it was the hard one, but as I parked outside the convenience store in Harmony, I considered that I'd made the wrong choice because it was the easy one.

I wandered the aisles, searching for something that didn't have sugar as its first ingredient. I'd never left the house in that state before—not just not closed down but actively half-broken. I would need to get things arranged with the contractor and have him coordinate with the house's caretaker. None of which would fix the closed-down half-brokenness inside me.

Amanda was probably driving, thumbing at her phone as she blasted down the Cabrillo, singing in the same voice that had drilled holes in my eardrums from the bathroom that first night, her sexy little car careening directly into a divider as she multi-tasked—at which point she'd become the second woman to walk out of my life and disappear right off the map.

My phone vibrated with an incoming text, confirming my worst fears. Amanda was not paying attention and had sent me a flash-lit image of the crawlspace with an attached message.

*—Here, I thought you were
honest and willing to be vulnerable—*

Another picture of a different corner with damp, mold-stained beams. It was worse than I thought.

*—Here, I thought you were
powerful but also kind—*

Flattened insulation webbed with mold. A beam, soggy and near black, the boards near it half-rotted away. She'd fallen through them.

*—Here, I thought you were
passionately guarded and that
it would be worth someone's time
to get through that guard—*

She'd been wrong, obviously. The cost of breaking through a decade's worth of solid emotional armor, built for my good and the good of everyone I cared about, was too high. I could tell her that in a text, but I needed to explain to her face, to see how her body reacted and how well she understood. I needed to confirm that she wasn't hurt.

—Where are you?—

No answer.

—I hope you're not answering

because you're driving—

As soon as the message sent, I heard her voice and looked up to find her standing behind a rack of brand-new tabloids, covers splashed with an actor I didn't recognize. Her story was last week's gossip. Without that, she didn't need me. She was as free as she'd ever been; she didn't owe herself to anyone anymore.

Amanda's living face was the only version of itself in the store, and she was looking upward slightly, face open and receptive as she listened to the man standing too close to her.

I'm not going to beg you to fuck me when you already agreed to it.

She smiled at him.

I'll find someone else to do your job.

I was pulled to her as if she were made of iron and the urge to touch her was a magnet under my skin until she reached for the man, and I can tell you—no magnet was strong enough to describe the force that attracted me in her direction.

She gently punched the man's arm in a gesture that made my blood run hot. My fingertips went numb when they closed into a fist, and the beating of my heart and the breath in my lungs pulled me forward even as I recognized the cold truth.

And whatever, I'll find someone else to do your job.

We weren't in the house anymore.

I didn't own her.

I'd walked away from her.

She wasn't mine.

And I knew that every time Logan had looked at me looking at her and thought he'd seen something wild and hungry, he'd been right.

I'll find someone else.

I came at the man, swiping the rack out of the way with a clatter and a rustle as the papers splashed across the floor, grabbing his collar as I pushed him against the counter. I was taller than him, but he was built like a truck. I was sure I could have broken him in two.

"Stay away from her," I growled.

This strange man put up his hands and looked at me as if I'd lost my mind, and I had, but he didn't reflect my rage back at me or react with violence, as if he'd kill me if he had to but wanted to make sure he had to first.

"Dante!" She cried from behind me.

"Dude," he said, unafraid.

But I wasn't afraid either. "Don't—" I hissed but couldn't finish.

Don't what?

Touch her?

He hadn't laid a finger on her.

She'd touched him.

A quick, hard pressure against my arm shattered my will, and I loosened my grip. It was Amanda, pushing me off.

"What is *wrong* with you?" she cried before shoving me hard enough to give me an excuse to let go and look around.

We were encircled by people. The cashier held up a baseball bat.

I felt ridiculous.

"Sorry," I grumbled to the man, holding my hands up in surrender. "I thought..."

You'd found someone else to do it.

Finishing that sentence was a great way to lose the opportunity to say more, so I got myself together in time to recover.

"Are you all right?" I asked the guy.

"I'm fine." He turned to Mandy. "You want me to walk you to your car?"

She looked from me to him, and I thought she might not accept his offer—but she should have. I wasn't stable enough to keep her safe, and every face in the small crowd confirmed it.

"Please," I said, taking out my wallet, "I'd appreciate it if you did."

"Excuse me?" Mandy said, her beautiful brow screwed tight with irritation. "That's my decision."

Her eyes were intent on me, and I couldn't bear being in the skin of the man she saw.

I slid out a hundred-dollar bill and laid it on the counter.

"For the damage," I said to the cashier lowering his baseball bat. "Apologies."

Head down, I left without saying another word. I paced to my truck, started it remotely, and got in as if it were on the far side of a tunnel with nothing existing outside it. Only when I drove out of the lot did I see another human. It was her, standing by her sunshine-colored car with her curls flicking in the breeze, waving goodbye to the strange man in a plaid shirt who had protected her when I should have. I almost caved in to my instinct and stopped, but I beat it back with a force of will that felt blinding and cold to turn onto the entrance of the Cabrillo.

Done.

One stupid thing… maybe two, but done.

I was free to live in the world as I'd built it, which should have given me relief. Yet there was nothing in my heart but grief. I'd walked away again, more reluctantly than before and for a better reason, but I'd still walked away, and there was no going back.

Traffic was light, but I stayed in the right lane. I wasn't in the mood to pass anyone, wasn't feeling strategic or motivated. So, when the car behind me honked, I ignored it because I was already in the slow lane. And when it passed me, I almost didn't glance at it, except that it was an impossible-to-ignore shade of daffodil yellow.

I rolled down my window, and Amanda opened hers on the passenger side.

"Pull over, you shit!" she screamed over the whoosh of the wind, leaning toward the center of the front seat so I could see her face as it went from the road to me and back again. "I'll run you off the road."

She was going to run herself off the road if she didn't pay attention.

I told myself that was why I pulled over, but I didn't believe it.

She blew past me and turned onto a private drive a few hundred feet away. Private driveways dotted the Cabrillo, set miles apart, each with a gate visible from the main strip. She couldn't get far once she turned, so I followed at my own pace to give myself time to think.

Which I didn't do at all.

Because if I'd been thinking, I would have kept on going, but I needed to tell myself I was a man who considered all the variables and known quantities before taking an action—not a man who'd follow a woman he'd just tried to beat up a refrigerator to protect and whom he had no future with inside the boundaries of Los Angeles.

Past the trees clustered around the spot where she'd turned, I found her standing in the shade. The buttercup Jaguar was parked against the white split-rail fence that bordered the entrance to the private road, and I parked perpendicular to it, blocking the sight of her from the highway. When I opened the door, I heard birds, crickets, and finally, when I got out, I caught the whoosh of a passing car.

When she spoke, her voice was low and certain. "You still owe me."

"Are you serious?" I said as if she couldn't be, but I was moving toward her with no intention of stopping.

What had she called me? *Powerful but kind.*

At that moment, I was neither. I was a weak man, enslaved by emotion and trapped inside biology. Even the mind I elevated wasn't more than a lump of electrically conductive proteins trapped in my bowl of a skull, and every cell, every neuron, every atom, and every yawning space in between wanted her.

"Stop," she said.

I drew up short before I laid a finger on her, grateful because once I started, I wouldn't be able to stop. "Say it, Amanda." We danced around each other like boxers. "Whatever it is."

"We're too complicated. Between Logan, my reputation, and the show you just put on? This is it. Once we're in LA... if we run into each other somewhere, we're cordial—friends."

"If I run into you around the pool at Chateau Marmont and you have a cabana—"

Her smile was razor sharp. "I won't even say hello."

On the other side of my truck, a car zipped by on the freeway, then another, then nothing disturbed us but the crackle of the wind in the trees.

With my truck behind her, wearing my clothes with surrender in her eyes, she appeared fully assimilated to me, exactly where I wanted her.

"Don't move," I said, approaching her slowly, drawing out the sweet agony between us.

She tilted her head back and bared her throat but kept her hands on the fence. She'd learned so quickly to be obedient. I could only imagine what she'd do if I had more time. She'd learn to say yes in a hundred ways to a hundred different things she'd never thought possible.

Without touching her with my hands, I pressed my face to her neck and whispered, "My little fucking slut."

She whimpered.

"Didn't get enough the first time, did you? I told you you'd beg for my cock. I didn't expect you to do it in public, but..." I slipped a hand into her hair and gave it a tug. "That's how bad you need it."

"Yes," she breathed.

I waited.

"Yes, *sir*."

I kissed her for that, long and slow and thorough. Her hips

were already working against mine, seeking friction, so I pushed her against my truck with one hand and slid the other one into the crotch of the sweatpants I'd loaned her only to discover that there was nothing else between us, just her warm, bare skin.

"You fucking whore," I murmured, sliding deeper to find her folds wet and ready. "Is this how bad you want cock?"

"*Your* cock."

She was slick enough to take two fingers and gasp at the sudden intrusion, gripping around me as if she wanted to hold my hand there, but my cock hardened to bury itself in her center, pushing with the quivering rhythm of her pulse.

I slipped my fingers out and placed them on her lower lip. "Suck it off. Taste what a perfect little cunt you have."

Thrusting my fingers along her tongue, I let her close her lips around them and suck, taking the opportunity to get my dick out. I could barely think straight; I needed to be inside her. If this was going to be the last time, she was getting every inch I had.

"Turn around," I said, spinning her before I was even finished with the command. "Hands on the truck."

She spun and gripped the hood as I yanked down the rolled-up sweatpants, exposing the sweet curve of her ass. I smacked it, and the sound got lost in the trees. When I spanked her again, she grunted from the sting.

"Hush now," I said, sliding the head of my dick between her ass cheeks. "Be a good girl. Stay still when I take you."

With the head of my cock at her dry ass, she was still and silent.

This was trust. This was control.

This was all I needed. Moving my head down to her wet cunt, I slid inside it, fucking her deep in one long, clean thrust.

"Touch yourself," I demanded. "Use your left hand."

She took her left hand off the fence and dropped it between her legs.

"When you get back, you'll fuck yourself with your left hand when you think of me. Because no one else"—I thrust into her so hard she whimpered again—"is going to fuck you like this."

She rubbed furiously at her clit while I pinched her nipples and fucked her harder with every stroke, trying to maintain control as she fell apart around me. Her orgasm left her clinging to me, limp and exhausted, and I held her tightly, pushing deep until I couldn't bear another second.

I pulled out and came on her ass, marking it as mine, as if my promise that this was our last time meant nothing at all. I pressed my face to her neck and let myself imagine, for one brief moment, that she was something I could allow myself to keep.

I got a handkerchief from my pocket and wiped the sticky come off her, reaching between her legs to massage her clit a little. She tried to pull away from the contact.

"Too sensitive?" I asked. "You sure you can't come again?"

"I can't."

"Are you *sure*, Mandy?"

We both froze as if time had stopped. I'd learned long ago not to take anything said during sex too seriously, but somehow, this was a massive slipup.

Mandy.

The word echoed between us, drowning out the birds and the wind in the trees.

She turned to face me, and I held my hands up like a man who'd said "I love you" on the third date.

In this case, I could hardly apologize or say I didn't mean it.

"I can't," she said again, a little more firmly.

Pocketing the handkerchief, I tucked my dick back into my pants. She bent forward to pull up my sweats, rolling them up as she avoided eye contact.

"Thanks for that." She sounded as distant and professional as if we'd just closed a business deal.

"Thank *you*," I replied.

"Glad we got that out of our systems." She glanced at her car as if calculating how many steps she'd have to take to get inside it and away from me.

"I'll see you in LA," I suggested.

The world pressed in. On the other side of my truck, the frequency of whooshing cars seemed to double.

"Yeah." She stepped away. "Maybe lunch at Mantillini."

Like a newcomer to Los Angeles without a clue how things were done, I almost thought we'd actually meet for lunch at Kate Mantillini, on Wilshire, and walk a few blocks for an afternoon fuck at the Sixty Hotel, or even the Four Seasons if we had time.

But before I opened my mouth, I remembered that Kate Mantillini had closed years ago, and in LA, you said you'd meet for lunch but never did, and also that I was a sad, sorry excuse for a man.

And then, for what I promised her was the last time, I watched her leave, and I smiled to myself because she didn't know something I did.

I was going to see her again.

CHAPTER 27

MANDY

GOOD. FINE. GREAT.

That was how I felt on the way out of Harmony. I put music on. Everything was cool. I was going back to Los Angeles. I loved my city, and no matter where I was coming from, I was usually relieved to be home.

But this time as I dropped out of the Angeles National Forest, the metropolis spread before me looked tired and dry. I navigated the bumper-kissing traffic and tried to be sorry about taking the time to fuck Dante in that driveway—getting caught in rush-hour was an amateur mistake—and couldn't. He'd said my name right, and that single victory made it all worth it.

A lone paparazzo waited outside my house, and the sight of him snapped my spine straight. I couldn't idle in memories of the past when there was a threat right in front of me.

I parked in my driveway, and he waved as I got out of the car.

"Hey, Mandy," he called as his camera clicked. "Love the outfit." He sounded like a store clerk whose manager was hovering nearby, listening to make sure he gave the corporate-mandated greeting. "Did you wash that man right out of your hair?"

The tabloids loved this—as soon as they couldn't sell the story of a woman's villainy anymore, they'd turn around and make her into a saint. Apparently, this week I could be a bravely rebounded go-girl heroine instead of their tacky whore.

And you know what?

I was strong enough to play that game.

"Right out," I said, talking about Renaldo while wrapped in Dante's clothes, surrounded by his smell, with the taste of his pussy-soaked fingers still on my tongue.

Now I would look great on page twenty-three.

* * *

THE SECURITY GUARD Logan and Ella had hired to watch over the house recognized me. I thanked her and let her know I was taken care of. I could watch the place on my own now.

My phone had buzzed and dinged all the way home, and I continued to ignore it. Once I checked my notifications, the Cambria experience would be really and truly over.

I dropped my bag in my room, stuffing everything that had been in it into a sack for my laundry service to take care of, then I took a long shower, scrubbing off the physical evidence of memories I'd never shake. Dante's hand connecting with my ass for the first time. Coming with his tongue on the dinner table. The sweet desperation of his side-of-the-road fuck when we both knew it was over for us. I cleaned my sore pussy and remembered him there.

You'll fuck yourself with your left hand when you think of me.

I took my hand away and stared at my wet palm as if I'd never seen it before in my life.

Without thinking, I'd been using the nondominant left.

Dante Crowne wasn't just in my head—he was in my muscles. He was controlling me through time and space, and I'd worked too hard to be my own woman.

He'd called me Mandy. Not *amea*. Not Amanda.

Mandy.

I got out, dried myself, threw a nightgown over my head, and texted Ella.

—I'm back—

—You're back!—

I'd left her only a few hours before, but a lifetime had passed. Yes, I was back, and bone tired.

—We were supposed to meet for dinner tonight, but I'm so tired. ZZZZZ—

—Go to bed. When do I see you?—

—You're busy with the WearHaus thing. So, maybe after that?—

Ella's company was sponsoring a red-carpet event showcasing young fashion students from backgrounds that—because of limited opportunities—didn't usually produce high-end designers.

—Girl, spa with me tomorrow. I need it—

Eight words was all it took to show me a friend who was thrilled I was home safe, in my own bed.

—Loft Club?—

—I'll book. Yay!—

She'd be so disappointed if she found out I'd submitted my body to her brother-in-law, and even more if she saw my newfound confidence was sewn together with the thread of his dominance. And when she noticed my sadness that he and I were only ever temporary, she'd write me off as a failure.

Ella would never.

She could have left me behind a million times, and she never did.

But fear had slipped through from somewhere, like stuffing through a weak seam.

I flopped on the couch and checked my notifications for a distraction. Making a concerted effort to not care that Dante hadn't called or texted, I listened to the voicemail.

"Hey, sweetheart. It's your mother."

She often thought I'd forget her voice.

"I know you're out in the boonies, but when you get this, give me a call. Ella invited me to the WearHaus party, and I don't want to go alone. Hint, hint. I love you. Bye."

I called her, and she rang back on a video call, her mud-masked face smiling from under the crack in the glass.

"Mandy!" She adjusted the towel on her head and took me on a walk out of the bathroom. "How was your trip?"

Of everyone in the world, my mother would have been thrilled at the slightest possibility of me in a relationship with Dante Crowne. He was rich, single, handsome, and stable. Then she'd find out our relationship—if you could even call it that—was a temporary thing, and she'd spend the next decade trying to turn it permanent. So, I spared her the truth.

"Exactly what I needed."

"Good! Did you get my message?"

"I'm meeting Aileen and Millie. You can join."

"Fantastic." She propped the phone on the coffee table and sat on the couch. "Do you know who's going to be there?"

She wasn't asking—she was leading into a relay of information, and my first thought was, *Dante,* but my next reaction was to soothe myself with the knowledge that she didn't know about him. Then I thought she meant Renaldo, but her tone was laced with gleeful anticipation, not worry or disgust.

"Here's a hint." She pantomimed fishing, reeling in the big one, then collapsing into a sad frown face.

The big one got away.

"Caleb Hawkins," I guessed. His name had new connotations, and like everything else now, they were tied to Dante.

"I saw his stepmother at Amelia's. He's single, but not for long."

"He probably wants to be single."

"You can strike while the iron's hot."

"Stitch in time," I added absently.

"Exactly! So, I told her to have him call you!"

I rolled my eyes. Caleb had dumped me years ago. He wasn't calling me for any reason, much less because he was conveniently single, but I had to give my mother credit for using sunny optimism and constant interference to secure her ambitions for me.

Now if only I could do the same for myself.

CHAPTER 28

MANDY

ONE OF THE BLESSINGS OF THE LOFT CLUB WAS THAT EVERYONE there had been the subject of the paparazzi's interest at least once in their lives, so no one gave me a second glance as Ella and I strode through the spa's public lounge to our private room, where we wound up belly-down, draped in warm towels, bathed in sunlight from the wide-open doors to a private courtyard while hot rocks cooled on our backs.

"Thank you for thinking of this," I said with my face squished.

"Mm," Ella said as a "you're welcome."

"You must have the WearHaus thing under control."

"More or less. How's your back after that fall?" Ella asked.

My back was fine. It was my arms that were sore—from holding myself up against Dante's truck as he'd fucked me.

"My mother's trying to set me up with Caleb again," I said as the masseur's hands firmly stroked the muscles of my back. It felt good, but not as good as it would have felt if Dante—

No. Not Dante.

"She's persistent."

"She says he broke up with… I forget her name. The head of that preschool Beyoncé sent her kids to—"

"The Center."

"You had that on the tip of your tongue."

Pause. Did she fall asleep?

"Ella?"

"You haven't told me anything about Cambria."

"It rained a lot," I said. That was true. "Dante and I argued." Also true. "It was good to get some time away from the city though, just to clear my head."

"I hope the arguing wasn't too serious," she said.

There was a long, loaded pause, and I knew she hadn't fallen asleep. She was waiting for me to fill in the blanks, but Ella would tell Logan, and Logan would drag it back to Dante.

"Nope," I said.

"So, you really didn't know about Logan's theory?"

"Which one?"

"That Dante's always had a thing for you?"

I laughed into the massage table's donut.

"There's no way in hell," I said truthfully.

"Could be like pigtail-pulling. You know?"

"He's not a pigtail-pulling type." Again, the truth. His hair-pulling was much more serious, and when he decided to hurt me, it was more painful and delicious than any schoolyard game.

"No, I guess not." She took a deep breath. "I'm sorry I went up there. I was just worried about you. And when I saw you, I thought there was something going on with you guys."

The denial was halfway out of my mouth when the truth muscled past.

"There was."

"What?" I heard a rustle and the thump of a rock falling to the carpet. When I looked over, Ella was up on her elbows.

"Ella, please," I said with a gentle firmness I'd learned from Dante, "it's fine. He's fine. It was a thing… a fun thing, but it was temporary. I used him. He used me. Done. I'm not emotionally attached at all."

That was a fat lie. I was, and the attachment nagged at me. It was wrong. It was a weakness I didn't need to shore up.

"But…" After I put my head back down and closed my eyes, I made a conscious decision to continue. "I don't think I'm cut out for casual sex."

"So, it was bad?" Ella said as she went horizontal.

"No, no, no. Not at all. It was—"

"Skip the details, please."

"I want more. That's all. I want to be unrestricted, and if I can't have that, I'll just hang out with my girlfriends and have fun."

The idea was appealing the way I'd phrased it. I could have easily said, "If I can't have Dante, I'm fine being alone," but I didn't because Ella would have seen that as an emotional five-alarm fire when it wasn't. I really was fine being single.

"You sure you're okay?" she asked.

"Fully. Really. It was exactly what I needed, but it wasn't real."

That felt like such an unexpectedly huge lie I almost choked on it.

"Logan's going to fuck him up anyway."

I chuckled at the thought and put my head back down, trying to forget that I'd lied to Ella about how real my time with Dante had been because the truth was too hard to swallow.

CHAPTER 29

DANTE

After the austerity and quiet of the Cambria house, the glass high-rises of Crowne Industries HQ came off like a game show host officiating a funeral.

My father, Ted Crowne, the patriarch of the companies we simply called Crowne, was seated on the brown leather couch in what used to be his office, going through the contents of the box with me. He'd ceded this space to Logan when my brother got married, but with his white hair and graceful command of what he'd built, my father still acted as if he was officially in charge. I'd taken a seat in an armchair, where I felt oversized and awkward. Ted Crowne was probably the only person in the world who could still make me feel like an ungainly adolescent dragging around the secrets of his misbehavior.

Ernie had perfectly transcribed both tapes in two hours, but I missed Mandy's hunting and pecking, her look of studious concentration, the ambition to get it right coupled with the knowledge that she wouldn't. Those transcripts meant nothing to her, and she could have stayed in the house even if she'd misplaced a thousand commas.

She'd wanted to be perfect because I'd asked her to be. She didn't need another reason.

I'd paid an arm and a leg for those transcripts, and I could barely read them. All I could think about was the woman who'd typed up the first few pages with two fingers and the *tappa-tappa-tap-ding* from inside her room.

"You have nothing." Dad leaned back and looked at me with his hands laced over his chest.

With Mandy on my mind, it had taken me that long to go through the transcript, but I tossed it on the table with the nothing contracts.

"What about the FCC conversation? It could be a bribe."

"He said four words, and the chairman refused." Dad plucked up the transcripts even though he knew what was in them. "This was a fishing expedition, and you came home with an empty bucket. It happens."

"They won't let me buy them out without a threat."

"Mm," he muttered, scanning the pages again but leaning back this time, as if he could trick himself into being surprised by something in them. "She didn't take an opportunity to renegotiate her prenup. Why?"

"We were going to run away together." I kept my voice as smooth as possible. "Run private clubs an ocean away. Why bother with a renegotiation?"

"Technically"—he plopped the folder back onto the table—"she was breaching both the infidelity clause and the criminal activity clause. And you were underage. You weren't a safe bet."

My answer was that she was safe with me. We'd set up businesses overseas. We were going…and soon. I'd had it all under control.

But it struck me differently today—maybe because I'd spent so much time with Mandy, a woman who reminded me viscerally of how young I'd once been, how untrained and untried in the world. For years, when I'd remembered my relationship with

Veronica, it had been from inside the experience of it: all of the passion of loving her and the rage of losing her.

Now I could see it from the outside, and it looked more like what my parents had always insisted it was instead of what I had once known it to be.

"Maybe." I crossed my legs. "Maybe she was hedging."

"Maybe you were too."

When I looked at him as if I didn't know what he was talking about, he took a deep breath and leaned forward. "You spent a lot of time at Crowne chasing Delilah Doctorow."

"Is it chasing if I caught her?"

He smiled and nodded. "You guys were attached at the hip for months."

"That's not how I remember it."

"Do you remember your mother sitting you down and asking you how serious you were about her?"

If I thought hard enough, I could call up a vague memory of my mother casually mentioning it by our pool and a sharp, clear remembrance of terror so thick I'd jumped in the water to dilute it.

"Even when you were little," he continued, "you wanted a say in everything. You had to lay down one rule. If we said bedtime was nine, you said no, it was 8:55. Not 9:05, because we would have said no. But you'd give up five minutes so we'd agree, and you'd be the one in charge of your life."

"Maybe I was tired."

"And maybe you let Veronica Hawkins use you because you liked it."

There had been plenty to like, but the sex wasn't what he was talking about.

"She was there," Dad said. "She'd never commit to you, no matter what she promised, no matter how many clubs you financed for her. It was a game. She said nine, and you said 8:55. You called the shots, but she set the limits."

"You know a lot about my relationship."

"I know a lot about you. You're still hedging."

"You're telling me to let go of the clubs."

"You think you're in charge if you keep them, but you're barely even there anymore. You're not getting any joy from them, and here you are"—he spread his hands to show me the trove of documents I'd stolen—"trying to completely own something you don't really want."

The idea behind pushing the Hawkins' out was to expand an unencumbered business, but why? Mandy worked for just enough. She created what she wanted, made the money she needed, and enjoyed the remainder.

I was keeping the clubs because I couldn't let go of Veronica's memory.

The realization came so hard and fast I laughed at myself, and before my father could ask what was so funny, Logan threw open the office door, slamming it behind him so the walls shook.

"Oh, here you are," Logan said, approaching what was now his desk. "At *last*. You didn't get 'delayed' in Cambria again?"

"No." I mocked his finger quotes.

My father looked impassively between us. He had never had any interest in mediating our fights. His attitude was that our strength as a family came through conflict and its resolution, so Logan starting a fight was as unsurprising as his continuation of it.

"Mandy's been one of my best friends since high school, and you—"

"Logan." I held up a hand and watched with satisfaction as his mouth shut. "If you're going to worry about someone, it should be your wife, who clearly doesn't understand her limits."

"Don't you start on Ella." He said it as if I'd threatened the love of his life with bodily harm.

"The same goes for Amanda," I said even though she clearly, *clearly* wasn't the love of my life. We'd agreed on that, so it must have been true. "She's a grown woman. She doesn't need you to set boundaries for her."

"I was setting them for *you*."

The hair on my arms stood up. He could ask me not to see Mandy, and he could tell me not to hurt her. One was a request, and the other was unlikely. But when he set limits for me and put her outside of them, my cells reacted before my brain even heard him.

She was mine.

She's not yours in Los Angeles.

The lizard part of my brain couldn't fight the facts, so it made its own reality.

Mine.

"Gentlemen." My father rose. "Let's put these back the way we found them. Have them sent to the Bel Air house. I'll ship it to Thoze from there with an apology. We have nothing on the Hawkinses."

"Shocker," Logan said, sitting behind his desk.

"Sorry it didn't work out, Dante." My father put a comforting hand on my shoulder as he passed.

When he was gone, I pulled together the papers on the table.

"So," Logan said, tapping into his laptop as if he wasn't speaking at the same time, "you and Mandy in Cambria."

"Don't start. Dad's not here to pull me off you."

"You finally realize you like her."

"What makes you say that?"

The typing stopped for half a second, then resumed.

"Your jaw's clenching that way it does when you've got your lid screwed on too tight."

"My lid?"

"She's not your type anyway." *Tap-tappa-tap* at the keyboard, with a *smack* on the ENTER key. "She's cool. You're a dud."

In the barrel of all the things that could have rubbed me the wrong way, he'd reached down to the dregs and found the one that would bother me the most. Mandy wasn't a dud or a bore, and if I was, that meant Logan was right. I wasn't her type. Logan knew it. Ella knew it. Mandy knew it. The only person with their head up their ass was me.

"I'm not a dud."

"Sure, dud."

"First of all, ask her before you decide what I am. Second of all"—I plopped a pile of papers into an envelope—"we have plenty in common."

"Sure." *Tappa-tap.* He sounded nonplussed, and my lid was screwed on too tight to realize he was drawing me out.

"She knows how to waltz, for one." I closed up a second envelope. "We can both cook. We have the same sense of humor. She's willing to do things she never did before—"

"Stop." His hands flew up to block the rest. "Too much information."

I was thinking about the crawlspace, not the bedroom, but words were pouring out of me too fast to backtrack. "She's smart and resourceful." I slid the tapes into the last envelope and closed it. "Loyal to a fault."

"You were talking about what you have in common."

"She sings like metal bending, but she feels it. She means every word, happy or sad. The worst lyrics in music history come out of her mouth... and I believe every bad note because she does."

A silence followed. I'd stopped talking, and Logan had stopped typing. The envelope with the tapes swung from my fingers, and I was staring at an undefinable point between myself and the floor while the Mandy in my head danced and sang with everything she had.

She only made a few beautiful dresses a year and had her heart broken so often for the same reasons. She didn't know how to do anything halfway. Not make a dress or love a man. Not make a promise or offer her body.

"Are you..." Logan sounded as if he couldn't believe what he was about to say, so he started again. "Are you *in love* with Mandy?"

"That's ridiculous." I got the box from under the table and put the envelopes in it. "It was nothing. Two consenting adults."

"Holy shit. You love her."

"What would be the point of that?" I shouted.

"I have no idea." He turned back to his computer to *tap-tap* at his keys. "If you figure it out, let me know."

Picking up the box with one hand, I got out of there in three steps. I didn't know why I was annoyed, but I felt two inches to the left of my body all the way to parking lot.

What would be the point of loving her?

None. There was no point to it.

I'd kept the truck home in favor of the Bugatti because I wasn't hauling anything or rocking up muddy hills. The trunk sprang open when I hit the key fob. I slung the box in and tried to slam it closed, but the hydraulics stopped me.

With a deep breath of patience, I waited, letting go of this one thing that was out of my control.

* * *

Forgetting Mandy was easy. Generally, I didn't think about her at all.

She didn't show up in my thoughts until the moments when the morning light hit my closed eyelids and exploded into bursts of yellow. When I opened my eyes, I was reminded of her by the sunlight on the wall, and I stared at it so long I realized it was blue, not yellow. I was only eager to tell her this so she could explain what her obsession with yellow was about, which I didn't consider thinking about her as much as wondering about her and regretting that I hadn't wondered sooner.

When the contractors called with estimates, she came to mind, but only because she'd fallen through the ceiling and spoken truth to me though the roof they were fixing.

One of them complimented the ingenuity of the umbrella contraption, and I remembered her suggesting it, then us working together to design it and put it together until the sun came up.

I lived my life, did my business, ate, slept, spoke, walked, bathed without her on my mind—except when I was awake, and when I wasn't, I dreamed about her.

Our encounter was supposed to stay in Cambria, but she'd followed me to Los Angeles, where I never thought about her unless I was breathing.

Was the problem our city?

Or the breathing?

There was only one way to find out.

* * *

She wasn't hard to find.

I could have called or texted her, but I needed to see her smile, smell her shampoo, hear how her laugh vibrated through the air. I needed to see the shade of yellow she was wearing to know how she was doing and how she felt when she woke up in the morning.

Her office was in a West Hollywood building off La Cienega. I had no excuse to be there, but I came up with one. At eight thirty in the morning, I waited in my car in the parking lot of the nearest coffee shop.

Cars came in and out constantly. Mercedes and bent-up Chevys. A white dually had to park diagonally, taking up two spaces so it didn't stick out, and a woman yelled at the driver anyway. Birds were flipped, but no humans were hurt.

An open box of fries from the Carl's Jr. across the street sat at the curb. Next to it, a bun lay upside down, like a distressed turtle, with bent spikes of cigarette butts sticking from it.

At ten to ten, a man snapped open the padlock of the smoke

shop and pushed open the black accordion gates, chatting in Spanish with a mustached man carrying a tray of coffee cups. Irritated, he pointed at the inverted ashtray bun as if to say, "How are people such slobs?" which was what I was thinking.

At 10:07, a buttercup Jaguar pulled into the lot and took a spot behind me. In the rearview, I saw her park crooked and too close to the line, just another Angeleno not paying attention.

She got out. White jeans. Yellow top. Sunglasses. Tote. Curls flying. Wrestling with her jacket because she had her phone in one hand. I was about to get out when she caught a glimpse of something, dropped her shoulders, and got back in.

"Where are you going, *amea*?"

Her brake lights flashed, and she backed out, stopped, then pulled in again, but straight this time, with enough space between her car and the one next to her. Then she started over again but with her jacket on and her phone in her pocket, and I realized she'd be fine. She'd figure herself out. She might not get it right the first time, but she was a separate, evolving human being who was going to be okay.

Mandy Bettencourt didn't need me to fix her, and I didn't need her. I could live the rest of my life the way I was living now and be no the worse for it.

And not one bit better.

When she went inside the coffee shop, she brought the sunshine and the possibility of me becoming anything brighter, better, bigger.

So, I did what I'd come to West Hollywood to do and went in for a cup of coffee.

CHAPTER 30

MANDY

My iced latte took a minute, so I scrolled through my email, marking what I had to take care of from the office and yes-or-no-ing the rest, which was why I didn't see him, but his voice cut through the air, shot through my spine, and dropped between my legs.

"No milk, thank you."

It was Dante Crowne, paying the cashier at the crappy Fairfax Starbucks with an Amex Black. He didn't look in my direction, even when I moved. He took his cup and walked out without seeing me, which seemed wrong and irritating and even somehow insulting.

"Hey!" I called, catching up to him in the parking lot.

"Hi," he said with a smile, leaning in for a kiss on the cheek, which I accepted.

I took in the feel of his body so close, his lips on my skin, the raw, earthy smell of him. His face lingered near mine as if he was taking me in the same way, then he backed up, clearing his throat.

"You look good," he said.

"Thank you. So, what are you doing here?"

"On the ass end of WeHo?"

"We call it home but okay."

"There's a penthouse on Doheny I'm looking at for a new club. I was thinking about you." He changed the subject whiplash quick, before I could feel good or bad about his thoughts. "For my mother. She has a thing. An event. She has a room full of gowns but says she doesn't have anything to wear."

His smile could light up the city, but there was something off about it. The instinct to ask him about it was hard to quash, but I had to. His family was none of my business, and prying would be awkward under circumstances I'd describe as sexually tense and emotionally fraught.

"She can call me," I said, tapping the button on my key fob. "It was nice to see you."

"You too."

I walked to the car, turned, and found him still standing there with his paper cup.

"What?" I asked.

His reply was to come two steps in my direction—all he needed to tower over me.

"I remember how you feel." He whispered the seductive reminiscence as if it was as normal as it was arousing. "When you come, I have to hold you down to keep you on my cock."

I felt him inside me, stretching the muscles, demanding my body accommodate him, and the rewards of its submission. "Are you asking if I remember too?"

"I'm asking if you want it again."

The city pressed against me—its noise, its people, its eyes everywhere.

"We're not in Cambria."

He smirked and touched my collarbone, watching his fingertips as they traced a slow line along it. "I'll strip you naked anyway. Open your legs. Tease you until you cry and beg. Let you come, then make you come, then break you until you come again."

His finger stopped, and his eyes flicked up to mine, checking to see if I was flushed, panting, lips parted and eyelids fluttering—then he split-second smiled and lowered his hand, leaving my skin tingling for more.

"One night?" I asked. "Or two?"

"Make it three."

He thought he had me, and there was a time when he would have, but I was tired of limits and sick of fear. I was the way I was, and though I didn't have to give my heart away to the wrong man ever again, I didn't have to pretend my heart was hard either.

"And then?" I asked.

"What do you want?"

"I'm not built to use you," I said, moving my gaze away from his with a monumental effort.

"So don't."

"Are you offering something with no rules?" I put my hand on his chest, where his heart beat, sure he was ready to refuse me. "More than sex, Dante."

He pressed his lips into a line. Had I said too much? Asked for more than I was entitled to?

No. I hadn't. Not at all. But he was going to refuse me because they all did. Every man I'd ever wanted walked away when I asked to be loved just a little more.

"Yes, Mandy. Yes, I am offering you that and everything else. I won't try to protect you or—God help us—myself."

My hand slid down, but he grabbed it before it could fall to my side.

"You're saying yes?"

I couldn't believe it. I didn't think he was lying. He wasn't trying to get in my pants. He wasn't toying with me. He was giving me what I wanted, and when he kissed my palm, my heart stopped beating with the shock of it.

"You're mine," he said. Intensity radiated from him like the ring of light around a solar eclipse. He was blinding. Hotter and brighter than he seemed, with a dark circle blocking the best and most dangerous parts of him.

Even sure that I deserved to be loved without boundaries or limits, I didn't know what to do with being accepted.

Maybe Couture Mandy was as bullshit as Discount Mandy.

Maybe I needed to be a completely different person that couldn't be defined by price.

"I have to go." I backed up a few steps before I melted from the heat of his intention. "Give your mom my number."

"Can I use it?"

I had to pause for a moment. He was asking. *Asking.* Not demanding or assuming compliance, but requesting permission to call. I was already off guard, but that pushed me outside myself, as if I was living two lives at once.

"Sure," I said. "Any time."

* * *

I DIDN'T KNOW what to do with what Dante had given me. It was like wishing for a Maserati your whole life, then finding it sat lower than you thought it would and the engine was louder, and both those things were fine but unexpected, and a driver had to get used to being loved instead of shunned. So, I went about my life waiting to feel different, or shiny and new, or sporting more horsepower, but nothing like that happened.

I was still me—but with a few more choices.

"This is your color," my patternmaker, Pia, said, big, brown eyes bordered with lines, softened with years, and sharp with expertise and experience. She stepped back to look at me in the bank of mirrors.

The dress was perfect from every angle, the shape of my body sheathed in the sky blue of Dante's eyes. It had been a full day since I'd seen him last, and I couldn't stop thinking about the heat in the cold color.

"It is."

"Any changes?" she asked.

"It's perfect." I twisted to see the place where my waist and my back met. Yup. Perfect.

Pia gathered her pins and chalk into the gray plastic box she brought to fittings. "You'll wear it on Saturday?"

"I will."

"In blue?" She smiled as if that pleased her.

"In blue," I replied, not mentioning the inspiration for the color.

"Good."

She left, leaving me on the platform, surrounded by multiples of my reflection in a new color for the new woman I was.

My phone dinged from my bag. I fished it out and found Dante's name on the screen. My belly went liquid, and my spine tingled.

*—Have you used your
left hand yet?—*

I had, and the sight of his suggestion flooded my body with warmth again.

—Maybe—

My coy answer resulted in a wait for the next text, as if he wasn't prepared to be unsure.

*—The roof is fixed now.
Ready for the next rainy season—*

Rain was so infrequent in Los Angeles that we celebrated when it came, walking around without umbrellas, eating on open patios, and laughing at our lack of proper shoes and coats.

But I missed it for a different reason—the patter of raindrops on an umbrella would always remind me of him.

—I still have your clothes and boots—

—At the risk of saying something cliché... what are you wearing?—

I took a picture of myself in the mirror and sent it, remembering that the last time he fucked me, I was in his clothes. They were washed and folded, sitting on the chair next to my sink. I thought of him when I brushed my teeth, when I curled my hair, when I took a bath.

—What do you think?—

—The color is shocking—

—To me too. I keep looking at myself in it. I wonder if anyone will recognize me—

—They will. And they won't be able to stop looking at you—

I didn't expect him to show up for Ella's event. In all the years I'd known him, I'd only seen him out a handful of times. He wasn't a gala kind of guy. He was the kind of guy who wore a four-thousand-dollar suit five days a week and barely pulled his jeans down to fuck you against his truck the other two.

Three dots trailed at the bottom of my screen. I couldn't take my eyes off them because he was probably going to say something perfectly nice, and I would be disappointed. We'd agreed not to fuck, and this wasn't fucking, but it was a breach just the same—a breach I shouldn't have let him make.

And yet, I wanted to be broken, torn open, rendered down to heat and liquid.

*—Pick up your dress and
show me what color you
are underneath—*

The relief was so strong and came so fast I nearly sobbed, then I smiled.

I picked up the skirt, faced the mirror again, and showed him yellow underwear that was just starting to get damp.

Again, I stared at those three dots, heavy where my legs met, nipples hardening under sky-blue silk.

—That's not what I meant—

My cheeks and chest flushed pink. Had I assumed too much? Had I humiliated myself?

I started to type an apology, deleted it, started over with something sexier, and tapped the backspace key as another came in from him.

—I meant...—

More waiting. What would inspire him to hit SEND after "meant," for fuck's sake?

Control.

Keeping me waiting gave him control over me, and my willingness to accept it gave him even more. Those two things together soaked the panties I'd just shown him.

—Spread your legs—

My knees almost stopped working completely.

Another text came right after.

*—It stopped raining, and your
cunt is still mine. Show it to me,* **amea.**

Let me see what a whore you are for me—

I had a choice to say no, but I didn't. Every nerve ending in my body vibrated to do what he demanded.

Sitting on the platform, I hiked up the skirt, spread my knees, and moved the crotch of my panties aside to reveal the aching, glistening mess between my legs.

I didn't pause before I took the picture, but I hesitated for a split second before I hit SEND.

If the pictures got out, I'd be humiliated again. If Dante was even slightly careless, it would be all over the internet.

But he wasn't careless. He was careful. And I trusted him at the same time as I didn't care.

SEND

—My beautiful little slut—

The arousal hit so hard I gasped.

This was on.

I was all in.

*—I'm a dirty whore.
I need a good spanking—*

My bottom had healed since he'd punished me, but it tingled with the memory.

—Spanking's too good for you—

—Show me how you touch yourself—

All in was all in. I took a picture of myself with my left hand under my panties. In the dull, unromantic lighting, sitting on a platform covered in gray industrial carpet with silk charmeuse gathered around my waist so I could expose my pussy, I looked degraded and vulnerable—a whore being skillfully used by the one man she'd intended to use.

Perfect. I sent it.

*—Sluts as filthy as you
get special punishment—*

    I ran my fingers along my clit.

—Tell me how you're going to do it—

—You won't like it—

—Will it hurt?—

—Yes. But you'll come when I allow it—

—Now?—

—No—

—Tell me, please—

He told me in a series of texts that came one after the other, except when he made me wait, as if he could time my orgasm from wherever he was.

*—You'll be naked in front of me,
On your back. You'll draw your
knees up and spread them.
You'll lay your hands on your ass
and spread yourself apart for me.
I'll push your knees back farther
until I can see your tight little asshole.
My cock will already be wet with your
spit, but I'll be kind, and I'll put my
fingers inside your cunt to wet you more.
My filthy little whore loves it, but when*

I put the head of my cock against your virgin asshole, your eyes go wide, and I push in. I destroy you. Stretch you so wide you think you're going to die. I thumb your clit. You don't know whether to cry or come. I won't let you do either until you say what I want to hear—

The pause was too long. I ran every possibility through my mind, then decided to come no matter what he said, but I couldn't. My pussy was wet and swollen to bursting, but it wouldn't release without his permission.

Then I knew what he wanted to hear.

—I am yours—

—Good girl—

His words filled me from the inside, ripping me open as if I'd been overstuffed with choices and will. Consciousness spilled out onto my fingers with his simple command to accept that my orgasm belonged to him.

—Amanda—

His next text came in when I was still panting, on my back with my dress around my waist.

Shit.

I'd been so good, then I'd given in so I could sext.

What was wrong with me?

—Thank you for that—

—My pleasure—

—Come to my place tonight. Show me what it looked like when I gave you permission—

Before I left for Cambria, I'd said I wanted to use a man the way I'd been used, but I hadn't. Dante and I made an agreement and fulfilled it to both our benefit. The implications in Los Angeles were wilder, less restrained, and though I didn't want boundaries around our potential, I needed to protect myself and fast.

—I have to go—

He hadn't used me in Cambria.
But with the casual avoidance of the content of his last text, I'd used him.

CHAPTER 31

DANTE

Since arriving back in Los Angeles, I'd felt out of sorts and hadn't realized it.

Taking control of five minutes of Mandy's time had snapped me back to life. I'd gone to Cambria intent on finding dirt on the Hawkinses, gotten distracted by her, and with a few texts, been brought back to life by her.

I still wanted Caleb Hawkins out of my affairs, but now I had even more incentive. I wanted to go to Mandy again, fully open to anything she wanted from me, but I had to be free of anything that could hurt her, including an enemy.

He didn't stall or play games but agreed to meet me at the InterContinental bar that night. The executive lounge was a fine and quiet place to meet, but he insisted on the bar with its throbbing music, boys with backward caps, and women in shirts with no backs. He was against the far wall in a bank of leather couches, slouching with a beautiful woman who seemed delighted to be in his company.

I stood in front of him. He looked up at me, a fall of blond hair crossing his left eye.

"Dante fucking Crowne," he said as if I was an old friend

before turning to the woman and saying something I couldn't hear over the music.

When she left, Caleb's eyes followed her, and he bit his bottom lip over the shape of her ass.

His eyes were half-lidded. Drunk? Stoned? Or was it an act?

"Have I told you you're disgusting?" I said.

"What?"

I needed to be heard, so I sat next to him.

"You want something?" he asked. "They'll spike it with whatever I say."

"I'm not here for the company."

"Poor Crownies. Can't afford to have the sticks removed from your asses."

"I'm not here for medical advice either."

"So." He lazily swung his arm. "Why are you here?" He turned to look me in the eye, and his suddenly weren't at half-mast. "Motherfucker."

"We have a box."

"Congratulations." He looked away and flicked his fingers at a waitress who was bending over us in a heartbeat. "I'll have another one of these." He swirled the ice around his glass. "And bring my friend here a Crowbar." Just when I thought he was done, he called her back. "That girl over there? With the ass? Get her whatever she wants." He leaned back.

"Are you done?" I asked. "Stalling won't change anything."

"I'm done. Tell me about your box, Dante. I'm all a-fucking-quiver."

"It was Dave Fallon's. From Thoze."

"May he rest his case in peace."

"It's got documentation of blackmail."

He turned toward me as if I'd piqued his interest but not his fear.

"Oh, well, that's just the kind of thing we'd leave around, so tell me more."

I'd worked out the story carefully, cutting it from a whole cloth and checking it for runs and holes. "The tapes are from 2005—"

"Tapes?"

"Phone calls. Your lawyer, Dave Fallon, and the FCC chair."

"*Privileged* phone calls?" He pushed himself up from a deep slouch to a crouch and put his drink on the table. "From when I was eighteen? And you were? How old? Oh… right. Fucking my mother."

"Your ass isn't on the line, but it's going to affect your father and your bottom line."

"Sure." He laughed derisively.

Our drinks came, and he stalled, buying one for another woman across the room. When he was done, he handed me mine and clicked it quickly before drinking.

"So," he said, centering the glass on his coaster. "You want to make a gentleman's deal. You and me. You give me this box or whatever, and I give you… what? It's a little late for my stepmother, bro. She had three kids already."

"You let me buy you out."

"Buy me out? Of the clubs?" He laughed. "Right."

"Market price and I destroy the box."

"Yeah. Sure." He drank, and I wasn't fooled into thinking he was agreeing to the deal. "You know why I agreed to meet you? Because I thought you'd come with something relevant to discuss, but you came with this shit. FYI – Thoze & Jensen? Those assholes? They weren't handling our licensing until 2007. So, okay, you're misguided, but if you have tapes that touch you in places that make you feel sad?" He shrugged. "I could take a look at them."

"Market price," I said.

"Out of respect for my mother's memory, I'll buy the clubs at twenty percent under market."

"Discuss with your father first. You sell, or I go to the DOJ."

"You're sexy when you put your foot down," he said with a wink. "And when another guy makes a move on your gal? Big-time sexy."

"Excuse me?"

"You really showed that magazine rack who was boss, tough guy."

I could have snapped back at his gibberish or walked away, but something told me not to. There was a thread of sense to it, and with every word, it untangled itself.

"What the hell were both of you doing out in the boonies anyway? I mean, Harmony? That's near Cambria. It's like a poor man's Morro Bay."

Cambria. Magazine rack. Another guy.

I thought I'd walked away from the Harmony convenience store a hundred dollars poorer but clean of scandal. There was video, but virality wasn't a guarantee, and not everyone knew how to get it into the media's hands.

Someone had though.

"I kinda destroyed Mandy Bettencourt's honor on the tail end of tenth grade, but you, my man? Defending it was quite the play. Kudos to you."

Kudos to me for putting her back in the public eye.

Of the two of us, I looked worse, but I didn't care. She'd be called names, be retied to Renaldo, and publicly shamed all because I'd lost my temper in public. That couldn't happen.

"What do you want?" I asked.

"Mandy's a downtrending commodity right now, but unless some celeb knocks up a maid, we'll have space for her again in about… say, eight days? Could be six. Never can tell. Video's always hot though. So, we're looking at four days for you to hand over those tapes and sell us the clubs for thirty under market."

He was railroading me, and I was letting it happen. I had to think fast before he turned the deadline into twenty-four hours… yet I couldn't just accept the entire offer.

"You can have the tapes but not the clubs."

"Dude," he said with exasperation. "Look, they belonged to—My. Dead. Mother. You're like this starfish sticking to them with the little underbelly suckers. You're lucky I'm offering anything for them, okay? Killing sweet video of your convenience store tantrum's just a token of my esteem."

I stood. This was going nowhere, and the offer wasn't getting any better.

"Kill the video, and I'll give you the tapes. That's the trade. We can talk about the other business later."

"That's not how this works, bro."

"It is now. Bro."

He waved a thought away, glancing around the room as if he was bored now. "Say hi to Mandy for me."

His last request was the most casual and least threatening of anything that had come out of his mouth since I arrived.

Caleb Hawkins was a little shit. I wanted to beat the life out of him, but Mandy didn't need Hawkins Media releasing a video captioned with her name.

CHAPTER 32

MANDY

It was Saturday morning, and I had a business to run. Maybe not much of a business, but it was mine and I liked it.

On the way to West Hollywood, I replayed Dante's insults from my first night in Cambria, when he implied I was a dilettante. He'd called my work a vanity project.

Well, fuck him and his private clubs. At least I showed up. He—

The phone rang as I made a mental point that would shut his dismissive words out of my head for good. I tapped the cracked screen to answer, and a voice from the past came over the Bluetooth speakers.

"Hello? Is this Ms. Bettencourt?"

"Caleb?" I narrowly avoided an accident.

"Hey," he said smoothly. "You remember me."

"Of course I do. How are you?"

"My stepmother said it was mission critical that I call you," he said with a laugh.

How many times had I cried to hear his voice sound so warm and relaxed? How many nights had I stared at the phone, trying to will a text or a call into existence? It was so long ago and still one of the clearest emotional memories I had.

"My mother casually threaded a needle about seeing you, but I didn't think you would," I replied, still getting over the shock.

"Call? Or want to see you?"

"Yes."

"How about it though?" he chuckled, and I remembered the charm of the sound, how it was so easy and relaxed, not too loud yet completely committed.

"How about what, Caleb?"

"How about we catch up? Maybe lunch?"

Lunch.

I could have parsed his intentions by the meal he chose and been utterly wrong or completely right, but the fact was lunch wasn't good for me and wouldn't be until the weekend. This was my last day off before I had to get back to my business.

"I have a lot to catch up on today." I turned into the parking lot under the building. "I can make a lunch tomorrow."

"How about Sunday brunch then?" he replied.

"How about that new place in the Grove?"

"How about one thirty?"

"How about…" I looked for another detail and found none. "You get the last word." The signal got fuzzy. "You win."

"I'm putting you in my contacts. You still Mandi with an I?"

"It's a Y now."

"Great. See you there."

I tapped off, remembering what I'd liked about Caleb.

He was charming, and he knew how to have fun. He was rich without being a snob and worked hard for his father's company without being overly serious about it. He was educated, smart, and handsome as hell. He looked great on paper.

He was made to love someone, but no matter how many adolescent tears I'd shed, that someone had never been me.

And though I wasn't going to cry about it the way I'd cried

over Caleb, I wished it had been Dante calling. I glanced at my phone, saw he hadn't, and pocketed it, determined to be the best dilettante I could be.

* * *

WearHaus was going to attract paparazzi, and even though the sizzle of my Renaldo drama was over, it was still fresh in my mind.

My mother told me not to worry about it as if she had it all taken care of.

I didn't know what she meant until we were on the red carpet. At WearHaus, she wore a white Chanel jacket and pencil skirt from the 1980s that she'd had altered to fit like their current spring line. She looked terrific, but that wasn't why she'd chosen it. The white blew out camera flashes set for darker colors, making pictures of her—and thus the two of us—useless without a touchup. The paps and tabloids would have better, easier pictures of real celebrities that would sell faster. She clutched my arm and stood in front of me when my name was called, smiling and waving as if one Bettencourt was as good as any other. Once we were inside, she let go to check the shine on her nose in a compact. She touched up, snapped it shut, and had it back in her bag in three seconds flat.

"Thanks, Mom," I said. "For running the gauntlet for me back there."

"Easier than I expected," she replied, taking my arm and pulling me forward. "I thought I was going to have to shove a Nikon up someone's ass."

Ella's team had turned the warehouse into a wonderland that felt both luxe and edgy. High heels clicked on concrete, and satin hems snagged on raw beams, but the walls were covered in a riot of vines and blooms, so the atmosphere was verdant, with huge chandeliers that brought old-world Victorian to a modern space.

Under a feathery cascade of flowers, jasmine and bougainvillea brushed my bare arms as we worked our way through the crowd. The best parts of Los Angeles, its riches and its roughness, had been gathered under this one roof for a single, glittering night.

"Mandy!" A woman's arm shot up. Millie. Logan's high school flame. A pink velvet ribbon around the base of the bun at the top of her head matched the bodice of her dress, which plunged at the neck. The color brought out the bronze of her skin, and her smile lit up the room.

Next to her, Aileen was a contrast in a navy suit dress. She tinkled her fingers at me. Her shyness had turned into reserve in manner and dress.

"Girls!" my mother said, hugging them before I did.

"My producer's been up my *ass* all week." Millie plucked a second glass of champagne from the waiter while the rest of us cleaned out the tray. "I haven't had a minute to breathe. I practically had to blow him to leave tonight."

"Cheers to that." Aileen lifted her glass, and the three of us clinked our rims together.

I had worried that once I was back in my element in LA, I would feel uncomfortable, out of place, or anxious, but I was strangely serene. The three of us had been attending events like this one together since we were teenagers. It was the easiest thing in the world to wear the hell out of my dress, to flag down waiters when I needed a refill, to gossip about work and men and money with my friends.

"I'd suggest we do a vacation," Millie said, "but *someone* already took one by herself."

"Where did you go?" Aileen asked. "I called to check in after the Renaldo thing hit, and you were *gone*."

"She was ready to send in the brigades," Millie added. "Ella talked her down, thank God."

"Did you miss me?"

"Were you at the house in Tahoe?" Aileen said. "Remember junior year? At the lake?"

We toasted to the lake.

"Everyone missed you," my mother said.

"God, he's really something, isn't he?" Millie murmured with an elbow nudge.

She could have been talking about anyone—these events were always packed to the brim with handsome men, celebrities from A-list to Z-list, with perfect pecs and thick hair, finance guys with melting smiles, young heirs freshly tanned from a trip to St. Barts.

And Dante Crowne, who wasn't supposed to be there.

He was in a three-way conversation with Logan and an older man I didn't recognize.

Our eyes didn't meet as much as his attention sought out mine.

He was as tall and broad-shouldered as ever, the height and solidity of his frame especially evident in a room where half the guys were actors—who were always shorter and less imposing in real life than they looked on TV. More than that though, I wasn't ready for the sight of Dante in one is his suits, crisply put together, the simplicity of the stark black and white tux making a lie of his inner complexity.

In Cambria, his clothes had been casual, rough, more often than not a little dirty from chores, and I had forgotten about how powerful he truly was. The way the silk double Windsor knot fit exactly right at his throat, he looked like a gift that needed unwrapping, a bomb that needed defusing, a man who could fuck me raw and senseless without removing his cufflinks.

"Oh," my mother sighed. "The Crownes."

The brothers reminded my mother of Samantha, and they should have done the same for me. Byron Crowne had found his fiancée, my sister, dead in the swimming pool, and I'd spent my time in Cambria juggling thinking of her while avoiding the connection.

"He's the kind of guy who marries a thirty-year-old when he's in his seventies and makes her pop out three babies before he drops." Millie twirled her glass by its stem, eyeing the last drops of golden liquid at the bottom.

"No," I said absently as Dante excused himself and made his way toward us. I couldn't have articulated what I was objecting to exactly. Luckily, no one asked.

"Well," Mom said from outside the tunnel between Dante and me, "those Crowne boys… you have to be careful. They'll eat a woman up and spit her out."

Was he really coming this way?

"Dante's more off," Aileen said. "Cold as ice. Guarded like Fort Knox, you know?"

Passionately guarded.

"He has his reasons," I heard myself say.

"Oh?"

Dante was halfway across the room. I wouldn't have time to answer fully before he arrived. He was nodding and shaking hands, avoiding conversations, only breaking our eye contact for moments at a time before resuming his path back to me.

We were going to fuck again.

His dirty texts had made it clear this wasn't over, but what I didn't expect was the level of intensity in his stride.

I was in danger. He was going to break my heart, and I was going to beg for him to shatter it.

"What reasons?" my mother asked skeptically.

I didn't have to answer. He would be here before I made the case, but then he looked away and another suit blocked my view. For the first time since he started across the room, he took his attention away for more than a second.

"All the money in the world," Mom continued. "Perfectly decent parents. And what do you get but five grown men with *issues?*"

"Everyone has issues," I said into my champagne, glancing at Millie and Aileen to see if defending him had set off any alarms.

But they weren't listening to me because their attention was fixed to my right—on someone about to descend on our group, and it wasn't Dante.

It was Renaldo.

He was still handsome. Denying he had a good face was pointless. But the thing was, I realized, he knew exactly what I saw when I looked at him, and that was in part because there wasn't much else to see. Next to Dante, Renaldo was smaller and thinner, less substantial, and that wasn't physical—it had to do with who he was on the inside. He was a gilt-edged mirror: beautiful and flat and empty until someone showed up to fill in the frame.

He greeted me last, after my mother made a mouth-twist of distaste over his shoulder during their hug, giving me time to unpack the reality of what he was and who he wasn't.

"Mandy." He kissed me carefully on each cheek.

We had so much practice greeting each other politely at events, appearing friendly but never intimate, that it almost felt normal. Except this time, it was.

Millie and Aileen had moved aside to give him access to me, watching me over his shoulder with exaggerated faces, Aileen mouthing, *Yikes!* as Millie gestured to ask if I wanted them to get him the fuck out of there.

I shook my head slightly and refocused on Renaldo. "Renny."

He was chewing gum. God, I hated the constant fucking gum-chewing.

"How are you?"

I hadn't heard his voice since before Cambria. He was giving me the full package—slick sincerity with his boyish charms turned to eleven. How had I missed that fact? That Renaldo was a boy and had never been close to being a man?

"Fine," I said.

"You look amazing." He stepped back to admire me from head to toe, and I didn't turn to the side, didn't cross my arms. I let him think he was undressing me because he wasn't doing any such thing. "This color, it suits you."

"Thank you."

"Please," he said more to my companions than me. "I need to borrow her attention."

Millie and Aileen were struck silent. Mom smiled over a sneer, reading my expression.

"One minute," I said, checking for Dante, but he was gone.

Good. I could handle this better without him.

Renaldo brought me to the bar. We ordered drinks, and once we were alone in the crowd, he pulled the same levers, turned the same dials, made the same moves he always made.

This time though, he was talking to a different woman.

"When I said you looked good," he said as he put his thumb on my hand to stroke it, "I meant you look like regret."

I used the hand he was touching to pick up my glass. "*Your* regret, you mean."

"Of course mine. It was so ugly. I never meant for it to be like that, Mandy. You have to believe me."

"Do I?"

"I made mistakes. Big ones."

"Okay. Well, you can improve for next time."

Our drinks came. More champagne for me.

"Tatiana's coming out next week," he said.

I almost choked on the fizz. "Out?" I whispered. "You mean *out* out?"

"Yes."

"Good for her. That's amazing."

He nodded, staring into his glass. "She doesn't give a shit how that makes me look."

"How does that make *you* look?"

He didn't answer. He just drank until an ice cube hit his upper lip, then he wiped it with a square napkin. The quick jerk of his jaw told me he'd tucked his gum between his cheek and teeth while he finished his whiskey sour. "I missed you. And I'm a free man now. More free than I've ever been."

"What about Gretchen?"

"Whatever." He shrugged. "I don't care about her." He took my hand between his. "I care about you."

Discount Mandy would have tried to determine what the touch meant, whether he was about to stroke his finger against my palm and start the whole thing over again. She would have decided to do that over the alternative—kick him in the shins and make a big scene.

Couture Mandy didn't consider either option.

Couture Mandy was tired of this nonsense.

"I care," Renaldo continued, "about what we had and what we lost."

I took my hand back. "Renny, sweetheart, I know you care, but I don't."

"No, no—"

"Your games annoy me. This? What you're doing now? I'm sorry." It wasn't an apology but the soothing of a self-possessed woman to a man she was too busy to bother castrating. "It's just not that interesting anymore."

I wasn't trying to hurt him. I hadn't sharpened the barbs to a point, and I hadn't aimed them at any of his specific soft spots. But I also didn't care if I hurt him. I didn't care if I didn't. I didn't care about a single thing he had to say… but he kept on talking anyway.

"This is the hurt talking." Shockingly, he was so bad at taking my cues he touched my hand again. "I can make it up to you."

"You. Bore. Me."

Then Dante was looming over us, his presence undeniable, his voice impeccably neutral and somehow all the more menacing for it.

"Renaldo DeWitt," he said. "I always knew you were a fool, but why do you insist on acting like a clown in front of everyone?"

He looked down at where Renaldo's hand touched mine, and the scorch of Dante's glare had Renaldo pulling his hand back as if he'd been physically burned. Dante hadn't even had to touch him.

Renaldo was a worm, and I'd spent too many days of my life thinking he wasn't.

And that was the last time I was capable of thinking about anything other than Dante. That same gaze he'd used to humble Renaldo swept over me. It didn't make me shrink. It made me feel powerful enough to get on my knees again, to feel his hands in my hair, his tongue in my mouth, his cock thick between my legs. He knew exactly how to put people in their place, and I had the agency to beg for him to open me up the way he had in Cambria, let me fall apart in his arms all over again.

That sense of controlled surrender. That exquisite, aching release.

"Nice to see you too," Renaldo said. "Is there something you want with this lady?"

I had to cover my mouth to keep in a burst of laughter.

Dante lowered his face a few inches to meet Renaldo's gaze at the same level. "Shoo."

Renaldo looked from Dante to me and back as if he didn't know what to do.

"Have a great night," I said, patting Renaldo's shoulder. "Thanks for the drink."

My ex straightened his jacket and walked away with the self-conscious steps of someone trying not to limp off the battlefield.

"You attract the worst men," Dante said.

"I do." I met his gaze helplessly, knowing he would see it on my face—that despite my firm promises in the parking lot, I wanted him again, wanted him now. I'd do whatever he commanded me to do.

Hadn't I just thought of myself as self-possessed?

My self-possession ended where Dante's ownership began.

"Come with me," Dante quietly demanded, and I was helpless to do anything but obey.

We walked through the crowds, and I imagined the punishment for indulging Renaldo—and the fight I could put up because I hadn't wanted to speak to him at all. Dante and I had agreed we weren't going to fuck anymore, so I had zero guilt, but what if the punishment was a spanking? Just to remind me what it felt like when the hurt was worth something?

Dante pulled me through a black door and shut it firmly behind us. We were inside a dark room covered in shards of mirror and glass, so what light there was reflected giddily and dizzily in every direction, shattering our faces and bodies against the walls.

"I'm sorry," I said between kisses. "Dante. Listen."

He let me speak by kissing my throat.

"I cut you off. After the texting, I shut down, and I'm sorry I treated you like that."

"You can't get rid of me that easily," he said.

An deep, intense hum emanated from him, drawing me closer, the before version of myself rushing into the blown-apart version reflected with his.

"You sure?" I laid my hand on his lapel.

"Are you?" He grabbed my hand, gripping hard but not pushing it away. "This is your last chance to break the deal."

"Break the deal. Break me. Break everything."

And then he was kissing me, tugging up the hem of my dress so that he could stroke his fingers against my slit over my underwear, the other hand hot and possessive at my waist.

"You're a provocation," he growled. "Do you know that?"

"I know what the word means," I returned because if I got a spanking for my punctuation, who knew what kind of painful pleasure he'd deliver with a vocabulary lesson.

"Do you though?" He dipped his mouth to nip at my collarbones, then lower, kissing each nipple through the fabric of my dress. "Your body changed the shape of my universe, and your words... your way of being."

He backed away enough to stare at the length of me, leaving his thumbs to brush against the tight bumps on my chest. I wasn't wearing a bra, and I'd have to walk out of here and let everyone see me ravaged and wrecked, my nipples hard, my cunt wet, my mouth swollen with the plunder of his kisses.

"You're gravity," he said. "No matter how high I jump, I come back."

"Does this mean you'll do it my way? You'll stop putting limits on us?"

"Yes."

He kissed me again, hands in my hair, pushing me against the wall as if we could disappear into it. I moaned my surrender against his mouth and clung to him, feeling him hard and ready against me. Had we sexted just a few days ago? It felt like a lifetime. Right now, I would have let him take me in the middle of the warehouse with everyone watching.

Anything to give myself to him.

I tugged at the fly of his pants. On the other side of the wall, the music stopped. This room—whatever it was—wouldn't be viable for privacy for long.

"Come home with me," he said.

Which meant I'd have to wait and get through all the times I'd try to talk myself out of this.

But it also meant I'd get more than a quickie in a room that was going to open at some point during the event.

"Yes, sir." My heart thundered in my chest. I nodded, then remembered where I was and who I had responsibilities to. "Ella. I can't just bail on her."

"She won't even notice you're gone."

"And my mother."

There was a long moment of suspended time while neither of

us moved. Then Dante stepped back and adjusted himself in his pants. He looked me over, eating me up with his eyes.

"I don't want anyone else to see you when you're like this," he said. "You're a whore, but you're my whore."

He slipped off his suit jacket and hung it around my shoulders. There was nothing to be done about my lipstick or my hair, but this way, it would be harder to tell that I'd been seconds away from sucking someone's dick in the middle of what was surely an extraordinarily expensive art installation. It was better that we weren't going to fuck in here, I reflected. Another five minutes and my back would have been against the shattered-glass wall, and neither my dress nor my skin would have survived the experience.

He guided me out of the room, back into the event. We skirted the edge of the crowd, his jacket over my shoulders, his hand tight on the back of my neck—a reminder of who owned me for the night.

We watched the fashion show from the back of the room. The walls of broken glass that Dante had pushed me against pivoted, opening to the runway, where the models walked with shattered versions of themselves as a backdrop.

It was a great show. Truly great, even with Dante's fingertips under his jacket, stroking the curve of my ass. And I was one hundred percent sure it was inspiring—but it couldn't be as inspiring as his touch.

The show had broken into speeches.

I tried to listen to the speaker and failed when he murmured from behind me, "I'm getting inside your ass tonight."

I swallowed.

"All the times I've mentioned it, you never said if you liked it." He grabbed my ass and squeezed. "I won't know how gentle to be."

"Be gentle," I whispered unevenly.

"How gentle?"

"Very. I haven't before."

"That's right. My filthy little slut is only mine."

The room burst into applause, and I joined in, but Dante didn't take his hand off my ass.

"Now," he said, and this time, I didn't disobey.

CHAPTER 33

MANDY

My group text with Aileen, Millie, and Ella had to be muted before the notifications asking who I was leaving with and why ran down the battery. My mother took the news well, apparently assuming I was taking off with Caleb Hawkins. My direct text to Ella didn't get an answer.

In the passenger seat of Dante Crowne's truck, I pressed my legs together to relieve the pressure that grew between them. I'd assumed he'd be handsy on the ride over, but he didn't touch me—hands at ten and two on the wheel, eyes on the road. He betrayed his impatience only by driving slightly over the speed limit, and I marveled at his control even as I longed for it to break.

His condo was one of the ones strung along Wilshire, a building with a green glass roof that lit up emerald against the night sky. The elevator was private, one long ride up to the penthouse, and he waited it out casually, hands in his pockets. The elegance of him in that suit was overwhelming. When I was done with him, I wanted to examine its stitches to see if whoever had made it was some kind of genius craftsman or if it only elevated him to such a godlike level.

"Someday," he said thoughtfully, "I'll have you strip while you ride up to see me so that when I open my door, you'll already be naked. Ready and waiting for my cock. You'd like that, wouldn't you?"

"I would."

"Good."

At last, the elevator dinged that we'd reached our floor, and when the doors slid open, the lights went on in a palatial foyer. Dante let me out onto the marble floor.

After the Cambria house, I hadn't known what to expect, but this place was less severe and much more modern. There was probably cell service and Wi-Fi, along with enough water for a bath and a connection to electricity that worked in the rain. But besides the obvious, the west-facing windows spanned from floor to ceiling, lording over the city and its threads of red lights as they moved to and from the dark horizon of the night ocean.

"Would you like a drink?" he asked, sliding his jacket off my shoulders.

My mouth had suddenly gone dry. "Water."

"Stay here." He went to the open kitchen and retrieved a plastic bottle from the fridge, but when I reached for it, he pulled it away. "Hands at your sides, *amea*."

"You're going to draw this out all night, aren't you?" I protested while keeping my hands at my sides.

"I don't have to." He touched the cold edge of the bottle to a nipple, waking it up again, then moved to the other. "This isn't our last time. We didn't make any promises I can't keep." He glanced up from his work on my breasts, meeting my gaze to check my reaction.

"And what if you wake up and want the promises back?"

"That I won't see you again?" He said it as if he was the one making the decision.

"That this is the last time," I said. "What happens when you change your mind?"

"It's going to hurt." He cracked open the bottle. "Me and you both."

He looked down at the bottle, tapping the rim in thought, then he touched it under my chin and gently pushed upward until I was facing the ceiling.

"Open your mouth," he said. "And I'll tell you why."

When I did what he commanded, he tipped the bottle to my lips and poured water over my tongue one drop at a time.

"You're reckless with your feelings. You say too much and think too little. You're unprepared, unrehearsed, and oversensitive."

When I tried to tell him to fuck off, he increased the water flow. I closed my lips around the bottle to swallow, sending the water streaming over my neck and chest. My dress was quickly soaked and stuck to my skin.

"You're fearless," he continued. "And I've lived in fear. You're everything I've been too afraid to become, and without you, I'll never be more than I am."

"Mnn."

He took the bottle away, put it down, and walked behind me. My dress had a dark-blue triangle spreading from my chest to the divot of my navel.

"You going to ask me what I want any time soon?" I asked.

He lowered my back zipper.

"Tell me what your heart wants." He pushed the straps over my shoulders and down my arms, exposing my damp skin to the air as he kissed the lines of my throat. "And your body will show me what it needs."

He took my hand and helped me step out of my clothes. He was still fully dressed, right down to the studs and cufflinks

"Let's do the body first," I said.

He smirked, taking a nipple between his fingers and yanking it hard enough to thicken a hot thread of pleasure that ran directly to between my legs.

"You are truly reckless with your trust." He said it as if it was a compliment. I shrugged it off. "Follow me. I owe you a bath."

I followed him up the granite steps to the master suite. The bedroom had a western wall of floor-to-ceiling windows, which made me feel shockingly exposed until I remembered that we were the highest thing in this part of the city. I could see Los Angeles, all of it spread out under us, but it couldn't see me.

The bathroom was stark white and gray, with a wall of mirrors obscuring the door to the toilet. The freestanding tub was long and bordered with a platform against one wall. Dante leaned against the counter, a predator alone with this prey at last.

"Wash your face," he instructed.

"I—"

"Wash your face."

The second time he made the request, I understood it. He was a man who took care of things that mattered to him.

I bent over his sink and soaped off my makeup, wiped away the rest of my lipstick, and with a lotion he presented, removed my eyeliner and mascara. When I was done, he came behind me and slipped the pins from my hair so that it fell, loose, around my shoulders. I regarded myself in the mirror: cheeks flushed, nipples hard as diamonds, my carefully thought out but hastily made dress in a pile downstairs.

In the mirror, he was still buttoned up, a man who held the world in his closed fist. I was still in my heels, nothing but upward breasts, wide eyes, and a wet cunt, my ribs heaving with the effort of every breath.

"Look at yourself," he said into my throat. "Look at what I do to you. Think about how much you want this. How you're willing to do anything for it." He touched under my chin and pointed it a little upward. "You should be proud to be my whore." He paused, then added two words. "My Mandy."

Dante had turned his resistance to my name into pure sex.

"Thank you," I said.

He smiled in the mirror and backed away, leading me to a leather bench opposite the mirror wall. I sat on the edge, and he stood over me with his arms crossed as if waiting for something.

Using the high heels for leverage, I opened my legs. He nodded and drew a bath, getting out of the way of the mirror.

You want this.

My want was all over my body and in the shadow where my legs met. I wanted it, and I was going to have it. The roar of the water reduced to a few spitting drops. Dante set the heater, then stood over me with his erection visible in the shape of his pants. I couldn't help myself—I reached up for it, and he grabbed my wrists.

"What are you looking for?" he asked.

"Your cock."

"Why?"

"Why do you think?"

"Say it."

"To suck it."

"You were a good girl tonight," he said as he unzipped his tuxedo pants and fished out his dick.

He didn't look half as undone as I felt. The shirt and tie were still on, but his dick jutted out from his pants, fat and red with a drop at the tip, undeniable proof of the animal he'd tried to hide under cufflinks and starched cotton—the animal I had coaxed out of him and whose prowl and pounce were all for me.

One hand gripped the back of my hair while the other guided his cock into my mouth.

"You like it like this," he growled, grunting as he shoved his length down my throat. "You're not hungry to suck any man's dick. You want me to fuck your face." He let me breathe, then used me again. "I'm going to ruin you, and you're going to let me."

The pulse between my legs receded to a distant pounding. I gazed up at him, wide-eyed, letting all the adoration I was starting to feel for this impossible man wash over me as he ruthlessly pounded my mouth.

"Tomorrow." He gasped, yanking me off by the hair. "You're going to beg me to keep you."

"Yes."

"Say yes in the morning." He let go, stepped away, and undid his pants. "Get in."

He indicated the bath, which he'd added soap to while I was observing my reflection. I kicked off my shoes, and I obeyed. The heater worked, and I had to slowly lower myself into the steaming water.

He stripped efficiently, giving me no time to appreciate the sight of his broad shoulders, or the definition of his chest and abs, or the hard thighs holding up the rigid glory of his cock. Without taking a moment to adjust to the scalding water, he sat across from me. I crawled on top of him, kissing him with all the passionate intensity I'd been lavishing on his dick.

Which was now right underneath my cunt, even hotter than the water around us. I ground down onto his length, then reached down to pull him inside me, where he belonged.

"No," Dante growled, and I stopped in my tracks. "Not tonight. Sit back."

I settled back and lifted my feet, putting each on the edge of the sides of the tub. He slid two fingers along my seam. My back arched when he got them inside me and thumbed my clit.

"You're wet." With his other hand, he reached to the ledge behind me.

"I am."

His hand came back with lotion on it, and he rubbed his thumb along the length of his fingers to spread it.

"I've had your mouth, and I've had your pussy," Dante said, hand back underwater to find my crack and part my cheeks to press briefly between them. "I promised I'd take your ass tonight."

He had.

He absolutely fucking had.

"And you're going to let me." His fingers rotated around my tight hole without entering, and he watched me with tense, hungry satisfaction as I adjusted to the pressure. "Aren't you, Mandy?"

My name in his mouth for the third time woke me out of the drug of pleasure long enough to answer. "Yes."

"Yes to what?"

"Fuck my ass." I whispered it so low even I could barely hear it. It wasn't half as loud as the shout I made when his slick fingers slid into my asshole, stretching me with a pleasure I didn't expect.

"There's your voice." With his other hand, he reached under the water and played with my clit. "Say it louder."

My body felt as if it was nothing but nerve endings—the ache of his fingers inside me, opening up the space he needed while his other hand stimulated my nub. "Fuck me in the ass."

"With what?"

He took my clit between two fingers and clamped it while fucking my ass with his other hand. The sensation was unbearable, and I wanted more.

"Should I let you come now?" he asked. "Or should I wait until you've taken my dick all night long, until you're sobbing for it?"

I shook my head. I knew what I wanted, which was more of everything, but I also knew what I needed, which was to let go of control completely.

"Use words."

"Whatever you want."

He removed his hands, and I almost cried *no*, but he stretched his body over mine and spoke softly into my cheek. "I want you to love it."

"I will. Just—" *Give it to me* was lost in a groan as the head of his cock pushed against my pussy.

"Are you comfortable?"

"Yes."

"Relax if you can." He got up on his knees and stroked lube on his cock.

I took a moment to wonder how he was going to get it inside me. "I'll try."

"You're so hot," he said, dropping back down. "So sexy. When I saw you tonight, in public, I knew you were mine." He put the head of his cock against my ass. "Now my dick is going to let you know it."

He pushed slowly, forcing the muscles to yield. My breath hitched.

"You okay, *amea*?"

"Yes."

He pushed farther, and I must have looked pained, because he stopped.

"Easy does it." He stroked my clit, and I groaned as the pleasure overcame the pain. "Your ass is clenching around me."

Flicking me under the water, he slowly drove deeper, and it hurt. It hurt the virgin muscle and my belly, but the pain nailed down the pleasure. To give up one was to give it all up.

"Mandy," he said. "It hurts…"

"Deeper." I grunted. "All the way."

The pain was subsiding, but he was still going easy. This wasn't how Dante's whore begged. I wanted it more than that.

"Fuck my ass," I demanded. "Fuck it hard. Please."

With a whispered yes, he leveraged one hand on my knee, pushing it toward my chest while flicking my clit. A second later, he shoved his entire cock deep in my ass. All I could do was take the brutal power of his thrusts, spread and split as he fucked his way deep inside me, then deeper, over and over again, fucking the pain out of me. I watched all of it happen: the ripple of the muscles on his torso as he moved and the flex of one arm holding the weight of his body while the other teased out my orgasm.

Finally, I heard myself saying, "Please, please, please, I need to come."

"You going to come for me, my filthy little whore?" His fingers tortured my clit faster.

"Don't stop," I begged, clutching his chest. "Please." I must have been sobbing, because my vision was clouded.

"Come while I fuck your ass."

He'd barely spat out permission, and I dissolved, with the ring of my asshole pulsing its hunger for him. I vaguely felt him coming, hot and wet and filthy, deep inside the most secret part of my body, and I thought I might never return from being taken apart and put back together, molecularly rearranged, as the aftershocks quaked through me and I screamed his name.

He slipped out carefully, but I keened as my body adjusted to the loss, and he pulled me into him.

"Was that all right?" he asked, kissing my cheek and jaw.

"My pussy feels left out."

He laughed. "I can't constantly have my dick inside you."

"Why not?"

"It's not practical." His hands moved softly over my body, offering sweet, soothing touches to the skin he'd abused.

"I don't care about practical," I said eventually. "I don't care about anything."

"You sure about that?"

I nodded against his shoulder, and he leaned back, pushing me away to look in my eyes.

"Then I'm revising the deal," he said, moving a lock of wet hair away from my eyes. He looked like a different man in that moment—real and approachable and warm, as if the cold, unavailable bastard had been worn down.

"*You're* revising it?"

"I am. Unilaterally."

"What if I don't agree?"

"You will."

"You're pretty sure of yourself." I'd do whatever he suggested. I knew that for sure, but there was no reason to make it easy for him.

"Do you want to hear it before you agree to it?"

My fingers were pruning, and I was getting thirsty, but I didn't want to leave the bath, so I turned around and curled into him, resting my head on the front of his shoulder at the waterline.

"Sure," I said, laying my hand on his chest. "Tell me."

"We'll do whatever we want for as long as we want. Fuck everybody. They'll handle it, or they won't. Not our problem."

I pressed my mouth tight so he wouldn't feel my uncontrollable smile, because he was right. I was going to risk getting hurt again and stupidly, recklessly, wholeheartedly agree to this change. "And Logan?"

"What about him?"

"He's not going to like it," I singsonged.

"He can fuck off," Dante sang back.

I laughed and settled into the bath, leaning against his solid form with his arms wrapped around me, protecting me from whatever might come.

Even a Sunday brunch with Caleb Hawkins.

CHAPTER 34

DANTE

My father hadn't sent the box back to Thoze. It was still at his house. I could pick it up and send it when I was satisfied Caleb had kept his end of the deal.

My parents lived in a modern palace in the Bel Air hills. There wasn't a house in Los Angeles harder to fill, but they'd managed it by using a corner of it and leaving the rest for parties and get-togethers.

I parked in the underground garage and came up the elevator to the second level, which looked over one of the pools. My mother waved to me from a lounger.

When I walked in her direction, she removed her bug-eye sunglasses and ran to meet me inside, her arms out for an embrace. "Dante!"

We hugged, and she kissed my cheek. Her hands shook when she slid them in mine—not from nerves or hunger, but from a form of Parkinson's that would eventually take her life.

"You look fantastic, Ma."

"Tell me more." She pulled me outside, where one of her staff set cookies and coffee on the table under the eaves.

"Radiant," I said. "Stunning."

"Is that all you have?" she asked as she sat.

"Are you working out, or is walking across this absurd house burning three thousand calories a day?"

"There's my acerbic boy." She laughed as I sat. "We ate lunch before my appointment, but if you want something…?"

"I'm good." I poured coffee for both of us. "Is Dad in?"

"Stay anyway."

I wasn't staying. I was meeting Mandy at Brandywine for a pre-fuck meal.

"What did the doctor say?" I asked.

She sighed and looked over the pool, pausing before telling the hard truth. "I just need to make it until I know all of you are settled with families of your own."

"Then you'll live a long, long time."

"Every pot has a lid." She waved dismissively. "Even you."

"Am I the pot or the lid?"

"You're not both, I'll tell you that much." She took a crunchy cookie and brought it slowly to her lips. Once, when she was having particularly bad tremors, she'd missed her mouth. Since then, she ate alone, or medicated, and even then she required measured intention. "I heard there was an incident in Cambria." She brushed a crumb off her chin.

"What did you hear?"

"So, there *was* an incident?"

"Incidentally."

With her cup suspended above the saucer by two shaky hands, she smiled at the familiarity of my avoidance.

"I was going to ask you to bring my typewriter home," she said before sipping her coffee, "but you were back before I had a chance."

"Next time."

"Hm."

"Hm? Is there a direct question you want to ask?"

She put down her cup and settled back in her chair. "You left the house with holes in it."

My parents had always insisted I hire out the work that needed to be done on the Cambria house, and sometimes—when the repair required expertise I didn't have—I did. So, I knew she wasn't annoyed that I'd walked away from two holes in the ceiling and a leaky roof. She was trying to open the box marked "Incident in Cambria" from the other side.

"Mom, you're much more fun when you just ask what you want to know."

"You always go up there alone, and this time, someone was with you. Your father says it was the other Bettencourt girl."

The "other" Bettencourt girl would be Mandy, Samantha's sister. The one who hadn't committed suicide. My mother was compassionate but had only witnessed the hurt Samantha's fiancé —my brother—suffered.

"She's nice," I said. "Does that kind of fashion you like. One or two things for too much money."

"You're pretending you don't know the word *couture*?"

"That. You should meet her. See her stuff."

Mom's eyebrow twitched, and that in particular meant I should stop bullshitting her. I'd read her hobbies and tastes correctly, but I'd fallen short in trying to play casual.

"Ella told Logan," I predicted. "And Logan told you."

"Logan told your father, and your father told me. Then you came here acting like it's about dresses. So... everything all right?"

"Everything's fine," I said, though Mandy was more than fine. She was perfect.

"Since I'm your mother, I get to ask how serious it is."

If I was ever going to admit anything about Mandy to my mother, this was the time. But she'd worry about how her perpetually single son would handle a breakup, then she'd worry that I'd picked an incompatible woman, because nothing about Amanda Bettencourt and I made sense. My mother didn't deserve to spend a moment of her life in emotional discomfort over any of her children.

"It is what it is," I said unhelpfully, "And the truth is…"

The truth was Mom's emotional discomfort caused by knowing I'd lied to her would last more than a moment.

"The truth is I don't know. I need to get away to figure it out." The rest of the words tumbled out of me unrestrained. "And I know I always say that before I go to Cambria, but this time… it's different. She's different. She's not who I expected, and now I'm not either because she's infected me, and I can't tell if I'm sick or if I'm cured."

My mother's gaze was fixed downward, and I followed it to my hand, which was tightened into a fist so tight I wasn't sure if I'd ever be able to let it go.

"D-Tay!" Lyric's toddler pronunciation of my name came from the house. She skipped out in a striped bikini and threw her arms around me.

My fist came loose to hug her. "Lick," I replied with what my very serious seven-year-old self had called her back out of a sense of spite and injustice.

Lyric threw herself in a chair and stacked three cookies in her palm.

"How about a plate, sweetheart?" Mom said.

"I'm good." She leaned back. Our mother handed her a plate, which Lyric took. "So, did you see the thing?" she asked me, taking half a cookie in one bite.

"Yes?"

"You look kind of badass."

"What thing?" Mom asked me.

"I have no idea," I admitted.

"Oh my God, really?" Lyric clicked the rest of her cookie onto the plate and slid it onto the table. "'I'm Dante,'" she mocked me in a comedic baritone while getting out her phone. "'I won't admit I don't know something.'"

"'I'm Lyric,'" I shot a falsetto back, "'and I think I know *any*thing.'"

"Fuck you, dude." She scrolled through her phone.

"You could have just answered her," Mom said.

"She could have asked a question with a proper noun."

As a reply, Lyric slid her phone to me, glass side up, and Mom came behind me to see the video of me making an ass of myself in the Harmony convenience store under the headline:

BILLIONAIRE CROWNE IN JEALOUS RAGE OVER RENALDO DEWITT'S HONEY

If a video like this had come across my sight with different players, I would have dismissed the enraged meathead making threats as a pathetic excuse for a man.

But there I was, in full color, trying to beat up a man three inches shorter but twice my size while a woman wearing my clothes tried to bring me to my senses before I was thrown out.

I shut the phone and slid it across the table.

Caleb was not to be trusted. I should have known that before I met with him.

"Is *badass* a proper noun?" Lyric asked.

"No," Mom and I said at the same time.

"Well, all my friends think you're one."

"All your friends haven't had a coherent thought since the last Taylor Swift album," I snapped, taking all the good-humored joking out of my tone.

Lyric flipped me the bird, eyes still on the shiny glass.

She didn't care. It could have been her in that video, and she wouldn't have batted an eyelash. The experience that almost broke Mandy would have rolled off my sister's back.

Mandy. She wasn't fully over the last time she'd been the

subject of a tabloid headline, and here she was again, viral for all the wrong reasons, because of me.

"Dante"—Mom put her hand over mine—"this is what you mean by not knowing if you're sick or cured?"

I ignored her, still latching on to my baby sister. "You think you're badass?" I said, half out of my seat. "You're Teflon? You want to know why you don't care what anyone else thinks?"

"What's your damage?"

"So you don't have to care about *anything*." I was standing over her now. "That's why. You don't give a single shit, and that's not a strength. That doesn't make you a quality person. It doesn't make you mature. It makes you detached and cold and dead, and I want better for you."

Lyric blinked, eyes big and blue, long, brown hair parted in the middle, looking soft and vulnerable without a comeback or a hand sign to protect her.

Who else was I going to hurt today?

I wanted to hurt Caleb Hawkins first, but it would be Mandy.

"I have to go," I said, coming behind my mother to kiss her on the cheek.

I patted Lyric's shoulder as I passed, hoping she had enough Teflon left to forgive me.

* * *

I NEVER FOUND out where Dad had left the box, and I didn't care. I had to get to Mandy before anyone else showed her the video. She had to hear my apology for dragging her out into the spotlight again. She'd be angry, and she'd be right.

That's not how this works, bro.

I could blame Caleb for breaking a deal, but it was my loss of control in Harmony that would hurt Mandy. He'd told me clearly that he had all the cards before I'd playacted at having a say over the video. I didn't because I cared too much, and the person who doesn't give a shit holds the winning hand.

I had a moral obligation to beat him anyway for being a liar and a weasel, for disappointing his mother, for avenging her over a relationship he didn't understand.

No one understood it.

Forget the infidelity clause. Forget the whole prenup.

Winding around the two-lane stretch of Sunset, I realized that maybe I didn't understand it either. Even if I'd been emotionally old enough to be in a relationship with a married woman in her forties, I hadn't been experienced enough to really know what was going on under the surface.

Maybe she hadn't told me everything.

Maybe I'd been too green to be there. Too easily manipulated.

Too young to fully relate to her.

Maybe that was why she chose me.

Because she died at the end of it all, I'd never ascribed any intention to the way things worked out. The clubs being in London. The structure of the silent partnership. My age.

I'd been used.

Caleb was truly devastated by his mother's death. His bitterness was as real as mine, but the whole thing had been a massive manipulation.

None of this excused releasing that video, but the blame was irrelevant. Culpability went back a few generations of feuding.

As I approached Mandy's block, I had a clarity over parts of my life I hadn't realized were obscured.

I texted her at a red light.

—I'm near your place—

—I'm at the Grove. I'll be home in an hour. Door code is 9182 if you want to go in and make

yourself comfortable—

She was shopping, and she'd answered me right away with an invitation. She didn't seem angry or distressed, which meant she probably hadn't seen the video yet.

The light changed before I could answer, but I'd already decided waiting wasn't an option.

CHAPTER 35

MANDY

Pink.

How had I never considered pink before?

Pink could be soft and passive as baby powder, or it could be as aggressive and in-your-face as a throat punch first thing in the morning.

Pink could be so orange it came in the side door after ringing the front doorbell. It could wrestle down deep red and make it sing soprano.

Where had pink been my whole life?

"And look at this!" I said, rooting around the Nordstrom's bag, one of the many at my feet. We were in an outdoor coffee shop at the Grove. The metal table was uneven on the cobblestones of the courtyard and piled with not just coffee, but unrelated objects in an array of pink shades.

I found the notebook I'd gotten from Nordstrom's.

"Brown-pink!" I handed it across the table and checked for a reply from Dante. If he was going to be waiting on my couch, I'd cut the coffee short and go right home, but he hadn't replied one way or the other yet.

"Dutch pink." Caleb ran his hand over the leather cover. "Pink used to mean brown-yellow, actually. *Pinkeln*. German for *piss*."

"Yellow and pink aren't even close."

"Same pigment as yellow madder, I think." He handed back the book. "I forget the name of the berry it comes from. Let me look." He took out his phone to fact-find.

Caleb seemed to have an interesting fact for everything I said, and I was reminded of how he'd gripped my attention as a girl. He connected unrelated bits of knowledge, uncovered surprising meanings, and relayed them without making me feel stupid for not knowing them already.

Five minutes into coffee though, I realized the exact mistake my young heart had made.

Caleb was interesting and smart.

He was fun to listen to.

He was handsome and charming.

None of that made him right for me.

Those were traits—they weren't a meeting of the minds. None of it made me the best I could be or enriched my inner life. He wasn't someone I should have been loving, and he'd known that. I'd been confused, he'd been a jerk, and we'd both been too young to know better.

"Oh." His brow knotted at something on his phone. "This just released and—"

Just as he was about to show me what had piqued his interest, a pigeon took flight a foot away from me, and I squeaked, jumping away. The bird tried to perch on the edge of one of my bags and fell in, flapping to get out in a burst of feathers.

"Oh!" I cried in panic. "Oh, no!"

The rest of the shoppers at the tables watched. Kids ran up to see. I didn't know what to do as the bag turned over and the bird stilled.

"Just wait," a man said.

The pigeon cooed, walked out of the sideways bag, crumpling the tissue paper a scarf had been wrapped in, looked around, and flew off to immediate applause with the tissue paper still tangled in its feet. It loosened and floated down.

As my eyes followed, I saw the man who'd asked me to wait. Dante.

I could tell it was him from his posture and bearing, but his head eclipsed the sun behind him, shadowing his face. We'd just texted a few minutes before, when he said he was close to my house, but he'd come here to see me sooner.

"Hey!" I said with a voice colored by all the joyful surprise I felt.

"Dante Crowne." Caleb stood, hand out for a shake. "I haven't seen you since—"

"Friday night."

"Come on." Caleb pulled out a chair. "Sit with us."

Dante rested his hand on the back of the chair but was disinclined to sit down. Caleb seemed to take it as a hint that Dante wasn't staying, so he sat, slouched in the cast-iron chair, and put his fingertips on his coffee cup.

"Five minutes." I put my hand on Dante's. "Caleb was just telling me—"

"That he had to leave," Dante finished my sentence, looking at Caleb, and I realized the tension in the air wasn't triangulated between the three of us. It was just them.

What did he think was going on here? Caleb wasn't Renaldo. He wasn't a threat, and the heartbreak Caleb had caused was way past its expiration.

"Actually, I was telling her the origins of the word *pink*, but you're right." Caleb stood. "It's time for me to go. Mandy"—he turned to me—"give me a call next week."

"I will." I was annoyed enough to promise something that may or may not happen. This was the third time since Cambria that

Dante had interrupted a conversation with a man who wasn't him. Once had been welcome. Those were not good odds.

"Later." Caleb waved to Dante and—with a last nod to me—left.

Once it was just Dante and me in the courtyard, my annoyance turned to something hotter and harder to contain.

"What the hell was that about?" I asked.

"You cannot see him—ever. Not—"

"I'm sorry, what?" I couldn't have heard him right.

"Without me present."

There had been a time, not long before, when I would have mistaken his demand for affection—but not this day.

"Are you kidding me?" I dropped my volume halfway through the sentence. If I made a scene, some well-meaning person would get between us and offer to walk me to my car. I wanted to handle Dante Crowne myself. "We were having *coffee*."

"*Amea*."

For the first time, the nickname wasn't used affectionately, but as a call sign for obedience, and I was too enraged to take a hint.

"Don't you *amea* me," I snarled.

"You don't know him."

"I don't know you either."

He flinched in a way that was so Dante Crowne I thought he was just blinking away a dust mote. The expression was gone before the next breath, but it proved he was vulnerable, and my need to explain proved I was too.

"Caleb and I had a thing in high school," I continued, putting my hand on his chest. "That's a lot of years. You have nothing to worry about."

"You can't see him again. Ever."

"I just told you—"

"There have to be rules." He took me by the wrist. "There have to be limits."

"And who sets them?" I yanked my hand away. "You?"

"Please sit." He put his hands up as if warding away my unease and telling me it was time to calm the fuck down. "Let me talk to you."

No. I wasn't going to be soothed. I wasn't going to listen to pretty words that wove me into a trap. I wasn't that person anymore.

"No." Gathering the pink things on the table, I put them back into their bags, avoiding eye contact that would weaken me. "You don't control me on this side of the bedroom door, and if you can't trust me, maybe we made a mistake."

"Mandy, I have to tell you something."

He was trying to calm a child, but I was a woman, and I wanted to go home.

"I don't want to hear it." I looped the bags on my forearm. "Not now."

"You're being unreasonable."

"This is who I am." I spread my arms, bags hanging, love me or leave me. "I'm emotional, sensitive, simple, shallow, and privileged… but I'm not stupid. This is the third time you got between me and a man I was talking to. The first time, you got a pass. The second was Renaldo and thank you. Both times I rewarded you with a fuck, but not now. No. This time it's a pattern, and I'm not rewarding it."

"I don't want a reward." He slashed the air between us with the edge of his hand. "I want you to sit down long enough for me to show you something!"

Now he was being loud, and I wasn't there to entertain a crowd with my personal life any more than I was there to take orders from a guy who constantly drew boundaries only to leap over them.

"I'm going home," I said. "Don't follow me. Stay away."

I walked away, head down, kicking up a splash of pigeons as I crossed the courtyard. I didn't look back, even for a moment, because there was no point to seeing his reaction unless I wanted to be weakened by it.

When I got to the parking lot and opened my trunk, I looked back. Dante hadn't followed me, and I was glad. Without the heat of his skin and the cool detachment of his eyes on me, I could discern the difference between who I was and who I wanted to be. If he was a bridge between them, great. If he wasn't, he had to go.

My bags had twisted around my wrists, and it took a moment to unwind them, giving me more than enough time to see the stack of headlines I'd tried to squash in my little corner of the world.

RENALDO & THE HOMEWRECKER:
HOW MANDY BETTENCOURT'S BIG PLANS BACKFIRED

One woman had planned a life with Renaldo and felt betrayed when it didn't work out. Another had bought this stack of papers and felt the weight of all the others in the world. Yet another had seen a similar stack in Dante Crowne's truck and felt cared for.

The woman putting her bags next to the old stack as she cataloged who she'd been knew nothing about who she'd become, but she knew what she wanted.

I slammed the trunk closed and got into my buttercup Jaguar.

I wanted a man I trusted, whom I could fight and love at the same time, and who'd challenge me to change. A man who'd set me free but keep me tied to him, who'd be his own man and mine at the same time.

Dante should have been that man.

Obviously, I'd been wrong about him.

When the car started, my phone dinged, then buzzed. I opened my purse to see it lighting up the contents. A receipt from Bottega Venetta. A blue lipstick tube. Mints. Dimes. A bag of unnecessaries.

The buzz stopped. I zipped up my handbag without looking at the notifications.

So much had happened. So much had changed. But the thing I'd left Los Angeles to do hadn't been done. I'd never been alone to think about what I wanted or what I needed, and now—before I saw him or spoke to him—I had to decide if Dante had a role where what I wanted and what I needed met.

CHAPTER 36

DANTE

MANDY'S ASS SWAYED IN HER JEANS, AND HER BAGS KNOCKED against her knees as the damp spray from the fountain cooled my cheek. She didn't look back at me, even though I waited, but turned the corner out of sight without a glance, leaving me with the shoppers and the pigeons.

She was a host of clichés. A tall drink of water. A long-stemmed rose with not a petal out of place. A whole human capable of intense emotion and painful candor. She could be deeply hurt and repeatedly walked into the pain with her softest vulnerabilities exposed because she couldn't bear to give anything less than everything.

I should have trusted her, maybe sat with her and Caleb or hung back until they were done.

I should have been patient and waited until she was ready to see the video, not insisted on satisfying my own need to get it over with and deal with the consequences.

Knowing she was right didn't change anything but me, and I was suddenly exhausted from the years and years of running in place.

Cambria had always been the cure for this feeling. The repairs were nearly done. I could spend a week or two alone in the house, separate from a world I hadn't built and couldn't change.

There was wood to split and a driveway that could stand to be repaved. The fruit was still on the counter. The ice cream was unopened in the freezer and the Ruffles in the pantry. A backward version of things that had changed me were stamped on the typewriter ribbon, ending with the first shot in the revolution in my heart.

Ive seen rivers, and you aint one baby.

Mandy had chopped the wood stacked against the side of the house and cooked in the kitchen. She'd begged at my feet in the driveway, offered me her body in the bedrooms, and now the spirit of Amanda Bettencourt—my pet, my treasure, my *amea*—was all over that house.

I couldn't go up there—couldn't run away, couldn't walk toward, could barely lie still in bed all night—because I knew I had to let go of everything in my past. All the fears that built the walls around me and the boundaries around her. I had spent so long avoiding freedom that I didn't know how to leave the cage I'd locked myself up in.

By the time the sun came up, I still had no idea how to do what needed to be done, so I was just going to do it… but first I had to see her.

CHAPTER 37

MANDY

The coffee shop was the same, but I ordered something different, and the cashier asked me if I was sure I wanted no caramel pump and two extra shots with that.

"I'm sure."

It was nice to be known—pinned to a place and time, connected to another person by habit and ritual—because I was otherwise unmoored from my own desires.

I'd woken up after a night out with Aileen feeling a little too headachey and dry for a single mojito. I hadn't stopped talking long enough to drink more, but maybe that explained the dehydration.

Guzzling a glass of water before filling a second, I recounted my relentless monologue of the previous night, when Aileen took me out, expecting me to be upset about going viral again. I wasn't upset about the new video at all, but seeing it had slapped me in the face with how much I missed Dante.

I insisted I felt generally better as a human. I'd taken control of my love life. I was a new, more complete woman. Except it'd have been better if I had him too. Like, I wouldn't give up feeling like this to have him, or at least who I thought he was, but if he wasn't that, then I wished we could be back in Cambria, where he was bossy but good bossy, not bad bossy.

And Aileen wondered if I was too hard on him, but I wasn't, because catching this stuff early is important. And I had. It was the right thing. And I was fine. Really, just fine.

But it was nice to feel owned. Possessed. Important enough to be his prize.

"And that, Mandy Bettencourt," I schooled my reflection, "comes from the same place as him setting the rules about who you can and cannot talk to."

Aileen had agreed, then I'd gone on about how I couldn't make this all work in my head because I wanted him to own me and free me at the same time, and it was wrong no matter how you sliced it. Like a pizza cut into, like, trapezoids or bunny shapes or something. How could it be both right and wrong? How could I be a better, happier person and miserable at the same time? Why couldn't this just be straightforward?

"It's not binary," Aileen said. "It's not 'he loves me, he loves me not,' or 'I need him, I need him not,' all the time. There are, like, variables. You have to solve them. Or not. Whatever. Are you going to finish that mojito?"

I thought about variables as I parked outside my usual morning coffee place.

What could change, and what had to stay the same?

I had never thought of myself as a rule follower, but where had I drawn the lines around myself? Around my work? Around the people I let into my life?

How many of those rules kept me safe while I recklessly threw my heart at anyone who'd catch it?

So, no caramel today and two shots because I was tired from a long night of talking to my friend about Dante—but not about him at the same time, because when I'd walked away from him at the Grove, his jealousy was half the reason. The other was that I needed to decide who I was, and he was getting in the way like it was his job.

When I stepped away from the counter, I was sure Dante was right behind me. I could feel his body filling the space the way it had in the little Cambria house, but when I turned, I was disappointed to find I'd only imagined him there.

I had to get over this.

CHAPTER 38

∽

DANTE

She must have seen the video, and I couldn't do anything until I was sure she was all right or I knew how bad the damage was.

That was my excuse.

This time, when I went to the strip mall parking lot outside the coffee shop, I didn't sit in the front seat of an outrageously expensive car, nor did I go inside when she did. With the car parked around the corner, I walked to the smoke shop, bought a steel lighter with a pissed-off eagle on the side, and browsed the window display from inside.

"You looking for a pipe, sir?" the guy asked, brushing back middle-parted shoulder-length hair. His orange T-shirt stretched over the bumps of his breasts and belly, and his light-brown beard had a recently adolescent unevenness.

"Just looking," I said, fiddling with the lighter in my pocket.

"That yellow one's Northern Waters Glass."

Just as he said "yellow," Mandy's buttercup Jag pulled into the lot and—without even slowing down—slid into the center of a spot and stopped right before the bumper. The car was lined up straight, equidistant from both painted lines—perfect, just like the woman who got out with the phone to her ear.

I couldn't see her face. Was she crying? Upset? Annoyed? Her gait told me nothing, but her head wasn't bowed in sadness and her hands weren't crumpling a soggy tissue.

As a matter of fact, she had a crispness to her stride, and when she spoke, her free hand waved as if the person on the other end could read her gestures.

"...out of the Upper Peninsula." The salesman's voice filtered back, closer now, but too far away to give a shit about. "That's in Michigan."

"That's interesting," I mumbled, craning my neck to watch her approach the coffee shop.

"If you want," the man continued, "I have some real nice Northern Waters stuff in the case."

Mandy opened the door and held it for a woman juggling a tray of coffee and a stroller. Words exchanged. Mandy turned her head to wave goodbye, and though I only saw her for a split second, it was all I needed to know how she was.

Fine.

She was fine.

Mandy Bettencourt—my *amea*—smiled at the mother in a way that couldn't be faked. Her genuine peace radiated outward, spilling surplus happiness like loose change.

Did she not know about the video, or did she just not care?

I could tell her. I could show her the thing and apologize and comfort her.

But if she knew and didn't care? Then she didn't need me or my past. She didn't need my rules or my dick. She was happier without me, and if I was a decent person, I'd let her have her happy life. The thought was a jolt from my chest outward—in her direction, pulling like one heart lassoed to another.

"Sir?" The salesman yanked me out of it.

"Yes."

If she didn't need me, then my plan was pointless. I had to know.

"Yes, the Northern Waters, here?"

Shit. Had I agreed to something?

"It's three twenty." The man held up a pipe with a huge ochre stone set in the base.

"Fine." I dug out my wallet, pinched away three hundreds and a fifty, and handed them over. "Wrap it up."

I left and ran across the parking lot, freezing at the window where I could see her ordering. Not just ordering. Chatting with the cashier. Nodding.

I put my hand on the glass as if I could touch her and feel a little bit of her comfort with herself.

What did I intend?

To burst in there and take her time? Steal her attention?

Break bad news or deliver information she already had?

If I went in there, it wouldn't be for her. It would be for me. There was nothing I could do for her. Nothing I could give her, buy her, offer her. All I could do was know her, and now I never would.

My hand fell away from the glass, and the version of myself I'd nailed together out of dominance and self-reliance fell apart as if it had spent years rotting away from the inside.

That shell had kept me apart from other people, and only when it broke did I realize what it meant to be alone.

* * *

A MAN DOESN'T GO to his parents when he's confused and upset, but I wasn't a man after I saw Mandy ordering coffee through a window and realized I was superfluous to her.

I was a boy.

I was a sixteen-year-old who had found purpose rescuing a woman more than twice his age and lost it when she died. Meaning had been pried away so fast the procedure broke me. My manhood was put together with spit and chewing gum. The act of dominance and control had been a hardened bond that had started thinning in the Cambria rain and melted completely in the solvent of a woman's smile.

"Dante!" my mother exclaimed when I appeared in the kitchen.

Dad handed her a water glass across the island, and a lazy Susan of amber pill bottles spun between them.

"Hey, son," Dad said, the picture of health and happiness in a gray polo and chinos.

We shook hands, and I fell into a hug that was supposed to last a masculine second but stretched out because I wouldn't let go. I'd always assumed I'd be like him but never understood what I had to do to get there.

"What is it?" Mom asked, coming behind Dad.

"I wasted all this time," I said. "Now it's too late."

"Oh, no, it's not," Mom said.

"You don't even know what he's talking about," Dad complained.

"I think I do." She took me by the hand and led me to the kitchen table, sitting me down like a trainer with a docile puppy. "My Lord, I haven't seen you like this since that horrible woman died." Her manner got grave. "Nobody died, I hope?"

"No," I said. "Nobody died."

"Was she upset?" Mom took a chair diagonal from mine. "I have an appointment with—"

"What's going on?" Dad asked.

"Don't," I said to my mother.

My father was getting impatient. "Who's upset?"

"No one," I answered. "No one's upset. Except me. I'm…" I had to take a moment to get out words I didn't associate with myself. "I'm upset. I'm confused. I'm…" The last one was a foreign language. "I'm… lonely." I dropped my voice for the last humiliating word, cringing as I articulated two syllables.

I was a solitary man. I answered to no one. I came and went as I pleased, unburdened by the need for company. I'd been that way for as long as I could remember.

Without her, my skin didn't fit around my soul.

"I can't carry it all anymore," I said. "I don't know how to let anything go. I didn't have to before. But we're in the real world, and there's just so much of it. I can't get a handle on it, and I don't know how to navigate it the way she does."

"I still don't know who we're talking about," Dad said. My parents looked at each other, layering meaning into a nonverbal language that could manage generalities but not enough specifics for my father. "Is it Samantha's sister?"

"Yes," I said, leaning back and looking at the ceiling because I couldn't meet the compassion in my mother's eyes or the surprise in my father's. "Her name is Mandy Bettencourt, and I'm in love with her."

The words hung in the air like physical things, then popped when my father spoke, as if they'd always been no stronger than soap bubbles.

"Okay," he said. "What are you going to do about it?"

"I give up, Dad. I don't know. I just give up."

He nodded as if I'd answered a tough question correctly. "Good start, son."

* * *

DAY 18

The location of my surrender was the Crowne HQ offices in the conference room facing the sea. The time was two o'clock, fifteen minutes before the sun peeked in from the corner, where the glass met the ceiling and the glare became unbearable.

Alone, I faced east with my back to the window because I was willing to go at this alone but not willing to do it at a disadvantage. William Hawkins sat across the table, next to Caleb, who flipped through the contract with Devin Thoze, his lawyer and the son of the firm's founder.

William didn't read contracts or wear ties. He preferred to show off his chest hair by leaving open his two top shirt buttons. His right hand was clenched in a fist on the table, and the other was laid over it as if he was holding himself back from punching someone.

Me.

In all the years my family had been connected to the Hawkinses, I'd never been in a room with William. My father had warned me that he was intense and tightly coiled for violence. Veronica had described anger that had been unleashed on her a handful of times, but I was full of myself. I'd believed Veronica and I would run to London, where I'd protect her from both poverty and pain.

But it had become more and more clear that I'd been the mark in a con I could still only half see.

"What happened?" William asked me. "With you? All these years you fight to keep us out of operations. You try to buy us out four times." He held up four thick fingers, one with a gold wedding band around the base. "What changed?"

"I think it's time to move on," I said placidly. A man like William Hawkins fed off the emotions of others, and I wasn't interested in being his dinner.

"Hold up," Caleb said. "When we break out the payment schedule, we end up basically at market."

"Yes."

"I said half market." Caleb slid the contract back to me and lied at the same time.

"You published a video you said you wouldn't." I slid it back. "The difference is payment."

"I'm not paying your therapy bills because people saw you

wrestle a magazine rack."

"I don't give a shit who sees me. But"—I leaned one arm across the table to point at Caleb—"you came for Mandy Bettencourt. That cost you. Then you sat across a table from her without telling her what you were trying to do to her. That cost you."

"How much to fuck her?" William said.

Punching him in the throat seemed like a viable option, but I wasn't going to be baited by a glorified frat boy.

"Full market, or the tapes go to the *Times* and the set of books I keep goes to the Crown Advocate." I folded my hands in front of me. "No relation. She can compare them to your books and whatever else she has on you. See how that goes."

I waited, watching the nonverbal communication between father and son—just as the sun dropped below the window and a blast of light hit Caleb in the face, forcing him to squint.

"When do I get to hear these tapes?"

"After you sign." I stood, blocking the sun.

"Because you have nothing," William added.

Once I won this, and I would, I'd be free of my ties to Veronica. Then I'd convince Mandy I could be different. No one would be out to get me or—by extension—her. We could start a new life without public temper tantrums or my fear of knowing a woman and being known by her.

"Sign in the next hour, and I'll fly to London to have this prepped to go for the next quarter. Delay and your accountant can explain the tax penalty."

I leaned down to gather my papers. The sun hit Caleb's face, and he put his hand up to block it.

"God, you are insufferable," he said.

"I'll leave so you can discuss," I said and walked out.

I would have sold them the clubs for half market just to get them out of my life, but they'd never believe there wasn't a catch. I didn't rush them for the same reason.

But I couldn't be patient with everything. My heart was starving. It needed her to sustain itself, and it had been too long without news. I didn't know what she was doing or feeling, and once I was out of the conference room, it drove me mad.

I went into an empty conference room and texted her.

—Are you there?—

CHAPTER 39

MANDY

—Are you there?—

My fingers flew over the glass to answer, then hesitated.

I was here but not for long.

After the feeling Dante was in the coffee shop, I'd called my mother and asked her for the keys to the Lake Tahoe house. I needed to be away from even the possibility that he was in my life, watching and protecting me, owning my body and my time.

I needed to take the solo trip I'd tried to take in the first place. Just me this time.

So, with his text on my screen, I kept hesitating because I was weak and indecisive and because I didn't know if I was here or there until my assistant poked her head in my office door.

"Your noon is here," she said, then cracked her gum.

"I thought we were sold out until next season?"

"Doreen Crowne? It's been in the book."

* * *

"Doreen!" I said, arms wide as I entered the showroom. Dante's mother was leaning into a mannequin, inspecting the embroidery on one of the first dresses I'd done. We exchanged a hug. "How are you?"

"Nothing to complain about." She gave me a good-natured shrug. "Not that that'll stop me."

We laughed at the old joke even though—in all the years we'd crossed paths—she'd never complained about anything.

"Gwen's going to get us a tray," I said. "Is there an occasion you're dressing for?"

She explained that she was more of a collector who wore her pieces, but all I could think about was how Dante had the masculine version of her wide jaw and how when she waved away her illness or the trouble with a house the size of a school district, she led with her first finger, the way he did.

It was pretty common for a client to come in and not even look at a single article of clothing. Sometimes I was booked years in advance and they wanted a spot in six months. An hour went by without us talking about an actual dress. I thought nothing of it until she was getting ready to leave.

"I'm glad I came by," she said. "I almost didn't."

"I'm glad you did too."

"Dante said it would be all right."

My smile froze across the bottom of my face. The mention of his name should have been enough, but the context shook me, and I had to think quickly to find a funny way to phrase my reply. "Does he curate your collection?"

"Oh, no!" She chuckled. "You two had a romance, and I didn't want to… you know, hurt his feelings."

"Ah." She was protecting him because that was what people did for each other.

"I hope that's all right," she asked, hitching her bag over her shoulder.

"It's fine. How's… um… How's he doing?" I tried to sound casual.

"Seems fine. He's off to London to close a deal."

"The clubs?"

"Yes." She drifted off as if she wasn't sure if she should say more. She was more taciturn than I was because I shouldn't have asked the question in the first place.

But since I'd gone that far, I figured I might as well go all the way. "I didn't think he'd sell them."

"Things change." We started out of the showroom. "Honestly, he should have sold out to his partners years ago.

His partners? The Hawkinses? Caleb?

"I hope..." I stopped at the door. "I hope he's not giving it up because of what I did."

"Mandy," she said as a prelude to something serious, "from what I understand, you didn't do anything. But Caleb Hawkins is slippery. He'd just promised Dante the night before not to release that video. The one of you both. And of course, he published them, so when Dante saw you two at the Grove together—"

"It wasn't jealousy." I didn't know whether to be relieved or angry, but clearly I was both. He wasn't trying to control me having lunch with a man. He was protecting me from a specific man because he had information I hadn't had.

"You'd have to ask him."

"I will."

I thanked her for coming in, gave her a truncated version of the song and dance every potential client got, and went back to my office.

—*Are you there?*—

There wasn't a follow-up text. He'd left it up to me to decide what I wanted without exerting his own will.

—*I'm here*—

CHAPTER 40

DANTE

—*I'M HERE*—

By the time her text came, I was already in the back of a car, getting driven to the airport. I hadn't given up on her, but I'd accepted that the ball was in her court and she wasn't hitting it back. There was nothing I could do unless I wanted to alienate her or take away the agency she'd earned.

"Mandy," I said to my screen when the text came in. "You're here."

A second later, the phone vibrated in my hand, and her name flashed on the screen.

"Hi," she said when I picked up. "I'm sorry."

"No, no, don't be. It was my fault."

"I should have listened. I'm just... I was afraid you were turning into a domineering asshole."

"I am a domineering asshole, Mandy."

The freeway popped under the tires at seventy miles per hour, and the city blurred into gray. I could be at her door in half an hour if there was no traffic.

I heard a sniffle on the other side. "Are you crying?"

"I love it when you say my name."

"And that makes you cry?"

"I'm relieved," she said with a sob. "You know me. My emotional thermostat's broken."

"No," I whispered. "The problem is that I don't know you. I don't know why you love yellow so much, or how you learned to sew, or what you'd do if I burned my hand."

"It was Samantha's favorite color, I taught myself, and I'd do whatever you did when I burned mine."

I was undeterred by the answers because they weren't the point.

"I bought you the flavor ice cream I liked and Ruffles, but I didn't ask you what you wanted, and that… It's going to change. I screwed up. I told you what I wanted and expected you to do it. From now on, if you let me—"

"I'll let you."

"I'm done telling you who you are."

"I'm yours."

"I'm *asking*."

"Is there a question?"

"Will you let me know you?"

She sniffled and took a deep breath, and though she'd already agreed to everything, she paused as if she wasn't sure.

"Yes," she finally said. "But…"

CHAPTER 41

MANDY

"But..."

I was leaning against the office wall when I left him hanging, which I wasn't trying to do on purpose, but I couldn't agree to be with him again while I was high on hope and so relieved I could take him back that I was sobbing.

I had to protect myself from my worst impulses, and nothing he'd said changed that.

After clearing the gunk out of my throat, I said, "But you're on your way to London."

"I can turn the car around and be there in half an hour."

"And I'm on my way to our old house in Lake Tahoe. So..." Another throat clear. "I need to go. Alone. I need to clear my head out. Get back to baseline. Just... not be so intense, you know?"

"You need to get off the roller coaster."

"Yeah. For a little while. Week. Ten days, maybe."

There was a silence on the other end that the whooshing and rumbling of the cars couldn't dispel. I slid down the wall and crouched on the industrial carpet.

"Dante?"

"I have a compulsion to come to wherever you are, pull your skirt up, and spank you raw for making me wait."

Before he was even done, I was telling myself he could do that. Right now, he could turn around, punish me until I came, and get back in the car for a later flight.

"Instead," he added, saving me from myself, "I'm going to make *you* wait."

"A week, then?"

"Ten days."

"Has anyone told you you're a domineering asshole?"

"The woman I love just did."

Then I cried so hard I could barely say I loved him too.

CHAPTER 42

MANDY

THE LAKE TAHOE HOUSE WAS HUGE. IT HAD ELECTRIC FROM THE grid and water right from the pipes. The roof wouldn't have leaked even if it was raining, which it wasn't. There was a real supermarket two miles away, and their *DMZ Weekly*s had the British royals on the cover.

Compared to all the wood-chopping, leak-fixing, and water-conserving I'd had to do in Cambria, our empty Lake Tahoe house was the height of American civilization. It even had a massive tub I could fill as high as I wanted.

And yet...

"Six days is plenty," I said as I strolled the bank of supermarket freezers.

"Self-actualization in less than a week?" Dante replied through my earbuds, calling from across the ocean. "You should sell a course, *amea*."

He should have sold a course in enforced distancing. We spoke once a day, and he refused to dirty talk or sext because he didn't want to interpose. No matter how horny I was, he insisted this was my time and we'd be together soon enough.

Domineering asshole.

I stopped by the Häagen-Dazs. "Do you want caramel ice cream?"

"You pick."

I opened the freezer door to grab a pint, but something else caught my eye. "Ohh, bitter chocolate could be interesting." I tossed it in the cart, then grabbed a vanilla in case interesting turned out to be too much. I let the freezer door *thup* closed. "How much longer is it going to take to sign papers and write checks?"

"A clean break's more complicated than that."

"Hm."

"Hm?" He seemed amused that I'd turned his favorite annoying word back around.

"I'm starting to think I should get on a plane." I pulled up to the potato chip rack.

"To London?"

"No, the fruited plain," I snapped. "Of course London."

"Why would you do that?"

"Boats make me seasick. Kettle chips or Ruffles?" I asked. "I think I have to call them crisps when I come?"

"Whatever you want."

Both kinds got flung on top of the pasta, cheese, broccoli, and wine. That was enough. I suddenly had the feeling I wasn't staying in Lake Tahoe much longer, whether I had his permission to come to London or not.

"It's time to get this thing moving," I said. "I'm ready to start my life already."

"Tell you what—if I'm not done by tomorrow, you get on a plane and come here."

"Really?" I stopped the cart. I couldn't walk and deal with this level of anticipation at the same time.

A guy in his twenties with a rock T-shirt and dark-brown scruff on his cheeks excused himself to get at a jar of salsa.

"Really," Dante said.

"We'll be together?" I whispered so Scruff Guy wouldn't hear me and think I was asking him on a date, because he was hovering by the rack, inspecting every bag as if he hadn't been on Earth long enough to find a favorite brand of fried potato.

"In the next two days," Dante said. "On one continent or the other, you'll be over my knee, getting the spanking you deserve."

That was the dirtiest thing he'd said to me since we were in Los Angeles, and it wasn't enough. I scooted the cart away from Mr. Discerning Chip Consumer.

"Then," he said softly, "I'm going to slide my fingers inside you and make you come."

"Day after tomorrow? You promise?"

"On one condition."

"Tell me."

"Beg."

I looked around the aisle. Scruff Man was there. A woman with a little boy in the cart seat. A young couple comparing peanut butters. Bright lights. Exposure.

"Please," I breathed. "I'll be your dirty little slut. Please just use me how you want."

"Not bad."

"I can't wait two days."

"Yes, you can." I heard a door open on his side. Since it was two in the morning there, he should have been inside, but it sounded like a front entrance. "Now finish up and go home, *umea*. Let me finish signing papers and paying lawyers."

We said goodbye, and I headed for the checkout line with wet underwear and a pulsing throb I'd have to take care of the minute I put the ice cream in the freezer.

* * *

ONE BAG OVER MY SHOULDER, I dropped the two I had in each hand at the front door so I could dig around for the keys. I'd bagged the ice cream on top so I could easily put that in the freezer before taking care of the urgency between my legs. As I fumbled with the door lock, I wasn't sure I'd even make it out of the kitchen.

Finally, I was in.

I swung the door open, grabbed the groceries, and kicked it closed the way I'd planned in my head. Not a beat was missed as I put the bags on the kitchen floor, threw the ice cream in the freezer, and slapped it closed.

Then I decided I could wait until I'd put the rest of the groceries away, which I did. The delay was deliciously distracting, and now I could give my needs the attention they deserved.

Pulling my jeans open, I realized I had to pee, so I went to the master bedroom to get naked before my left hand teased out the thought of him. When I stepped out of my jeans, I saw that the bathroom light was on.

I would have sworn I'd shut it off.

Wiggling out of my underwear and T-shirt, I went to the bathroom door, unhooking my bra on the way.

"Holy shit!" I gasped, grabbing the nearest weapon—a thick scented candle the diameter and height of a can of tennis balls—and held it ready to swing at the man in the tub.

He was laughing, of course—and in another heartbeat, so was I.

"You —" I didn't have another second to call him an asshole because he pulled me into the tub with him.

I went willingly, dropping my weapon so I could kiss him with my arms around his soap-slick shoulders.

"I thought you were in London," I said between kisses.

"You begged me."

"But you were already here."

"I've always been here." He put his hands under my ass and hitched me to straddle him. "And I always will be."

Looking into the warmest blue eyes I'd ever seen, I believed him—but more importantly, I believed in myself enough to trust him.

EPILOGUE

MANDY

"Daaaadddeeeeeee..."

In the dream, Samantha was on the other side of a wall in our house. It was a wall that didn't really exist, but the way our house had been built, there was no telling if the wall was dream logic or premonition.

"Da-da-da-daaadddeeeeeee...."

I went to the other side of the wall to look for her, but no dice. She'd moved behind another wall, but now there were doorways and windows everywhere, and I had no idea which one she was behind.

My dream self found that annoying, not scary, and I decided to stay still until she showed up.

"What time is it?"

My real self heard Dante's question. My dream self was still standing in an empty room with her arms crossed.

"Mm," Real Self said.

"Jesus Christ."

Dante's profane prayer woke me. The walls—the real ones—glowed dawn blue. Dante's question was rhetorical. The time was irrelevant and fell inside the parameters of *too damn early*.

"Da-da-daaaadeeeee," Samantha's voice entered from outside the room.

Dante was already at the window in nothing but thin cotton sweatpants with a waistband that hung three inches below his navel, where his happy trail met its destination.

"What's she doing out there?" I groaned. Our daughter seemed to know the best days to wake up too early were the days after her parents were up late. I had the sore bottom to prove it.

Dante cranked open the casement window and leaned on the sill, looking down into the backyard one floor below.

"Sweetheart," he said, voice carrying down without being raised, "it's not wake-up time yet."

"Dey cats."

He turned to me for a translation, thick arms still braced on the windowsill.

"She probably wants you to read the singing cat book."

"At five in the morning?"

I slung my feet over the edge of the bed. He'd kissed them last night, blindfolded me and tickled them before moving upward with his lips.

That was good.

"She's three," I said, joining him at the window.

Our daughter stood on the patio, looking up at us with blue eyes the size of saucers, black hair she insisted we cut short, and a nightgown with a truck on it. Favorite Monkey hung loose from one hand, and the other pointed at the deck her father had built with Teddy last summer.

"Dey. Baby. Cats," she insisted, jabbing her finger at the wood-planked deck. Then she splayed her fingers apart. "Five. I count. One-two-fee-fou-fife."

"Honey," I said, "if they're rats or something—"

"I'm on it." Dante pushed himself off the sill, kissed my cheek, and grabbed the shirt he'd thrown off to fuck me only a few hours before.

* * *

IN THE SEVEN years since our wedding, and seven and a half since selling off the clubs, Dante had partnered with his brother to do what he loved. Not Logan, who could crunch a number until it screamed, but Byron, the real estate developer who tore buildings down and built newer, fancier ones in their place.

Dante had sold Byron on a retrofitting idea for a piece in Mar Vista. He could have done it himself, but he needed Byron's expertise and salesmanship. Dante asked me to marry him in Lake Tahoe, in the tub, and I said we should wait, but when he came home with a yes from his brother, I'd never seen him so happy. We were both ready.

I accepted his proposal. We went to city hall the next morning. My mother was thrilled on one hand. On the other, it took her a couple of years to get over all the steps we skipped. Dante's mother took a little longer, and his father was still disappointed we didn't have a big thing.

I didn't grow my business. I didn't want to. The company was the size and shape of my dreams, and my husband was in his element—fixing, building, making things work. There seemed no limit to the talent that had lain dormant while he managed a foreign business he didn't really care about.

Teddy came first, with his calm control and sense of self. Then Samantha, who hated boundaries so much she fought her way out of my body three weeks early.

The house in Beverly Hills was secure, but our daughter always found a way outside. It started when Dante decided he was going to replace the footings under the porch himself. He'd had to tear off the front of the house, which left us with no front door.

One day, we woke to find our toddler kicking a soccer ball around the front lawn with the security guard who watched the front gate.

We sealed that up, but our girl was not only clever—she was

persistent. She defied childproof locks, safety gates, and barriers that would have stumped Harry Houdini. Every boundary was a challenge, and all challenges were accepted.

In the end, we just left the back door open, sealed off the yard, and moved hazards to a shed with three working padlocks and—just for her—a weaker fourth at the bottom, which she almost disabled by unscrewing the hinge. Only the limitation of her tiny hands prevented its complete removal.

We both went downstairs and joined her on the patio.

"Tell me what you saw," Dante said, crouching in front of Samantha.

Two minutes into morning light, I could see her feet were filthy and the front of her nightgown was streaked with gray dirt.

"Baby cats." Her speech impediment thickened the last S. "Unna da deck."

She pointed at the deck by the pool. We had a gate, but we'd taught her how to swim rather than trust a silly cast-iron railing to keep her from drowning.

Dante looked over his shoulder at me. Under the deck. There was no more than eight inches of crawlable space under the planks, but obviously—judging from the dirt on her elbows—it was enough.

"Did you touch them?" I asked, still fearing rats or possums or a nest of adorable baby squirrels with rabies.

She shook her head vigorously, dropped Favorite Monkey, and grabbed her father's hand, pulling him across the lawn. She was tall for her age, but Dante still had to crouch.

The oddly shaped pool was salt water, with a waterfall, and surrounded by plants and trees like a natural watering hole. The gate was open, of course. We'd check the security footage later to figure out how she did it, then apply preventative measures that would fail.

"Show me where," Dante said, still allergic to asking a question when a command would serve the same purpose.

But though we were on the wood planks in our bare feet, Samantha was already at the side of the structure, crawling into a space where a hole had been dug under the flashing.

"Hon—!" I cried.

But Dante had already leapt into action, grabbing Samantha by the hips and yanking her out. Her dirty face crunched. She was about to melt down and needed her attention diverted.

"I see them!" I said, pointing at a random spot. "Between the planks."

"No!" She wiggled out of her father's arms and ran to a spot in the corner, crouching with her nose touching the wood. "Dey here!"

We followed, crouching to look between the planks. Sure enough, five sets of kitteny blue eyes stared back up at us.

* * *

"I DON'T WANT A CAT," Teddy objected before shoving a spoonful of cereal into his mouth. The milk dripped back into the bowl except for one drop on the kitchen bar, which our son wiped away before it even settled.

"Dey five." Samantha splayed five fingers in her brother's face. Her other hand twisted vertical, catapulting cereal milk across the bar. She didn't clean it up. Her age was her excuse, but I was sure that wasn't going to change with the years.

"Personally," Dante said, arms crossed, leaning on the counter as though he owned the joint and everyone in it, "I don't want a cat either."

"Why not?" I asked, leaning against him. "They're cute, and they nuzzle up and go..." I purred into his cheek.

He put one arm around me while the other grabbed a rag from the backsplash. "They're chaos agents. We have enough chaos in this house."

His arms were long enough to hold me and wipe up Samantha's mess at the same time. He missed being alone sometimes, but when he went to Cambria by himself to take care of a cracked foundation or update the solar cells, he came home early.

He needed to be alone but wanted us.

Or wanted solitude but needed our chaos.

We didn't know. Probably all of it and something completely different.

"Just one," I said. "How much chaos can one cat cause?"

"A lot," Dante said.

"They poop in boxes. In the house. Gross." Teddy crunched his face at the fine print on the cereal box. He was six but so frustrated with his inability to read he'd already started learning. "What's high fruhc-toes corn sie-rup?"

"Poop in a box." I took it away and folded it up so he couldn't fill his belly with any more garbage. "Listen. They're like an unclaimed gift. We can put four up for adoption, but we have to take one. Just o—"

"No!" Samantha pounded her fist on the bar, catching the edge of her bowl, which spun enough to make a mess before it righted itself. "Dey *five*."

"We're not taking five cats, sweetheart." I reached around Dante to grab the rag.

"Picking one isn't fair." Teddy laid out his infallible logic to his sister. "The others will feel bad."

"One is—" I started to lay out my logic, but Samantha was bursting at the seams.

"Five!"

"Excuse me?" Dante said in his stern daddy voice that was a prelude to someone being in big, big trouble.

"Not one. All by himthelf and no brother. Who he nap with? Who lick him face when he dirty? Five it nithe. One it lonely."

"They're cats, sweetheart," I said, rinsing the rag. "They don't get lonely like people do."

But as I wrung out the cloth, I saw my husband looking at his daughter with a changed expression, and I put my hand on his arm.

"Honey?"

He shook it off.

"Let's go!" He clapped his hands once. "School, kid." He pointed at Teddy's bowl. "Finish up."

* * *

WE DIDN'T TELL Samantha what we decided because anything could go wrong in the weeks between.

She stole into the shadows to watch the mother cat come home as the sun set and was there when mama crawled out in the morning. The kittens came out to eat what we left for them, then scurried back to their safe place. When a red-tailed hawk screeched above, looking for a meal, we knew the time had come. We had to lure them out and take them inside.

"Are you sure?" I asked Dante as he put on a pair of gloves to protect his hands from scratches and bites.

"You want the hawk to start picking them off?"

"I mean… no. But five cats is a lot of chaos. They'll be in everything. They knock things over—"

"We can handle it."

"—and there's the poop in a box problem."

"We can hire more help."

"Here's the thing," I said. "It's more… not people, but more activity. There won't be peace. You won't be alone."

He smiled, looking down as he pressed the Velcro strap of his glove tight around his wrist.

"That's the point, *amea*." He kissed my lips. "That's the point."

And they lived happily ever after

* * *

This is the last Crowne book, but I have so much in store for you. A super, duper dark romance with a mafia guy, a kidnapping, an underground society, a forced marriage, betrayal, passion and the kind of hurts-so-good heat I love to write.

TAKE ME is coming out in January, but I have a SNEAK PEEK of the first three chapters. The books are going to be 5,99, but if you preorder *Take Me* now, you can get it for 3.99.

So keep scrolling to read the chapters, or just get it now.

TAKE ME

Have you read the other Crowne books?

Iron Crowne / Crowne of Lies

* * *

Follow me on Facebook, *Twitter*, or *Instagram (but don't expect much)*

Join my fan group on Facebook.

JOIN THE MAILING LIST *for deals, sales, new releases and bonus content.*

My website is cdreiss.com
email: christine@cdreiss.com
Check out Take Me....

TAKE ME

THESE CHAPTERS ARE UNEDITED

Between now and publication, things will change and hopefully improve. Except the idea, which is simple.

She's kidnapped on her wedding day, held by a man who wants vengeance on her father, married to him against her will, and forced into a world of betrayal, lies, and sexual deviance she's lived in her entire life…but never known it.

All she has to do to escape is destroy everything she's ever loved, and love a man she wants to destroy.

TAKE ME

* * *

Copyright © 2020 Flip City Media Inc. All rights reserved.

No part of these chapters may be reproduced by any electronic or mechanical means without permission, except for brief quotations in a book review.

This story came out of the author's head. Any similarities to persons living or dead makes you a sick puppy in good company.

CHAPTER 1

NEW YORK CITY

SARAH

The sun's first rays spill over the horizon, blushing the white silk of my dress a sweet, shimmering pink. It was dark when I woke, cool blue light rendering the world outside my window in smudges and shadow as I was helped into my gown, but now the sunrise is a riot of color in the slit of sky between the buildings of 37th Street.

I'm a pragmatic person. I don't believe in omens or a benevolent God. There is no capital-U universe. There's the world as it exists, and the people in it, and the collectively they're the only force that can change how they exist in the world.

All the same, I can't help feeling like the intense, singular beauty of the sky on my wedding day bodes well. I almost press my fingertips to the town car's window, but pull them away at the last moment, mindful not to leave a smudge that someone else will be responsible for cleaning later.

The warmth on my face feels like a caress, and I soak it up—allowing myself a little bit of indulgence on today of all days—the culmination of so much work and effort. My life will be realized before the witness of all of us—I become a wife.

From the other side of the black glass that hides me from the driver, I hear a rustling, then a murmur, and my thighs tense until it stops. I can't see the man driving me to my wedding. I assume it's Timothy, who's taken me everywhere since I was small, but the voice is deeper, more urgent, and even though I can't make out the words, they're more commanding than a driver's needs to be.

Definitely a new driver not used to my father—who never tolerates anyone else's lateness, but often arrives slightly behind schedule for his own appointments. I've never been able to confirm he's unapologetically late on purpose, but I'm sure of it. The only question is why, and my theories have swung between a need to show everyone waiting how powerful he is and a consideration for anyone beneath him who might be running behind. Either he's displaying his strength or showing consideration for those who are weaker. Maybe it's both. He'll never tell me anyway.

Right now, he needs me to be patient, and I can stay patient, even today.

I crack open the car's window and take deep lungful of the sweet morning air, my ribs working against the tightly-tied laces of my dress. Will the air taste different once I'm a wife? Deeper, or richer? Or a word I haven't learned yet for a sensation which will be revealed?

The doorman, William, sees me through the crack and tips his hat with a nod. He's one of us, and though his uniform means nothing to the rest of the world, we know how important and dangerous his job is.

I roll the window back up.

My father, Peter Antoine emerges, his gait as certain and unhurried as ever. On another man, his black tuxedo might be out of place in Murray Hill at five thirty in the morning, but he wears it like it like a second skin. With his slicked-back dark hair and gold eyes, his elegance is striking, even to his only child.

There's always a moment when I see him like this, out of context, as a stranger might, and wonder: how can he possibly be related to me? I have none of his power, and certainly none of his ability to wield an almost lethal authority. I am skilled at my duties, not an embarrassment or a failure, but I am my mother's daughter.

That's what I've been told, anyway.

William opens the car door and my father slips in next to me. The door snaps closed and the locks click. The driver pulls away from the curb without another rustle or muffled command.

There isn't much traffic this early, and I can feel more than see us picking up speed. The route to the Hollow is familiar. East on 37th. Right onto First Avenue. Left on 20th. Into Resident Services to stairs. Fourth level down. Through the unremarkable double doors, and into our world. I didn't even need to follow the colored lines on the floor anymore.

"Kyle's on time," my father says, putting his phone away as if he just finished a conversation with my fiancé. "Whole family, too. The Dows are filing in." He looks at his watch, then shakes it down his wrist. "Should go on without a hitch."

My palms sweat into elbow-length fingerless gloves. I fold them together, but that makes it even worse. Will Kyle feel the dampness during the ceremony?

"I'm glad."

My father senses my nerves, but not my overactive glands, and puts his hand over mine.

"I have something for you." With his free hand, he reaches for a pocket. "From your mother, for your new husband."

He holds out a zip-lock bag with a lacy fabric inside. I slip my hands from under his and take it.

This gift could be a mile away from Kyle's fantasies, I have no idea yet what my husband will like. We've met a couple of times. He's handsome and powerful. All I have to do is make him happy, and all he has to do is tell me clearly how to do that.

The streets of Manhattan whip by the window, a blurred melt of sunstruck color lighting up the buildings' gray. We're going down Second Avenue instead of First. There must be traffic.

I open the bag and release a circle of lace and elastic.

A garter.

My cheeks flush, and I look down at my dress to hide their color. I allow myself to finger the soft lace, reveling in the handmade luxury. Tonight with my husband I will feel much finer things than this, I know, and I'm breathless just imagining it: the caress of his mouth on my skin. The way my body will please him, and a twinge of worry that it won't.

No. I was prepared. Every part of my body had been trained to please. None would fail.

"It's lovely," I say. "I wish she could be here."

"The Colony survives," he says absently.

"And so it shall, my own life," I recite back, sitting straighter as I claim the truth. The endurance of the group is more important than the death of any, single individual. Even my own mother.

I've been looking down at my dress, then straighter, but when I look at my father's face, hoping to see happiness, he's frowning. Perhaps he senses the turn my thoughts were taking—my pride, and my anxiety? Should I have avoided mentioning my mother?

Men are easy to read.

Dow Hannah had drilled this into me, and I'd forgotten to think of my father as no more than a man. So I read him, and it takes half a moment to realize he's not frowning at me.

He glances past me, out the window again, to where another shiny black car is keeping pace with us. We'd passed the 20th Street Loop in Stuy Town, and were heading under the FDR. When I look over my father's shoulder, I realize that we have more neighbors, flanking us in every direction.

We are in the wrong neighborhood, and now we're in what seems like bad company.

For a glancing moment, I panic about being late to my own

wedding. The disapproving looks of the Dows. Kyle's disappointment. The Schenker giving him the opportunity to back out, and me the opportunity to beg in front of everyone.

"Sarah," my father murmurs with a tight vocal control he uses when he expects difficult obedience. "You will not speak." He takes his eyes off the window long enough to meet my gaze. "Or scream. Or do anything to show them you feel fear. Do you understand?"

"What's happening?"

"You are the Colony."

Then the phalanx of cars veers off the main street and turns sharply into the empty parking lot under the raised highway, stopping so abruptly that my father and I are jolted forward.

There's a moment of perfect stillness. Then the partition window that divides us from the driver rolls silently down, and he turns to us.

I don't know him, and I know everyone I'm supposed to know.

This driver—this man—he's not one of us. I can tell. It's not the inappropriate length of his hair, which drops below the driver's cap, over his ears and high forehead in dark locks, or eyes so black all the detail's been inked over, obscuring what has to be ten lifetimes of terrible stories.

He's combustible, with an interior so much bigger than his body that it presses against the shell of his skin like an overfull balloon ready to explode.

In fact, he looks like he wants to eat my father alive.

"Petyr Antoine," the man says, confirming this isn't all a big mistake.

It isn't until I hear him speak that I fully understand the gravity of our situation—or that gravity can even exist around this man.

"And who are you?" my father demands.

The man lifts his driver's cap from his head, almost a salute, and places it on the seat next to him. I realize that what I had at first taken for a trick of the light is something else entirely: the tops of his ears are missing. Between the locks of hair is only a flat black line where there should be familiar whorls of skin and cartilage.

I feel certain that he will be furious if he catches me looking at his disfigurement, but I can't help myself—I've never seen anything something missing make the whole seem so much more beautiful.

He trains his black eyes on me for only a moment, but that's all he needs to strip me, shred me bare, rummage through my heart and find the place I keep my deepest fears and desires before turning back to my father.

"You don't know who I am?" he sneers. Behind him, through the windshield, men surround the car. I take my eyes off the man long enough to look at my father, who's tapping his finger impatiently—as if this entire thing is a nuisance—and out the side window behind him, where more men surround us.

"No," my father replies. "Should I?"

"Of course not," he scoffs, then pulls out a gun and points it between my father's eyes. "You'll know before I kill you. You'll remember it all."

My father doesn't blink or stop tapping his fingers. He breathes in the same slow rhythm. He doesn't fear death. That's why he's First Watch.

"But will I care?"

I care. My fingers clutch palm sweat and my toes curl in my shoes. My lungs ache in their cage, and that's when I realize I haven't taken a breath since my father demanded silence.

"No," the half-eared man says, with a fascinating twitch in his lips that sends a bolt of unwanted arousal through me, and I wonder, deep in my core, who this man is. "You won't care who I am. Only what I can do to you if you don't accept this deal."

My father doesn't respond. He just taps the same beat. It's almost a sigh of boredom.

"You'll give me as much money as I tell you to," the driver explains. "And a list of names. The New York Council. Then I'll let you live."

A tremor of relief whispers through me, though I am determined not to let it show. We have plenty of money, and if he needs more, the Colony's coffers will cover whatever our private wealth cannot. A list of our elders—that seems less likely, but my father is an expert dealmaker: that's why he works in the Outside as a state senator, ensuring the laws favor Colony interests.

It'll be okay. It's always been okay, and so it will be, again, this time. My mind repeats this mantra like a prayer, but my father still hasn't responded, and the driver's still aiming a gun at his forehead. Against my will, my body shakes with fear, and I curse the bodice of my dress, which I had Dow Hannah lace as tight as I could bear this morning.

Don't cry.

You are Sarah Antoine, and today is your wedding day. You will not arrive at the Hollow late with ruined makeup. But you will be beautiful.

You will be pristine.

And you will beg for forgiveness in front of everyone.

My father shifts in his seat, and the driver and I both startle at the motion.

Once he's comfortable, he says, "No."

For a moment, I know I've misheard him—misunderstood the finality packed into that single, definitive syllable. He must have more to say than that—some plan, some argument, some *something*—but he doesn't. There's more silence than my heart can bear.

And then the gun swings left.

At the first sign of movement, I'm convinced the man's going to shoot my father, but he doesn't.

He aims it between my eyes, using the full length of his arm to place the barrel so close to my forehead, I can feel the chill of the metal.

"I won't hesitate," the driver says.

I squeak, kneading my hands together. Any thought of composure is gone. My heart races. My cheeks are hot, and then cold; sweat dampens my armpits and the backs of my knees. I try again to breathe but the dress is so tight, and I can feel my heartbeat everywhere, like my blood is trying to pound its way out from under my skin.

And through all of it, the edge of the bodice cuts into my breasts as they heave, and my nipples harden under the lace that was meant for a man whose name I barely remember.

"Hesitate or don't," my father says. "No names."

I focus past the gun, to the man holding it. He's intense. Confident. He's a man with nothing to lose because he's bet his life on this one moment.

"But the money?" The man seems to find the question amusing.

"You're not interested in money."

"I am not," he says. "I'm interested in those names. And your daughter."

His tongue flicks over his lower lip as he clicks off the safety.

An exclamatory *hm!* escapes my throat. My vision blurs, stars spangling themselves in the car's dark interior, and I long to be back in that quiet, peaceful moment in the rose gold of the morning sun.

"The Colony survives." My father's voice is as cold and flat as the driver's, but in speaking of the colony to an outsider, I know he's not as composed as he seems.

"So you say." The man's voice is blocks away, down the length of a tunnel that's getting dimmer and dimmer, leaving me taut, gasping, pulled toward him by an arousal that terrifies me.

"You aren't getting those names," my father says.

"Then I take her instead."

No. I cannot be killed by this firestorm of a man. I cannot die wet between my legs from my murderer. I want to turn to him—

to plead, to beg. Stall. Figure it out. Pay him money. Give the names.

"And so it shall," my father murmurs. "My own life."

Then I disobey my father's edict of silence with a hot scream that's louder than a gunshot, and the world goes black as death.

CHAPTER 2

I AM MADE OF WHITE LIGHT.

Death is final and unavoidable. Death is a shrug. Death is useful. Death of the individual is insignificant as that individual's life, and as utterly crucial.

The Colony cannot survive without lives, and without deaths, it dies.

My eyes blink open and then slam shut again. I curl in on myself; my eyes hurt, and my head hurts, and I can't get my thoughts in order, especially in that blinding brightness. I take a long, deep breath and it feels steady but hitched. Easy, yet constrained. But possible, and essential. So I take another, and another.

I am Sarah Antoine, and it's my wedding day.

The last thing I remember with any certainty with the car ride to the Hollow.

What happened to me? I don't feel injured, exactly, but I'm sore and achy, not to mention hungry and thirsty. How did I end up in so much pain?

Today, under my husband's command, my training ends and my purpose begins.

The looseness around my ribs suggests I'm no longer wearing my wedding dress, but my ankles are bare on a hard floor and yards of fabric bunch where my knees bend, suggesting otherwise. My hands are hot but my fingers aren't and one side of my face is pressed into soft, but uneven fabric.

I've fallen asleep with my head pillowed on my fingerless embroidered gloves.

Keeping my eyes closed, I touch where the seams have left tender grooves in my cheek, and then my dry, chapped lips. I can tell just by feel that my hair is a lost cause; the morning's perfect updo, constructed by Dow Norah before the sun rose, has dissolved into a disheveled wreck. Could this all be the result of a long, late party? Did I have too much to drink and manage to forget the day I've been waiting for my entire life?

I search for memories of my fiancé's face, of the food fed each other in a ritual consumption. Our mutual pleasure as I was at last allowed to put my training to good use, and give my husband the body I had saved for him.

But I come up with nothing. Instead, what surfaces is the stuff of nightmares: the line of my father's jaw, and the cold steel in his voice when he invited the half-eared driver to shoot me. The buzz and rattle of the FDR above us, and—between my legs—the throbbing heat caused by my terror.

It was too horrible to have been real.

My hands continue their path down my body, checking now for blood or scars, evidence of real, serious violence—whatever happened that I wasn't awake to remember. But it isn't there. I am intact, I realize.

Too intact.

There's no soreness between my legs, which is the final bit of proof that my memory is good. We didn't complete the marriage ritual. Didn't even make it to the Hollow.

I am still a girl. A burdensome child who takes and takes from those who can provide, and the knowledge causes me almost as much pain as the realization that this means that the memories I do have—the terrifying, paralyzing ones—are very, very real.

And now I am... where, exactly?

Gathering my courage, I carefully open my eyes, blinking until they adjust to the blinding light, focusing it into black-outlined rectangles, squares, shapes gone rhomboid from the distortion of perspective.

The shapes are glass and the dark outlines are the casings between them.

Winter sunlight falls in dazzling streaks through its dusty panes. The sun is nearly directly overhead, which makes it close to noon. I've been dumped into a greenhouse, where I've been out for half a day.

I sit up and gingerly get to my feet, but the world tips over, and I land on my hands and knees.

So, I crawl into the direction I'm facing. The floor is cracked tile, grouted with decades of dirt. I push past a green plastic nursery pot with hairy soil stuck to the sides. A flat yellow stick with a flower genus printed on the side.

Plant in full sun six weeks before last frost. Space seeds 4-6".

Sprouts will emerge in 5-17 days. Keep soil moist until 6" tall.

My head feels like it has a brick wired to each side, pressing down against my skull, forcing blood and fluid through the veins.

I'm alive.

Approaching a counter with two empty shelves under it, I have to remind myself through the headache that I'm alive. I can reach for the bottom shelf. I can feel the cold steel. I can get my feet under me. I can pull myself up high enough to lean on the second shelf and when my stomach cramps from hunger and a bodice that isn't as tightly strung as I remember. I can feel every organ in my body. I close my eyes against the pain.

I'm alive, but why?

For the good of all.

My brain sings the elementary school answer out of habit, like the second line of a jingle.

In the blessed darkness behind closed lids, I pull myself to a standing position.

Slowly, I open my eyes, and I am flying. There's no ground outside the windows. No street. No pavement. Nothing nearby. Only a ledge and then…nothing.

The horizon is cracked into the geometry of the city, and from this I get my bearings. The greenhouse is on a rooftop, several stories above the rooftops of all the nearest buildings. Manhattan is spread out around me on three sides, laid out as if it's within reach.

Chrysler Building this way.

Twin Towers there.

Brooklyn, endlessly into the haze of Montauk, and the Atlantic ocean, to the place my people sailed away from like their asses were on fire.

New Jersey.

Central Park, wildness inside the right angles of green frame.

I am west of Times Square and a little north.

I am in a boiling pot, twenty stories above the grind of Hell's Kitchen.

The dizziness has retreated. I'm warm enough, so the place must be heated, but it doesn't seem to be in use; a few metal shelves and racks are mostly empty, save for the occasional stack of trays or flowerpots, a stray bag of soil moldering on the tile.

My headache is all pain now, and I can manage pain. I can even turn it into pleasure, but now it's only a travel companion I can ignore as I push my way to the east side of the structure.

This side is set back from the edge, leaving roofing surface between me and the drop to the street. A white plastic chair surrounded by cigarette butts is pushed against the HVAC unit.

There's a door to my right. It leads into the building. Solid, flush at the edges with no molding. It's even painted the same color as the one wall as if it's supposed to be incongruous.

I'm not surprised when it's locked, but I'm frustrated.

I turn the knob. Pull. Yank. Leverage my foot against the wall as if muscle and bone could beat a deadbolt

"Hey!" I pound the metal. "Hey! Driver guy!"

I punch the door as hard as I can, screaming with every bit of air I can fit inside my lungs, and pound harder. Shocks of pain rattle my wrists and even with the gloves, the sides of my hand burn from the friction. I'm going to break a bone, shatter my insides, bash them to jelly before I even find out what happened.

Maybe that's for the best.

Maybe that's what needs to happen.

Or maybe this is pointless. I push myself away from the door and go back to the east side of the greenhouse.

I can see the building I've lived in since daddy was promoted.

I lay my palms on the cold glass, but the apartment we live in faces the other way. It has its back turned to me, and I've just started to understand I'm a princess, trapped in a tower, and I'm completely alone.

Stepping back from the edge, I search for a door in the glass and find it, but it's locked tight. I yank the cast iron lever anyway. It's that move that makes me realize how loose my dress is around me, the corseted top that should be sculpted against my ribs now a loose raft of fabric and boning. I reach for the laces that should be keeping me secure and realize with a start that they were taken while I was unconscious. No wonder it's so easy to breathe.

And suicide will be that much harder.

I have spent my life being educated in the womanly arts, being trained to spatchcock birds and knead dough, wield a sewing needle and calm any man's flaring temper, but they never covered escaping kidnappings. Luckily, I know how windows work. I take another step back and pick up one of the pots, a terracotta thing with some heft to it, and throw it against the greenhouse's wall with all my might.

It shatters on impact, and the glass absorbs the blow with a dull, disinterested thud.

I throw another, and then another, watching them explode, splintering uselessly into fragments and dust. I shriek out a sob of rage and fear, and the sound startles me—I clap my hands over my mouth.

You will not speak.

My father told me to be silent.

Or scream.

I'd forgotten.

Or do anything to show them you feel fear.

No one comes, and for a moment, it seems like a mercy.

Then I am confronted with the cyclops gaze of a camera I hadn't noticed before. It's mounted in a corner, too high to reach, its lens shiny and black, as menacing as the view down the barrel of a gun. Next to it, a red light blinks. I turn in a slow circle, wary, now, and see another camera, and then another, and another, each one aimed so that there are no blind spots in the greenhouse. They can see every angle.

Whoever they are, they're watching me closely.

I've always known the Colony had enemies, but until now that concept was vague and shadowy—as I got older, I started to think of them as nothing more than bogeymen Dows used to keep little girls in line.

Of course the Outside People would destroy our way of life if they knew about it—but they don't know about it. How could they? We are stealthy and smart. Law-abiding citizens, fully integrated into the system for generations. We're nothing more than a web of invisible connections.

The cameras creep me out, and I instinctively hide my face behind my hand, then look for something to hide under—a table, a chair, a pile of burlap, anything to shield me from that impassive, all-seeing gaze. But there's nothing: just empty racks and broken pots and my ruined dress hovering inches from my yet-unruined body.

The camera can see down my top. I press the neckline to the skin and look right at the camera.

"Are you just a pervert?" I ask it. "Pathetic."

The door to the greenhouse bangs open. I whirl around to find myself once again face-to-face with the half-eared driver, now dressed in plain clothes: dark pants and a white button-down, open at the throat. The sleeves are rolled up to reveal his forearms; though he's thin, I can see that he is corded with muscle, his body coiled like a whip. He's tall, too, and surprisingly broad-shouldered; despite his being slender, I don't think I stand a chance if I attack him outright. Especially since the cold façade he presented in the car has cracked open to reveal a simmering cruelty that scares me more than anything I've seen yet today.

"Sarah Antoine," he says without an ounce of emotion. He's stating a fact and I am that fact.

You will not speak.

My voice catches in my throat, but he doesn't seem interested in what I have to say.

"Only daughter of Petyr Antoine, six-term New York state senator and one of the most powerful Watchers in the Colony."

I had known he knew about us—when he'd asked my father for a list of our elders in the car, there had been no mistaking what he meant. But still, it's a shock to hear someone from outside the Colony say its name. And mine.

One of the first things a Colony child learns is how to deny her world if Outsiders ask. I respond automatically, my voice surprisingly proud for someone who's shaking in her skin.

"I don't know what you're talking about."

His laugh is mirthless. "Don't lie to me."

"I'm not—"

"Sarah," he says, and the way he says it, I remember the feeling of the gun at my head, his look of determination, the way a potential for violence seeped from his pores, making me feel terrified and alive.

He knows about us, and he means us harm.

And yet, the force of him is like a vaccine, inoculating me against fear by giving me a dose of it.

I bow my head.

"Do you feel pathetic?" he asks. "You should," he continues with an audible sneer, like the name itself is a curse, "you're neither as powerful, nor as pure as you think."

I remain silent.

"You think your little group, your secret society, will protect you. That it cares about you. You believe that it *matters* to be among the chosen."

He's drawn close to me, but he doesn't reach out and touch me. The malice radiating off of him is as palpable to me as his body heat.

"You were wrong

"It is my wedding day," I say to the floor.

"I don't have any sympathies," he assures me. "So if you're trying to appeal to them, you can save your energy. You'll need it."

My eyes settle on the hollow of his throat, near where his pulse pounds, and I think: *okay*. He can claim that he had no human side, but he is still a man. I have been trained to please men. Perhaps that will work to my advantage.

"Why don't you ask me the names? You have me. Just ask me who the *elders are."

"And you'll tell me?"

"Yes."

"You're quick to promise what you can't deliver."

When I try to put my gaze back on the floor, he takes me by the chin and points it up until I'm looking right into the dark emptiness of his eyes.

"Don't they teach you to keep your chin up for everyone but your husband? Chin up, legs open. Right?"

If I ever found solace that he couldn't know us inside and out, those comforts are no longer. He knows everything about what I know, and what I'm not permitted to know.

"What do you want then?" I ask. "You know I can't give you names I don't know. You know I don't own anything. You know I'm useless."

His hand falls away from my chin, and I make an effort to point it upward without his help.

"Maybe I just want a forbidden plaything."

"They'll find you and kill you."

He points his index finger at the ceiling and wags it once.

"Correct. They'll let me torture and abuse you before I kill you, as long as they're little hive isn't disrupted. They'll let you die for the good of the group. But if I stick one piece of me inside one of your well-trained holes, they'll erase me from God's memory." He shakes his head and takes one step back. I suddenly feel air on my breasts where the loosened bodice falls away. The man isn't baited. "If, in your Colony education," he says, "they taught you the world was fair, they lied to you then, too."

I look up, and look him in the eye. I will not reveal anything to him, I vow. Not one drop of information.

"At least," I say, "Tell me your name."

"Darius."

"Darius, I—"

"Be quiet, princess."

My jaw snaps shut. He circles me, taking in my dusty dress and tear-streaked face, making it clear that he'd just as soon spit on me as have to keep looking at me.

"You've always thought you were special, so much better than other people, haven't you?"

I look down again. He's managed to hit a sore spot—I *have* always been prideful about my sewing, no matter how hard I tried to avoid it. I was congratulating myself on my gown just this morning. And my father's position of power, both within the Colony and in the Outside, has certainly shielded me from certain harms. I always knew I'd marry. I'd never have to give my body as a quean. None of the girls in my cohort could be as sure.

"I'm not a princess," I insist. "I'm not special. You see it from the outside. You think you know who we are, but you're just another pathetic Outsider who doesn't get it. No one is special. No individual is greater than the group. If you want to abuse me, go ahead. If the council needs to kill you to protect us, they will. If my death protects all of us, then my life is forfeit. Proudly. I have no name. I have no face. I am one of many and we are one."

Darius looks at me and doesn't say anything, stretching the silence between us until his attention is so taut I squirm.

"I know that's what they teach you," he says before breaking his gaze to come behind me. I feel him there. I feel how my dress hovers away from my body. Feel his eyes probe in the space between, looking for the place the shadows cast my body into mystery. "But I never met anyone who believed it."

I feel his breath on my skin, and I want him to touch me so badly I have to swallow back a plea.

The Dows told us horror stories when we were little—tales of what depraved Outsider men have done to Colony women who thought they were too important, too special to stay under the group's protection. Seduced by promises of love or money or freedom, as if having no place in the world was a blessing and not a curse.

The men lived for nothing besides themselves, using them and threw them away, leaving their soft parts consumed and discarding the husks on the street.

Every lurid detail rises around me in vivid Technicolor, Darius' threat so vivid that when I try to breathe, my lungs fail me again.

"How do you know so much about us?" I ask, distracting

myself from the heat of his body and his animal scent. I'm facing east, in the direction of the apartment building that has its back turned on me. If I can keep my attention there, I won't fall to my knees.

"How I know?" His voice and breath move from one shoulder to the next as if he's stroking me with a fingertip. "Irrelevant. Ask me *what* I know, and I can spend all day telling you about you."

"You don't know us."

"No?" He pauses, and I'm convinced he's going to touch me. "I know that you haven't had anything to eat or drink since sundown yesterday. And I know why."

The afternoon sunlight is starting to make me sweat, a clammy thing that spreads at the backs of my knees and my neck as my pulse hammers too hard in my wrists.

"Good for you." I whisper. I know why I'm hungry and dehydrated and I don't need him to recite it.

He does anyway.

"Because after the wedding is the Intercession."

"Yes. I know."

"Where he tells you what he expects you to submit to. Before he takes you to the bridal chamber of the Hollow. He leaves his mark in an empty vessel. No food. No water. Just his filthy leavings inside you."

"You're ignorant and you're a prude."

"Have you ever wondered why the Intercession is after the wedding? When it's too late to refuse?"

"No," I lie.

He steps away. A piece of clay pot crackles under his heel, and I start at the sound. For the first time since I broke the pots, I realize that the pieces are sharp enough to shear skin and soft, vascular tissue.

Darius stands to my right and pushes a shard away with the toe of his shoe.

I could kill myself. End it all. Remove the possibility of him finding my weaknesses. Whatever Darius wants from us, he wants badly enough to kidnap me. If I'm his only leverage and I remove myself from the equation, he won't get what he wants.

"You broke the pot you were supposed to shit in." He flicks the shard away. It skips and clicks a few feet, landing on top of another one and transferring its energy until they both take off in opposite directions.

"I need water," I say.

"I know." He's in profile—not fully turned to me when he says it—and I can see where the top of his ear ends in a surgically straight line.

Turning away, he opens the door just enough for me to see light on the other side, then slips through and closes it behind him.

The deadbolt clicks. I drop to my knees and weep, and the sadness sedates me into something that I mistake for sleep.

CHAPTER 3

THE SECOND TIME I WAKE UP IN THE GREENHOUSE, IT'S DARK. My legs are cold, and at some point in my unconscious state, I must have taken off my gloves, because my hands are free. My joints ache and my entire head hurts. I'm hours past hunger pangs. A mass of glue and sand has lodged itself in my throat.

The minutes crawl like hours while my vision gets used to the light. I spot a glove resting by my shoe, and it's not until I reach for it that I realize my skirt's hitched over my knees.

Did he...?

No. He didn't.

He wasn't interested in raping me. He was interested in watching me starve. Or maybe someone else was watching me.

Leaning forward for the glove, I check the camera. The red light glows steadily.

Darius hadn't been speaking lightly when he threatened my survival, but it wasn't pure sadism. He was after the Colony.

The only way to keep him from getting what he wants is to take myself out of the negotiations. Just then, my eyes adjust to the shapes on the tile. He removed my laces to keep me from killing myself, but he left the shards.

Well, that was his mistake.

Grabbing the glove, I gather my skirts, slyly picking up a triangle of pottery to tuck into the base of my palm.

To mask what I'm doing from the camera, I pretend to put the glove back on while—under the fabric—I tuck the pointy side of the shard into my wrist. Once I cut it open, all I have to do it curl up and bleed out. They won't notice until I'm already dead. They can't stop me, and they'll lose. We'll survive.

My starving brain decides it's a good plan, until the edge of the ceramic is pressed to my skin, and all I have to do was put the glove on quickly. It's then that I realize that the *elders could be on the video feed. They might miss it and give up everything, or they might be building a plan that included me dying at some other, more strategic, point.

I keep the shard in my glove, flat side against my skin, but I can't use it.

Even suicide's too risky, too self-involved, too much an individual decision.

The best way to help the colony is to be predictable.

My thoughts degrade into colors weaving together. Fear is green and yellow. Thirst is brown and burgundy. They become a whirring, spinning loom that clatters around my head.

***

Kylah's family had come from the Good Hope Colony in Connecticut. Her father was an accountant who must have been extremely talented at weaving together our web—with its secrecy and fiscal traditions—and the Outside—with its taxes and disclosures, because relocation was rare and had to be approved by a plurality of Council members across regions.

She was fourteen—the same age as me—when she came to Preparation. I'd just gotten my blood a few months before and was still excited about the daily routines of preparing me for my sixteenth year, when I'd enter Training, and learn how to please a husband.

I knew traditions were different in other parts of the country, but she was wearing a skirt. We weren't supposed to wear skirts until we were married.

"I heard about the Hollow," she said on the first day as I showed her the underground lunchroom. She seemed fascinated by the stone archways between rooms and vaulted ceilings of the largest chambers. "That these are beer fermentation tunnels built by Father Anselme himself. Is that true?"

"I wasn't there, so…here's where we keep our lunches cool. We can't draw electricity so we use this—"

"You can feel the history," she said, looking at the ceiling with fists balled in excitement.

"Lift the lid," I continued. "But don't forget to put it back. Okay. So, the library is this way."

She gasped, slapping her hands over her mouth as if she needed to keep an escaping butterfly inside it. Her nails weren't polished, but they were well-kept and longer than appropriate.

"Are there histories?" she asked as I followed the yellow line to the library. "Books? Primary sources?"

"Excuse me?"

"I'm just so loving the idea of writing down everything about us. And this place. Back home, everything's done in this supposed Catholic church they built in like, the fifties but—"

"You can't write it down," I stopped her in the hallway before she could go further. "And you can't say you're going to. Not out loud. Not ever again."

"But…no. I'm sorry. I mean like…as fiction!"

She was so sunny and bright that I hated her and craved her company at the same time.

"Listen." I held my hands up, whispering urgently in the stone hallway. "You even think of doing that and you're going to be in big trouble."

Her expression was all question marks. I didn't know how to

be any clearer with her. She was one of us—and safe because of it—but she was also walking across a minefield in clown shoes.

"And get pants until you're married," I said. "You're not supposed to be accessible."

"Pants won't keep a man from thinking or doing anything."

"That's not the point. It's tradition. Please. I don't want you to end up in the Palace."

Her face fell, and I hated that I did that to her and loved knowing I'd saved her at the same time. I could have predicted our relationship would be one of contradictions on day one.

"You have those here?" she asked. "Palaces?"

With tight lips and crossed arms, I exhaled. How was I supposed to explain that we didn't consign women to communal sexual servitude any more, but that the threat of it was as real as it was before we stopped the practice? I couldn't even explain this particular bogeyman to myself, but I believed in it just the same.

"Just follow my lead on everything," I said. "Until you've got your feet under you. Okay? Wear what I wear. Clip your nails. And please…write regency romance or something. Don't borrow from real life."

She nodded, casting her eyes down, and I thought I'd done a good thing.

I thought I'd fixed her in time.

***

I don't need to be fixed. This isn't my fault. My father saw everything. He knows it wasn't my choice.

When this ends, I will still be a worthy bride. I'll need more time to sew another gown. The intricate beading on this one is pulled. Its silk fabric stained with dirt and tears. And it's stained with invisible memories that will never wash out.

Besides, after this, I'm going to eat like a pig for a year. It won't fit around the ham and soft cheese.

Coffee.

I want coffee.

And sausages. Miles of them.

Lèige waffles drowned in chocolate, like when I was a kid, but no limits. I'll need a gown ten times the size, but I'll definitely still need a gown, because I'm still pure, and worthy, and desirable.

Water.

Gallons and gallons of water.

I have not been tainted, not by a man's body, and not by Outside. I cling to that as the endless hours unfold.

This wasn't my choice, and I can still belong to only one man.

But every time I try to reassure myself with this thought, another set of memories comes rushing in: half-remembered snatches of gossip, tales of women who *had* queaned themselves, as if our bodies didn't belong to everyone. As if the treasure is theirs to spend.

They are not banished. No one is ever banished.

Sometimes, though, they are gone. Just gone. Not for wearing a skirt before marriage or anything like that. But when a woman willfully—and without permission— associates herself with Outside People, she's never the same, even if she stays.

The sun slips below the horizon and in the night's darkness I try to sleep. Rest is fitful, uneven, and my dreams are all nightmares: the horrors of Reconditioning*, or what I've heard of it, anyway, chasing me through my sleep. The worst Colony criminals are imprisoned underground in our tunnels, passages built by our brewers long before Manhattan was a city, and just before dawn breaks I am trapped in a feverish delusion of being stuck down there, punishing darkness enclosing me, surrounded by the skittering sounds of criminals and madmen.

I'm half-mad myself by the time the sun is overhead again, shimmering down brilliantly at me from the cold blue sky. It's lower than where it was when I woke the day before, which means I've now been missing for more than a day. I clutch the sharp piece of pottery under my glove. It's a safety blanket. A choice I can make in a situation where my decisions are meaningless.

Hovering in half-consciousness, my eyes are closed when the door bangs open again, and Darius enters, carrying a tall glass of water. He sets it on a dirty counter in front of me and then leans against the table, crossing one long leg over the other.

I get to my feet and approach the glass, wary but unable to stay away from its promise. I've never been this thirsty in my life; my eyeballs burn and my tongue's made of layers of cardboard.

Darius watches me silently, but then, as I reach out to take the glass, he slaps my hand away. I am already weak and dizzy, and the force of the blow makes me stumble and spin.

"Please!" I cry. I realize I am on my knees. I had intended to be strong, to refuse to let him see me suffer any more, but I am so, so thirsty.

"Take that stupid dress off."

I shake my head. I'm past caring about modesty. I care about the dress. It's ruined, but it's mine. I worked on it for months, my fingers numb from stitching, my eyes and back aching as I worked into the night. It may be the only piece of the Colony left to me besides my own body and I will not take it off.

He shrugs and picks up the glass of water.

I remain defiant.

He turns to go.

And I think, with blinding clarity: *I cannot die here.*

"Okay," I say.

He stops, turns around, but does not take another step.

I slip the dress off slowly, regretfully, because as awful as it looks, the fabric is still fine, soft and sweet, a reminder of who I was and what I expected just yesterday. The gloves stay and so do the undergarments I'd worn to please Kyle, because Darius just said to take off the dress, and I'm weak but not dead. I'm not giving him anything he didn't ask for.

He places the cup back on the table. Then he sweeps a hand

through the dust and dirt on its surface and sprinkles them into the water. I watch helplessly as it clouds with gray.

"Down to the skin," he says. "Show me every inch."

The suggestion in his command floods my dry veins with resistance.

"No. You said the dress." I hold out my left hand, the bare one without the distorting piece of pottery under the glove. "Give it to me."

This time, he takes a discarded nursery container and pinches out white-flecked potting soil. He drops it in like a chef seasoning too heavily.

"It's going to be mud soon," he says. "If you aren't naked."

"Where's my father?" I squeak without spit. "Did he give you the names?"

"Haven't spoken to him since the car, when he told me to do what I wanted with you."

"I don't believe you."

"We tried. He won't negotiate with outsiders...so. Take your fucking clothes off."

I do everything I can not to cry as I lower my underpants and slip out of my matching bra, my hands shaking the entire time. I leave the glove for last, hoping its beside the point.

"I know what you're hiding in your glove. You're not going to kill me with a broken flowerpot."

"It wasn't for you."

He nods, then flicks his finger at me. I peel the glove off. The shard clatters to the floor.

I am finally bare before him, exposed as I have never been before a man.

My breath skips, and I cry, but I don't make tears or snot over this destroyed moment—the first time a man's eyes see my skin, my nipples, my utter vulnerability and power.

This was supposed to be one of the most beautiful moments of my life. Instead, it is a violation.

He isn't satisfied yet though.

"Stay still," he commands.

He walks behind me, hovering for a moment before grabbing my hair and yanking it back, so that I'm gazing up into the camera's merciless eye.

"Can you imagine how good it will feel," he murmurs, his breath hot against my neck, "when I let you drink? That cold, sweet water, sliding down your throat?"

I'm barely holding myself upright. I nodded helplessly, swallowing a lump of garden pebbles.

"Even with a little dirt, a little dust, you'll take it all down, won't you? And then you'll beg for more."

"I'll beg," I agree. "I'll do it."

"You need it," he says, and I can *feel* the cruelty of the smile in his voice.

"Please," I whisper. "Please—please—"

"Say it for the camera."

Who's on the other side? His boss? His partners? The entire Outside?

"Please give it to me."

"Let me swallow it," he whispers thickly.

"Let...let me swallow it all."

"I know what your body needs. And what you'll do to get it." And then, just as abruptly as he'd grabbed me, he spins me around so that I'm facing him, and then he lets me go.

I sink to my knees, dropping my face to hide my fury and shame.

"Okay," he says after a moment. He's bored again, casual. "You can drink now."

I do. I am shameless and desperate, and I savor every drop in the glass, dirt and all.

He leaves before I finish, apparently not interested in watching me debase myself any further.

I lie naked where he left me, legs in the letter K, bare skin on cold tile, the empty glass a few inches from my hand, watching the clouds form in the grid above me.

There door clicks and whooshes open. The room spins when I bolt to a sitting position. A tray of food, accompanied by a whole pitcher of water, is pushed across the threshold.

The door claps shut again and the deadbolt is smacked home.

I glance at the camera. He's watching. He has to be.

I should stand up and walk like a human, but by the time I finish making that decision, I'm already crawling on my hands and knees like an animal.

We eat hearty food, but the tray contains food I've never eaten: a plastic clamshell with a sandwich inside—pink meat spills from a circle of bread split into a pocket.

Taking it slow, I peek into the pocket and find cheese and the familiarity of mayonnaise. A pink container of yogurt that proudly proclaims—next to a bulbous strawberry—that it has REAL FRUIT inside.

I rip it open, ready to suck it down, but I stop.

Kylah had confessed to me that she'd tried Outsider food once. She'd snuck out and gone to a restaurant where they served things she'd never heard of, raw fish on rice with salty, spicy dipping sauces. "It was disgusting," she'd said, giggling. "But... kind of fun, too." Some girls thought it fun to flirt with the Outside, to get a taste of what the men in our community were protecting us from, just to see, but I had never had such impulses, because I am Sarah Antoine.

I am the Colony, and I live for the good of all.

I stand up carefully, my head still swimming from the heat, my hunger and thirst and poor night's sleep. I walk over to my discarded pile of garments first, though, and put them on again: the underwear and bra, the ruined dress, my shoes. I leave the glove and shard.

Then I put the tray onto the counter, right a white plastic chair that matches the one on the roof, and—dressed in silk garments that had once been a hopeful symbol of my purity and were now nothing more than a painful, ridiculous reminder of everything I have lost—I nourish myself, dreaming of the day I murder Darius.

*　*　*

Take Me is the first of three, and it'll release on 1/12.

GET TAKE ME

Subsequent releases — *Make Me* and *Break Me* will release with four to six weeks between. I'll get preorders up as soon as I can.

TAKE ME - 1/12

MAKE ME - 2/16

BREAK ME - 3/23

For the time being, these books will be wide. I reserve the right to change my mind for any reason including, but not limited to laziness.

THE NY TIMES BESTSELLING GAMES DUET
He gave up his dominance when he married her. He wants it back.
Marriage Games | Separation Games

THE EDGE SERIES
Rough. Edgy. Sexy enough to melt your device.
Rough Edge | On The Edge | Broken Edge | Over the Edge

THE SUBMISSION SERIES
Jonathan brings out Monica's natural submissive.
Submission | Domination | Connection

CORRUPTION SERIES
Their passion will set the Los Angeles mafia on fire.
Rogue | Ruin | Rule

CONTEMPORARY ROMANCES
Hollywood and sports romances with heart and a lot of heat.
Star Crossed | Hardball | Bombshell | Bodyguard

Printed in Great Britain
by Amazon